The Dutiful Elf

"The humans stole nothing. They meant no harm, and in truth the only harm they did was to a clan reviled of gods and elves alike."

Kiinyon Colbathin regarded Galaeron coldly. "And what of the lives lost? The lives of *your* patrol?"

"That was fate's doing," said Galaeron. "And if not fate's, then my own."

The Beautiful Stranger

"The line will tighten if you pull." Galaeron normally preferred to let captives discover this for themselves, but he feared the elven rope would crush Vala's ankle if it grew any tighter. "It can be removed only by the one who put it on."

"Is that so?" Though the binding had to hurt, Vala's pale eyes betrayed no hint of pain, only cold ire. "Then I suppose I mustn't try to escape."

The Mysterious Wizard

Galaeron heard Melegaunt Tanthul before he saw him. The human's deep voice came from the shadowy side of the moonlit cairn, growling out the arcane syllables of a bizarre spell. The incantation was unlike anything Galaeron had ever heard, even among the corpse-stealing drow who occasionally worked their evil in the isolated crypts of the Desert Border. The words were booming and raspy, loaded with power and danger, but also intricate and enigmatic, full of cleverness and deception.

FORGOTTEN REALMS

RETURN OF THE ARCHWIZARDS

Book I

The Summoning
TROY DENNING

Book II

The Siege
TROY DENNING
December 2001

Realms of Shadow
EDITED BY LIZZ BALDWIN
April 2002

Book III

The Sorcerer
TROY DENNING
September 2002.

FORGOTTEN REALMS

THE SUMMONING

Return of the Archwizards

BOOK I

TROY DENNING

THE SUMMONING
Return of the Archwizards, Book I

©2001 Wizards of the Coast, Inc.

All characters in this book are fictitious. Any resemblance to actual persons, living or dead, is purely coincidental.

This book is protected under the copyright laws of the United States of America. Any reproduction or unauthorized use of the material or artwork contained herein is prohibited without the express written permission of Wizards of the Coast, Inc.

Distributed in the United States by St. Martin's Press. Distributed in Canada by Fenn Ltd.

Distributed to the hobby, toy, and comic trade in the United States and Canada by regional distributors.

Distributed worldwide by Wizards of the Coast, Inc., and regional distributors.

FORGOTTEN REALMS and the Wizards of the Coast logo are registered trademarks owned by Wizards of the Coast, Inc.

All Wizards of the Coast characters, character names, and the distinctive likenesses thereof are trademarks owned by Wizards of the Coast, Inc.

Made in the U.S.A.

The sale of this book without its cover has not been authorized by the publisher. If you purchased this book without a cover, you should be aware that neither the author nor the publisher has received payment for this "stripped book."

Cover art by Jon Sullivan. Map by Dennis Kauth.
First Printing: March 2001
Library of Congress Catalog Card Number: 00-190762

9 8 7 6 5 4 3 2 1

UK ISBN: 0-7869-2031-9
US ISBN: 0-7869-1801-2
620-T21801

U.S., CANADA,
ASIA, PACIFIC, & LATIN AMERICA
Wizards of the Coast, Inc.
P.O. Box 707
Renton, WA 98057-0707
+1-800-324-6496

EUROPEAN HEADQUARTERS
Wizards of the Coast, Belgium
P.B. 2031
2600 Berchem
Belgium
+32-70-23-32-77

Visit our web site at **www.wizards.com/forgottenrealms**

For Eric Boyd
With many thanks

Acknowledgments

This book would not have been possible without the help of many people; thanks to you all! Some who deserve special mention: Eric Boyd, for guiding me through the forest and pointing out just how much reading I still had to do—and for providing it when no other source was available. Ed Greenwood, for the loan of a very special character—I hope he finds his way home! Skip Williams and Jeff Grubb for talks both shadowy and magical. Jim Butler and Rich Baker for their invaluable comments on both outline and manuscript, and for making the 3e coordination as painless as possible. Rich, again, for his excellent work on *The Shadow Stone*, and to Clayton Emery for reasons that should be apparent by the end of the book. Phil Athans, my editor, for his usual patience, good humor, and insight. Mary Kirchoff for turning me loose on the Realms again. Sean K. Reynolds, Rob Heinsoo, and James Wyatt for their give and take; Duane Maxwell, Julia Martin, Anthony Valterra, Roger Moore, Steven Schend, Michele Carter, Dale Donovan, and the entire FORGOTTEN REALMS 3E board and product group for their many ideas and insightful suggestions. As always, thanks to Andria for support, patience, and encouragement.

And thanks to the FORGOTTEN REALMS readers, without whom there wouldn't be a FORGOTTEN REALMS first edition—much less a third!

CHAPTER ONE

*20 Nightal,
the Year of the Unstrung Harp (1371 DR)*

Like every burial cairn Galaeron Nihmedu had ever entered, this one stank of the bodies and breath of those who had opened it. The air was permeated by the odor of saddle soap and camp smoke, and the reek of musty human armpits and sour human breath. What Galaeron did not smell was blood, which meant these crypt breakers were more skillful than most. Usually at least three fell to traps and magic during the entranceway excavation.

As Galaeron led his patrol deeper into the cairn, his dark sight began to illuminate the passage walls in shades of cool blue. Inscribed into the flat wall stones were ancient elven glyphs recounting the lives and deeds of the ones buried within. Like most entrance tunnels, this one was low and narrow, with just enough height to stand upright and barely enough room for an elf's slender shoulders. How the burly humans had found room in the cramped space to clear the corridor he could not imagine, but they had deftly spanned the death pits with rough hewn planks and braced the deadfalls with oak posts.

Galaeron followed the tunnel to the burial chamber. He was surprised to find the room both quiet and dark, given that a pair of his elves were outside guarding twenty shaggy horses and three red-faced sentries. Nor could there be any doubt the humans had reached the crypt. The bronze shield that had once served as a door had been melted almost into nothingness, a crude but effective entry that hinted at plenty of magic.

Galaeron slipped cautiously into the chamber. Seven elf dead lay undisturbed on their ancient biers, their flesh and hair perfectly preserved by the crypt's now shattered magic. Their bejeweled weapons and gold-trimmed armor were lying untouched beneath a thick layer of dust. By their amber skin and ornate bronze armor, Galaeron knew these to be Aryvandaaran nobles, high lords of the aggressive Vyshaan clan who had touched off the First Crown War and plunged the entire elf race into three thousand years of carnage. Though he wished them no peace in their sleep, he would bring their crypt breakers to justice. As a tomb guard, he had sworn to protect all elven burials.

In the tomb's far corner, Galaeron found a knotted rope leading down into a freshly opened hole. The shaft had been excavated by the same magic that destroyed the bronze door, for there was no dirt or rubble heaped around the collar. Trying to imagine what the greedy humans might be seeking down there more valuable than the priceless armor and enchanted weapons of the Vyshaan lords, he led the patrol down the rope.

Thirty feet later, the shaft opened into a labyrinth of low, square-cut dwarven tunnels. By the looks of the working, it had been old when Evereska was young. Dust clung to the walls two fingers thick and lay on the floor a foot deep. The humans' path twined its way eastward through the powder, looking for all the world like a trail through snow.

Galaeron sent two scouts ahead, then, as the last faint light from outside faded, he took a pinch of stardust from his pocket and flung it into the corridor ahead. Though the phosphorescent dust was too faint to be seen by humans, it provided light enough for the sensitive eyes of elves. Recalling the care his quarry had displayed in defeating the crypt traps, he ordered a three-elf rear guard to follow behind. Stooping almost double beneath the low dwarven ceiling, the patrol moved into blackness. Galaeron left his sword in its scabbard and took his customary position three places back from the leader. Though all tomb guards could fight with both spell and steel, he usually served as the patrol's primary magic-user. Not only was his magic more versatile than that of most elves, he had learned in his few battles that crypt breakers often targeted spell-flingers first, and he preferred to shoulder that burden himself.

The human trail ran eastward for a thousand yards, circling past a dozen ancient cave-ins. Narrow seams of sand began to appear in the ceiling, suggesting to Galaeron's experienced eye that they had crossed under Anauroch itself. Not long after, the distant clatter of falling rock started to echo through the tunnels, and his favorite scout returned to report.

We must be careful with these spiders. They look to have venom. A svelte Wood elf with a cupid's bow smile and brown eyes the size of a doe's, Takari Moonsnow's slender hands streaked through the near darkness in finger talk. *And their pet has fangs of its own.*

Pet? Galaeron's fingers weaved a basket of lines before him. *What kind of pet?*

Takari smiled coyly. *Better you should see for yourself.*

She spun away and started up the passage, leaving Galaeron knowing little more than he had before her report. He shook his head and followed. If he wanted a Wood elf for a scout, Takari had to be allowed her fun.

Aragath, the second scout—a moon elf—lay near the inside

wall of a gentle curve, his head silhouetted against a flickering blue glow that filled the tunnel ahead. The clatter of falling rock was louder, punctuated by the gruff talk of men at work. Galaeron lay on his belly and crawled up beside Aragath. After stooping so long, it was a relief to stretch out on the floor— even if it did mean breathing through his fingers so the dust did not make him sneeze.

Galaeron peered around the corner and almost cried out in shock. Less than ten paces away hovered a leathery orb of gray-green flesh, nearly three feet in diameter and shaped more or less like a head. A huge eye bulged out from the center of its face, and beneath that gaped an enormous mouth filled with sharp teeth. Atop its pate writhed ten thick tentacles, each ending in a single bulbous eye. Nine of these tentacles had been folded over a small length of wood and bound so that the eyes could look only at the top of the gruesome head. The tenth tentacle was sweeping back and forth, spraying a brilliant blue beam across a four foot width of stone wall. Wherever the light touched, six inches of stone deteriorated into yellow smoke.

Galaeron swallowed, hardly able to believe what he saw. The creature was an eye tyrant, one of the rarest and most feared killers of the Underdark. Galaeron had never fought one himself, but he had seen a trophy specimen in the Evereskan Academy of Magic. According to the Histories, the monster had taken possession of King Sileron's crypt in the Greycloak Hills, then gorged itself on two patrols of tomb guards before the great Kiinyon Colbathin finally killed it.

So stunned was Galaeron that he barely noticed the creature's companions until a section of roof collapsed and several men crawled forward to clear the rubble. All were heavy-boned and huge, with thighs as large as an elf's waist and dark braids of hair swinging about their shoulders. Their high boots and battle-worn scale mail were trimmed in black sable, while the belts that girded their thick middles were made from white dragon scales.

As the men worked, the eye tyrant's blue gaze drifted downward, cutting a swath of smoking emptiness inches above their backs. They dropped to their bellies and grunted something in a harsh, rasping language, then a small fist appeared on the other side of the monster and clasped one of its bound eyestalks. Though the hand was hairless and smooth, it was also strong, pulling so hard Galaeron thought the tentacle would pop off.

"Shatevar!" a voice called.

A female face appeared in the narrow gap between the ceiling and eye tyrant's head. Her features were heavy and rough by elven standards, yet striking and surprisingly beautiful, with hair the color of honey and eyes as blue as tourmalines.

Her second hand came into view and pressed a dagger to the trapped eyestalk, then she said in Common, "Try that again, and I'll make a cyclops of you."

"Then keep your oafs out of my way." The eye tyrant's voice was deep and gurgling. "I'm too tired to watch them."

"Tired or dead, your choice."

As the two argued, Galaeron tried to take count of the humans. Behind the eye tyrant stood two men holding what appeared to be glassy black swords. The weapons might have been obsidian, save that they were perfectly molded, with shadow-smooth blades and none of the conchoidal flaking marks he would have expected. Four more men squatted along the near wall, their scabbards resting across their knees. Judging by their shimmering pommels, these weapons were also made of black glass. It was impossible to see how many men might be lurking beyond the eye tyrant, for the brilliance of its disintegration beam washed out Galaeron's dark sight. Still he did not think his patrol too badly outnumbered. There had only been twenty horses outside.

Galaeron backed away from the corner then issued his orders in finger talk. He did not relish trying to capture someone who made slaves of eye tyrants but had little choice in the matter. Word of such a strange encounter was bound to circulate through Evereska, and any leeway given the humans would reflect badly on the entire patrol. The matter would not trouble Galaeron overmuch. It was his reputation as a malcontent that had landed him a posting along the Desert Border in the first place, but there were some among his elves who still hoped to make names for themselves in the Tomb Guard.

Once his warriors had readied themselves, Galaeron used a spell to turn himself and four more tomb guards invisible. Trusting the rest of the patrol to follow, he led the way around the corner, the magic of his boots smothering all sound as he skulked along opposite the crouching humans.

Unfortunately, even magic spells and elven boots could not keep dust from billowing when someone walked through it. Two paces from the eye tyrant, one of the humans pointed at the gray cloud around Galaeron's feet and spoke in his harsh language. When the warrior started to rise, the heavy pulse of bow strings throbbed through the passage. Four white arrows streaked out of the empty air and struck their targets in the unarmored calves, the heads sinking only to the depth of a fingertip. The astonished humans leaped up, banging their skullcaps on the low ceiling, then their eyelids rolled down and they collapsed facedown into the dust.

Rendered visible by their attacks, Takari and three more elves rushed forward, exchanging bows for swords and pausing to turn the heads of the sleeping warriors sideways so they would not smother in the thick dust. Behind them, another half dozen elf archers appeared in the low tunnel, three kneeling in front and three standing hunched behind them.

"Elves!" hissed the female human, still the only woman Galaeron saw in the band. A trio of threatening arrow tips appeared out of the darkness to each side of her broad shoulders, and she glared over the eye tyrant at Takari. "My men better be alive."

"They are only sleeping—as are the sentries you left outside," Galaeron said. Trying not to let the woman's apparent lack of alarm worry him, he annulled his invisibility spell. He signaled Takari and the three elves with her to wait against the opposite wall, then waved at the sleeping men. "These are now our prisoners—as are you. Lay down your weapons and explain—"

"No."

The interruption took Galaeron by surprise. "What?"

"I said no." The woman spun the eye tyrant so that its largest eye faced Galaeron. "We will not lay down our weapons, and we have no need to explain anything to you."

"You have broken a crypt," he said. "In these lands, that gives you much to explain. Surrender now, or you will be the first to fall."

The woman merely looked past Galaeron's archers and called, "Sterad?"

"Here."

A trio of muffled thumps sounded from the rear of the tunnel. Galaeron glanced back and was relieved to see his archers still standing. He was not so relieved to see a pair of burly human warriors standing behind them, looming over the unconscious bodies of the rear guard he had assigned to watch the patrol's back.

"Your rear guard will have a few lumps when they wake," said the woman. "Their headaches will trouble them no more than the wounds in the legs of my men."

As she spoke, the front rank of elf archers spun on their knees to aim at the newcomers. The rear rank ignored the peril at their backs and continued to train their arrows on the woman. If she noticed, she did not seem to care. She said something in her own language to the two men who had delivered Galaeron's rear guard, and they laid their black swords across their breasts. Though the move was not overtly threatening, Galaeron noticed that it placed their weapons at a good height for hacking his archers in the neck.

The woman looked back to Galaeron. "You've no idea what you've blundered into here, elf, but know I mean no harm to you or your people. You may leave while that remains so."

"Pay her no heed, my princep," said Louenghris, one of the archers in the rear rank and the patrol's only Gold elf. "Let them cut my throat. My aim will still be true."

"Thank you, Louenghris, but it won't come to that," said Galaeron, hiding his annoyance. At only a hundred and ten, Louenghris was the youngest of the patrol's elves and still foolish enough to put the humans on their guard by inviting such things. Allowing a nugget of coal to drop from his sleeve into his palm, Galaeron looked back to the woman. "Perhaps you meant no harm, but in breaking the tomb's seal, you have caused it. Now you must come before the *erlagh aneghwai gilthrum!*"

Slipping smoothly into a spell incantation, he crushed the coal nugget and brought his hand forward. A fan of pink radiance shot from the eye tyrant's huge central eye, speckling Galaeron's vision with pale light. Even through the red spots in his eyes, he could see that the tunnel remained as bright as before.

The woman tapped her dagger above the monster's huge central eye. "Haven't fought many beholders, have you? Magic's not much good around Shatevar."

"I am aware of an eye tyrant's power." Galaeron lowered his gaze to address the creature directly. "But I had not heard they were such faithful slaves. We have no quarrel with you, Shatevar."

Shatevar twisted his toothy maw into a sheepish grin. "Sadly, your warriors are not the ones holding darkswords to my back. Should that change, rest assured I will serve you as loyally as I have Vala."

"Vala?" Galaeron repeated, guessing the reason the eye tyrant had spoken her name. Charm spells were much easier to use when a caster knew his quarry's name, and they did not require anything so clunky as hurling coal dust at someone. "What kind of name is Vala? *Meshim deri—*"

"Enough!" Vala pricked her dagger into the eye tyrant's head, drawing a single bubble of brownish blood.

Shatevar's central eye widened, and again the pink flash filled the corridor. Galaeron's spell died on his lips.

"Try that again, elf, and there will be blood." Still keeping the eye tyrant's largest eye pointed at Galaeron, Vala cut another eyestalk loose from its bonds and aimed it at a fist-sized hole the creature had inadvertently drilled into the wall. "You've eleven eyes. Back to work."

"As you command, mistress."

The eye tyrant began to sweep its blue beam across the wall again, revealing a strange square of glimmering radiance deep inside the hole it had created. Content with a standoff for now, Galaeron dropped his hand and used a pair of curt finger gestures to issue two instructions, the most important being to wait. With a little patience, he might learn what the humans were doing and—more importantly—not get anyone killed.

The eye tyrant continued to melt the rock away, shaping something that looked ominously like a doorway. As the opening grew, so did the shimmering square of radiance, though it seemed little more than a sheet of silvery light. Shatevar's blue beam passed through undisturbed, continuing to disintegrate stone on the other side, while the rocks that occasionally fell from the ceiling tumbled back through into the chamber. Given their location, Galaeron wondered if he might be looking at the fabled Sharn Wall, a barrier of ancient magic rumored to lie buried along the perimeter of Anauroch. If so, he could not imagine what the humans wanted on the other side. The few veteran tomb guards who gossiped about such things claimed the hell beyond was rivaled only by the slave pits of Carceri.

Vala kept a wary watch while Shatevar worked, and the patrol was still awaiting Galaeron's signal when the blue beam began to leave black nothingness in its wake.

"We've broken through," reported a human.

Vala's eyes shifted, and Galaeron knew this to be the best chance he would have. He curled the tip of his index finger, signaling the attack, and a trio of white arrows flashed past. He was already diving as the shafts struck home, two above Shatevar's central eye and the third in Vala's cheek. Though the arrows sank only fingertip deep, that did not prevent the victims from crying out.

To Galaeron's surprise, no human arrows clattered off the wall behind him, and no elf voices cried out in pain. As he rolled, he glimpsed Louenghris falling beneath the blow of a human sword's lustrous pommel and saw two more archers lying in the dust unconscious but unbloodied, then Takari and her companions swept past him, flinging sand and uttering spells of sleeping.

Galaeron came up face-to-eye with Shatevar. Though the lid of its central eye was drooping, the eye tyrant had not yet fallen to the sleep arrows and was swinging around two unfettered eyestalks to attack. The blue beam swept past above Galaeron and tore a six inch hole across Aragath's chest. The scout did not scream; he simply dropped his chin and stared at the red mess spilling down his stomach, then he fell into the dust.

Galaeron was already raising his hand to spray magic at the eye tyrant when a black sword fell on it from behind. The shadowy blade slid through the leathery head almost effortlessly, splitting the skull down the back and spilling the ghastly contents onto the floor. Shatevar's many eyes grew foggy and vacant, then the blue disintegration beam died and left the tunnel in darkness.

"You fool," growled a gravelly voice.

Galaeron looked up, struggling to see. The silvery radiance was still glimmering in Shatevar's door but did not seem to *cast* light so much as *be* light. As his dark sight returned, he found a mustachioed human staring across the eye tyrant's deflated orb at him. By the look of utter contempt on the man's face, it was clear he could see in the dark as well as any elf.

"You have no—"

Takari interrupted the human by catching him across the jaw with the dull side of her blade. He staggered backward, then stumbled over Vala's legs, protruding from beneath Shatevar's cleaved skull, and landed on his back. Takari placed a boot across the back of his neck and kicked his sword away, but the precaution was hardly necessary. The man was sleeping as soundly as his commander.

"Don't break his neck." Galaeron rose. "They aren't killing, so neither should we."

Takari glanced at Aragath's body, then said, "The beholder was theirs."

Despite the bitterness in her voice, she scuttled off to join the hunched battle at the head of the tunnel. It was a strange fight, with stooped figures on both sides striking with hilt pommels and flat blades, the walls echoing with the ferocious yelling of any combat, but no one wailing in fear or grief. Galaeron was not pleased to see that his elves were winning only by dint of magic and numbers—and had the humans been willing to kill, even these advantages would have failed to achieve victory. Determined to end the fight before someone made a mistake and turned it into a mortal brawl, Galaeron summoned to mind the incantation of his sleep spell.

"Can you fools not be silent out there?" The voice was wispy and dark and as deep as the tunnel itself. Galaeron stopped and looked to the hole in Shatevar's doorway, but the voice seemed to be coming from everywhere around him. *"You have led the devils straight to me!"*

The remaining humans fell silent and lowered their swords. Takari knocked one unconscious, and two moon elves slipped quickly forward to take charge of the prisoners and prevent them from restarting the fray. Galaeron used finger talk to divide his patrol between caring for his fallen archers and binding the humans, but he kept Takari at his side. He did not want the unpredictable Wood elf venting her grief over Aragath's death on their prisoners.

Turning to the nearest of three humans still standing, he asked, "Who did that voice belong to?"

The humans looked blindly about, uncertain as to who Galaeron had asked, and he realized they could see in the dark only with their swords in hand. He touched one on the chest.

"Who was that voice? What are you doing down here?"

"No harm to Evereska," answered the man. "That's all—"

The last few words were lost to the crack of a magic blast, then the cavern vanished into an instant of murk thick enough to feel. The clatter of falling stones echoed through the tunnel, almost inaudible to Galaeron's ringing ears, and his vision slowly returned, spotty and filled with strings of spidery darkness. He motioned the guards to continue watching the prisoners then turned toward the source of the explosion.

The head and shoulders of a burly human protruded through a saddle-sized cavity in the back of Shatevar's doorway. Behind the screen of silvery radiance, he looked pale and ghostly, despite what Galaeron guessed to be a swarthy complexion and hair as black as jet.

"Melegaunt?" called one of the prisoners. "Melegaunt Tanthul?"

The figure nodded, then thrust a beefy arm through the hole and shouted, "Help!"

The humans started forward at once, trying to bull their way forward despite their bound hands. It was a bad mistake. Takari laid one out with an elbow to the nose, and the other two fell to their guards' pommel strikes. Fortunately for Melegaunt Tanthul, half a dozen elves were rushing forward in the humans' place. They slowed as they passed through the silvery barrier, then caught hold of his arms and began to pull. The human slipped forward, then abruptly stuck and screamed for them to stop.

The shocked elves obeyed, and the human vanished back through the hole. There was a muffled thump but no scream.

Takari looked to Galaeron for orders, as did the elves inside the silver barrier.

Galaeron shook his head uncertainly but started toward the doorway. "I guess we should see what—"

Something that looked like a mouth surrounded by four arms shot through the hole and began to slam itself around, catching elves between its scaly head and the doorway's rocky walls. One elf tried to scream but instead poured forth a torrent of frothing blood. Another fell with her flattened helmet still on her head. The survivors tried to draw weapons and back away. The creature lashed out with its four arms, catching two of the elves by their throats and arms, then came slithering the rest of the way out of the hole.

With a spiked, slug-shaped body tapering back from its huge mouth to a thin tail, the creature was the strangest living thing Galaeron had ever seen. It had no eyes or ears but was aware enough of its foes to jerk its captives away from the two elves who had escaped its grasp. As they moved to help their comrades, a black bolt materialized out of thin air and struck one down. The second warrior fell when the thing hurled one of its prisoners into her head. Both elves fell with broken necks.

"What hell did these human bastards open?" Takari yelled, reaching down for a second sword. When her palm closed around the leather-wrapped hilt of human's sword, she hissed and dropped the black blade then displayed a welt of frozen skin. "By the Night Hunter, even their weapons are profane!"

On the other side of the wall, Melegaunt's muffled voice rose up, sounding pained and quivery as it growled out a string of arcane syllables. Something long and spike-covered floated past the hole, then the bearded wizard finished his spell. The only effect Galaeron could see was a set of scintillating shadows.

"Bows—choice of arrows!" Galaeron yelled.

"What of Ehamond?" Takari asked, referring to the elf still struggling in the creature's grasp.

Galaeron started forward without bothering to answer. Of all the elves in his patrol, Takari had been with him the longest, and they shared an almost instinctive rapport. He nudged her toward Ehamond, indicating he would attack and she should rescue.

"When wolves mount porcupines!" she snapped.

Pushing Galaeron behind her, Takari snatched up the human sword and hurled it at the strange beast then sprang forward behind the tumbling blade. Galaeron followed close behind, his spell ready on the tip of his tongue.

The human sword passed through the silver barrier and buried itself to the hilt in the creature's squirming torso, then Takari pushed through the light and was on the creature, slashing and slicing. Galaeron danced through behind her—the barrier dragged at him like a curtain of cold spider silk—and slid over behind Ehamond. The elf was coated in blood, screaming, hacking wildly at the thing's teeth.

"Calm yourself, guard!" Galaeron dodged a claw, then caught a free ankle. "We can't help you like this."

Takari parried a claw, dodged the creature's snapping mouth, then brought her blade down on an arm holding Ehamond. The sharp elven steel bit deep, nearly slicing the limb off at the elbow, and Galaeron pulled Ehamond's right side free. Crying out in elation, Ehamond brought his own blade around and lopped off the hand still holding him. Galaeron stumbled back through the silvery barrier, dragging Ehamond after him, and saw the monster's barbed tail arc around behind Takari.

"Behind—"

The barb struck her between the shoulder blades, piercing Takari's leather armor as though it were parchment. Her arms dropped and her body arched forward. The tail began to pulse, pumping its contents into her body. Galaeron dropped Ehamond's leg and leveled his hands at the tail then cried out an incantation. Four bolts of golden magic shot from his fingers and blasted the barb off the tail, freeing Takari to collapse back through the silver barrier.

She had not even touched ground before a flight of black

arrows sizzled past Galaeron to strike the creature. The first three bounced off the thing's thorny hide, but the final stuck deep in its mid-section. The archer who had fired it spoke a command word, activating its death magic.

A puckered white ulcer appeared around the wound, but the strange creature did not fall. It did not even sag.

Leaving Ehamond to scramble off on his own, Galaeron grabbed Takari and dragged her away. Her eyes were open but glazed, more shocked than frightened. Another flight of arrows hissed past, but the creature's hide turned gray and stony, and all four bounced off harmlessly. The small number of shafts filled Galaeron with despair, but with Ehamond and Takari wounded and three more elves unconscious from the fray with the humans, only four warriors remained to him.

Much to Galaeron's relief, the creature stayed in the cramped cavity between the silvery barrier and the hole at its back. It snapped the single arrow that had wounded it and tossed the ends at the elf who had fired the shaft.

Galaeron rolled Takari to her side and plucked the creature's barb from her back. The wound was already swollen and pestilent. Deep in the puncture was something small and round, glowing hot scarlet in Galaeron's dark sight. Knowing better than to attempt removing the thing now, he called Ehamond over and pushed Takari into the arms of the battered elf.

"Take her and go. If we don't follow, make a report."

"You'll follow," said Ehamond, glancing toward the strange creature. "You'd better—who'd believe this if you don't?"

With that, he pulled Takari into a cross-shoulder carry and vanished up the tunnel. Galaeron started to toss the tail barb aside, but thought of what Takari would do and threw the spike contemptuously across the silvery barrier. The creature caught it, then rose a few inches and floated to Galaeron's end of the cavity. Though it was impossible to perceive anything resembling emotion on the faceless thing, Galaeron had no doubt that were it able to attack across the silver barrier, he would be dead.

The creature was still hovering in front of Galaeron when a beam of purple magic crackled through the hole, catching the thing in the back and slamming it against the barrier. It writhed madly, loosing an ear-piercing squeal that sounded like it would bring the roof down.

"Now!" It was the same voice that had filled the tunnel earlier. *"Take up my swords and kill it now!"*

The remaining elves reached for their weapons and started forward, but Galaeron did not want them anywhere near the creature. "Not swords! Magic bolts." He raised his hand. "On my count . . . now!"

Shafts of golden magic began to converge on the creature. Some sank into its stony hide with no effect whatsoever, but most struck powerfully, hurling the thing back into the purple beam, blasting off thorns and pieces of hide. Galaeron's first spell had barely left his hand before he repeated it, firing another flurry of raw magic even as the creature tumbled away from the first. His bolts flashed through the silver curtain and met the beam of purple magic coming from the other side.

The result was not exactly an explosion. There was a flash of a thousand colors and the roaring silence of the void, then a horrid prickling and the bewildering realization that he now lay slumped against the tunnel wall. The air reeked of burning iron, and everything ached. There was a crimson ring on the silvery barrier, flickering and steadily growing dimmer as it expanded outward. On the other side of the curtain lay the strange creature, its body pocked and pitted with blast marks, strips of peeled hide showing long strips of green flesh. As Galaeron struggled to comprehend what he was seeing, the thing rose off the ground and floated over to the barrier, then stuck its head through the smoldering hole.

Galaeron's stomach grew hollow, and his stunned elves began to fill the tunnel with low groans. The huge mouth seemed to smile, then the creature floated the rest of the way through the hole. It plucked an unconscious human off the floor, then delicately pulled off his helmet.

Galaeron forced himself to his feet. "Stand if you are awake!" he yelled, reaching for his sword. "Defend yourselves!"

Only a handful of figures stirred, but it was enough to make the creature drop the human. The thing's mouth swung toward Galaeron, shooting a plume of black fog out between its teeth.

There was no time to shout a warning. Galaeron barely managed to close his mouth before the cloud rolled over him, burning his eyes and nostrils and making his lungs cry out for air. The sound of coughing and retching filled the tunnel, anguished and frightened and all too brief. By the time Galaeron could summon to mind the words of a wind spell, half the voices had fallen silent. By the time he actually uttered it and sent the deadly fog whirling down an empty side passage, the rest of the voices were also quiet.

Knowing he would be the next to fall, Galaeron did not fight the terrible rage rising up inside him. Anger bred folly, but it also bred desperate courage and mad strength, and he had seen enough of this devil-creature to know what he needed most. He charged after the receding edge of the black cloud, still holding his breath and swinging his sword blindly into the murk. He felt the edge bite once, then inverted his grip and lunged, driving forward with all his strength.

The blade sank perhaps a foot before slowing to a stop. Galaeron dropped to a squat and heard two arms whistle past his head, then he jumped back and saw two more come slicing out of the swirling cloud. He pulled a glass rod from his sleeve. The fog spun away and left the creature's body floating not five paces away, his sword lodged up near its mouth. Hoping a lightning bolt would prove more effective than the rest of his magic, he leveled the rod at the thing's body and started his incantation.

"Not magic," boomed the deep voice. "I said swords!"

Galaeron glanced over and saw the swarthy wizard stepping through the barrier, dark robes swirling around him like shadow. The creature whirled toward the human, twenty tiny tongues of flame already crackling on its fingertips. Melegaunt circled his hand, creating a wheel of cold blackness in the air before him, and stepped confidently forward. The flames shot straight from the monster's hands into the shadowy wheel and vanished.

Galaeron was already moving, snatching a black sword from the hands of a fallen human and leaping to the attack. Even with the leather wrapped around the hilt, it was so cold it burned his flesh, instantly turning his fingers numb and stiff. He attacked anyway, bringing the edge down two feet from the creature's tail.

The dark blade sliced through effortlessly, cleaving the tail off cleanly.

The creature shuddered in pain and whirled on Galaeron but stopped when it nearly impaled itself on the dark blade. Galaeron lunged for its throat, nearly dropping his weapon when the thing pulled back and his frozen fingers could not adjust.

Galaeron changed hands. In that instant, his armor grew so hot it began to glow, filling the tunnel with eerie pink shadows and washing out his dark sight. He screamed in agony but rushed forward slashing wildly. The creature had no choice except to fall back—straight into Melegaunt Tanthul.

The wizard pushed forward, driving the thing onto Galaeron's blade. It gave the same pained squeal it had earlier, but he could hardly hear it over his own wail. He found the strength to twist the blade and drag it along as he fell.

A pile of green entrails landed on the dust before him, and the creature drifted slowly to the floor at his side. Galaeron screamed and rolled away, fumbling for his dagger.

Melegaunt Tanthul placed a restraining foot on his stomach, then kneeled at his side. "It's dead. Well done, young fellow. Now hold still." The wizard passed his hand over Galaeron and spoke some strange magic, and the armor cooled. "Better?"

Galaeron nodded. "What—"

"No time for talking. There are another dozen on the way." The man pulled Galaeron to his feet, then gestured at the hole in the silvery curtain. "And now they can get at us."

Biting back a scream of pain, Galaeron asked, "They?"

"Later, or we'll be as dead as everyone else."

The wizard started to pick his way through the bodies. Elf and human alike, their faces were contorted into masks of anguish, their chins covered with beards of red froth.

Melegaunt stopped beside Shatevar's deflated body and pointed at Vala's legs. "That one's still alive. Bring her."

Though the wizard looked capable of carrying his own wounded, Galaeron pulled Vala from beneath the eye tyrant. Much to his astonishment, her chest was rising and falling with breath, just as the wizard had said it would be. Galaeron loaded her over his shoulder and started after the wizard, paying no attention as her black sword dropped silently into the dust.

Melegaunt spun on his heel and pointed at the weapon. "Her darksword, you fool."

"I can't carry it." Galaeron displayed his frozen palms.

The wizard stepped closer, running his gaze over Galaeron's face. "What are you doing here?" he asked, seeming to notice Galaeron's pointed ears for the first time. "You can't be of the Granite Tower . . ."

CHAPTER TWO

20 Nightal, the Year of the Unstrung Harp

In the month of Nightal, the sand winds turned wild and bitter, sweeping in from Anauroch full of stinging grit and stabbing cold. At night, no elf in uncloaked armor could long abide their frigid blasts, yet Galaeron's scalded flesh raged at the extra weight of his thkaerth wool cloak. His hands, still dead and white from touching the black sword, had moved beyond pain to agony, and even that did not seem punishment enough. Takari sat slumped on a big human horse, so weak and delirious that Ehamond had to sit with her. Ehamond himself was webbed with claw slashes and puncture wounds. Nimieye and Dynod remained uninjured, having stayed outside the cairn to guard the prisoners, but they would have to scout ahead, and one or both might yet fall to some dragon or griffon drawn by the smell of so much blood. The rest were gone. Of the seventeen elves who had entrusted their lives to Galaeron's command, he had lost thirteen. For such a failure, he deserved more punishment than a simple scalding—far more.

Galaeron fumbled the last binding over Vala's foot and jerked the loop tight then wrapped the end around her boot and stirrup. When he pronounced a mystic word, the line snaked up her ankle, fastening her into the saddle. He did not realize how hard he had tugged until the magic line, taking a cue from his angry yank, cinched itself down so tightly that boot leather bubbled between its coils.

"The line will tighten if you pull." Galaeron normally preferred to let captives discover this for themselves, but he feared the line would crush Vala's ankle if it grew any tighter. "It can be removed only by the one who put it on."

"Is that so?" Though the binding had to hurt, Vala's pale eyes betrayed no hint of pain, only cold ire. "Then I suppose I mustn't try to escape."

The edge in her voice suggested she had no intention of escaping, not until she repaid Galaeron for the deaths of her men. Though it was a vengeance she would never have, she could at least take consolation in the price he would pay to his own masters. Not since the days of Kiinyon Colbathin had a patrol of tomb guards taken such losses—and never along the Desert Border South, the quietest of any area the tomb guard patrolled.

Galaeron started to walk away, then thought better of it. Without turning around, he said, "We are sorry for the deaths of your men. Know that we would have saved them, had it been in our power."

"But it wasn't, elf." Vala's voice remained unforgiving. "As I said then, you have no idea what you're dealing with."

Galaeron bit back the urge to make a sharp retort. "Then why don't you tell me?"

Vala looked away. "It is not my place."

"Very well," Galaeron said. "Then what about yourself? Where is the Granite Tower?"

Vala's eyes flashed, whether in alarm or anger was impossible to say. "That is not for you to know, elf. We are hardly friends."

"No, I suppose we aren't."

Galaeron turned and walked away. It hardly mattered where the woman and her three sentries were from. In all likelihood, they would soon be joining their fallen companions. The Hill Elders rarely made hasty decisions, but when a tomb guard brought captives before the council, there was seldom much to decide. The sentence for crypt breaking was as certain as it was harsh.

Galaeron heard Melegaunt Tanthul before he saw him. The human's deep voice came from the shadowy side of the moonlit cairn, growling out the arcane syllables of a bizarre spell. The incantation was unlike anything Galaeron had ever heard, even among the corpse-stealing drow who occasionally worked their evil in the isolated crypts of the Desert Border. The words were booming and raspy, loaded with power and danger, but also intricate and enigmatic, full of cleverness and deception. Though it was the third enchantment of caging the wizard had cast since leaving the battle site, Galaeron, who usually had an instinctual feel for all things magic, had yet to grasp this wizard's art.

When he rounded the corner, Galaeron found Melegaunt working the shadows into an impassable maze of moonlight and darkness, swirling them into dead-end spirals, folding them into meandering corridors that rounded a hundred corners and came back to their own beginning. The wizard himself was nearly impossible to find, his black robes and swarthy complexion blending into the night the same way Wood elves melted into the forest.

Though Galaeron did not think he had made any noise as he approached, Melegaunt glanced in his direction and nodded. He finished his maze by feeding its only exit into a hole of fuming darkness, then simply melted into the shadows beneath his feet.

Galaeron stood outside the maze feeling perplexed and foolish. Before his indifference to the ritual tedium of the Academy of Magic had landed him across the glen at the Academy of Arms, he had spent more than two decades studying the basics of every known spellcasting system, and he could not even guess how Melegaunt had vanished. There had been no gestures or words to trigger the spell, nor even a twitch or sharp breath to activate a ring or magic pendant. The wizard had dissolved into the shadows as though by an act of will.

"The umbral maze should hold until dawn."

The voice came from the ground beside Galaeron. In spite of himself, he hopped away and looked down. The wizard's body was rising out of the shadow, peeling itself up like a turning page.

"And they won't like the daylight at first."

Melegaunt braced on the ground then brought his feet beneath him in a practiced motion. As he stood, his body resumed its shape, filling out like a glove inflated with breath.

"We have until tomorrow dusk, no longer."

"We?" Galaeron had to scurry after the wizard, who was already rounding the corner of the cairn. "To do what?"

"To set things right, of course. I'll need at least one company of good wizards and a trio of high mages." The human spun on Galaeron, bushy brows furrowed in concern. "Evereska does have three?"

"I—I couldn't say." Galaeron assumed the city had at least that many, but high mages were not something Evereskans discussed openly and certainly not with humans. "First, we must talk about—"

"We'll talk while we ride." The wizard whirled away and rounded the corner. When he came upon Nimieye and Dynod standing guard over Vala and the other three prisoners, he stopped. "What's this?"

"Your friends are crypt breakers." Though Galaeron had been dreading this moment since coming to realize how powerful the wizard was, his duty was clear. "They must be taken before the Hill Elders, but you were not with them. You are free to do as you please."

"Of course I am." Melegaunt's black beard twitched as though he might laugh. "But this won't do, elf. I was the one who told them to break the crypt. Do you intend to tie me, too?"

Galaeron swallowed and reached for a binding rope. "I have sworn—"

"What you have sworn makes no difference."

Melegaunt gestured at the ground, and icy ribbons of shadow spiraled up Galaeron's legs, squeezing his bones and numbing his flesh. The wizard glanced down and shook his head in an expression of dismay then turned toward the horses. Galaeron tried to go after him and found his feet rooted in place. He flashed a finger command to Nimieye and Dynod, ordering them not to engage the human in what would certainly be a futile attack.

Melegaunt stopped next to the horse carrying the humans' confiscated weapons. "We have unleashed a terrible foe on your people," he said, drawing a black sword from its scabbard. "You will either work with me to return it to its place, or you will wait here until it kills you."

The wizard stepped over to the first of Vala's captured sentries and touched the sword to his binding. Galaeron was not really surprised to see the shadowy edge slicing through the magic cord. Melegaunt handed the weapon to the man and motioned for him to continue then turned back to Galaeron.

"Which shall it be?"

"Death or battle? What choice is there?" asked Galaeron. "But you must promise to do no harm to my people. Otherwise, I choose death."

"No harm I can prevent—and that's the best promise you'll get, given the circumstances." The wizard gestured, and Galaeron's shadow bindings dissolved. "You've chosen wisely, elf. These devils have already laid low an empire, and I would not like to see the same fate befall Evereska."

"You keep calling them devils." Galaeron walked over to undo Vala's bindings, touching each one and whispering a command word. "Is that what they are?"

"Close enough," said the wizard. "Do you know what that silver curtain was down there?"

"The Sharn Wall?"

"Is that what you elves call it? An apt name. Then you must know what lies on the other side."

Galaeron hazarded a guess. "The sharn?"

"I see your high mages have kept their knowledge to themselves." Melegaunt snorted, half-amused. "Perhaps I should honor their wisdom until I know why."

"I hardly think it a secret." Galaeron released Vala's last bond. "Most tomb guards know the legend of the Sharn Wall."

The wizard cocked a brow. "Brazen for an elf, aren't you?" He plucked Vala's bare sword from the pack horse and brought it over. "Very well. The sharn are not the trapped ones—they are the ones who made the wall."

"Then what were—"

"Phaerimm," said Vala, taking her sword. "You do know what they are?"

"I do now." Like the Sharn Wall itself, they were the stuff of Tomb Guard legend, mysterious killers who could wipe out whole patrols. From what Galaeron had seen, the description fit. He looked back to Melegaunt. "You were lost in their tunnels?"

"Not lost." As he answered, the wizard turned his attention to Vala. "You are the master of this company?"

"What's left." She cast an angry glance at Galaeron, then dismounted and dropped to a knee before the wizard. "Vala Thorsdotter, daughter to Bodvar's grandson, at your service."

"We've no time for such silliness," Melegaunt said, motioning her up. "But a great-granddaughter to Bodvar! It does my heart good to see his line so long continued."

Vala laid a hand to her scabbard. "A blessing of your gifts, Mighty One."

"No doubt—and call me Melegaunt. You'll find I answer to it more often." Melegaunt waved her to her saddle, then looked down the line of big human horses and frowned. "I don't see Sable."

Vala's jaw dropped. "Milord, Sable has been dead these eighty years." She pointed to a husky black stallion near the end of the line. "But Raven there is of her line."

A flash of grief filled Melegaunt's dark eyes. "Of course. I should have realized." He motioned a human to bring Raven forward, then turned to Galaeron and pointed westward, where a jagged wall of shadows marked the impassable peaks of the Sharaedim. "I trust you elves have a quick way across those?"

"There is a pass," said Galaeron, "but it is watched and warded. You'll have to wear blindfolds and bindings, or none of us will reach Evereska alive."

"Be careful, Mighty—er, Melegaunt," Vala said. "Once he has us bound and blindfolded, we'll be at his mercy, and this elf is a sly one."

"You have a better way?" Melegaunt asked.

"I have heard stories of shadow walking."

"I'd need to know the way, and there is no time to find it."

"Nor would it work," said Galaeron. "Evereska is well-warded against such magic."

The look that passed between Vala and Melegaunt was as quick as it was knowing, but Galaeron pretended not to notice. Whatever they believed—and whatever the truth about these phaerimm—the humans would be under his control when they entered the city.

"The only other way is to circle around and enter through the Halfway Inn. That would take a tenday by horse." He looked to Melegaunt and added, "Only three if you can fly us."

"Still too long." The smile that came to Melegaunt's lips might have been knowing or confident. "We will wear the elven bindings."

CHAPTER THREE

21 Nightal, the Year of the Unstrung Harp

The scent of spruce resin filled the darkness, and Galaeron knew they had completed the Passing. His dark sight began to function again, and the human horses snorted as they sensed the ponies' joy in returning to Evereska. Even Takari perked up, leaning back in Ehamond's arms to draw a breath of crisp air.

Though Galaeron knew that a hundred elf archers watched from the hidden galleries high above, he did not look up. Any sign of acknowledgement would bring a flurry of spells and arrows down on his prisoners, a precaution contrived to keep secret the defenses of the Secret Gate.

The path rounded a curve then arched over a smoky-bottomed abyss on a marble bridge. Galaeron spoke a word of passing and led his companions across, then stopped in a cramped vestibule sealed by a thin sheet of muscovite mica. A stern-faced moon elf in the silver-gilded plate mail of a Vale Guard *kanqat* stepped into view and touched his fingertips to his heart.

"Glad homeagain, Nihmedu." Though the kanqat stood on the other side of the mica, his voice was as clear as his image. He was Orem Arvaeyn, a classmate from the Academy of Arms who—like nearly everyone else—was rising much faster than Galaeron. Orem looked past Galaeron to sneer at the humans. "I see you have crypt breakers. Shall we expect the rest of your patrol soon?"

"No, Kanqat. They won't . . ." The words caught in Galaeron's throat, but he forced himself to meet Orem's gaze. "I couldn't recover their bodies."

The kanqat's face grew even paler. "I see." He studied the prisoners, clearly trying to reconcile the fact that they were mere humans with Galaeron's loss, then asked, "This happened in the Desert Border South?"

Galaeron nodded, confident any account he gave would only make him look worse. "If you please, my scout needs care."

"Of course." The kanqat looked away and nodded, then he stepped aside as the mica barrier rose out of sight. As Galaeron's pony passed by, Orem said quietly, "No need to be short, Galaeron. Not that you'll get one now, but I always thought you merited a better assignment."

Surprised by the kanqat's unexpected kindness, Galaeron pulled aside and let Ehamond lead the others ahead. "My thanks, Orem. Your words may be the only kind ones I hear tonight."

"You were the best of our regiform, Galaeron." Orem shook his head. "You just shouldn't have been so arrogant. There's more to this business than spell and steel."

"Arrogant? What is true is not . . ." Galaeron caught himself then nodded his agreement. "Good advice given too late, I'm afraid."

"It may serve you tonight, if you keep it in mind," said Orem. "Nothing would take the tomb master more by surprise."

"This is a matter for more than the tomb master." Galaeron glanced at Vala and Melegaunt, who were sitting on their horses bound, blindfolded, but far from frightened. "The humans play only a small part in this, and none at all in the deaths of my guards. I'll need to speak with the Hill Elders at once."

"At once? This morning?"

Galaeron nodded.

Orem studied the empty saddles behind Dynod and Nimi-eye then said, "I'll arrange it."

Galaeron offered his thanks and resumed his place then led the column down a hanging gorge into the forests of the Upper Vale. The trees were ancient and enormous, mostly spear spruce tall enough to scratch the sky. The trail descended sharply, winding through ravines and around craggy outcroppings where the treetops grew thin enough to show streaks of distant cliff.

Though Galaeron was free to remove the humans' blindfolds at any time, he did not. He was convinced that Melegaunt had some way of seeing other than eyes. The wizard sat in his saddle easily, holding his body upright and still even when his black mount slipped or stumbled. In contrast, the other humans rode comfortably but loosely, swaying to every twist in the trail. Vala's jaw remained clenched and tense, her red lip raised in an indignant sneer.

Her patience lasted only a quarter hour, until the trail left the steep slopes of the Upper Vale and descended into the terraces of the Vine Vale.

"How about these blinders and bindings, elf?" she demanded. "I can tell by the wind we're out of the Passing."

"The blinders, yes." Galaeron stopped and motioned Nimi-eye forward to remove the blindfolds—actually leather half-hoods enchanted to confuse the wearer's sense of direction. "The bindings remain."

"What?" Despite the question, Vala did not seem overly surprised. "I should have known not to trust an elf."

"I promised nothing."

"It was implied," Vala snarled.

"Careful, child. We are in no position to lecture Galaeron about his ethics," said Melegaunt. He let Nimieye remove his hood then locked gazes with Galaeron. "Much will depend on whether he blames us or simple accident for the loss of his patrol."

"Then we are lost," said Vala. "Men make better scapegoats than misfortune."

" 'Tis so, but I think our friend smarter than that." Melegaunt continued to watch Galaeron. "What say you, elf? Will you call us crypt breakers and thieves, or victims like yourself?"

"That's for the Hill Elders to decide," said Galaeron. "My duty is only to tell what happened."

The answer was a dodge, for the truth lay somewhere between the extremes laid out by the wizard. The humans had broken an elven crypt, but the ones inside had been nobles of the much despised Vyshaan clan, and even then nothing had been stolen. And while the humans had resisted the patrol's attempt to capture them, they had risked their own lives to avoid injuring elves. Given these facts, Galaeron's attitude would carry more than a little weight with the Elders.

What Galaeron did not know was how much to trust the humans. There was an undeniable aura of darkness about Melegaunt, and it had crossed Galaeron's mind that the battle in the Vyshaan crypt might be no more than an elaborate ruse to sneak a powerful and evil wizard into Evereska.

Melegaunt smiled crookedly at Galaeron's response then watched as Nimieye removed the hoods from Vala's followers. The three men—Vala had introduced them as Burlen, Kuhl, and Dexon—blinked and glowered at Galaeron, portending the black look Vala shot him when her own hood came off.

"Mind how you tell your tale, elf," she said. "Helm has a memory for word breakers."

"That might concern me, were I a word breaker or a human." Galaeron was beginning to feel a very humanlike anger at the woman. "As it is, I'm a tomb guard holding a band of crypt breakers in custody, with no reason to trust them."

The woman opened her mouth to retort, but Galaeron cut her off by glancing over to check on Takari. The scout was still slouched in front of Ehamond, not quite slumbering, but in some state far deeper than Reverie. It was a bad sign, for elves did not sleep unless they were ill or badly wounded. Galaeron started down the trail at a trot, determined to have Takari in a healer's hands before Eastpeak's shadow left Moondark Hill.

Despite the many concerns facing him—or perhaps because of them—Galaeron found himself bitterly disappointed by the humans' indifference when Nimieye removed their blindfolds. This section of the trail was the most striking part of the return to Evereska, with a vast staircase of vineyards descending toward the city in a series of mist-shrouded terraces, and not one human had stopped glowering at him long enough to notice the view.

In the bottom of the valley lay a rolling patchwork of fields both gold and black. From Galaeron's perspective high in the Vine Vale, these farmlands formed a deep crescent in the bottom of the valley, with the thousand foot cliffs of the High Sharaedim ringing it on the exterior and Evereska looming up in the center. Though the city was often described as walled—usually by bombastic humans who based their "eyewitness" accounts on tales bribed from elves half-drunk on the Halfway Inn's potent elquesstria—the walls were in fact the smooth-polished cliffs of the Three Sisters, the largest of the dozen hills upon which Evereska rested.

Behind the cliff tops rose hundreds of towers, soaring up out of a thick bluetop forest to make the city look like a many-spired crown. Most spires rose to twice the height of the surrounding trees, some even higher than the peaks of the High Sharaedim. Their exteriors swarmed with lines of antlike figures, residents of the city going about their daily business with no thought as to how strange it looked from below.

Such was the magic of Evereska, jewel of the mountains, and Galaeron considered anyone who failed to gasp at its wonders worthy of doubt. He led his prisoners down the Vine Vale terraces via a series of gentle switchbacks, then traveled down a narrow lane to the walled pasturelands that surrounded Evereska. As they approached the boundary, Galaeron spoke a word of passing. The gilded gate swung open, admitting the column into a rolling meadow dotted with boulders and bigcone firs. Like many of Evereska's defenses, the gate's purpose was not obvious. While it was not magical, it marked the perimeter of the city's most priceless treasure and best-kept secret, the mythal.

As intangible as it was invincible, the mythal was a mantle of living magic woven by the high mages of old. Galaeron did not fully understand its nature—when the masters spoke of it at all, it was only to claim that no elf alive could comprehend a mythal's intricacies—but most elves believed it to be a mesh of mystic energies spun from the life-forces of its ancient casters, the favor of Corellon Larethian, and the fabric of Faerûn's magic Weave. What Galaeron did know was that first and foremost, the mythal was Evereska's most potent defense, capable of plaguing foes with a dazzling array of assaults—including the famous gold bolts so often attributed to Corellon's guardianship. The mythal also provided other blessings, such as the ability of the city's inhabitants to climb vertical walls. In return, it required only that the elves maintain the health of its sustaining lands.

As the rest of the column crossed the mythal's perimeter, Galaeron glanced over his shoulder to look for any sign that Melegaunt perceived the magic field. The wizard's eyes remained as dusky and unreadable as ever, exhibiting neither curiosity nor surprise as they scrutinized the meadow's green grass and the butterflies still bobbing along in the breeze. Vala and the other humans were a stark contrast to Melegaunt's nonchalance, gawking about with fallen jaws and craning their necks to stare up Evereska's thousand-foot cliffs.

Satisfied that neither Melegaunt nor any of the humans sensed the mythal, Galaeron led the column across the meadow to the Tomb Guard Livery. A simple three-walled shed with a station for each patrol to store its harness and tack, there were no pens or stalls, nor even any mangers or watering troughs. Galaeron dismounted and made his assignments then unbound the humans' feet and helped them dismount as well.

"Nimieye will unsaddle and curry your mounts." He slung the humans' sword belts over his shoulder, taking care not to let the glassy pommels touch his skin. "But we don't corral our beasts."

"It is no bother," said Melegaunt. His hands remained bound like those of the other humans; unlike the others, he did not seem irritated or particularly worried by it. "Raven will bring our mounts when I send for him—though I trust we won't be returning to the Desert Border on horses."

"That much we are safe in assuming, yes," said Galaeron.

Vala gave him a dark look, then stepped out from beneath the livery shed and tipped her head back to stare up the cliff. "How do we get up there?"

"Dynod will lead the way."

Galaeron nodded to Dynod, who took Takari from Ehamond's arms and entered a small, irregular chamber hewn into the cliff base. He vanished from sight, as did Ehamond when he followed. Galaeron motioned Vala and the other humans to follow, then stepped through himself. There was a golden flash and a brief feeling of falling, and when he put his foot down again, it was onto a marble-paved lane filled with the zesty scent of dusktop blossoms.

Vala and her men stood at the edge of the street, silently gawking at the wondrous forest around them. White-paved paths curved off in every direction, twisting through an eye-boggling tangle of towers and trunks. In the sylvan shade, it was difficult even for Galaeron to tell which was which. The trees were uniformly as large around as castle towers, with cross-striped bark ranging from white to gray, and branches so high overhead it was not unusual for mist to form *beneath* the leaf canopy. The towers were sometimes smaller than the tree boles and sometimes larger, but most were almost indistinguishable from the mighty bluetops that dominated the outer rim of the city.

With the sun just rising above Eastpeak's craggy shoulder, it was the busiest time of day. Elves were everywhere, gliding along the ground paths, popping out of high doorways to clamber headfirst down the tower exterior, sometimes even soaring from one building to another like flying squirrels. Even with the unpleasantness to come, Galaeron found himself feeling more content and peaceful than even the calmest desert afternoon lounging naked in a pool of cool canyon water. This was Evereska, Lasthaven to all the elves of Faerûn, sanctuary to Galaeron and all Tel'Quess who would hold some home for their race against the relentless tide of human expansion.

"I believe we are to follow Dynod and Ehamond," said Melegaunt, nudging Vala and the others up the lane. "Galaeron will inform us when we should turn off."

"Follow them all the way." The long ride had fatigued Galaeron more than he thought. Though he always enjoyed his return to Evereska, he usually did not come so close to slipping into Reverie the instant he entered it. He shook himself alert and started up the lane. "We will see Takari to the Hall of the High Hunt."

Melegaunt stopped, finally seeming to take exception to Galaeron's instructions. "Do you think that wise? We wouldn't want to keep the Hill Elders waiting."

"You will do as I say, human." Galaeron pushed Melegaunt after the others but quickly regretted his tone. His anger had more to do with the danger he had unleashed on the city than anything Melegaunt had done. In a gentler voice, he added, "We'll be speaking with the elders sooner than you think, Melegaunt. In Evereska, we have our own ways of doing things."

The path ascended along the bank of a small stream, passing several waterfalls artfully arranged to spill from the mouths of deep emerald pools. As they walked, elves young and old paused to stare at Galaeron's prisoners in open disgust, in part because some had never before seen a human, in part because they knew by the captives' bound hands and Galaeron's Tomb Guard cape that these were crypt breakers. Vala and her warriors did their best to fulfill expectations by sneering and glowering, but no one seemed to take these threats seriously. Galaeron wondered how that might have changed had they witnessed what he had beneath the tomb of the Vyshaan.

By the time they began to traverse Moondark Hill toward the Hall of the High Hunt, a small band of elderly elves had completely encircled the humans. Though none rose any higher than the chest of Vala's shortest man, they did not hesitate to laugh at the captives and make fun of their barbaric appearance, often in languages they knew the prisoners could understand. Though Galaeron could see the humans chafing under this abuse and would certainly have been insulted by it himself, he did nothing to prevent it. To Vala's great credit, she had only to issue one stern command to rivet the eyes of her men straight ahead and render them unresponsive to the mockery.

Finally, the tallest of the elves pulled back his hood and stepped to Galaeron's side. "Glad homeagain, young Nihmedu," he said in Elvish. "I see you've brought us some crypt breakers."

Galaeron looked over to find himself looking at a moon elf

with silver hair and a dignified bearing borne of great age and long service.

He bowed without stopping and answered in Elvish, "Lord Duirsar."

The elf lord nodded to someone behind him, then the tomb master, Kiinyon Colbathin, stepped up on the other side. His expression was far easier to read than High Lord Duirsar's—and Galaeron had good reason to wish it was not.

"We've been given to understand that in addition to losing your patrol, you could not wait to make your excuses," the tomb master said, sneering at Melegaunt's back and speaking in Common. "I hope it took more than these five."

Allowing herself a luxury she denied her men, Vala spun on the elf. "It wouldn't have taken that many, had I intended them harm."

"That's enough, child." Melegaunt forced Vala up the path. "Let the fools have their fun. We will make our case to the elders."

Galaeron had to restrain a smile. Whether Melegaunt knew it or not, he and the other humans were already making their case. The elves abusing them *were* the Hill Elders, and they had already begun the trial that would determine whether the crypt breakers lived or died. Kiinyon Colbathin reached out and shoved Melegaunt hard, causing him to trip and stumble into Vala.

Melegaunt merely raised his chin and continued on without speaking, as did Vala. Kiinyon shoved the wizard once more. When Melegaunt made no response except to catch himself before he stumbled into Vala, the tomb master turned his acerbic tongue on Galaeron.

"So, how did the great Galaeron Nihmedu lose his patrol to a band of thieving human murderers? Tell us."

"Be careful who you call thieves and murderers." Vala did not look back as she spoke. "We took nothing and killed no one."

Lord Duirsar cocked a querying brow, and Galaeron nodded.

"That much is true," he said. "We tracked them through an opened tomb, but they left the bodies and treasure untouched."

Galaeron went on to recount how he followed the crypt breakers into the dwarven working beneath the tomb and found them using a beholder to disintegrate a section of wall. Kiinyon Colbathin raised his brow and regarded the humans with newfound respect, for he knew himself how difficult the creatures were to destroy, much less enslave. Galaeron went on to describe how the beholder had killed Aragath and how the humans had refused to surrender but avoided fatal attacks. Vala could not help pointing out here that had she not restrained her men, the matter would have ended with the death of Galaeron's patrol, which would have been a much better outcome for everyone concerned.

Noting the look of condemnation that flashed through Kiinyon's eyes, Galaeron found himself wondering if the woman was trying to get herself killed. He went on to explain how he had heard Melegaunt calling for help then ruptured the Sharn Wall by ordering his patrol to attack the phaerimm with magic missiles.

"*You*, Galaeron? Puncturing the Sharn Wall?" scoffed Kiinyon. "You've always had a high opinion of your talents, but this is a bit much even for you."

Lord Duirsar was not so quick to dismiss the account. "Kiinyon, if he didn't rupture the Sharn Wall, how do you explain the phaerimm?" The high lord shook his head in despair. "Galaeron, how did you do this thing?"

Melegaunt turned to address them. "Not that Galaeron has any need to explain himself to you, but the fault wasn't his. It was an unfortunate, ah, *blending* of magic that ruptured the Sharn Wall. If there is any blame, it belongs on my shoulders, not his. I should have foreseen the possibility. Now, if you will excuse us, good lords, we really must be on our way."

Melegaunt grabbed Galaeron by the elbow and pulled him up the trail, and it was only then that Galaeron realized they had reached their destination. The Hall of the High Hunt was a great colonnade of soaring shadowtops that enclosed the Singing Spring of Solonor Thelandira, a gurgling fountain of silver waters whose sacred melodies could cure any wound. Dynod and Ehamond were already disappearing between the trunks of two shadowtops, holding Takari aloft between them and calling for High Huntsman Trueshot.

"I know all elves share a special bond, but we must alert the Hill Elders," Melegaunt said, still unaware of who had been tormenting him. "Remember, we have only until nightfall."

"Until nightfall?" echoed Kiinyon. "Why until nightfall?"

"In good time," said Melegaunt. "Now, as I said—"

"It is only a guess." Galaeron ignored the wizard's insistent tugging and continued to address the tomb master. "In truth, they may be free already, but this human laid some spells that he hopes will delay them until this evening."

"This *evening*?" Lord Duirsar cast an uneasy glance at Kiinyon. "That is no time at all."

Melegaunt glanced thoughtfully from Galaeron to Lord Duirsar then finally seemed to realize to whom he was talking and stepped forward to address the elf lord. "Milord, I know the time is but an instant by elven measures, but I assure you that if you can spare me only a small company of wizards and three high mages, I will have the situation under control before then."

Lord Duirsar stared at Melegaunt as though he were mad. "*You*, human? I should say you have done quite enough." He turned to Kiinyon. "Gather what forces you need, Tomb Master, though I agree with the crypt breaker in this much: a high mage or two may be in order, if their studies can be interrupted."

"*If?*" Melegaunt growled. "Milord, perhaps I did not explain clearly enough. You will need me and three high mages—"

"Do not presume to tell me what I need," said Duirsar.

"Evereska was old before your ancestors left their caves. I think us more than capable of cleaning up any mess you can make."

"It is a wonder your head is not as pointed as your ears!" Vala snapped. She stepped toward the elf lord and instantly found herself facing the tips of a dozen sharp swords, Galaeron's among them. She stopped but seemed completely nonplussed. "You have no idea who you—"

"That is enough, my dear." Melegaunt raised his hand to silence her. "If the elves will not accept our help, there are others who will."

"Perhaps so, but they will be difficult to reach from the inside of a bone cage," said Kiinyon. "Evereska is not in the habit of freeing crypt breakers."

Kiinyon glanced around the crowd, and Galaeron realized he was already calling for the Hill Elders' verdict.

"If it pleases the council, I should point out that the tomb they broke was Vyshaan," said Galaeron. While Melegaunt was being both presumptuous and rude in assuming the ancient magic of elves to be less than his own, his only intention was to help, which bound Galaeron in honor to speak on behalf of the humans. "The humans stole nothing. They meant no harm, and in truth the only harm they did was to a clan reviled of gods and elves alike."

Kiinyon Colbathin regarded Galaeron coldly. "And what of the lives lost? The lives of *your* patrol?"

"That was fate's doing," said Galaeron. "And if not fate's, then my own."

This drew a soft whistle from Vala, who said softly, "The worm grows a spine. . . ."

Galaeron ignored her and gestured at Melegaunt. "All the humans save this one were our captives when the phaerimm attacked, and I owe it to him that any of us survived."

"So you say the humans committed no crime?" asked Duirsar.

"The council should not rush to judgment." As a tomb

guard, Galaeron could hardly contend that crypt breaking was not a crime. "There is much to consider here."

Lord Duirsar studied those around him. Though no human could have read the indecision in their expressions, it was plain enough to Galaeron. Elves were neither cruel nor hasty, and they would not sentence even a human to death without all due consideration.

At length, Duirsar turned to Galaeron. "Until the Hill Elders come to a decision, we will leave our guests in the care of your family." He turned to Kiinyon Colbathin and added, "Unless the Tomb Guard has more pressing duties for him?"

"Nothing that will interfere." The tomb master glared at Galaeron and tipped his slender chin toward the Hall of the High Hunt. "See to Takari and Ehamond. We'll talk about the lost ones when I return."

Kiinyon turned and the other Hill Elders left without another word, leaving the humans to look after them in puzzlement. The captives' expressions grew even more bewildered when Galaeron began to undo their bindings.

"They have freed us?" Melegaunt asked.

Galaeron shook his head. "You are my guests."

"But the phaerimm . . ."

"Are Evereska's concern," said Galaeron. "You have warned the Hill Elders, and now you must await their decision on the matter of the crypt breaking."

The humans looked at their unbound hands and seemed more confused than ever.

"My family does not treat its guests as prisoners," Galaeron clarified.

"And if we leave?" asked Melegaunt.

"You must not," Galaeron said. "My family has guaranteed your conduct."

"It has?" Vala asked. "When did you do that?"

"*I* didn't." Galaeron returned her sword. "You did, when you reacted to the Taunting with both honor and restraint. Those are virtues held in much esteem by the Hill Elders."

Vala's eyes lit with sudden understanding. "But you spoke for us." She gave him a rugged smile. "You surprise me, elf. I take back half the bad things I've ever said about you."

CHAPTER FOUR

21 Nightal, the Year of the Unstrung Harp

By the time Galaeron slipped into the leaf-shadowed Hall of the High Hunt, Takari lay naked in the Singing Spring, her complexion returned to its normal bronze and her eyes lucid for the first time since being wounded. Behind her stood an aged moon elf wearing no more clothes than she, his arms hooked beneath hers to hold her above the shimmering surface. The air smelled of moss and sweet water, and the song of the silver fountain trilled through the woody pavilion in gay melodies. Ehamond sat beneath the lilting spray as naked as the others, his cuts and bruises already fading. Dynod stood on the bank with two minor priests, describing the destruction of the patrol.

As Galaeron entered the grove, one of the priests nodded in his direction. There was no hint of embarrassment as Dynod turned toward him. Elves seldom relished the failures of others and therefore had few misgivings about discussing them. Having suffered more than his share of pitying looks and sympathetic encouragement, it was one of the few traits Galaeron wished he could change about the Fair Folk.

Dynod's eyes slid past Galaeron toward the edge of the pavilion, where the humans stood waiting, Melegaunt looking tentative and the others even more awestruck than usual. Knowing the glade of Solonor Thelandira to be the one temple in Evereska where humans would not be an intrusion, Galaeron motioned them forward and turned back to Dynod.

"Then the humans were absolved?" asked Dynod.

"Closer to it than I," answered Galaeron.

Dynod and the priests exchanged knowing looks, then one of the priests offered one of those compassionate little comments Galaeron had learned to loathe early in his studies at the Academy of Magic. "You mustn't worry. Tomb Master Colbathin is a stern commander, but a fair one."

Dynod rolled his eyes and looked away, and Galaeron said, "Had we spent the last two decades in the Greycloaks instead of the Desert Border South, I'd be more inclined to believe that." Ignoring the surprise on the faces of the two priests, he kneeled beside the water and called to Takari. "How do you feel?"

"Like a moth with a fang hole in its back." Her voice was cheerful, if rather weak. "Sick, but happy to be alive."

"I have healed the wound," said Pleufan Trueshot, the aged huntsman holding her. He rolled the scout over to display a inflamed lump where the hole once was. "But I can't rid her of the pestilence."

"It may not be an infection," said Melegaunt, stepping to the bank beside Galaeron. "May I have a look?"

Pleufan nodded. "You are welcome in the Singing Spring."

Much to Galaeron's astonishment, Melegaunt stepped into the water without removing so much as his boots. Dynod and Ehamond also raised their brows, but the high huntsman and his two assistants, who often numbered humans among their worshipers during the monthly Ceremonies, showed no surprise.

Galaeron glanced over at Vala to see if she found the behavior odd, but her expression was one of such total astonishment he could not tell what she was thinking. Her men, however, were staring at Takari with such a look of feral hunger that he began to worry the Hill Elders had misread the humans' reaction during the Taunting. This puzzled him even more than Melegaunt's odd behavior, since the humans had known Takari only as an incoherent battle casualty. Under the circumstances, they could hardly have developed any feelings of love for her, so it was hard for an elf to understand why the mere sight of her naked body should inflame their passions.

Trailing a murky cloud of mud from his trail-worn clothes, Melegaunt waded to the center of the pool and stopped beside Takari. He prodded the sore then looked back to Galaeron.

"The phaerimm did this with its tail, did it not?" Without waiting for a reply, he continued, "Did you see it inject anything?"

"The tail pulsed," said Galaeron. "Later, I saw something small and hot at the bottom of the wound."

Pleufan looked up. "I've tried every poison antidote I know."

Melegaunt shook his head. "Phaerimm don't inject poison," he said. "They inject eggs."

"Eggs?" Takari craned her head around so hard she twisted free of Pleufan's grasp. "What do you mean 'eggs'?"

"Only one at a time," said Melegaunt. He looked to the high hunter. "This is how they reproduce."

"Like caterpillar wasps?" Takari paled to a sickly saffron. "Kill me now! I want nothing eating me from the inside."

"It won't come to that." Melegaunt turned to the high

hunter. "Cut out the egg and treat her as for an ague. If she rests, she'll be fine in a tenday."

Takari did not look convinced. "Easy for you to say—"

"Yes, it is. I've cut out six—and no healer to see me through the fever." Melegaunt patted the scout on the cheek, then nodded to the high hunter and waded back to shore.

"Dynod, you'll see that she does as instructed." Galaeron looked to Takari and added, "Then you are to return to your own people for a year."

"Thank you," Takari said, her eyes turning sad, "but I'll wait until after Kiinyon—"

"No, go as soon as you are able," said Galaeron. "Even if he has not spoken it, Kiinyon has already made his decision. I want you gone while the order is mine to give. It has been too long since you walked the High Forest."

Takari's eyes grew liquid. "I will—"

Galaeron raised his hand. "We'll talk before you go," he said. "See me when you're able."

Takari nodded then allowed herself to sink back into Pleufan's arms. "Till next."

"Till next."

Galaeron told the priests to thank the high hunter for him and gave them a gold lion for their goddess, then waited as Melegaunt climbed out of the water. The human rubbed his fingers together, running through the gestures of a minor drying spell, but nothing happened. He frowned and tried it again.

His clothes remained as wet as before.

"Allow me," said Galaeron, more than a little puzzled by the wizard's failure. The mythal would turn back the spell of any non-elf attempting harmful magic within Evereska. But a drying spell was hardly harmful, and Melegaunt would have suffered some adverse effect, had he meant to cause injury. Instead, the enchantment had simply failed. "Is there an incantation?"

Melegaunt raised his bushy brow but shook his head.

Galaeron ran his fingers through the same gestures as the wizard then felt the Weave's magic course through him. There was a sizzle and a small flash, then Melegaunt's clothes were dry and smoking.

Melegaunt patted out a small flame. "Did you copy my spell?"

"It's a small talent I have," said Galaeron, glossing over the long explanation of his enrollment in, then expulsion from the Academy of Magic. "It wasn't as strange as your other spells."

"Amazing," said Melegaunt. "You could learn a little control, but amazing nonetheless."

"Would that you were a master in the Academy of Magic," Galaeron laughed.

He turned and led the humans out of the grove. As they returned to the marble-paved lanes outside, Vala came to his side.

"You should have kissed her," she said.

Galaeron nearly stumbled. "Takari? Why would I do that?"

"Isn't that what elf lovers do when they part?" asked Vala. "Or do only humans kiss?"

"We kiss—though not as often as humans, judging by how you breed," said Galaeron, "but Vala and I are not lovers."

"I take back the twelve nice words I've said about you," said Vala. "Only a tusker would treat a woman in love so badly."

"Tusker?"

"Orc," explained Melegaunt. "And Vala, it's hardly a guest's place to interrogate her host about such matters."

Vala lowered her eyes at once. "Of course. I apologize." She fell a step behind and allowed Melegaunt to take her place.

Galaeron glanced back, a little troubled by how quickly her spirit vanished at any hint of the wizard's disapproval. He had been trying to puzzle out their relationship since departing the Vyshaan crypt, but whenever he mentioned the Granite Tower or their past, Melegaunt always changed the subject. Vala told him to mind his own business.

Deciding the best way to win Vala's confidence was to be open himself, Galaeron said, "There's no need to apologize, Vala, but we have never been lovers." He could tell by the look in her eyes that she knew there was more to the story. "We could have been, but such things always come to bad end between moon elves and Wood elves."

"Really?" It was Melegaunt who asked this. "I wasn't aware of that."

"Perhaps because you are not an elf," Galaeron replied.

Ignoring the curious—and sometimes hostile—looks of the pedestrians they passed, Galaeron led the way across the great sunning meadow at the base of Bellcrest Hill and started up Goldmorn Knoll. Apparently sensing the melancholy that had come over him, Melegaunt allowed Galaeron a few minutes of introspection before speaking again.

"They're going to get killed, you know."

Galaeron did not need to ask who the wizard meant. "It would be a mistake to judge our high mages by my skills." He spoke in a low voice, and even then only when they were near no other elves. "Lord Duirsar was not exaggerating when he told you how old Evereska's magic is."

"Old yes, and powerful as well, I'm sure," said Melegaunt. "But how much do your high mages know of the phaerimm? You didn't even know what they were, and your priest wouldn't have realized what was wrong with Takari until the hatchling ate its way through her entrails."

"And how do you know so much about them?" asked Galaeron.

Without answering the question, Melegaunt said, "The phaerimm have spent the last thousand years starving beneath Anauroch, barely sustaining themselves on the few Bedine their slaves can kidnap or lure through the Sharn Wall. And now we—you and I, Galaeron—have given them a chance to escape. I promise you, they will be quick to seize it."

"Which still does not answer my question. Why do you know so much about them?"

"Because I have spent the last century studying them," said Melegaunt. When Galaeron remained silent, he added, "That's all you need know."

"And all you need know is that I won't break my word to Lord Duirsar," said Galaeron. "Not on your say-so. Not on my own life."

"It is not your life I'm worried about."

"Then tell me why," said Galaeron. "If I'm convinced, we will speak again with the Hill Elders—"

"Who would rather see Evereska fall than accept help from a human."

"Who have dealt with enough humans to know their help is never free," said Galaeron. "I'm not a fifth their age, and I have learned that for myself."

They rounded the corner and came to the granite bank of Dawnsglory Pond, where two dozen laughing elves were availing themselves of the morning light to bathe and play in the steaming waters. Galaeron led his companions along to a quiet corner, where a pair of winsome Sun elf sisters were washing the tangles from their hair.

The eldest, a stunning beauty with violet flecks in her eyes, looked up. "Glad homeagain, Galaeron. We heard about Louenghris and your silvers. He will be missed."

Galaeron winced at how fast the news was spreading. It would arrive at his father's before he did. "As will they all, Zharilee." He gestured behind him, where he could almost feel the heat rising off the humans at the sight of the naked sisters. "These are in my care until the Hill Elders decide their fate, and I'm sorry to say they have need of a bath before I take them to my father's."

The youngest wrinkled her nose. "Keep a close watch on them." She rolled onto her back and started toward the center of the pool. "I don't like how that crooked nosed one looks at me."

There was the sound of a heavy blow, then Vala growled, "Close 'em or lose 'em, Kuhl."

Galaeron gave the sisters a moment to retreat, then waved his guests into the pool. "If you please." He glanced toward Melegaunt and added, "It's customary to remove your clothes."

The men's expressions changed from hungry to nervous, and they looked to Vala for instruction.

Vala shrugged and said, "Why not?"

She unbuckled her sword belt, then sat down and began to unlace her high boots. Her men reluctantly followed her example, and ten minutes later they were splashing in the water like pup otters. The men all looked like rothé, with thick tangles of dark hair across their massive backs and huge barrel chests. Vala was stout but much smaller, with rounder curves than an elf woman and—thankfully—only small tufts of hair growing in the appropriate places, but her idea of sport was as rough as that of her men. When they began to play keep-away with one of her boots, she did not hesitate to yank things most elves would have considered it impolite for even good friends to touch. The men responded in kind, grabbing whatever they could in order to keep her at bay. They even tried to include Galaeron in their games, tossing her boot—and Vala herself—at him. So surprised was he to see her eyeing him with the same hungry look he had noticed in the men that he forgot to defend himself and let her hand dart past his guard—and he was even more surprised by what she grabbed. She bowled him over backward and, burying his face in her soft chest, snatched her boot from his grasp.

Galaeron came up coughing, and found Vala holding her boot coyly in one hand. "What's the matter, elf?" She gave him one of those hungry human smiles, then tossed the boot on the bank. "Still too dirty?"

"Not at all." Suddenly feeling very self-conscious, Galaeron turned toward the bank. "My house is not far. We'll break our fast and see to cleaning your clothes and armor later."

They all climbed out of the water and bundled their armor inside their cloaks. Without their clothes, the humans looked a lot less intimidating and drew far fewer sneers, and it was not long before they reached the summit of Goldmorn Knoll. Located well into the interior of Evereska, the knoll was not as high as the Three Sisters nor as large, but it was home to a sizable grove of rare sycamore trees that had left Cormyr during the Time of Troubles and sought refuge in Evereska. Galaeron could not help smiling when he recalled the sight of that endless line of trees marching past his camp along the Desert Border and vanishing into the Sharaedim. He came to the base of Starmeadow Tower—before the sycamores arrived, it had stood in the heart of a favorite meadow for stargazing—and pointed at a hole-shaped doorway seventy feet above.

"There is my home. If you are ever lost in the city, ask for Treetop in Starmeadow, and you will be returned here."

"Treetop," repeated Dexon. The burly human craned his neck, watching a pair of elves crawl past the doorway head-down. "Where's the ladder?"

Galaeron smiled. "There is no need for ladders in Evereska."

He tucked his armor under one arm, then pressed one palm and the sole of the opposite foot to the wall. Thanks to the magic of the mythal, they held fast to the stone, and he began to climb.

"Always use bare skin. Never wear gloves or shoes."

Vala and the others watched him warily for a few moments, then finally pressed their own palms to the wall and started to follow. They were even more delighted than at the pond, and it was not long before they were embarrassing Galaeron with excited whoops and yodels.

Only Melegaunt, who in truth looked like he needed to use more muscle and less magic, did not seem to relish the experience. He stood on the ground for several moments trying to cast a flying spell, which failed as utterly as had his drying magic, then he finally gave up and clambered up the wall. By the time he joined Galaeron and the others beside the door, he was huffing and puffing so heavily he could hardly speak. Galaeron showed the humans the safest way to enter and leave a door hole, which was to approach it from the side rather than clamber over the bottom, and entered.

Inside Treetop was airy and light, all smooth curves and softly glowing walls. A staircase swirled down from the upper floors, rounded a corner in the foyer before them, and flowed into the lower house. Along the walls sat benches of white marble and tables of translucent alabaster, often with a delicately embossed vase or ethereal statuette placed carefully on top.

Galaeron's youngest sister, eighty-year-old Keya, appeared in the doorway.

"Galaeron!" She rushed across the room in a streak of long blue hair and gold-threaded gown and embraced him. "Glad homeagain! This past year has seemed a tenwinter!"

Happy for a change to hear nothing about his lost patrol or how his chances with the tomb master are better than he thinks, Galaeron dropped his armor and hugged her to his chest.

"Keya! More the lady each time I see you." He held the embrace for a moment, then disengaged himself and turned to present his companions. "The Hill Elders have asked me to care for these guests."

"I know." Keya took one look at the looming mounds of hairy flesh and said, "I'm sure one of your tunics will fit the woman."

"Vala," said Vala. She offered her free hand and studied Keya as though sizing up an object of prey. "Well met."

Keya retreated from the stocky appendage in confusion.

"You're to clasp it," Galaeron explained. "A human gesture of friendship."

Keya looked up at Galaeron, her gold-flecked eyes clearly asking if such a thing were truly necessary.

Galaeron took her hand and placed it in Vala's. "You'll have to forgive Keya," he said, laughing. "I'm afraid my sister has never heard humans called anything but thieves and murderers."

"Sister?" Vala's expression softened, and she pumped Keya's hand warmly. "Don't you believe everything Galaeron says about us. I hope you and I will be great friends."

"I'm sure that would be, um, interesting. I've never had a human friend before."

Keya turned to the men and reluctantly offered her hand to each in turn, looking slightly puzzled as they blushed and struggled to cover themselves. Even Melegaunt seemed embarrassed, though he did a better job of hiding it than most.

"I can probably find a cloak that will fit the plump one, but these others . . ." Keya shook her head. "I doubt our blankets are large enough to go around their shoulders."

"Their waists will do, I think," said Galaeron. "Is Father here?"

"In the contemplation." Keya gestured through an archway toward the back of the house, then looked to Melegaunt. "He asks you and Melegaunt to attend him at once. A messenger has arrived from Lord Duirsar."

"From Duirsar?" Melegaunt allowed himself a superior smile, then started for the archway. "Come to his senses, no doubt."

"If you would be so kind, Keya. . . ." Galaeron said.

He motioned to Vala and her men, then went after Melegaunt. He steered the wizard through the circular great room, where the family took its meals on the rare occasions when there were enough of them to fill it, then stepped through a broad archway into the contemplation. His father was standing at the back of the tome-filled chamber, staring over the treetops through a theurglass window. A white snow finch sat on his outstretched finger, chirping and tweeting rapidly—no doubt passing along the latest gossip from

Cloudcrown Hill, where the palaces of Lord Duirsar and the great nobles sat scattered among the trees.

Galaeron cleared his throat. "Father? We've arrived."

His father turned at once, a broad grin bringing a little light to his morose eyes. With silver hair and sagging shoulders, he seemed older and smaller than he had the last time Galaeron had been home.

"My son. Glad homeagain."

The bird chirped a greeting as well, though Galaeron was not versed in peeptalk and could only return it with a polite bob of his head.

Galaeron gestured to Melegaunt. "Meet Melegaunt Tanthul, a human wizard of strange magic and no small power."

Galaeron's father inclined his head. "Welcome to Treetop, uh, *Wizard* Tanthul."

"I am a prince in my own city," said Melegaunt, noting the elder Nihmedu's uncertainty about how to address him. "But in truth I've been away so long I have all but forgotten the fact. Call me Melegaunt."

"And I am Aubric."

"Well met, Aubric, and my thanks for opening your home to us." Melegaunt peered around the contemplation, his eyes sliding past the Reverie couch and reading stand as he searched for another person. "I was given to understand there is a messenger?"

Galaeron's father raised the snow finch on his finger. "This is Manynests, attendant to Lord Duirsar."

Manynests chipped in greeting, then launched into a long series of tweets and whistles.

"Lord Duirsar sends his greetings and salutations," translated Galaeron's father. "He reports that Evereska's wizards—" A peep from Manynests prompted him to correct himself. "—that our *high mages* required over an hour to solve your shadow maze."

Melegaunt's eyes widened. "Only an hour?"

The bird began twittering again, and Galaeron's father

translated, "Lord Duirsar was surprised that it took them that long. He sends his compliments and inquires whether you would be willing to supply them with the passwords for the traps in the dwarven workings. As entertaining as the high mages find your work, there is a certain element of time involved."

"Yes, of course." So shocked was Melegaunt that he dropped onto the Reverie couch, drawing a wince from both Nihmedus as his hairy rear touched the pristine marble. "The first is purpledusk, the second darkmorn."

"Purpledusk and darkmorn?" Galaeron's father repeated, translating for Manynests.

When Melegaunt nodded, the bird peeped its thanks and took wing, darting through the theurglass window almost before the elder Nihmedu could utter the command word rendering it permeable.

Galaeron went to Melegaunt's side and said, "You surprised me, but it's good that you did not try to use the passwords to coerce your way into battle."

Melegaunt's eyes were still round with shock. "It wouldn't have been much of a coercion. If it only took an hour to break the shadow maze, they would have been through the other spells by midmorn."

"Still, it speaks well of your intentions that you did not hesitate," said the elder Nihmedu. "Manynests will report your cooperation, and that will count for much when the Hill Elders discuss the matter of your crypt breaking."

"I hope it will count for as much as Lord Imesfor's anger," said Galaeron. "I happened across Zharilee and Gvendor when we bathed, and the Golds have already begun to discuss Louenghris's death."

A cloud came over his father's eyes. "I doubt Louenghris's death will count against the humans. Manynests tells me that Lord Duirsar is already thinking of suspending Lord Imesfor from any deliberation related to his son's death. Your fate is a different matter. Kiinyon sent young Imesfor to the Desert

Border for a reason, and he'll blame you for any ill will that befalls the tomb guards because of the lad's death."

"He'll blame me for any trouble he can," said Galaeron. "He's already made that much clear—and perhaps I deserve it. I *did* lose two thirds of my patrol."

"And did more good than you will ever know." Melegaunt stood. "I don't mean to speak immodestly, but had you left me to the phaerimm, it would have been a great loss to the world."

"Because?" asked the elder Nihmedu.

"Because it would have been a cowardly thing to do," Melegaunt dodged, no more eager to reveal himself to Lord Nihmedu than to Galaeron. "And your son is no coward. Under the circumstances, he did all that could be asked and more. Kiinyon Colbathin will come to understand that, if he and the others are lucky enough to survive."

"Then we have nothing to worry about." Galaeron's father clasped both Melegaunt and Galaeron on the shoulders and steered them toward the great room. "Kiinyon Colbathin always survives. Now perhaps we should break our fast. With the passwords in hand, the high mages are likely to have the phaerimm destroyed by midmorn, and I don't want you facing the Hill Elders on an empty stomach."

CHAPTER FIVE

23 Nightal, the Year of the Unstrung Harp

The high mages did not have the Sharn Wall patched by highsun of the twenty-first. They did not have it repaired by dusk, nor even deepnight. Grateful for Melegaunt's earlier aid, Lord Duirsar kept the Nihmedus informed via his bird messengers. Kiinyon lost a company of tomb guards when they bypassed Melegaunt's second trap and surprised a pair of phaerimm. The high mages slew the two monsters in a flurry of lightning and fire, but the battle left them so exhausted they had to retire to the surface.

Melegaunt sent word to avoid attacking the phaerimm directly, as they could often absorb magic and fling it back at the caster, or use its energy to heal themselves. Lord Duirsar thanked him for the advice and said he would pass it along.

By the time more high mages and another

company of tomb guards teleported from Evereska, half a dozen phaerimm had slipped into the dwarven workings and vanished. Two more companies of tomb guards were teleported in from the Greycloak Hills to track these down. One company was never heard from again. The survivors of the other returned with the good news that they had wounded one of the creatures.

Melegaunt offered to bring Vala and her men and join the battle. Lord Duirsar thanked him for his interest, but said it would be better for them to remain in Evereska. All Evereskan tomb guards were told to report to the College of Magic and Arms. Galaeron was not included in the alert, and Takari had already left for the High Forest. Ehamond and the others were attached to someone else's patrol.

Kiinyon Colbathin reached the Sharn Wall with ten tomb guards and two of his three high mages. After examining the hole, the mages concluded they needed a third to repair it. Kiinyon, who understood the intricacies of high magic no better than any non-mage, flew into a rage. While he screamed, two phaerimm emerged from beneath Anauroch. During the battle, Kiinyon stumbled across a darksword and used it to slay both phaerimm, freezing his hand but saving one high mage. Before retreating, he had the four survivors of his patrol search the tunnel for more darkswords. They recovered sixteen, which Vala requested be returned to her, as they were family heirlooms passed down for five generations.

Unimpressed by the pedigree, Lord Duirsar nevertheless promised to return the weapons after the battle. Until then, he hoped she would not mind if Tomb Master Colbathin put them to use—and was there anyway to keep the hilts from freezing the hands of those who wielded them? Sadly, there was not. The magic was attuned to the family that owned it. Melegaunt offered again to join the battle with Vala and her men. Lord Duirsar thanked him for the offer and noted he had suggested the same thing to Kiinyon and the Highest Mage, whose name was never revealed to a human. After much discussion, it was agreed they would keep the offer in mind, though for now they feared a mixture of fighting methods would cause more problems than it cured. The Vale Guard, the Feather Cavalry, and the Army of Evereska were all placed on alert. All tomb guards capable of teleporting themselves were ordered to report to the Vyshaan cairn at once, and the remainder were ordered to ride for it. There were no longer enough wizards to transport them by spell.

Galaeron tried to relieve his frustration by taking Vala and her humans on walks through Evereska. They visited the Floating Gardens of Aerdrie Faenya, the Groaning Cave, the Tower Higher than Eastpeak—from the top of which they could see the Vyshaan cairn and the elf army encamped around it, or so they fancied. Finding Vala much more open around him, Galaeron asked again where her home was and what her relationship to Melegaunt was. She went so far as reassuring him that his people had nothing to fear from hers. The Granite Tower was far, far away and hardly strong enough to pose a threat to Evereska—and that was all she was going to say on the matter while she remained a prisoner. Galaeron decided it would have to be enough.

By highsun of the twenty-first, Galaeron began to notice as many glares directed at him as at the humans. By dusk, people were rebuking him for endangering Evereska through his poor judgement. For one elf to be the object of so much public scorn was unheard of. Galaeron fell into a depression and no longer wished to leave Treetop. Vala told him to get over it. She wanted to see the statue of Hanali Celanil.

On the twenty-third day of Nightal, the phaerimm claimed the dwarven working, forcing Kiinyon and his last tomb guards to the surface. Reports circulated of strange monsters appearing in remote locations. Galaeron snapped at Keya, then realized she and Vala had become good friends indeed when Vala drew her dagger and threatened to geld him. He apologized, and the giant eagles of the Feather Cavalry darkened the skies for a quarter hour as they departed to reconnoiter the phaerimm breakout.

Melegaunt suggested to Lord Duirsar that the Hill Elders command Kiinyon and the unnamed Highest Mage to accept his help. Lord Duirsar responded rather tersely that the Hill Elders had no more right to interfere with the field commanders than a human had to interfere with the governing of Evereska. After that, no more messages came for a while, though Aubric Nihmedu learned from other sources that the Army of Evereska was being dispatched to all corners of the Sharaedim, the Vale Guard had been ordered to establish a perimeter in the mountains around the vale, and the senior regiforms of both academies of the College of Magic and Arms had been ordered to stand ready. Melegaunt approached Galaeron to broach the idea of joining the battle without permission, and Galaeron was so frightened he almost agreed.

It was late that day when Vala came to Galaeron with puffy cheeks and tears in her eyes. At first, he thought Melegaunt had broken his word and left, but he dismissed that notion when she took his hands and held them to her lips.

"Galaeron, I'm so sorry to be the one to tell you."

"Tell me what?" Galaeron could not imagine anything that would make Vala cry. "Have the phaerimm broken through?"

She shook her head. "It's Aubric."

"My father?" Galaeron did not understand. He had seen no sign that his father was preparing to journey west. "There's nothing wrong with my father."

"No." Tears spilled down Vala's cheeks. "No longer."

Pulling Galaeron by the hand, she entered the contemplation, where Aubric Nihmedu lay on the marble reverie couch, his eyes open wide and a tome spread across his chest. He looked happier than Galaeron had seen him in decades, his lips curled into a slight smile and the furrows gone from his forehead.

No longer puzzled, Galaeron folded his hands over Vala's and backed into the great room. When he judged they would not be overheard, he whispered, "Thank you."

Vala frowned. "Is that all? Don't elves cry?"

"When there is cause."

"A father's death isn't cause?"

"Dying?" The statement was so absurd that Galaeron guffawed, drawing a startled cry from the other room.

Vala glanced through the arch and grew as pale as a moon elf. "He's back!"

"Back?" Galaeron's father appeared in the archway. "Where was I?"

"D-d-dead!" Vala's knees buckled, and Galaeron caught her.

"Dead?"

Aubric looked to Galaeron for an explanation, but Galaeron was laughing too hard to explain.

"Your eyes were open," Vala said. "I thought you were . . . gone."

"Gone?" Finally, Aubric seemed to understand. "Oh, the eyes. You thought I was—"

"Dead," Vala confirmed. "You weren't moving."

"The Reverie," Galaeron said, still laughing. "Haven't you wondered why we have no beds? Elves don't sleep."

Vala looked wary. "Everyone sleeps."

"Not everyone," said Aubric. "Though I suppose the Reverie could be considered a kind of sleep."

"A little, perhaps." Galaeron did not want to confuse the poor human.

"It's a waking dream?" Vala asked.

"Not a dream, exactly," Galaeron said. "We revisit the events in our lives."

"Or we join with the community," his father added.

Vala looked confused.

"To share our feelings," said Galaeron. "It's restful."

Vala narrowed her eyes. "You all thought-speak?"

"It's not speech, but we share." Galaeron tried to think of how he could describe the Reverie. "You must have a family."

Vala frowned, insulted. "Do I look like I was *spawned*?"

"Do you ever feel what they feel? Do you ever know what they need without asking them, or experience their pain from afar?"

Vala's eyes lit. "Sometimes with my son. You feel that with all elves?"

"You have a son?" Galaeron was so surprised he did not register her last question.

"Yes, I have a son." Vala ran her fingers down her sides. "You've seen me naked. Did you think this body could be barren?"

Galaeron felt the heat in his cheeks. "Of course not, but elf women—"

"Have no hips. Giving birth must feel like a gut stab." Vala narrowed her eyes, then said, "Maybe that's why you have such slim heads."

"Without doubt!" Galaeron's father clapped a hand on Vala's shoulder. "You've a tongue on you like a Wood elf, my dear."

Vala's expression changed to self-reproach. "I'm sorry. I forgot myself."

"Not at all." The elder Nihmedu shook his head in mirth. "I haven't enjoyed an argument so much since Morgwais was here."

"Morgwais?" asked Vala.

The gaiety vanished from the old elf's eyes as suddenly as it had appeared. "Galaeron's mother. You won't be meeting her."

When no explanation was forthcoming, Vala looked to Galaeron, and a moment of awkward silence followed. Galaeron was spared the trouble changing the subject by the sudden flutter of wings. A streak of white circled the room three times before Manynests grew calm enough to perch on the elder Nihmedu's outstretched finger.

"I was in here." Aubric had to speak through the snow finch's warbling. "Was it so much trouble to use the door?"

This quieted the bird somewhat. He continued to *zeee* and

chirp, and even Galaeron's father had to concentrate to keep up.

"When did Lord Duirsar last hear from them?"

The bird peeped, then continued for another twenty seconds. Finally, Manynests cocked his head, his wings twitching as he awaited a reply.

"Tell Lord Duirsar that the Swords of Evereska will leave within the hour," said Aubric. "I took the liberty of planning for such a summons."

The bird launched itself into the contemplation and was nearly at the window before Aubric could speak the command word to render the theurglass passable.

"That finch is going to break his neck," said Melegaunt, entering the room ahead of Keya and the other humans. "Why so excited?"

"The Hill Elders lost contact with Kiinyon and the high mages an hour ago."

"An *hour* ago?" Melegaunt fumed. "And they're only telling us now?"

Galaeron's father raised his hand. "There's more. They can no longer contact anyone outside the Sharaedim."

"What do you mean?" Keya frowned. "That can't be right."

"I doubt Lord Duirsar is mistaken," said her father. "There is no response to his sendings, and those using the gates never return."

"So any help Evermeet sends won't arrive through Evereska," surmised Melegaunt. "They'll have to fight their way in from outside, with the troops sent by your other allies."

"Other allies?" asked Aubric. "What allies would those be?"

"I've heard Evereska holds a special place in the heart of Khelben Arunsun," said Melegaunt. "Surely he is already mobilizing Waterdeep's forces."

"You are well informed," said Aubric. "Khelben was the first human to visit Evereska, but we elves are a proud people."

"He hasn't been told?" Melegaunt closed his eyes. "What about Evermeet?"

"They were told, but no help was requested. Lord Duirsar has ordered the remnants of the Feather Cavalry to inform all elf-friends of our peril."

"They'll fail," said Melegaunt. "The phaerimm would not overlook such an obvious thing."

"Then it may be some time before Evermeet sends help," said Aubric. "In the mean time, I must excuse myself. Duty calls."

"Duty?" asked Vala.

"Father is the Blademajor of the Swords of Evereska." Keya's voice was as frightened as it was proud.

The elder Nihmedu nodded. "Lord Duirsar has asked us to scout and report."

A look of relief crossed Melegaunt's face. "Good. We're coming with you."

Galaeron's father smiled warmly. "Would that you could, my human friend." He shook his head.

"But as the commander, surely Lord Duirsar will listen to your wishes," Melegaunt objected.

"No doubt, Lord Duirsar would," said Galaeron. "But the Swords of Evereska are a noble militia. The title of blademajor rotates, and it could easily be rotated to someone else through the scheming of a few high nobles."

"My command is tenuous enough." The elder Nihmedu made no mention of why, but they all knew it was because of the blame being heaped on his son's shoulders. He turned to Galaeron. "Manynests mentioned twice that the spell guard is watching the city exits. You and your friends would do nobody any good hanging in bone cages."

Galaeron studied his father. "You have nothing to fear on our account. I only wish we had nothing to fear on yours." He clasped his father to his breast. "Remember what you have learned from Melegaunt about these devils. No one knows them better."

"I have marked every word." Galaeron's father returned the embrace, then separated himself and turned to Keya. "I am sorry to leave you alone, my daughter. Will you care for Treetop until next I return?"

"Of course." Keya buried herself in her father's chest. "And you won't be leaving me alone. Galaeron and his friends will keep me company."

Galaeron and his father exchanged a look over Keya's head, then the elder Nihmedu turned to Vala. "It may be that we do not meet again, human. Should it prove so, know that your wit and beauty will be a treasure to me always." He nodded toward Galaeron. "And it would do an old elf's heart good to know you will watch after his son."

"Then I'll be glad to be of some use to an old elf." Vala gave the blademajor a hearty embrace, but the bewilderment in her eyes suggested she did not yet fully understand what he was saying. "Sweet water and light laughter, my friend."

The traditional parting caused Galaeron's father to raise his arched brows. "Another day in Evereska, and there'd be no telling you from an elf." He laughed and turned to the other humans. "Sweet water and light laughter to you all."

Aubric was barely out of the room before Keya turned to Galaeron. "That was a strange thing to say. Where does he think you're going?"

"He doesn't know—and that's how it must remain," surmised Melegaunt. Not waiting for a confirming nod from Galaeron, he plucked at Vala's silky green shift. "Get out of this and into your armor."

"Armor?" Keya's jaw dropped, and she turned to Galaeron. "You mustn't let them."

Galaeron took his sister's hands. "Keya, I'm not letting them. I'm *taking* them."

CHAPTER SIX

23 Nightal, the Year of the Unstrung Harp

Once they had descended Starmeadow Tower, the humans moved with surprising stealth, considering their armor and the difficulty of traveling in an invisible group. At times, Galaeron and Keya could not even tell the warriors were behind them. They descended Goldmorn Knoll and slipped past Dawnsglory Pond without drawing a second glance, and Galaeron grew confident their plan would work. They had to stop once and listen to a silver-haired matron assure Galaeron that no one blamed him for freeing the phaerimm and only Golds listened to Lord Imesfor anyway, but even she did not seem to sense the invisible humans.

The forest ended abruptly at the edge of Moon-dark Hill, where a low stone wall was all that separated them from the empty air. A crescent of green pastureland lay far below, flecked with gray boulders, brown ponies, and emerald stands of fir. Beyond the pasture, the rolling patchwork of black-and-gold winter fields rose toward the mist-shrouded vineyards. The Swords of Evereska were visible on the highest terraces, their long column of ponies wagging like a tail as they rounded the last switchbacks into the forests of the High Vale. There were no other companies in sight, though Galaeron knew there would be a handful of Spellguards posted at the livery stations and the other entrances to the city.

"Now is as good a time as any, unless we want to wait until dusk," he said.

"We dare not wait." Melegaunt's voice came from the air behind Keya. "With the phaerimm, every hour is an eternity."

Galaeron extended his hand. "I'll need the rope."

An invisible hand laid a thin coil of elven rope in his palm. Galaeron looped it over his shoulder and climbed a big duskwood, then crawled out on a sturdy limb well past the wall. He secured the line and fed the bottom out until it touched the pasture. No human rope—at least not that one person could carry—would have stretched so many hundreds of feet, but enough elven cord remained to create a large coil on the ground.

Galaeron returned to his companions and climbed down next to Keya. "All is ready. Stay away from the cliff. If you touch it, Evereska's defensive magic will cancel my spell."

"We're all going at once?" asked Vala.

"We must all stay within ten feet of you or become visible," explained Melegaunt.

"That thread won't hold five of us," objected Kuhl.

"It would hold five stone giants." Keya's tone was anything but patient. "That's an *elven* rope."

The explanation was met with a wary silence, then Vala said, "On with you, Kuhl." There was a lot of scuffing and grunting, then the thick branch sagged dangerously. "We'll be waiting at the bottom, Galaeron."

"I'll be along directly."

Galaeron allowed the humans a few moments to begin their descent, then embraced his sister.

"Too long away," he said, "too quick gone."

"Next time." She smiled bravely and touched her long fingers to his cheek. "Bring me no phaerimm eggs."

"Of that, little sister, you may be assured." He stepped onto the low wall, then glanced at the duskwood branch. "You'll retrieve the rope?"

She nodded. "They'll never know of your leaving. Sweet water and light laughter."

"Back soon for soft songs and bright wine."

Galaeron cast a spell to turn himself invisible, then fixed his gaze on the coil of rope far below and stepped off the wall. His plunge was at first a breathtaking blur of wind and color, but the mythal's magic prevented any native of Evereska from being injured by a plummet from the cliff tops. As he neared the bottom, his fall slowed to a mere descent. He landed lightly on his feet and was there waiting when the invisible humans stepped onto the ground.

Keya pulled the cord up. Galaeron had the humans link hands, then he led them across the pasture to the perimeter of the mythal. He climbed over the wall into a field of winter wheat and stopped in a corner shade bower.

"Melegaunt?"

"Here."

"The Spellguards will be watching the Secret Gate, and we can't pass through unnoticed. Now would be a good time to use your shadow walk to move us to the other side of Eastpeak."

"I'd be happy to, but I think you have noticed my magic doesn't work in Evereska."

"It will now," Galaeron said.

"Really?" There was a pause, then Melegaunt asked, "I wonder why would that be?"

Though he knew the wizard could not see it, Galaeron shrugged. "You have your secrets, I have mine."

"So it seems." The wizard chuckled, low and foreboding, then added, "Very well. I suppose what the master claims cannot be denied the novice. Everyone find me and grab hold."

Though it had been more than forty years since Galaeron had considered any wizard his master, he did as instructed and took hold of an arm. Melegaunt's gravelly voice rose in an incantation, and the world turned dark and indistinct. Five blurry silhouettes appeared around him, then one of the smaller shapes separated itself from the others and started forward.

"We are walking the border between the world of light and the world of the dark," said Melegaunt. "It is easy to lose your way, so you must not release me. Time and distance have no meaning here. If you lose sight of me for even the blink of an eye, I may never find you."

Galaeron found himself clinging to a small arm that could only belong to Vala. She was holding hands with one of her huge warriors, and the warrior's other hand was clamped to Melegaunt's collarbone as tightly as a vise. Though every hand between Galaeron and the wizard possessed at least twice the strength of his own, his eyes soon began to burn for fear of blinking. To one side loomed flat purple shapes. Sometimes they were as high as mountains, with jagged profiles that suggested peaks and ridges. Other times, they were slender trunks with scarecrow arms, swaying in an unfelt wind, reaching down to clutch at Galaeron with fingers of darkness that could not touch.

Opposite the shadows shimmered a vast horizon of yellow radiance, blinding and bright and as hot as the Anauroch sun. Despite Melegaunt's warning, Galaeron found himself longing to walk into the light. Its familiar warmth was an enticing contrast to the cold eeriness of the shadows, and there was something young and frightened inside him that longed to be away from the darkness. He fixed his gaze ahead, forcing himself to concentrate on Vala's back.

Finally, slivers of radiance began to break off the horizon

and tumble along to both sides of the companions. Some rolled completely by and passed out of sight. Others landed flat on the ground or lodged themselves between shoulders of purple darkness, creating a ghostly landscape of gullies and hills. Despite the cascade of splinters, the light never grew smaller. The yellow horizon merely flattened out and spread itself into a rolling plain that Galaeron soon recognized as the sands of Anauroch.

Instead of continuing toward the desert, Melegaunt dropped to his knees and tipped forward. Galaeron thought the wizard would fall, but his body merely extended itself at a slant and hung over the ground until the rest of the party followed his example. When they were all leaning forward at the same angle, Melegaunt had Galaeron cancel his invisibility spells, then led them downward into darkness as black as coal. The sensation of descent vanished within a dozen steps. A few minutes later, they stopped, and Galaeron's dark sight began to function.

"Your shadow vision will work now," Melegaunt whispered to the humans.

Vala and her men briefly touched the hilts of their swords, then blinked the sight back into their eyes. The group was standing in a small chamber hewn from solid rock. The walls had been cut so smoothly they seemed almost polished. Along one side of the room lay a sleeping berth, covered with a billowy black mattress of shadow made solid. On the other side sat a small stone desk.

From the front of the chamber came the sound of grunting and scuffling. Galaeron turned and found himself looking through a foot-wide crevice, where a haggard human was scuttling past in a high squat. The man's hair and beard were long and unkempt, his gaunt body coated in sweat-streaked filth. He was dragging a wooden chest crammed so full of parchments, books, and scrolls that the lid would close only partially.

Melegaunt motioned for quiet and stepped to the crevice.

He ran through a series of mystic gestures, both cupping his hand to his ear and rubbing the tips of his fingers on his forehead. Galaeron and the others cast puzzled looks at each other and wondered where they were. Their answer came a moment later, when a huge-toothed maw surrounded by arms floated into view. Galaeron raised his hands to summon a bolt of magic, and the humans reached for their black swords.

Melegaunt stepped away from the crevice. "No!" He pushed Galaeron's hands down. "Your magic would have them on us like crows on a battlefield."

Galaeron glanced toward the crevice, but the creature floated past with no hint that it had seen them, its thorny body writhing through the air in a motion part fish and part serpent.

"It's angry with its slaves for being so slow," whispered Melegaunt. "It's complaining that the best holes will be taken. They'll be faster next move, or they'll be egg bags."

As the barbed tail rippled out of view, Galaeron asked, "Where's it going?"

"And where are we?" added Vala.

Melegaunt answered Galaeron first. "I think you know where it's going."

"The dwarven workings?"

"Somewhere in the Sharaedim," Melegaunt corrected. "They must consider it safe haven now."

"Safe haven!" Galaeron could not keep the outrage from his voice. "Never!"

Melegaunt touched a finger to his lips. "Quietly. This cloaking magic was meant to muffle snores, not shouts." He answered Vala's question next. "We're in my last refuge, not far from our rendezvous point in the dwarven workings. The phaerimm will place their WarGather at the breach in the Sharn Wall, to make sure it stays well guarded."

"So we came to *their* side of the wall?" she asked.

Melegaunt nodded. "The phaerimm are as intelligent as they are evil. They'll be ready for scouts. With luck, they won't expect them from this direction."

Galaeron thought of his father, riding out of Evereska on the mission Melegaunt described. "But the Swords—"

"Are still in the Secret Gate," said Melegaunt. "Time is different in the Shadow. If we are lucky, we will have discovered everything Evereska must know before the Swords leave the High Peaks. If we are not lucky . . . In that case, I fear your father must face the risk."

Galaeron nodded. Evereska had to learn the extent of the enemy's victory. If he and his human companions failed, then it fell to the Swords of Evereska to win the information themselves—no matter how poor their chance of success. Seeing that the phaerimm was gone, Galaeron motioned to the crevice.

"Shall we?"

"In a minute," said Melegaunt. "The phaerimm have spells to detect intruders . . . and it would be good if you were able to understand the phaerimm for yourself. Can you copy the spell I just cast?"

"Perhaps . . . a simple combination of eavesdropping and thoughtspeech?"

Melegaunt cocked his brow. "You are a truly gifted *innatoth*."

"Innatoth?"

"Innate one," said Melegaunt. "What my own people would have called an ArcNatural, but which is better translated in most of Faerûn as 'sorcerer.' "

"What's the difference?" asked Vala.

"Not much to you, but a great deal to me," said Melegaunt. "Even to the best wizards, magic comes slowly and with difficulty. Not so to sorcerers. For them, it is a gift, a natural talent that can be improved with time and practice, but a gift nonetheless. Needless to say, all those wizards who must work at their art tend to be suspicious of those who don't."

"That's an apt description, if ever I heard one," said Galaeron. "Are you an innatoth?"

"Would that I were!" Melegaunt laughed. "I take it you found your Academy of Magic less than accepting?"

"Far less." Galaeron tried to keep the bitterness from his voice. "My father used every political favor he was owed to secure me a place in my regiform, and a more terrible waste I've never seen. I never fit in. Eventually, they accused me of dark magics and demanded to see my spellbook. Unfortunately, I had never kept one."

"Now you're making *me* jealous," Melegaunt said.

Galaeron smiled sadly. "No need. It took Lord Imesfor's intervention to win me a place in the Tomb Guard." He fell silent, recalling the bad end that the high noble's patronage had wrought for his son. In truth, the Gold lord could hardly be blamed for the things he had been saying. "And even that favor has had its price."

"No need to feel sorry for yourself." Melegaunt's voice was at once reproachful and consoling. "It will be your magic that saves Evereska, or I've never cast a spell."

"Did you not say that his magic would draw the phaerimm's attention?" Vala's tone was respectful but concerned. "This is the last place I'd want one of those things to trap me."

Melegaunt smiled. "It would be a better place than you think, but you're right about what I said." He looked to Galaeron. "We must teach our friend to cast magic differently."

"Differently?" Galaeron asked. "That will take time."

"Not for you, I think," said Melegaunt. "Not if you are as brave as you are talented."

"I'm here now."

"Yes." Melegaunt's eyes turned as black as obsidian, so dark that even Vala gasped. "You're brave enough when you meet the monsters outside. Let us see if you have the courage to face the one within."

Melegaunt's face became strangely elflike, his bushy brows rising into arches, his brow becoming high and smooth. His ears grew longer, pushing their sharp tips out through his dusky hair, and his eyes assumed the malevolent gleam of a drow demon.

"Corellon's lute!" Galaeron's head whirled in confusion.

This could not be the human who had told him he would be the savior of Evereska—but then again, ever were demons the deceivers of mortals. "What are you?"

"More than you think, I am sure," came the answer.

Knowing he would never have time to cast a spell—and that even if he did, he could not hope to best Melegaunt in a duel of magic—he dropped a hand to his sword. The demon's own hand lashed out as quickly as a jumping spider, caught Galaeron by the throat, and slammed him against the stone wall. A pair of ivory fang tips jutted out beneath Melegaunt's lip, and his shadowy beard changed into a grotesque chin. The humans gasped and murmured, but seemed too bewildered to act. Galaeron tried to draw his sword, but the demon pinned his wrist to the wall.

Vala was the first to recover even a little. "Mighty One!" She freed her blade and stepped forward. "What are you—"

"Stand clear!" Melegaunt glanced over his shoulder. "By the Oath of Bodvar, I charge you obey!"

Vala ground her teeth, but stopped and lowered her sword, then signaled her men to stand fast. When Melegaunt looked back to Galaeron, his eyes were glowing purple, and his fangs were as long as a viper's.

"Do you know what I am, elf? Are you brave now?"

"Y-y-yes." Galaeron could barely choke out the word. Like most surface elves, he feared the drow as much as he hated them, and he could imagine no fate worse than becoming the undead servant of a drow vampire-demon. "Let me have my sword—"

Melegaunt slammed Galaeron against the wall. "I think not." He smiled. "But I give you a choice."

Melegaunt thrust his palm out behind him. "Darksword!"

Vala flipped her hilt around, but hesitated before handing it over. "What are you going to do?"

Melegaunt glared at her, his neck filling the room with unnatural cracking sounds as it turned farther than it should. "Nothing that is not my right by the Granite Tower."

Vala's face fell, and she laid the hilt in his palm. Melegaunt glared at her a moment, then pressed the icy hilt into Galaeron's left hand.

"I give you the choice, elf." He grabbed the weapon by its blade and set the tip beneath Galaeron's jaw. "Serve me or not—your choice."

Galaeron knew no vampire would give him the chance to slay it—but he also knew it would be just like a drow to give him the opportunity then taunt him with his cowardice through the rest of time. He lifted his chin and flipped the black blade forward, drawing the edge across Melegaunt's throat and chest.

The glass passed through the wizard as though his body were smoke. Melegaunt smiled, then plucked the sword from Galaeron's hand.

"Coward." He returned the weapon to Vala, then pinned his captive's head against the wall.

Galaeron struggled, but the drow-demon was too strong. Melegaunt lowered his head, and Galaeron felt two cold pangs in his throat.

"No!"

He brought his knee up into Melegaunt's groin, but even that did not drive the demon away. An icy numbness spread through Galaeron's neck, then Melegaunt raised his head. There were a pair of slowly cooling blood runnels on his chin, and his eyes were glowing damson with mad hunger.

"Do you feel the fear?" he demanded. "Open yourself to it, Galaeron. Embrace it."

Galaeron had no need to open himself to anything. His fear was coursing through him. He could feel it in his hollow stomach, in his heaving chest and hot huffing breath, hear it in his pounding pulse and the wail rising in his throat.

The scream did not quite reach his lips before Melegaunt covered his mouth. "You can't scream, Galaeron." The wizard's face was returning to normal, his pointed ears vanishing into his dusky hair, his arched eyebrows growing straight and bushy. "You mustn't, or the phaerimm will give us all something to fear."

Galaeron pushed Melegaunt away. The wizard sailed across the chamber and slammed into the opposite wall, now looking completely human.

When Galaeron managed not to scream, Melegaunt nodded encouragingly. "Good. Now use it, Galaeron. Use that power inside to cast your spell."

"You're mad! The only thing I'll use it for is to kill you."

Galaeron drew his sword and was instantly separated from Melegaunt by Vala and her men.

"Not like that, elf!" Melegaunt's voice grew stern and commanding. "Will you master your fear, or be its slave?"

Something in the wizard's tone reached Galaeron. He touched his neck where the demon had bit him and felt smooth skin.

"Now, Galaeron!" urged Melegaunt. "Cast the spell!"

Finally beginning to understand, Galaeron let the sword fall and ran his fingers through a series of mystic gestures, then finished by cupping his palm to his ear. His fear did not evaporate as expected, but burned down through him, branding him with raw ribbons of pain that trailed through his body and vanished into the darkness beneath his feet.

Galaeron rolled his hands through the second half of the spell. When he began to rub his brow, the ragged ribbons of pain turned cold, filling him with a biting numbness that started in his feet and shot up through him like icy lightning.

Then Galaeron's mind was filled with wispy voices, all talking at once in half-formed sentences. He let out a groan and covered his ears. Melegaunt stepped past Vala and the others, then took Galaeron by the shoulders and looked into his eyes.

It's a bit confusing. The words sounded inside Galaeron's head, reverberating above a dozen other voices. *You're hearing the thoughts in all of our minds. Think of them as wind, and pay attention only to what you want. It helps to talk until you're accustomed to it.*

Galaeron removed his hands from his ears. "What did you *do* to me?"

"I showed you your shadow self." As Melegaunt had promised, the other voices faded into the background. "Think of it as the wellhead tapping another kind of magic."

"What kind of magic? Vampire? Or drow?"

"Neither—and don't blame me for that thing," chuckled Melegaunt. "What you saw, you made."

Galaeron glared at him. "I didn't make that."

"Not consciously," said Melegaunt, "but whatever a man—or elf—makes, he also makes the shadow of. If he makes himself brave and honest, then he makes a shadow of himself that is not."

"So a man makes a shadow of himself that's a woman?" Vala asked.

"No, that would be the opposite," Melegaunt explained. "A shadow is not opposite, only absence. In the day, it is the absence of the light that your body blocks. In a man, it is the absence of the male, not the presence of the female. In the case of Galaeron's shadow self, it is the absence of kindness and loyalty."

"That thing wasn't part of me," Galaeron insisted.

"No, it wasn't," agreed Melegaunt, "but you created it, and through it, you touched a new magic."

"Then it must be an evil magic." Galaeron retrieved his sword. He could still feel the strange ribbon of coldness that connected him to the ground. "I would that you had never shown it to me."

"Do not let the guardian frighten you." Melegaunt laid a hairy human hand on Galaeron's shoulder. "The greatest treasures are always protected, and this one is key to defeating the phaerimm. It is the only magic they do not understand. If we are to save Evereska, you will need to wield it well, and wield it often."

CHAPTER SEVEN

23 Nightal, the Year of the Unstrung Harp

The phaerimm WarGather lay exactly where Melegaunt had said it would, in the dwarven workings just beyond the breach in the Sharn Wall. A green spell glow hung in the air, barely bright enough to illuminate the room and render Galaeron's dark sight unnecessary. The tiny chamber was packed with phaerimm, the last two feet of their tails dragging on the floor so they could float upright beneath the low ceiling. They were surrounded by swirling clouds of dust, stirred up by a cacophony of strange whistling winds similar to the sand devils he occasionally saw spinning across the sands of Anauroch.

In the back of the room, barely visible through jostling phaerimm and swirling dust clouds, a cage of polished bones barricaded the entrance to a side passage. The vertical bars were made of sturdy human thigh bones, stacked one atop another and fused together with magic. With a lighter color and generally more delicate form, the crossbars were probably elf. The door was a grillwork of ribs interlaced around four skulls, two human and two elf, with sad eyes still floating in the sockets.

The door was hanging ajar, and the attention of the phaerimm seemed to be centered on the tunnel wall beside it, where a pair of elves sat against the stony wall. Through the forest of phaerimm bodies, Galaeron recognized the gilded seams of Kiinyon Colbathin's plate armor. The other figure Galaeron could not identify, though the glimpses of gold thread and red silk suggested it was a high mage.

It was difficult to see more. He and Melegaunt were on the far side of the Sharn Wall, squatting opposite each other to peer through the hole that had been opened by the beholder Shatevar. Vala and her men were a hundred paces away, keeping watch in case any more phaerimm appeared. Even at that distance, their thoughts poured through Galaeron's mind in a constant stream. He tried to focus on the three phaerimm nearest the two prisoners.

Your crudeness has given us nothing but corpses, Tha, said the one nearest Kiinyon. Though it seemed to be addressing its fellow through the swirling winds, Galaeron could understand it only by concentrating on its thoughts. The effort made his head ache, for the message itself was often lost in an emotional muddle of jealousy and contempt. *It is time to let someone more skillful rack them.*

Perhaps, Zay—if there were one more skillful, responded Tha.

The others have screamed their throats raw and told you nothing, countered Zay. *First we must break their will. Only then they will tell us the words.*

Melegaunt tapped Galaeron's arm. *Words?* The wizard did not speak, but only thought the question.

Probably words of passing. Galaeron intentionally avoided any mention of the mythal.

I should have known, Melegaunt responded. *There's a mythal.*

Galaeron scowled. *I said nothing about a mythal.*

Melegaunt shrugged. *Words have shadows, too.*

So I've noticed, Galaeron thought. *But what would Evereska's mythal explain—if there was one, that is?*

Melegaunt smiled knowingly. *Phaerimm need magic in their environment to survive, just as you and I need air. Without it, they starve.*

Then why are they still alive? Galaeron asked. *There can't be much magic in Anauroch.*

More than you think. What do you imagine the Sharn Wall is?

The barrier that imprisons them sustains them? surmised Galaeron. *Cruel.*

Perhaps, but not as cruel as what will they will do to Evereska—if it has a mythal, said Melegaunt. *Phaerimm are solitary, contentious creatures, but there are almost forty of them living close together in the ruins of Myth Drannor.*

Galaeron nodded, already taking the wizard's meaning. The ancient mythal that had once protected Myth Drannor had not perished with the city. Though it had deteriorated over the ages, it was still very powerful—powerful enough, apparently, to nourish a colony of phaerimm. And if the deteriorating magic of Myth Drannor's mythal was enough to sustain forty of the creatures, he could only shudder at the thought of how many Evereska's far stronger mythal might support.

Galaeron shook his head at the thought of the evil he had unleashed.

Melegaunt tapped Galaeron's knee. *You did not unleash this. You were executing a sworn duty. If the blame lies anywhere, it lies with me.*

Galaeron shook his head. *I knew we were in above our heads the instant I saw Vala's beholder, and she warned me so. Had I listened—*

You would have violated your oath to protect the crypts of your ancestors, which is not something Galaeron Nihmedu would do, Melegaunt said. *And had I not been so eager to escape, I would not have instructed Vala to break even a Vyshaan crypt in order to find the dwarven mine. At the least, the fault is ours together, and there is no use second-guessing ourselves. Know that had you been a coward and turned your back on me, the evil you did would have been far greater than this. We are going to set things right, you and I together, but this matter is bigger than Evereska—much bigger. Even were we to fail and Evereska to fall, what you did would still be worth it.*

To a human, perhaps, Galaeron thought.

Though he did not think it consciously, he knew that if Evereska fell, his name would be vilified in the coming ages as terribly as that of the Vyshaan or the drow. On Faerûn, at least, Evereska was the last haven of elven civilization—all that remained of the empires that had founded mighty cities such as Cormanthor and Siluvanede. More determined than ever to find a way to stop the phaerimm—to destroy their entire race, if need be—he turned back to the WarGather.

Having won the argument about the best way to proceed with the interrogation, Zay was holding Kiinyon Colbathin spread-eagled above its—his—toothy maw, flicking his barbed tail across the bloody rents in the tomb master's battered armor.

Would you like that, elf? The phaerimm was using thought-speech alone to talk to his prisoner, for the wind language of the phaerimm was clearly not one most elves were likely to speak. *It would be an honor to carry my egg.*

The barbed tail arced down to touch Kiinyon's lips, then the creature motioned to several fellows. They leveled themselves horizontally and ran their own tails over the elf's body, probing for holes and seams in his armor.

Perhaps I will let you carry eggs for all my friends, taunted Zay.

Kiinyon seemed barely conscious enough to notice. His

eyes were swollen half shut, his broken nose spread across both cheeks, his lip split so badly that the tip of his tongue showed where there should have been teeth. It was more difficult to tell the condition of the body beneath the armor, save that the deep creases and puckers bespoke plenty of bruises.

Would you like that, slave? All those larva growing inside, slithering through your entrails, eating the food from your stomach?

Impossibly, Kiinyon shook his head and said, "No."

The word was so garbled that Galaeron barely understood it. He was surprised to discover he felt none of the tomb master's pain. Elves who lived even in reasonably close contact were so connected to each other—through the Reverie and the Weave—that they shared at least some shadow of each other's emotional experiences. Instead, Galaeron sensed Kiinyon's anguish and fear only through Melegaunt's eavesdropping spell. There was even—he was ashamed to admit—some small part of him that actually took pleasure in the tomb master's pain.

Galaeron found the strange emotion as puzzling as he did frightening. Elves were not spiteful, for their emotional bonds tended to curb such low passions. In a very real sense, to wish pain on another was to wish it on oneself, and not even the most arrogant Gold was foolish enough to do that. The vile sentiments Galaeron was experiencing seemed all too human.

The phaerimm continued to hold Kiinyon a long time, allowing his fellows to run their barbed tails over the elf's body, until a strange, rhythmic moaning rose from the tomb master's lips. Galaeron did not recognize the sound until the other captive, the elf in the high mage's robes, began to say the Prayer for the Dying.

"Behold, there in the West. There I see my comrades and my lovers, my childhood friends, those who have gone before me and those still to come. There I see them in the tall oaks, high in the limbs where the golden sun lights their faces.

"They are calling my name. They are calling my name. They are calling me West, and there I am going."

The voice was unmistakable. It had not only the clear articulation and eloquent intonation so typical of the Sun elves, it had the same plumy timbre Galaeron had come to know so well over his last two years of duty. The voice belonged, undoubtedly, to Louenghris's father, Lord Imesfor.

One of the phaerimm backhanded the high mage, silencing him, then Zay raised his tail and brought it down hard on Kiinyon's breastplate. The barb penetrated the mithral steel and sank to its base, but Galaeron saw no convulsing muscles as he had when Takari was implanted.

No? Then you must give me a reason, said the phaerimm. *Tell me the first word, and I will let you die without eggs.*

"Goldheart," Kiinyon whispered. "The word is Goldheart."

Liar!

Zay motioned to his fellows, and a dozen barbs pinged through Kiinyon's armor. A couple of the tails began to convulse, but the spasms seemed weaker and more sluggish than the ones that had implanted the egg in Takari. The tomb master screamed, and his body grew puffy and rose toward the ceiling. Only the phaerimm's grasp prevented it from floating all the way.

As astonished as Galaeron was by the strange effect, he was even more astonished to discover he could actually stand to keep watching. By all rights, he should have felt so sickened that he found himself either attacking madly or cowering in fear.

My congratulations, Zay, said Tha, now speaking in the phaerimm's wind language. *The same false answer.*

Zay pushed Kiinyon into the bone cage, where the tomb master floated to the ceiling and hovered helplessly, pinned in place by the strange magic with which the phaerimm had injected him.

The answer cannot be false, said Zay, *only our understanding of it.*

All the same, it has not opened the portal. Tha plucked Lord Imesfor off the floor. *There is only one thing we have not tried.*

Perhaps the dead can be made to tell what the living cannot.

Galaeron's heart sank. The phaerimm could be talking about any of several portals into Evereska, but it seemed most likely they meant the Secret Gate, the only way through the mountains from this side. It was also the route by which the Swords of Evereska were leaving the Vale, and Galaeron did not care to think of what might happen when his father emerged from the portal into the arms of a band of phaerimm.

Lord Imesfor began to recite the Prayer for the Dying, this time for himself. Galaeron retreated and turned away. With so many phaerimm in the chamber, he saw no way to effect a rescue, and given the strange, vengeful emotions he had been experiencing, he was not sure he wanted to find out how he would feel when the high mage was killed.

Galaeron felt a tap on his knee and looked up to see Melegaunt. *Come along. We don't have long to plan.*

The wizard slipped past Galaeron, moving down the tunnel to where Vala and her men were gathering. He had to scuttle along like the slave they had glimpsed earlier, for the passage was only four feet in diameter and shaped like a tube—much more comfortable for floating phaerimm than walking humans. Galaeron joined the others and kneeled, his back sore from hunching.

Melegaunt drew a hand across the ceiling and uttered a quiet incantation, creating a curtain of shadow between themselves and the passage into the WarGather. He assigned Dexon to keep a watch on the other side, then turned to the others and motioned for them to speak softly.

"We could slay two or three, but not seventeen," said Melegaunt. "That rules out fighting, so we'll have to do this another way."

Galaeron raised his brow. "If you are thinking of a rescue, you should know that it is Evereskan tenet never to risk many lives in the desperate hope of saving a few."

"And how often is that tenet followed?" asked Melegaunt.

Galaeron smiled. "Not very often."

"I thought so," the wizard said. "Did you see how I opened the shadow path?"

"It was a bit above me," Galaeron admitted. "Though if you took a few moments to teach—"

"No!" Melegaunt's hiss came near to a yell. "That way lies ruin. It is well and good to test yourself with the tame magic of elves, but do not try such a thing with what I have shown you. You will be consumed by your own shadow. Do you understand?"

Somewhat taken aback by Melegaunt's sternness, Galaeron nodded. "I'll use only spells I can handle easily."

"And never mix the two magics." Melegaunt motioned vaguely toward the hole in the Sharn Wall. "We have seen what comes of that."

Again, Galaeron nodded.

"Good. Now, here is what we'll do." He explained his plan, then finished by looking to Vala. "I've seen enough of Kiinyon Colbathin to know he'd hesitate before trusting a human, and there's little reason to imagine a Sun elf high mage would be any less prejudiced. I'm afraid Galaeron must go with you."

Vala studied Galaeron for a moment, then glanced at his scabbard. "Can you handle that thing?"

Suspecting she would be unimpressed by his third place regiform steel-ranking, Galaeron simply nodded. "I can, but the blade wasn't much good against the phaerimm last time."

"Their magic," Melegaunt explained. "Even enchanted steel won't bite."

Vala turned to Dexon. "Will you trade with him until this is over?"

A corner of the human's mustache rose as though he'd rather not, but he nodded. "As long as he understands."

"Understands?"

"If you lose the weapon, his son's name will be lost," said Vala. "In our valley, the noble's title goes with his sword."

Melegaunt frowned at this. "That was never my intention."

"You have been gone a long time," said Vala. "That is how matters have come to be."

"It doesn't matter." Galaeron raised his palms to decline the sword. "I can't hold the sword. The last time I tried, my fingers nearly froze off."

"You will not feel the cold this time," said Melegaunt.

He nodded to Vala, who removed her scabbard and leaned it against the wall, then kneeled facing Galaeron. He removed his own scabbard and passed it to Dexon, and took his own place across from Vala. Melegaunt struck a torch. He had both Galaeron and Vala bound and gagged and stationed a warrior behind each. He took his glassy dagger from its sheath, and kneeling alongside Vala, began his incantation.

A pall of shadow darkened Vala's eyes, and her expression changed instantly to one of vanity and suspicion. Still uttering the syllables of his spell, Melegaunt ran his glassy dagger along the floor beside her, cutting free the shadow cast by the lit torch. Vala's eyes grew instantly feral and angry. She spun on Melegaunt, hurling herself into the air sideways and slamming her knees into his ribs despite her bound feet. Kuhl threw himself over her, pinning her to the floor beneath his big body and holding her there motionless.

Now separated from its body, Vala's shadow rose to its feet and stood upright, bending along the tunnel's curved wall in a way her body never could have. The shadow retrieved the scabbard from where Vala had leaned it, then turned to wait for Galaeron.

Galaeron could not tear his gaze from the thrashing body pinned beneath Kuhl. As Melegaunt kneeled beside him and began the incantation, Galaeron's heart pounded wildly. The thought that he would go as mad as Vala terrified him. Elf spirits were, after all, different than human souls, and he was not at all certain he would find his way back to his body. Still, he forced himself to remain calm and motionless, for he was troubled by the vengeful emotions he had experienced earlier and determined to redeem himself—in his own eyes, if no one else's.

Galaeron had the feeling of being drawn into the stone, then found himself looking up at his own body, trying to peer past Melegaunt as he drew the glassy knife along the ground beside his leg. He could actually feel the blade, icy and sharp, cutting him free of his body. As the wizard finished, Galaeron was seized by a terrible coldness. His body became a wild thing, whirling around at the waist in a mad effort to slam its head into Melegaunt.

Dexon hurled himself onto Galaeron's body, slamming it to the ground and pinning it there. Galaeron felt a pang of concern for the wild thrashing thing, but put it out of his mind and lifted Dexon's scabbard off the man's belt. He hung it where the hooks would have been on his own belt, as Melegaunt had instructed, and the scabbard melted into his form. Galaeron reached down and felt the hilt beneath his palm, but sensed no weight on his hip. Nor did he notice anything particularly cold about the weapon. Rather, it seemed to him that the whole world—the tunnel walls, the darksword, his own form—had become the very substance of cold.

"Ready?" Vala's voice was wispy and deep.

Galaeron nodded and followed her up the tunnel, not walking so much as flowing along the walls. He suffered a moment of disorientation as he slipped through the shadow curtain Melegaunt had hung across the passage, then continued toward the phaerimm's spell glow. Vala glided across the ceiling as he slid across the floor, and together they streamed through the opening into the dwarven workings.

Zay was clutching Lord Imesfor in two hands, holding a third hand over the elf's mouth to keep him from uttering any unexpected enchantments, and using a fourth hand to tug at the high mage's golden rings. Because many of the rings were too small to fit over the elf's broken fingers, the phaerimm was carefully popping each digit off at the appropriate knuckle. Lord Imesfor accepted this with remarkable calm, glaring at his torturer more in anger than pain.

Beneath Lord Imesfor lay a veritable pile of amulets, bracers, girdles, and other magic items Zay had already removed from the high mage's body. A half dozen of the other phaerimm were floating inches off the dusty floor, pawing through the treasure and arguing about who had the right to claim what. Tha already held the high mage's book of war spells in one hand, but that did not prevent the monster from snatching a silver diadem from one of his fellows. Galaeron hoped the greed fest was enough of a display to hold the attention of the others. Without knowing where their eyes were located, he had the constant feeling that they were watching him.

Vala drifted into the shadows on the ceiling and started toward Lord Imesfor. Galaeron slid along the wall, creeping along in small, flickering motions that he hoped would look like normal shadow movements. Melegaunt had assured him that while the monsters could see normal magic as easily as an elf saw at night, the creatures had never detected any spell he cast using his "other source of magic." The wizard had been unable to tell Galaeron whether they could see normal things—like shadows.

Galaeron made his way along the edge of the chamber, then entered the darkness in order to cross the tunnel. As he did so, he felt something cold pulling at him, trying to draw him deeper into the darkness. The spell glow became a green sphere in the far distance, and it took him a moment to realize it was growing smaller. He bit back a cry of alarm and concentrated on moving toward the green light. It grew as large as before, filling the chamber in front of him. Deciding he would rather be discovered by the phaerimm than dragged into the darkness by whatever had grabbed him, he crossed to the other side at the edge of the light and slipped between the bone bars.

The cage was cluttered with listless elves, all with an inflamed puncture wound somewhere on their torsos. They were in various states of ague, and many had fallen into a sort of comatose trance beyond all hope of recovery. The worst had arm-sized snakes writhing beneath their skin, usually along the path of their intestines, but sometimes coiled over their hearts or girding their ribs.

In the center of the cage floated the great Kiinyon Colbathin, stripped naked and clawing at his wounds. Unlike the wounds of the other prisoners, his punctures showed no sign of inflammation or infection. Recalling how Takari had immediately fallen into a stupor and how her wound had swollen, it seemed unlikely that the tomb master had been injected with an egg. Galaeron streamed across the ceiling and pressed himself to the tomb master's far side.

Kiinyon shuddered and cried out. Galaeron slipped a shadowy hand over the elf's mouth and felt it sink into flesh. The tomb master's voice shrieked through it unmuffled.

Several nearby phaerimm turned their open mouths toward the cage. Galaeron wrapped himself around Kiinyon's body and hoped he was truly as unnoticeable as Melegaunt had promised. The tomb master began to shiver. The phaerimm kept their mouths pointed toward the cage. Finally, Kiinyon could no longer contain himself and let out a single groan of fear.

The phaerimm swung their heads away, chuckling in their strange wind language. Galaeron waited until they had turned back to the pile of magic treasure, then pressed his shadowy lips to Kiinyon's ear.

"Master Colbathin, hold your tongue or I swear by the Black Arrow I'll leave you here," whispered Galaeron. "Understand?"

Kiinyon's eyes grew round as plates.

"Do you know who this is?"

Kiinyon nodded, though his eyes held a thousand questions.

"Good. I won't waste time asking whether you are happy to see me," said Galaeron, "but if you want to live, you must comfort Lord Imesfor with the Prayer for the Dying."

The tomb master remained silent, looking first to his own wounds, then to the inflamed punctures of an elf lying nearby.

"Whatever the phaerimm injected you with, it wasn't eggs, or you'd be as sick as everyone else," said Galaeron. "Now, say the prayer if you wish to live."

Instead of obeying, Kiinyon whispered, "What of the others?"

Galaeron looked at their listless forms, and his heart grew as heavy as gold. "They're not going to move themselves, and you felt what happened when I tried to cover your mouth. Do you have a way to carry them?"

"No." Kiinyon closed his eyes, no doubt coming to the same conclusion as Galaeron. Their only choice was whether to leave and let the others die alone, or stay and die with them. "This isn't right."

"No, it isn't, but we'll do what we can." On the ceiling outside, Galaeron saw a shadow flicker back and forth and realized Vala was signaling him. "We're out of time. Speak if you wish to live."

Kiinyon shook his head at the awfulness of the decision, but said, "I *must* live." A cry of fear sounded around the corner, and Kiinyon looked toward the door. "Have strength, Imesfor. Behold, there in the West—"

The prayer was interrupted by the deafening trill of an anguished phaerimm. Galaeron slipped to the front of the cage, then took a position on the wall. On the floor beyond the door lay a crooked phaerimm arm, severed cleanly at the biceps and resting in a pool of rusty blood. Lord Imesfor lay on the chamber floor, holding his mangled hands to his chest, his neck craned back to stare up in shock at the stump of Zay's amputated arm.

Zay shrieked something too fast for Galaeron to understand even with Melegaunt's eavesdropping spell, then reached for Imesfor again. Vala's darksword drove down from the ceiling, appearing out of the shadows as though wielded by the rock itself, and buried itself in Zay's thorny back.

Zay screeched and spun in the air, pulling Vala half off the ceiling. For an instant, her torso hung stretched between the ceiling and the writhing phaerimm, a vaguely female silhouette holding a very three-dimensional glassy black sword. Then she turned the blade into the roll, and the shadowy edge began to cut again. Zay's body opened around the middle and spilled steaming gore into the dust. Vala barely had time to pull herself back onto the rock before a storm of fire and lightning blasted the ceiling.

Galaeron slipped around the corner, then spoke in High Elvish. "Into the cage with you!" He had to shout to make himself heard. "To Kiinyon's side, and into the tunnel of shadow!"

The high mage's eyes went wide, but he rolled to his knees and, using his mangled hands like forepaws, scrambled for the cage.

It's the yellow one! trilled Tha, pointing at Lord Imesfor. *It's his—*

Galaeron drew his borrowed darksword and saw it appear in the air. He silenced Tha with a vicious slash across both jaw hinges, and the phaerimm's mouth fell open gurgling blood. Galaeron sheathed his sword and continued across the floor, streaming safely away even as the stone behind him erupted into a spray of molten magic.

Melegaunt's deep voice rose briefly from the direction of the Sharn Wall. A shaft of spinning shadow shot from the breach across the chamber, knocking shocked phaerimm aside like a battering ram. It extended through the cage door and stopped. Tiny tendrils of shadow twirled off the end like threads off a fraying sweater cuff, weaving themselves through the bone bars of the cage.

This time, the phaerimm were quicker to recover—far too quick for Galaeron's liking. A dozen whirled around, flinging every manner of magic at Melegaunt. Whether the attacks troubled the wizard was impossible to say, for the instant the spells touched the Sharn Wall, they exploded into searing heat. Those attacks aimed into the breach simply vanished into the whirling shaft of shadow, then came spinning back out a few seconds later.

The remaining phaerimm turned their attention to Galaeron's side of the chamber, flinging meteor swarms and ice storms toward the bone cage. The brunt of the attack vanished into the shadow net spinning off the end of the shadow column, but enough of the spells penetrated to fill the air with the stench of scorched flesh and half-lucid elf screams.

Galaeron flowed across the floor and took a position on the wall opposite the door, ready to attack when the phaerimm tried to pass through the net of shadow. Through the mesh of dark tendrils, he could just make out the figure of Lord Imesfor struggling with his fingerless hands to shove sick elves into the mouth of the shadow tunnel. Kiinyon was helping as much as possible, but trapped as he was against the ceiling, he was even less efficient than the high mage.

Galaeron started to wonder where Vala's humans were, but his question was answered when he saw a pair of thick hands pulling a sick elf into the mouth of the tunnel. The other two men were, of course, continuing to wrestle with his body and Vala's.

Realizing their magic was no more able to pass through the Sharn Wall from the outside than the inside, the phaerimm on Melegaunt's side of the chamber concentrated on the whirling column of shadow. As before, their spells simply vanished into the blackness, then came spinning back out. One of the phaerimm even tried to break into the shaft. He lost two arms to the whirling darkness. Another created a blazing orb that illuminated the whole chamber in brilliant silver light, but of course where there was light, there was shadow. The shaft became a writhing, snake-like thing weaving along through the dark corners of the cavern, bowing up behind the moving phaerimm, then disappearing into the dust beneath their floating bodies.

The phaerimm on Galaeron's side of the chamber were more successful. A pair floated alongside the shaft and paused before the cage. The polished bones fell away from each other, collapsing into a heap on the floor and leaving only the shadowy mesh that had spun off the end of Melegaunt's tunnel. One dared push a finger through the mesh. When it passed through without being torn off, the creature pushed an entire hand through—and promptly lost it to Vala's darksword.

The phaerimm's reactions were far quicker than they should have been, at least by elf standards. The creature simply lashed out with its remaining hands and caught hold of the sword hilt, easily jerking it free of Vala's shadowy grasp. The creature trilled at the weapon's icy touch, but held on as its companion blasted the wall with lightning and magic.

Galaeron was on the thing in an instant, flowing across the tunnel ceiling and slashing his own blade across the width of its body. The phaerimm all but exploded, spraying the tunnel with a green ichor and dropping to the floor in a heap of thorny flesh.

It was harder to kill than that. The thing rolled to its back, spraying the ceiling with a long stream of fire. Galaeron shrieked as the heat struck his leg. He flowed down the wall and along the floor, placing the other phaerimm between himself and the one he had just wounded.

Whistling in anguish, the creature on the floor dragged itself away through the dust. Galaeron searched the walls and floor for Vala, but she was as hidden to him as to the phaerimm.

Coward! accused the phaerimm he was hiding behind. Switching Vala's sword from one hand to the other, the creature pushed through the icy net toward the fleeing elves. *They're just shades!*

Galaeron brought his darksword up and severed the hand holding Vala's weapon, then caught the darksword as it fell. He whipped the blade around and plunged it deep into the yelling phaerimm. The creature reacted by spraying the floor with raw magic. Galaeron flowed up the wall, screaming at Kiinyon and Imesfor in High Elvish.

"That's it! We've saved all we can."

The wounded phaerimm turned toward his voice and blasted the wall with lightning, but Galaeron was already back on the floor, slashing at the thing's underside with both swords to hold its attention. Kiinyon and Imesfor did not make things any easier. There were only three elves left in the cage, and the high mage paused to snatch one up in his dismembered hands before hurling himself into the shadow tunnel. Kiinyon grabbed the other two by their collars and slowly kicked his way across the ceiling, dragging them along behind him.

Galaeron escaped another flurry of fire and ice by flowing onto the ceiling, then glanced back to see half a dozen phaerimm floating through the shadow net. Realizing he would never stop them all with his swords, he slipped the weapons into his belt—or, rather, where his belt would have been—then plucked off a lock of his shadowy hair. Moving along the ceiling to avoid being impaled by a spear of golden light, he opened himself to his fear as Melegaunt had taught him.

With so many phaerimm approaching, fear was an easy commodity to come by. It flooded into him, bringing with it that eerie, cold energy he had felt earlier. He tossed the tress of hair at the phaerimm and uttered an improvised wind spell.

A howling gale tore through the cage, blasting the phaerimm with a solid wall of dust. The spell was hardly enough to injure them, but it made them pause in a moment of caution. That was all Kiinyon needed. Carried along by the gust, he floated past the blindly slashing claw of the last phaerimm and vanished into the shadow tunnel.

Thinking to make the best of the opportunity, Galaeron drew his swords again and swung around to finish off his wounded enemy—then felt a shadowy hand grab his wrist.

"Time to go, elf," Vala called. She jerked him into the shadow tunnel. "And give me my sword!"

CHAPTER EIGHT

24 Nightal, the Year of the Unstrung Harp

Galaeron's body hung on him like human armor, heavy and hot and painfully ill-fitted. His shoulders ached, his head throbbed, his neck wouldn't turn. The hand holding his corner of the floating litter was so frozen he doubted the fingers would unbend, and still he counted himself lucky. Dexon, who had been holding him down, had two black eyes, a missing tooth, and so many bruises that they looked like camouflage in the dusky realm.

A gurgling shriek rose from the center of the litter. Galaeron and the other stretcher bearers—Kiinyon, Vala, and her three men—stopped and spun toward the sound. A catatonic elf was thrashing about, coughing, choking, and clubbing fellow patients. Even from the edge of the platform, an arm-sized phaerimm larva could be seen writhing about under his skin, flickering across his breast as it worked its way up into the elf's throat. Galaeron instinctively stretched out a hand, as did Kiinyon on the other side, but the victim was surrounded by a dozen fellow patients and well beyond reach.

"Keep him quiet!" Melegaunt rushed back and vaulted onto the litter, paying no attention to those he stepped on, then slapped a hand over the elf's mouth. "Put us down."

Galaeron and the others obeyed. By the time Melegaunt dragged the warrior off the litter, only the larva tail remained visible, a fingerlike cord worming up toward the gullet. The wizard dropped a knee across the elf's chest, then slipped his dagger tip under the skin and exposed a spine-covered tentacle as big around as Galaeron's arm. He pulled the thing out of its victim and pinned it down while he sliced off the tiny mouth atop its body.

The wizard was not quite finished when the elf's foot swung into the murk alongside their path. He started to slide into the darkness, but was too weak to do more about it than whimper. Galaeron lunged for his arm—then was nearly knocked off his feet by one of Melegaunt's huge arms.

"Don't!"

"Something has him!" Galaeron tried to push past.

Melegaunt held him back. "And it will have you, if you're fool enough to challenge it!"

As the warrior was dragged off, his glassy eyes rolled toward the wizard's face and remained there until he vanished into the shadows. The wizard turned away, his own expression as hard as it was unreadable.

"Take up your friends and keep moving." He motioned to the big shadow stretcher. "We must go before more *shadator* come."

Only Kiinyon did not reach for his corner. "We can't leave him."

"We can and we must." Melegaunt started forward again. "Shadator seldom come alone."

Kiinyon did not move. "Elves are not cowards. We do not abandon the spirits of our dead to places such as this."

Melegaunt turned, this time with an expression of genuine sorrow. "I am sorry for your friend, but there is truly nothing we can do. When the rest of the shadator arrive, they will strike at more capable prey. They'll attack from below, at first taking only one or two of us. But the feeding frenzy will start quickly, and all our spirits will be left to the dark. Is that what you want?"

"Of course not." Kiinyon's face was silver with rage. "But I've seen enough of your magic to know you can do something."

Melegaunt's eyes went dark. "Sadly, you are mistaken." The wizard started to walk again. "You may stay if you wish. It is all the same to me."

Eyes bulging, Kiinyon started after him. "You . . . will . . . not!"

Realizing the tomb master had been robbed of self-control—and perhaps even his wits—by the past few days of death and defeat, Galaeron blocked his way.

"Master Colbathin, if Melegaunt says he has done everything possible, he has. It's only because of him that you are here at all. I was ready to give you up for dead, but he insisted it was possible to rescue you."

Kiinyon's fiery gaze shifted to Galaeron—a definite improvement, since Galaeron was not likely to grow impatient and blast the tomb master into shadows.

"Why am I not surprised?" Kiinyon said. "You and your lazy magic—I should've known you were a coward, too."

"That's enough." Vala stepped to Galaeron's side.

Though her tone was calm, the blow that followed was not. The tomb master was rocked back into Burlen's waiting grasp, where his arms were pinned to his side. Vala produced a black cord and tied his hands.

"Galaeron deserves this abuse no more than does Melegaunt." Whether she was speaking to Kiinyon or Lord Imesfor was unclear. She was looking past the tomb master toward the high mage, whose glassy eyes barely seemed to notice the confrontation. "Nor do we have time for it."

"Do as you must." Lord Imesfor held his arms crossed in front of him, his mangled hands pressed to his chest. "The tomb master will understand when he returns to his senses."

The high mage inclined his head toward their backtrail.

Galaeron looked and saw a ghostly silhouette crossing the light between two shadow hills, four short tentacles where there should have been a nose. He looked away casually, then asked, "Illithids?"

"They've been following us for some time," said the high mage. "I was wondering if they're native to this plane."

"No." Despite the softness of his voice, Melegaunt sounded angry. "They're servitors to our enemy. The phaerimm, I fear, have figured out how to track us."

He gestured in Burlen's direction. The warrior gasped in surprise, then blinked in confusion.

"You will grow accustomed to it soon enough," said Melegaunt. "Someone must keep watch behind us."

Burlen waved a cautious hand behind his helmet. "You might have warned me. This is . . . unnatural."

Melegaunt waved at the maze of shadow and light around them. "Four eyes are as natural as anything here."

The wizard nodded to Vala, then started to walk away. She tossed Kiinyon onto the shadow litter with the patients, then Galaeron and the others took up their positions and followed.

Lord Imesfor scurried to catch Melegaunt. "Perhaps we should tarry. If the shadators are attracted by sound, we might use them to spare ourselves the trouble of ambushing the illithids later."

Melegaunt continued to walk, and quickly. "A good plan, but one we've no time for. Now that the phaerimm have finally discovered where we are, they'll move to cut us off."

"Finally?" asked Lord Imesfor. "The high mages *did* try shadow walking."

Earlier in the journey, Imesfor had related how Evereska's army had stumbled into a phaerimm ambush, then been unable to escape via teleport spells, magical gates, or dimension doors. Each time, they ran headlong into another trap, until all that remained were handfuls of scattered survivors. The final blow came when Imesfor attempted to planewalk to Evermeet, only to emerge where they had found him.

"I'm sorry," said Imesfor. "We won't escape through the shadows."

"If we hurry," said Melegaunt. "The shadows are a big place, and there are only two ways to track someone through them."

"Of course. One is to follow physically." Lord Imesfor craned his neck meaningfully toward the rear. "The other is far easier. Track their magic."

"Exactly." Melegaunt's smile managed to be both patient and condescending. "Tracking elven magic is easy, but mine is another story."

Galaeron resisted the urge to look back, for he saw what the wizard was planning. As long as they believed themselves unobserved, the illithids would bide their time and wait for the phaerimm to attack. If Melegaunt and the others could slip away before then, they could reach Evereska unmolested.

Lord Imesfor did not share Galaeron's faith. "You're telling me the phaerimm cannot see your magic?"

"It's true," Galaeron said, speaking from his place near the front of the litter. "Nor can they defend themselves from it. You saw how the darkswords cut through their shieldings."

Imesfor glanced at Galaeron, then back to Melegaunt. "How?" His tone was not as disbelieving as thoughtful, but there was a hint of condemnation to it. "I don't understand."

Melegaunt's voice grew harsh. "What is there to understand? All you need know is that I can get you past the phaerimm. Do you wish that, or not?"

"Of course." Lord Imesfor kept his voice carefully level.

"But there is no sense returning to Evereska. Perhaps you could guide us to Waterdeep?"

"Waterdeep?" This from Kiinyon. "You would ask humans for help?"

Imesfor looked back, sneaking a glance toward their pursuers. A flash of concern suggested he had seen one.

"I mean to ask help of whoever will give it," said the high mage.

"Human help comes at a dear price," Kiinyon said.

Imesfor's eyes narrowed. "I am sure our companions—no, our *rescuers*—understand the strain you have been under."

"We do," said Melegaunt. "Regardless, we cannot take you to Waterdeep."

"I thought as much," said Kiinyon. "Just like a human to open the floodgates of hell and run for high ground."

Finally losing patience, Melegaunt wagged a crooked finger back at the tomb master. "The place I am running is to call the only help that will save your miserable kingdom, which is more than your kind . . ." Melegaunt let the sentence trail off, then his face turned as dark as his hair. "Elves! You are too full of tricks for your own good."

"Perhaps so," said Lord Imesfor. "But then again, your kind have always seemed to measure what is good for others by what is best for yourselves."

Melegaunt's bushy brows came together. "*My* kind?"

Now it was Imesfor's turn to smirk. "Whatever that may be. No normal human would have the power—or reason—to live so long in the caverns of the phaerimm."

Melegaunt studied the high mage a moment longer, then glanced at Kiinyon, and finally looked to Vala. "You may as well cut Master Colbathin free and let him pull his share. He and Lord Imesfor have been playing us a little bit for fools, I think."

Vala drew her darksword, and without breaking stride, slashed the tomb master's bonds off. "We have a saying in my home," she said darkly. "The fur of the clever fox is the finest."

Kiinyon smiled and jumped off the litter. "Then I shall have to take care you don't skin me."

Melegaunt turned to Lord Imesfor. "I'll see you safely out of the Sharaedim, then you can teleport to Waterdeep or wherever you like to ask for help."

"I see." Imesfor's golden eyes betrayed his disappointment. "I thank you for that much, at least."

"Thank me later, when I return to Evereska with the only help that will save it," said Melegaunt.

"Very well, I will thank you then." The high mage still did not sound convinced. "Unfortunately, there are a few minor complications . . ."

The complications were anything but minor. First, there was the matter of teleporting. Even with his fingers torn off, Lord Imesfor was capable of casting the spell, as it required nothing more than a complicated string of mystic syllables. Unfortunately, he had used all such enchantments in the attempt to save Evereska's army and could not teleport himself or anyone else until he studied the spell again.

Melegaunt solved this problem—rather reluctantly—by lending his own spellbook to the high mage. This occasioned hard feelings when he caught the elf puzzling over other spells, especially since Imesfor's accusatory manner in defending his actions suggested the enchantments were of a dangerous—if not outright corrupting—nature. Melegaunt's only response was to nod curtly and turn back to the spell Imesfor was supposed to be studying.

The second problem proved more difficult. Even at his best, Imesfor could not teleport all of the wounded elves to Waterdeep. Galaeron suggested a detour to drop them off at Evereska, but when they turned in that direction, the illithids rushed to catch up. Melegaunt veered away from the vale. When the illithids fell back, he gave Kiinyon a small light, telling him to take Vala's men and the litter and follow the light to safety in the Secret Gate. Eager to look after Keya and find out how his father and the Swords of Evereska were faring, Galaeron volunteered to accompany Kiinyon on the perilous journey back to the Vale. Melegaunt had other ideas, asking for Galaeron to accompany him so he would be able to reenter the Vale when he returned with help. This arrangement did much to reassure Lord Imesfor, who approved the plan wholeheartedly, sternly announcing that if he could sacrifice a son to the war, Galaeron could stand not knowing the fate of his father and sister for a few tendays.

Galaeron stayed. Melegaunt masked Kiinyon's departure with a shadow illusion, and the illithids did not seem to notice until much later, when the illusory shapes of the missing party members finally faded into wisps of black fog. Even then, the creatures seemed rather confused, sending a trio of scouts to search for their missing quarry. Two of the scouts vanished into the shadows and never returned. The third met some horrible end, as evidenced by the hissing screech that came from the direction it had gone.

The sound was more than enough to convince the rest of the illithids that the time for stealth was past. More than a dozen tentacle-faced silhouettes materialized out of the darkness, seeming to float forward in their long robes. Neither Galaeron nor Imesfor needed to be told to run. The creatures considered thousand-year-old elf corpses something of a delicacy, and the tomb guard was always having to fight them off.

Vala, on the other hand, did not seem to understand what the creatures could do if she allowed them to see her eyes. She drew her darksword and turned to face them—then screamed, grabbed her ears, and collapsed in a quivering heap.

Melegaunt spun and attacked without looking at the creatures, spraying a long chain of ebony bolts in every direction. "Get her!"

Galaeron was already scooping the woman into his arms. In her heavy scale armor, she weighed half again as much as he did, but there was no time to cast a spell to levitate her.

Once the creatures were close enough, they could blast the thoughts from a victim's mind without making eye contact.

As Galaeron hefted Vala over his shoulder, the darksword slipped from her grasp and disappeared on the dark ground. Knowing what she would do to him if he rescued her but not her sword, he dropped to a knee and ran his hand through the shadow mist until he hit something and felt his fingers go cold.

"What are you doing?" Melegaunt let loose with a long chain of black lightning bolts. Something hissed and fell, and he growled, "Hurry!"

Galaeron grasped the sword by the blade and lifted it out of shadows. Trying not to notice he had just sliced the pads off two fingertips, he tossed the weapon into the air and managed to catch it by the hilt. His palm began to sting with cold.

"Got it!"

He turned to flee toward Lord Imesfor, who stood a dozen paces ahead shaking his useless hands in anger. Melegaunt caught Galaeron by the shoulder and guided him past the high mage.

"This way!"

Melegaunt paused to make certain Lord Imesfor was keeping up with them, then ducked down a corridor of shadow. They ran no more than twenty paces before the first illithid rounded the corner behind them, its breath hissing down the dark gorge. Melegaunt flung a finger over his shoulder and unleashed a storm of black meteors behind them.

Burdened as Galaeron was with Vala's armored body, he was breathing so hard he barely heard the illithids' strangled shrieks. Melegaunt led the way around a bend in the dark passage and came to an intersection, one route veering off between two hill shapes toward a distant wedge of light, the other snaking deeper into the darkness.

Melegaunt pushed Lord Imesfor toward the light. "That way, no more than a hundred paces! You'll come out near the Marsh of Chelimber."

The lord's eyes grew wide. "We've come that far?"

"Yes!" The soft sound of hissing began to sound around the corner behind them. Melegaunt pushed the high mage toward the light. "Run, and cast your spell the instant you see the marsh."

Lord Imesfor sprinted for the light, groaning in pain as he pumped his mangled hands. Galaeron turned to flee in the opposite direction, but was surprised to feel a beefy hand catch him by the shoulder. He turned to see Melegaunt holding a finger to his lips, then watched in growing puzzlement as the wizard drew a veil of shadow down in front of them.

The illithids reached the intersection a moment later. Galaeron was so frightened he barely noticed the icy numbness creeping up the hand that held Vala's sword, but the creatures turned away and rushed after Lord Imesfor.

As Galaeron listened to the procession hiss past, he began to feel steadily sicker and more revolted. He kept waiting for Melegaunt to spring his trap, to step from behind the shadowy screen and spray the horrid creatures with some immensely powerful spell that would slay them all instantly. Melegaunt remained silent and motionless, save that he reached over to take Vala's sword when he noticed how white Galaeron's hand was growing.

Finally, Galaeron's shock gave way to the realization that the wizard had no intention of ambushing the illithids, that he had simply been using Lord Imesfor as a decoy. He dumped Vala's limp form onto the shadow-misted ground, then drew his own sword and started past Melegaunt.

The wizard planted a hand in the middle of Galaeron's chest, stopping him short. "Pick her up. You'll attract a shadator."

Galaeron shook his head. "I see how it is with you humans." He pressed the edge of his blade to Melegaunt's throat. "Save yourselves and sacrifice us!"

"You see less than I thought." Melegaunt wrapped his free hand around Galaeron's sword. Such were the wizard's protective enchantments that even its magic blade did not cut him. "Lord Imesfor will survive, so long as he does what I told him to do."

"You can't know that."

"Can't I?" He pushed Galaeron's sword away. "Even if I could not, would Lord Imesfor hesitate to use you as a decoy? Would you *want* him to, if it meant saving Evereska?"

Galaeron lowered his sword. "You should have warned him."

"Would he have trusted me?" Melegaunt returned Vala's sword to its scabbard, then picked her up himself. "Whatever you think, *we* are the ones who must reach our destination. Any help Imesfor finds in Waterdeep—or even in Evermeet— will do no more to stop the phaerimm than Kiinyon and his tomb guards. You, at least, have seen enough to know that is true."

It was one those rare moments that were growing ever rarer, when Khelben "Blackstaff" Arunsun was both idle enough to join his lady Laeral for her highsun "nap" and relaxed enough to enjoy it—when his troubles were far from mind and no worldly problems weighed on his shoulders, and so he was most decidedly *un*happy to hear the boots of an apprentice ponding up the stairs.

"Master Blackstaff!" It was young Ransford, the most excitable of the novices and—at that moment, at least—the most reckless. "Lady Silverhand!"

"Ouch." Laeral turned her head and raised a dreamy green eye toward Khelben. "Gently, my dear."

Khelben looked down and saw that the knuckles of his hands—the hands that had, until two seconds ago, been gently kneading Laeral's shoulders—had gone white. He forced them open, then forced out a calming breath, then forced his voice to remain calm.

"Sorry, love."

"Awake, my lord!" Ransford's cry grew more urgent as drew nearer. "My lady, awake!"

Listening to crunch of his own grinding teeth, Khelben swung his knee over Laeral's back and placed both feet heavily on the floor. "If this is about three-legged frogs again, I'll have that lad's tongue for a potion of ventriloquism."

He pulled on his black robe, then tossed Laeral's silver shift to her.

Ransford reached the landing and pounded on the door. "My lord, *wake*—"

"Quiet, lad!" Khelben jerked the door open so quickly that Ransford came stumbling across the threshold all elbows and knees. "Don't you know what 'nap' means?"

"I'm sorry, Master Blackstaff, but—" Ransford caught a flash of pale skin as Laeral slipped into her shift, then blushed and fell into a fit of stuttering. "B-b-but—"

"What?" Khelben grabbed the boy's ear. "Out with it."

"Th-th-there's an e-e-elf," he stammered. "A-a-and an, an ill-ill-illillill . . . just come and see!"

Ransford took Khelben by the hand and led him over to the window, but the boy was so excited that Khelben had to speak the word of transparency himself. When he did, he was so surprised he nearly began to stutter himself.

In the courtyard outside, a mangled elf with no fingers was kicking and flailing at a single mind flayer, trying in grim desperation to pull one of the thing's tentacles out of a small round hole in his skull.

"By the Weave, Laeral!" Khelben thrust a hand toward his namesake staff and, in the same instant, felt the familiar comfort of its polished wood. "I think that's Gervas Imesfor down there!"

CHAPTER NINE

24 Nightal, the Year of the Unstrung Harp

It seemed a lifetime since Galaeron had last felt the glaring sun of the Desert Border on his face, or bathed in the moon's milky light, or glimpsed even a star's blue twinkle, and he felt hungry for light— not the flat, toneless white radiance of these endless shadowlands, but real light. Light he could feel, hot and stinging against his skin, light that would make him thirsty and burn the musty smell of sweat from his cloak. Light that would give him some sense of direction, that would mark the passing time by its ebbing and flowing.

They had been marching for what seemed hours, but might have been mere minutes or days unending, winding through a labyrinth of sinuous shapes and sharp-edged silhouettes. Galaeron's mind had long since stopped trying to make sense of the patterns and merely classified them as passing forms. If the lack of light troubled Melegaunt, he showed no sign of it. He simply marched along, leading the way ever onward at the same brisk pace.

Vala, now recovered from her brush with the illithid, followed close on the wizard's heels. Though she never complained, Galaeron could tell by the weariness of her stride and the way she craned her neck skyward that she missed the light as much as he did.

They seemed to be approaching some sort of shadow border, a curtain of utter darkness that Galaeron kept glimpsing at the far end of long shadowy channels, or looming up beyond hill shapes. Whenever the curtain came into view, the stretch he saw was longer. Sometimes he saw two stretches at once, one spanning a broad shadowbed, the other rising behind a nearby slope. Each time, the curtain seemed higher and darker and somehow deeper, as though it were not so much a barrier, but a vast expanse of pure, unlit darkness.

Finally, they rounded a corner and saw nothing but black curtain in any direction, its billowing crown silhouetted against the lighter purple of the shadow sky, its dark feet rooted in the swirling black ground mists. Vala's shoulders slumped, and a sigh almost too faint to hear slipped her lips, and Galaeron knew he had to say something to Melegaunt before he and Vala went mad.

"Melegaunt, wait."

The wizard spun on his heel, his dark eyes searching the dusky landscape behind his two charges. "What's wrong?"

"Nothing, except I'm about to lose my mind," said Galaeron. "Doesn't this bother you?"

"This?" Melegaunt looked around. "After the Phaerlin? You must be joking."

The wizard started toward the shadowy curtain ahead. Vala started after him, but stopped and looked back when she realized Galaeron was not following.

"Are you coming, elf?" she asked.

"Not in there." Galaeron gestured at the blackness ahead. "I'm not going any deeper until I've had a few minutes of sunshine."

Melegaunt turned. "Deeper?"

"Into the shadow." Again, Galaeron pointed at the dark curtain. "Just a few minutes in the light—please?"

Vala nodded her agreement. "In truth, this gloom wears on the nerves. I could use a little sunshine myself—especially if we're going deeper."

"Deeper?" Melegaunt scowled and looked into the darkness ahead. "Deeper into what?"

"Shadow," Galaeron said. "Even I can see that—"

"It's a forest," Melegaunt growled.

Galaeron frowned. Now that the wizard mentioned it, the curtain did resemble the gloomy edge of a deep wood, and the billowing crown was shaped like a forest's outer canopy.

"The Forgotten Forest, to be exact," said Melegaunt. "I'd never take you beyond the Fringe."

"The Fringe?" asked Galaeron.

"The boundary between the worlds of light and the Shadowdeep." Melegaunt waved his arm at the surrounding terrain. "Neither of you would last a hundred steps beyond the Fringe."

Vala scowled and started to object, but Galaeron cut her off by asking, "*Worlds* of light?"

"There are many worlds, young elf. The Shadowdeep connects them all. It's the one mirror that shapes their many lights." Melegaunt started forward again. "And now, if you'd please start walking again, you will see your precious light again in Dekanter. I'd like to be there before the Shifting."

Galaeron raised a questioning brow to Vala, who shrugged and started after the wizard, grumbling, "Better not to be left behind."

Feeling no less distressed for the explanation, Galaeron started after his companions. Once they had formed a neat line again, Melegaunt turned his head a little so it would be easier for Galaeron and Vala to hear him.

"You have noticed how the shadows change as the sun crosses the sky?" Melegaunt asked. "And how they dance in the light of a candle?"

"Of course," said Galaeron.

"What happens when the sun sets?"

"There is darkness." It was Vala who said this.

"There is *shadow*," corrected Melegaunt. "The sun has not vanished, only sunk out of sight. It's light is blocked by the horizon."

"A fine distinction," noted Galaeron.

"But an important one," said Melegaunt. "On Faerûn, there is only shadow. Everything that people call 'dark' or 'night' is nothing more than light blocked by the world itself."

"Even in caves?" asked Vala.

"Even caves. If they weren't surrounded by rock, the sun would light them," the wizard explained. "But there are places—other planes—where there is no sun or any light. There, no shadow exists, only darkness—true, black, darkness."

"And this has *what* to do with the Shifting?" asked Vala.

"Only this," said Melegaunt. "Darkness is by nature motionless and without life, but shadows are all motion and vigor. They dance and swirl and flicker and continually beget strange creatures, and only light ever fixes them in place."

"So when the sun goes down, they lose form and go into motion," surmised Galaeron. "The Shifting."

Melegaunt nodded. "One could almost say they *become* motion." He craned his neck around to smile at Galaeron. "We'll make a shadow shaper of you yet, elf."

"I'm sure the Hill Elders will like *that*," said Vala.

Though she made no complaint, Galaeron could tell by how she dogged Melegaunt's heels that she had realized the same thing he did. If they wanted to feel any sunlight on their faces in Dekanter, they had to hurry.

As they approached the forest, the darkness resolved itself into a fence of charcoal depths, laced by black tangles of undergrowth, striped by the ebony columns of impossibly thin tree trunks. Knowing it to be the forest, or more accurately the absence of one, Galaeron began to feel a little more at ease. Elves, even those who dwelled in cities, were at home in the woods. If he could feel safe any place in the Fringe, it would be there. He moved closer behind Vala and spoke to Melegaunt over her shoulder.

"Is Dekanter where we'll find the help you promised?"

"Sadly, no," said Melegaunt "My, uh, friends are a few days farther north—and west, I believe. But I've always wanted to see Dekanter, and as it happens to be on our way, I thought it would be a good place to rest for the night."

Dekanter was the last place in Faerûn—that Galaeron knew of, at least—where the ruins of ancient Netheril could still be visited. Little more than a few towers and dozens upon dozens of holes in the ground, the city was not much to see and even less of a camping spot, but Galaeron suspected the goblins and gargoyles who normally plagued visitors there would quickly see the wisdom in giving any camp of Melegaunt's a wide berth.

"It would ease my mind to know who these friends of yours are, Melegaunt," said Galaeron. "What makes you so certain they can stop the phaerimm when Evereska's high mages could not?"

"Have you heard nothing I've told you?" snapped Melegaunt. "I'm certain because ridding Faerûn of this evil is what they have prepared themselves to do. It's unfortunate they will have to do it in Evereska instead of Anauroch, but they will succeed nonetheless."

"Unfortunate?" Galaeron had visions of his beloved vale being reduced to a ruin of shadow and smoke. "How?"

Melegaunt's voice grew impatient. "How do you think? The phaerimm have already killed hundreds of Tel'Quess and may well kill thousands more." The wizard reached the forest edge and continued forward, then suddenly began to grow translucent. "But there is no need to fear for Evereska itself. We will not allow . . ."

The wizard's voice grew softer as his body grew more transparent, then finally faded altogether when he vanished.

Vala pulled up short, and Galaeron stumbled into her from behind, nearly knocking her into the forest after Melegaunt.

"Mighty One?" she called.

Galaeron shouted, "Melegaunt?"

When no answer came, they drew their swords. Galaeron's first instinct was to look for shadators—as though he could actually see one—and illithids and beholders or any of the other deadly creatures of wickedness he was beginning to associate with Melegaunt and their phaerimm enemies. Vala's reaction was more direct and to the point. She grabbed Galaeron and started forward into the forest.

"Vala! Are you . . ." Galaeron made it only that far before he realized she was doing exactly the right thing. "All right, I'm coming!"

A cold afternoon wind began to whip his hair about his ears, then he found himself standing ankle deep in cold Nightal snow, staring at the winter skeletons of a thick forest of oak, walnut, and shadowtop. Melegaunt was no more than three paces ahead, surrounded by a semicircle of eight trees, all still holding their leaves. The largest of the trees, a twenty-foot oak, was blocking their path, shaking a gnarled branch at Melegaunt and rumbling at him in a voice as deep as thunder.

"Through my wood, Melegaunt Tanthul, you do not go!"

"But it is the shortest path, Great Fuorn," Melegaunt protested, "and the only one I know."

"Matters not," said the tree.

Now that he had recovered from his astonishment, Galaeron could make out the twisted bark faces of the eight trees. They had knotholes for eyes, jagged hollows for mouths, crooked limb stubs for noses. Their lips and brows were formed of gathered bark, their cheeks by lumpy burls. Galaeron's mother had once introduced him to a treant in the High Forest, and he recognized these plants as creatures of the same kind.

"Your magic is a thing cold and dark," said Fuorn, "and this wood it shall not enter."

"If my magic feels strange to you, it is because you have never seen its like or power before." Melegaunt pointed east toward Anauroch. "I employ it in a good cause, against the wicked creatures that turned the old forests into barren sand."

Fuorn looked east. "Yes, I recall the magicgrubs." His crown of scarlet leaves swayed back and forth in a sort of nod. "Little larger than men, but with a bite like dragons. We have seen a pair sniffing around our forest, peering into the shadows beneath our branches."

Melegaunt's shoulders squared. "The very ones. The phaerimm. I have come to undo what they have done."

Again, Fuorn seemed to nod. "Then well I wish you—but not here. I will have no battles in my forest."

"I thank you for the warning, tree," said Melegaunt. "You have my promise that no harm will come to your forest."

The wizard lowered his arm and cupped his hand beneath his sleeve, and Galaeron knew something terrible was about to happen. He clipped Vala's heel with the arch of his foot and knocked her to the ground with a sweep of his arm, then slipped forward and used the same technique to knock the wizard off his feet.

Melegaunt bellowed and started to raise the suspicious hand, but stopped when Galaeron's foot pinned his arm to his chest.

"No, my human friend," said Galaeron, "not even for Evereska."

Though he still held his sword, Galaeron was careful to hold the blade away from Melegaunt—and not only because he knew it would never pierce the wizard's magic. Vala had already leaped to her feet and was stepping toward him, dark-sword ready to strike.

"Have you lost your mind, elf?" Though there was a hint of grief in her expression, the set of her jaw and the hardness in her eyes left no doubt of her intentions. "You know I'm sworn to defend him."

"A little late for that, my dear," chuckled Melegaunt, "but no harm done."

The wizard motioned her to stand down, then brought his hand out of his sleeve and displayed a large black kernel.

"To help the treants protect their wood in the battles to come." Melegaunt handed it to Galaeron, then his voice grew pained. "You couldn't have thought I meant to attack them."

"I didn't know what to think." Noting that the treants were watching them with expressions ranging from bewilderment to suspicion, Galaeron sheathed his sword and examined the seed. It was about the size of an acorn, but as shiny as coal and full of swirling darkness. "I apologize. What is this?"

"Shadowstorm seed." Melegaunt heaved himself up and faced Fuorn. "Hurl it down, and any being not rooted to the ground will be swept into the shadowdeep. There will be wind and lightning, but any battle likely to be waged near your forest would be stopped at once—or at least moved to where it could do no harm."

Fuorn considered this, then asked, "And rain?"

"If you throw it into the air," said Melegaunt. "But do so only in great desperation. The deluge it brings will quench even the fiercest fire, but the waters will be black and cold—far colder than any ice storm."

This drew a leafy shudder from the treants, for only burning was considered a more awful death than being split down the trunk by the weight of an ice-crusted crown. Fuorn lowered a twisted bough, and Galaeron laid the seed in the cusp of his woody palm.

"With your gift, I will be very careful." Fuorn tucked the kernel into a fold of bark. "And in return give you the favor of a warning word. Of late, the northern shadows have often taken the shape of great wings and long tails."

"Shadow dragons," surmised Melegaunt. "Shimmergloom?"

Fuorn's leafy crown quivered in a contrary sign. "It is sung on the winds that the longbeard Battlehammer slew the great wyrm when he reclaimed Mithral Hall, but it may be that Shimmergloom's seeds have begun to sprout and show themselves. You would do well to walk the shadow way carefully after you round the forest."

"Round the forest?" echoed Melegaunt. "You still refuse us?"

"We thank you for the shadowstorm seed," said Fuorn, "but what did you risk in its giving?"

Without waiting for an answer, Fuorn stepped back among his fellows. He stretched upright and stood motionless, not so much staring at the travelers as waiting for them to make their decision. Not wishing Melegaunt to come to the wrong one, Galaeron reached for his arm—and felt Vala's strong grasp on his own.

"You surprise me once," she said.

"Don't be ridiculous," Galaeron said. "I mean him no harm."

"Good." She smiled artificially. "I'd miss you."

Melegaunt spun away from the treants and started eastward along the edge of the forest. Vala motioned Galaeron ahead of her, then slipped in behind him, and they both had to scurry to keep pace with the wizard's long strides.

Galaeron was not sure when Vala finally sheathed her sword, but it was in its scabbard when they reached the Lonely Moor just before dusk. Galaeron and Vala took a minute to bask in the sun's fading radiance, then set up camp and cooked a meal of marsh voles over a black-flamed fire Melegaunt had struck. Despite the glyphs and wards the wizard set around the perimeter of the camp, they divided the watch into three shifts and settled in for a wet night.

As it turned out, Galaeron could have taken all three watches himself. Whether it was because of Vala's distrust or worry for his father and Takari back in Evereska, he was never able to slip into the Reverie. He spent the whole night huddled in his cloak, staring at the stars and wrestling with feelings of guilt so vague and ambiguous he could only guess at their source. Of course, he was troubled by the part he had played in releasing the phaerimm, but his regret over that was real and tangible, an emotion so manifest he could almost touch it. The thing bothering him was much more subtle, a queasy hollowness that smacked of disloyalty and betrayal, though he was left to wonder just who he had betrayed. Had he been wrong to distrust Melegaunt? Or to accept so easily the wizard's explanation for the casual betrayal of Imesfor? Whatever the answer, Galaeron feared he would not enjoy a revitalizing Reverie until he had it.

Dawn found them all cold and awake, ready to warm themselves with a brisk prebreakfast march. Before departing, Melegaunt insisted on kneeling between Galaeron and Vala, holding his hands in their shadows, peering first into one, then the other, from the moment the sun broke the horizon until the moment the bottom edge no longer touched it. Only then did he rise.

"Come along, sun lovers. There will be no shadow walking for us today."

"Not that I'm complaining, but why?" asked Galaeron.

"Because I have read the day to come and have no desire to fight shadow dragons. The bugbears will be much easier."

"Bugbears?" Galaeron gasped. "The phaerimm have bugbears?"

Melegaunt shrugged. "Perhaps. The phaerimm control many creatures, most who do not even know it, but I cannot tell everything. I'm only reading shadows." He started northward, motioning Galaeron and Vala to follow. "Keep a sharp watch. We should be all right as long as we don't let them surprise us."

This proved much easier said than done, of course. They slogged northward across a few miles of peat moor, then slipped around the northern tip of the Forgotten Forest and started northwest across the Forsaken Dale. As they crossed the snowy flats, Galaeron kept a watchful eye on the birds, but knew they would not have much to worry about until they reached the Greypeaks in the distance.

Just after highsun, the foothills drew near enough to make out individual gullies, and the pinnacles of the snowcapped mountains themselves began to show above the horizon. Galaeron's thoughts kept returning to his inability to enter the Reverie the night before. The explanation Melegaunt had given for using Imesfor as a decoy was sensible enough, but it still smacked of deceit, and it occurred to Galaeron that he was placing a great deal of trust in a human he really did not know very well. He allowed Melegaunt to drift a short distance out of earshot, then spoke over his shoulder to Vala.

"If I offended you by doubting Melegaunt, I apologize," he said. "Perhaps if I knew more about him . . ."

"You know he is trying to save Evereska." Vala said, prodding Galaeron in the back, urging him to catch up to Melegaunt. "You know he is trying to undo a mistake you made. How much more do you need to know?"

"How much do *you* know?" asked Galaeron, doing his best to ignore the barb about his "mistake." "He claims much, but reveals little."

"He is a good man."

"From where?" asked Galaeron. "I have never seen the likes of his magic before."

"That does not mean it is evil." Vala's voice was sharp enough that it caused Melegaunt to cock his head to one side. "The Melegaunt Tanthul I know is not evil."

"But *I* do not know him," Galaeron said. "I might find it easier to trust him if I knew more about your relationship. Now that you are no longer Evereska's prisoner, perhaps—"

"Very well," Vala sighed. "A hundred years ago, my ancestors were living in log longhouses roofed in thatch and chinked with mud, battling the orc hordes with weapons of cold-forged iron and losing children to worgs and gnolls faster than our women could birth them."

"And I suppose Melegaunt changed that?"

"He did," said Vala. Twenty paces ahead, the wizard seemed to nod smugly to himself. "In return for a pittance of service, he offered to build my great grandfather an impregnable keep of black granite, and to arm twenty warriors with black swords that would cleave any enemy's armor."

"A bargain your ancestor obviously accepted," said Galaeron.

"Not as quick as you believe, for we Vaasans have always been hard bargainers," said Vala. "The debt would be called at some time in the future, when a company of warriors armed with those same black swords would be summoned to service. Bodvar agreed, providing only that all of the swords remained unbroken and the granite keep was never breached."

"I take it the conditions were fulfilled."

Vala nodded. "My own father heard the voice less than a year ago, but he was too old and sick to lead the men. It was left to me to take up the sword."

"And that's all you know of Melegaunt?" asked Galaeron.

"It's all I need to know." Vala's tone was almost soft. "The service of twenty warriors for the kindness he has done my clan? You elves are too distrustful."

"Perhaps so," allowed Galaeron. "We weren't always distrustful. That we learned from humans."

He spied the long valley that led to Dekanter and began to angle toward it, his thoughts consumed by questions of why Melegaunt would want to visit the ruins if the help he sought wasn't there—and what kind of help he might be seeking if it was.

They caught up to Melegaunt and entered the gulch together, and Galaeron was instantly too busy looking for bugbears to concern himself with anything else. The gully was perfect for an ambush, with an abundance of cliff-flanked narrows and blind corners, but they resisted the temptation to climb to higher ground for fear of making themselves more visible to phaerimm searchers. Twice, they were actually ambushed by goblin tribes, but a simple display of magic was enough to send the creatures skittering away.

When they reached the head of the gulch without meeting any bugbears and climbed into the hills themselves, Galaeron began to think Melegaunt was not as infallible as he appeared. The ruined towers of Dekanter were just visible in the distance, a short row of absurdly twisted and impossibly leaning spires silhouetted against snow-blanketed slopes, and the sun was already sinking into the narrow rift of the Bleached Bones Pass.

The sight of the towers seemed to invigorate Melegaunt. Abandoning all effort at keeping a low profile, he clambered along a boulder-strewn ridge toward the sunken roadbed that had once connected Dekanter to the rest of the Netherese empire. Vala scurried after him, apparently abandoning her resolve to never again let Galaeron behind her.

"Melegaunt, what about the bugbears?" she asked.

"Yes, yes, I'm sure they're here somewhere," he said. "But the ruins are still a good mile away, and I must be there when the sun goes down."

The wizard continued forward at a near run, giving Vala and Galaeron no choice except to keep a watchful eye and hope for the best. Soon enough, the towers resolved themselves into jewel-colored oddities of architectural corruption, grotesque forms that arced and twisted in impossible directions with no thought of form or function. Some had no doors or windows, one seemed to be a single warped door spiraling into the sky, another looked to be a huge window with no interior depth at all.

The towers were scattered among the great mines that had been the reason for Dekanter's existence in the days of Netheril. Now long played out, all that remained of the ancient workings were snowy dumps of waste rock and the yawning portals and abysmal shafts of the holes themselves. Even Melegaunt seemed to sense the melancholy insanity of the place. He walked among the ruins silently, inspecting each warped spire like a wandering son returned home to find his house occupied by another family.

When the bottom curve of the sun finally touched the distant saddle of Bleached Bones Pass, he kneeled in the shadow of the door tower and pressed his brow to the dark ground. He spoke a few syllables in some tongue Galaeron did not understand, then lifted his body and shook his head slowly.

"The folly," he said. "The unbelievable folly."

When the tears began to roll down his cheeks, Vala went to his side and slipped a hand under his arm. "Is there time to try another tower?" she asked. "Every story can't be the same."

The thought seemed to cheer Melegaunt. He allowed her to pull him up, then started along a boulder-lined trail toward the window tower. "Yes, another tower would be good."

They had taken no more than a dozen steps when Galaeron noticed a trio of crows circling overhead. Instead of calling to each other in their usual raucous voices, the birds were unusually silent, like anglers afraid their voices might frighten the fish.

"Stop."

Galaeron had barely spoken the word before Vala had her darksword in hand and Melegaunt behind her.

"Where?"

"I don't know," Galaeron said. "Here."

A half dozen paces up the trail, a pair of pointed ears appeared over the top of a horse-sized boulder. Vala spotted them instantly and gestured silently with her sword. Grousing under his breath, Melegaunt fetched something from his robe pocket, and Galaeron realized the emergence of the ears had been too convenient. Bugbears rarely made such foolish mistakes.

"Melegaunt, wa—"

He was too late. The wizard pointed a finger and spoke a

single word, and a shadowy bolt of darkness drilled straight through the boulder. There was no thud or anguished roar or any other sound to suggest the attack had hit anything living. Rather, a slimy mauve face with a snout of tentacles rose up behind the adjacent snow bank, fixing Melegaunt with a white-eyed stare.

The wizard screamed once, then clutched at his eyes and crumpled to the ground.

"An illithid?" Even as Vala shrieked the question, she was flinging her darksword at the creature in a backhand flip. "Melegaunt said nothing about illithids!"

The blade pirouetted through the air and took the illithid's head off cleanly.

In the next instant, a dozen bugbears sprang from behind boulders, rock dumps, and snowdrifts to both sides of the trail. Galaeron pulled his sword from its scabbard with one hand and reached into his cloak pocket with the other.

"Vala," the elf shouted, "sword!"

He tossed the sword toward her hilt-first, then pulled his other hand from his pocket and flung a pair of green leaves in the direction of the nearest bugbears. The brutes were huge, a full head taller than Vala's burly men and far broader across the shoulders, but with ugly batlike snouts and gleaming red eyes. Vala caught Galaeron's sword with her off hand and whirled the blade around to point at the charging beasts.

Galaeron uttered his incantation, but instead of feeling the magic flow into his body from the all-encompassing Weave, it surged up through his legs in a cold bolt. With a dozen screaming bugbears on the way, there was no time to be shocked. He simply waved his hand across the hillside, and a cloud of putrid brown miasma filled the air around the bugbears' heads. Four out of the first five creatures collapsed gagging. The fifth perished when Vala dived at its feet, then somersaulted between its legs and slashed Galaeron's magic blade across the front of its belly.

Galaeron slowed the remaining beasts with a pinch of

sand and a quick word of magic, sending two into a deep slumber. Vala toppled another with a knee slash, then caught a heavy axe swing against the flat of Galaeron's blade. The bugbear continued to push, confident its strength would simply collapse Vala's guard.

She thrust a hand out in the direction of the dead illithid, and her darksword came flying back into her grasp. She brought the black blade beneath her attacker's big belly, driving the point clear to its heart. Galaeron pointed at the bugbear nearest Vala. Again, the magic shot into him from the cold ground, and the shaft that leaped from his finger to tear open the bugbear's chest was as black as night.

Seeing they were still three paces away from Vala and unlikely to get any closer, the last two beasts turned to flee. There was no question of letting them escape, for their illithid companion made plain the identity of their masters. Galaeron blasted one down from behind with another magic bolt. Vala sprang after the other as it bounded over the edge of the hill, and a strangled howl echoed up the slope.

Galaeron used a pair of lightning bolts and a fireball to finish the bugbears he had incapacitated with his earlier spells. He felt the same surge of cold magic when he cast the first lightning bolt, but found that by concentrating on the living Weave all around him, he could create spells normally. Still, Vala returned from her trip down the hill to find him shivering with cold; it seemed to be welling up inside him, as though the marrow in his bones had turned to shadow.

"Something wrong?" She returned his sword. "You look like that's the first time you ever killed anything."

"Would that it were." Galaeron pulled his cloak more tightly around him. He turned to face Melegaunt, who was lying glassy eyed and drooling on the ground. "I'm fine, but what about him?"

Vala considered him for a moment, then shrugged. "Well, at least he saw his towers."

CHAPTER TEN

25 Nightal, the Year of the Unstrung Harp

When Galaeron climbed down into the rocky basin where they had made camp the previous night, he found Vala lying next to her unsheathed sword, staring into its glassy blade with a vacant expression. On an elf's visage, her arched brow and wistful smile would have suggested a not-altogether-unhappy loneliness, but he was not sure what the look signified on a human face. His first reaction was one of envy, as he himself had again passed the entire night without a moment of reverie. Then he remembered: humans did not have the Reverie.

"Vala?" Galaeron reached out to shake her.

Her hand came up and caught his wrist in a lightning-fast trap block. He barely managed to pull free and fling himself backward before her dark-sword cleaved the air where he had been kneeling.

Galaeron somersaulted over a shoulder and pulled his own sword to block.

Vala rolled to her hip, her pale eyes vacant and dangerous.

"Vala!" Galaeron called. "It's me—the elf . . ."

Her brow knitted, then reason returned to her eyes. She scowled at the weapon in Galaeron's hand.

"What's that for?" If Vala noticed that she was pointing with her own sword, her face showed no sign. "Trying to kill me in my sleep?"

"You weren't sleeping. Your eyes were open."

This seemed to stir her memory. "That's right . . . I was visiting." Now she scowled. "And you interrupted me?"

"Visiting?"

"The Granite Tower." She jammed the darksword into its scabbard. "Dream walking. You know."

Galaeron shook his head. "Is this like the Reverie?"

"Not really." Vala glanced eastward, where a brightening band of gray horizon foretold the coming dawn. "You didn't wake me for my watch."

Galaeron shrugged. "I couldn't rest. I thought you might as well."

"Thanks, but you should have tried. You look like hell." More gently, she explained, " 'Visiting' is my word for it. Over the years, every darksword seems to inherit a few foibles from its family. Burlen's hums in combat, Dexon's talks in its sleep."

"And yours 'visits'?"

"Spying might be a better term." Vala's cheeks darkened. "It likes to, uh, show me what's happening in the bedchambers of the Granite Tower."

Galaeron raised his brow.

"It's not something I like."

"Of course not," Galaeron said, enjoying a rare opportunity to bait her. "Though you did seem to be smiling."

"I was watching Sheldon sleep." Though there was no indignation in Vala's voice, her tone grew solemn enough that Galaeron regretted chiding her. "He's my son."

"Can you two not be quiet?" rumbled Melegaunt. The wizard sat up, palms pressed to his eyes. "What happened to my head?"

"Illithid," Vala said. "With the bugbears."

Melegaunt pulled his hands away. "Then the phaerimm are a step ahead." He ran his fingers through his dusky hair and hefted himself to his feet. "We'll leave as soon as I've read the day."

They gathered their gear, then climbed to the rim of their campsite and stood in the light of the rising sun. Melegaunt knelt between Vala and Galaeron as before.

"A day of meetings," he announced, "but nothing to fear. So long as we are cautious."

"How cautious?" asked Galaeron.

"Bad things in the mountains." Melegaunt gestured westward toward Bleached Bones Pass. "But the shadow way looked clear to the north. Good news, is it not?"

Vala and Galaeron eyed each other with looks of dread, then Vala asked, "How bad were the things in the pass?"

"Shadow dragons are fearsome creatures, even in a world of light," said Melegaunt. "More importantly, though, there is speed to consider. The phaerimm will not find it easy to breach Evereska's mythal, but if we give them too long, they will discover a way."

Galaeron gestured the wizard forward.

Melegaunt cast a last, wistful look at the twisted towers of Dekanter, then spoke the words of his shadow walking spell. The world around them grew dull and featureless, with a jagged ridge of purple mountain shapes to the left and a subdued morning glare to the right. Galaeron felt instantly cold and isolated, and saw by the disquiet in Vala's eyes she felt the same.

Melegaunt donned the cold gloom like a favored cloak, letting out a sigh of satisfaction and setting off at a near dash. Vala motioned Galaeron to follow, then fell into position behind him.

"How did you two manage the battle without my help?" Melegaunt's voice was overly innocent. "With a mind flayer present, I imagine the fight was a difficult one."

"Not particularly," said Vala. "I killed it first. Galaeron took care of the rest with his magic."

"Truly?" Melegaunt peered back over his shoulder. "And all your spells worked well?"

"I'm hardly a magic-user of your caliber," he answered carefully. The wizard's interest seemed to suggest certain expectations, and Galaeron found himself less than eager to confirm them. "They worked as well as usual."

"They did the job." Melegaunt looked forward again, his brow lowered in disappointment. "That's what counts."

Galaeron resisted the urge to keep from demanding an explanation of exactly what the wizard had done to him. The question would give away more than he cared to, and he had already seen that Melegaunt was not someone who yielded his own secrets easily. They traveled onward in silence, twisting and winding their way through a maze of hill shapes. The jagged silhouettes of the mountains always remained to their left, but otherwise Galaeron saw no rhyme or reason to their route. Melegaunt turned into the light as often as he turned away, followed shadow troughs as often as he walked through hill shapes, went down as often as up. As the day passed—or what passed for day in the Fringe—the band of radiance to the right rose higher in the sky, then divided into irregular shapes and scattered itself across the landscape.

When mountain shapes started to rise on all sides, Galaeron realized they were climbing into the Greypeaks. He quickly lost all sense of direction. In the Fringe, everything felt flat beneath his feet. When he thought they were ascending, they were descending, and when he thought they were going around, they were going through.

Soon, the shapes turned ghostly and blue, and Melegaunt began to hesitate before picking directions. When the silhouettes grew transparent and gray; Melegaunt started to mumble and backtrack. Finally, the shadows vanished altogether, and Melegaunt stopped and began to turn in circles.

"What's wrong?" Galaeron asked. "Are we lost?"

"Lost?" Melegaunt spun in a slow circle, his eyes scanning the featureless gray fog around them. "I'm afraid so."

Galaeron groaned. "And you can't cancel the spell."

"It wouldn't be wise," said Melegaunt. "We'd probably return to our own Faerûn, but if I took a wrong turn somewhere . . ."

"What if we just went toward that campfire?" asked Vala.

"Fire?" Melegaunt asked. "Where?"

She pointed into the gray distance, but Galaeron could see no sign of fire.

Melegaunt slipped past him and peered over her shoulder, then smiled and clapped her back. "Well done."

Galaeron retreated two steps and peered over Vala's shoulder, then saw two tiny ribbons of yellow and white flickering around each other. "You're sure that's fire?"

"That's what it looks like from the Fringe," said Melegaunt.

Within half a dozen steps, the ribbons expanded into a small circle of flames surrounded by a whirling gray haze. Melegaunt motioned for Vala and Galaeron to ready their swords, then led them into the radiance of the campfire.

The flames turned instantly to their proper orange, and a mewling voice cried out in surprise.

"By the One!" On the other side of the fire rose a pudgy little man in a snow-blanketed cloak and hood, his pink hands held high to demonstrate they held no weapons. "Cause me no harm, and you shall have all I own . . . little as that may be!"

Melegaunt motioned the fellow to lower his hands. "You have nothing to fear from us, so long as we have nothing to fear from you."

The little man glanced from the husky wizard to his two well-armored companions and did not lower his hands. "Why would three so mighty need fear a humble beggar like myself?"

Though the man's cloak was travel worn and his beard disheveled, he hardly looked the part of a beggar. His face was round and soft, his belly ample, his eyes shifty. He had made his camp in a small side gulch high in the Greypeaks, where a tangled thicket of black spruce offered at least some protection from a driving snowstorm blowing in from the east—the cause, Galaeron suspected, of the strange paling that had forced Melegaunt to abandon the shadow way. A single sad-eyed mount stood tied behind a lean-to of dead logs, its saddle and bags tossed carelessly inside the shelter. The horse's expression seemed as down-trodden as that of its master, but its coat gleamed from daily currycombing, and—if anything—it looked overfed. Melegaunt studied the camp, his eye running from the fire to the lean-to to the horse as though everything were exactly where he expected.

Continuing to hold his hands over his head, the little man gestured to the log he had been sitting on. "You are more than welcome to share my fire." He started to close his mouth as though he were finished speaking, then suddenly looked surprised and added, "I couldn't stop you anyway."

"We wouldn't want to impose on you." Melegaunt looked around. "I'm a little turned around in this snow. If you'll point the way to Thousand Faces, we'll be on our way."

"Over the pass?" The little man shook his head vigorously. "You can't, not here."

This drew a scowl from Vala. "You think to stop us?"

The little man's eyes widened. "I d-don't—but even you three are no match for so many b-beholders."

"Beholders?" Melegaunt sounded less surprised than disappointed. "How many?"

"Enough." The little man shook his hooded head in despair. "My luck has been a curse all my life. First it was the mind flayers at Bleached Bones, then the Zhentarim at Dawn Pass, and now it is the beholders. Who knows what it will be at the High Gap? I tell you, we are not going to find a safe place to cross until we are past the Far Forest!"

"Perhaps not," said Melegaunt. "Let me have a look at these beholders. I sometimes have a way with them."

The little man raised his brow. "Truly? If you can get us across these accursed mountains, I would be forever in your debt—no doubt because I seldom repay a favor." A frown of dismay flashed across his face, but he cautiously lowered his hands and bowed to the companions. "Malik el Sami yn Nasser at your service."

Khelben paced at the foot of Imesfor's bed, two steps then turn, two steps then look, two steps then turn. To the mage's eye, the elf looked no better than the day he had arrived, save that he no longer had an illithid tentacle probing the hole in his skull. The lord's gaze was glassy and vacant, with a raccoon's mask of purple bruises ringing his eyes, and his sunken cheeks were as pallid as ivory. An inert tongue lolled out of his mouth with no indication it would ever speak again, much less soon.

Khelben took two impatient steps, turned, stopped, then looked to the aradoness leaning over the stricken lord. "You've been with him for nearly two days. When will he speak?"

The elf priestess fixed Khelben with a black-eyed glare. "Your concern for your friend is touching. Bear in mind that it is just that concern that will keep his spirit in his body."

"Lord Imesfor and I have been friends nearly five centuries," growled Khelben. "He knows how I feel about him—and I know how he feels about Evereska. If he knew what was happening there—"

"He does know," said the priestess, Angharad Odaeyns. "Isn't that why you're trying to wake him?"

Khelben gave her a black look. "You know what I mean. If he knew we couldn't get near the place. . . ." He let the sentence trail off, then ran his palm into the canopy post so hard he shook the whole bed. "Cloudblast!"

Laeral slipped a hand through the crook of his arm.

"Perhaps we should try another tact, Khelben." She pulled him to the side of the bed opposite Angharad, then used a cantrip to pull a chair across the room for him. "It was you Gervas came to see. Perhaps if you—"

"Lady Blackstaff, I don't think that wise." Angharad started around the bed. "A human touch is not the same. There is no emotional tie."

"Really?" Laeral fixed the elf with an icy stare. "Then why did he come to Khelben instead of Queen Amlaruil?"

The question staggered the proud Gold elf as no blow could have. "I'm sure there was a reason." She stopped at the foot of the bed to think of one. "Perhaps the mind flayer—"

"All we know is that he came to see Lord Blackstaff," Laeral interrupted. She looked to Khelben. "I see no harm in letting him know you're here. Speak to him as though he were awake. Tell him what's been happening."

Khelben's first thought was that Laeral was proposing a monumental waste of time, but he didn't say so. Laeral was the one person he never snapped at—well, that he *tried* never to snap at—and he was accomplishing little enough otherwise. He had tried to teleport into the Sharaedim a dozen times, only to find himself hip-deep in some stinking marsh or sliding down a searing sand dune, so far from his goal he could not even see the mountains, much less find out what was happening in Evereska.

Khelben took Lord Imesfor's hand. "Old friend, it's not going well. In truth, it's going damn poorly. I know you came here in need of help, but you've got to help *me*. I can't seem to get anywhere near Evereska—"

"Fie . . . ream." The word slipped from Imesfor's lips so faint and wispy that Khelben thought he had imagined it.

Angharad gasped, then rushed to the far side of the bed and looked into Imesfor's eyes. His gaze seemed to focus on her, then went glassy again.

Khelben felt Laeral's hand push him toward the elf. "Keep talking."

Khelben leaned over his old friend. "Fie who? What's wrong in Evereska?"

Imesfor's eyes came back into focus. "Fieream!"

"Fieream?" Khelben repeated, then it hit him. "*They* did this to you?"

Imesfor shook his head. "Not phaerimm . . . to me. Illithid."

"We know about the illithid." Khelben glanced to Laeral. "Do a sending."

Laeral nodded. "Already done. Elminster will be here—" She was interrupted by the soft crack of a teleport spell. "Now."

Still stinking of the pipe smoke in his study, Elminster stood in the center of the room, blinking and wobbling as he struggled to reorient himself to his new surroundings. Suppressing the irritation he felt at the showy display of power (Elminster being the only wizard on Toril who could defeat Khelben's wards and teleport directly into Blackstaff Tower), Khelben motioned the wizard over.

"Over here. He's just coming around."

The sound of Khelben's voice helped the wizard orient himself, and he stepped to the bed. "Gervas, ye look like something a carrion worm spit out."

Laeral slapped Elminster on the shoulder. "Be nice. Lord Imesfor isn't alert enough for raw wit."

"I'm alert enough to know . . . that awful fireweed smell." Imesfor tried to push himself into a sitting position, then winced and settled for keeping his eyes open. "My thanks for coming, Stinkbeard."

"My thanks for being alive when I arrived," Elminster said. "Now why don't ye tell us how that hole in your head came to be?"

"We were fleeing the phaerimm—"

"The phaerimm?"

Elminster looked to Khelben, who could only shrug and say, "It's the first I've heard about it, but who else could ward the entire Sharaedim against transport magic?"

"I can think of a few—any two of which would be preferable to the phaerimm," Elminster said darkly.

Gervas's eyes grew concerned. "You don't know?" He looked to Angharad. "How is that possible?"

The priestess looked away. "It wasn't my decision."

"But you *are* from Evermeet?" the elf pressed.

Angharad nodded. "I was told this is an elf problem." She cast an uneasy glance toward Khelben and Elminster, then leaned closer to Imesfor. "Evereska is our last bulwark on the continent. The Island Council feared that the humans would seize this opportunity to claim it for their own."

"What?" Khelben was so angry he nearly teleported over to strangle the priestess. At least that explained the stream of mages and warriors that had been emerging from the basement of Blackstaff Tower all day. There was an elf gate down there that allowed elves to pass freely between Waterdeep and Evermeet, and it had been in nearly constant use since he had asked Queen Amlaruil to send a healer for Lord Imesfor. "Evereska is being overrun by phaerimm, and your people are worried about humans?"

"Evereska is hardly being overrun," said Angharad.

"It is!" Imesfor said. "Not yet the vale, but our armies are gone." He turned from the priestess, who had gone nearly as pale as he, to Khelben. "They took us from behind, and when we tried to flee . . . it was unthinkable. I would have been dead, save for Melegaunt and his humans."

"Melegaunt?" asked Khelben.

"A shadow-shaper, involved in breaching the Sharn Wall," explained Imesfor. He looked to Angharad. "Surely, the council passed that much along?"

The priestess shook her head. "They did not even tell me."

"Then perhaps ye would be kind enough to tell them something for me." Elminster rounded the bed to place himself between Lord Imesfor and the priestess. "Tell them the council would do well to recall how many friends the elves truly have among men—lest they chase them *all* off with their boneheadedness!"

Angharad's eyes widened. "I couldn't possibly—"

"Ye could and ye shall." Elminster shooed her toward the door. "And be quick about it, before I make a caryatid of ye!"

Laeral held the door. "I suggest you hurry. You know how rash and impatient we humans can be."

Angharad glanced toward Lord Imesfor, but before she could ask what he wished, there came a knock at the door.

"Speak!" Khelben commanded.

"Milord Blackstaff," came young Ransford's nervous voice. "Lord Piergeiron seeks a word with you about the unusual number of elves that seem to be gathering in the city."

"Send word that I will attend him the moment I am free."

"I would rather discuss the matter *now*, Khelben," came the warden's deep voice. The door opened, and the towering form of Piergeiron Paladinson ducked beneath the lintel. "They are threatening to buy up every last horse in the city."

The warden's sharp eyes wandered once around the room, lingering just long enough on Elminster and Lord Imesfor to make plain his feelings about being left uninformed of such a gathering.

Laeral was the first to recover, ushering Angharad into Ransford's arms. "See the aradoness to the elf gate, Ransford, and see to it that she uses it—she has an important message to deliver to Evermeet."

Piergeiron stepped aside to let the elf leave, then scowled at Khelben. "Will someone tell me what the devil is going on here?"

"An excellent idea." Elminster summoned a pair of chairs out of thin air and levitated them into place on his side of the bed, then sat down and patted the seat beside him. "Why don't ye come and sit with me, and we'll hear the tale together."

Khelben nodded, grateful to his old friend for diffusing the situation so effortlessly. "Why don't you start from the beginning, Lord Imesfor?"

The elf nodded, then told them the whole story, starting with Galaeron Nihmedu's discovery of the crypt-breaking on the Desert Border, his capture of Vala Thorsdotter and her warriors, then proceeding to the subsequent appearance of the phaerimm and its advertent release. Here, he paused a moment to collect himself as he related the death of his son Louenghris, then went on to describe Evereska's disastrous efforts to reach the Sharn Wall and repair the breach. He finished with a description of how Galaeron Nihmedu had defied the Hill Elders to rescue him and Kiinyon Colbathin, and of how Melegaunt Tanthul had helped him escape through the shadow way.

When the elf finished, everyone in the room sat silently contemplating the story they had just heard and trying to come to terms with the horrible evil that had been unleashed on the world. Finally, Khelben patted his friend's hand.

"Evereska isn't alone in this, Gervas," Khelben said.

The elf nodded. "I know."

"It makes no sense." Elminster was looking at the ceiling as he said this. "I don't care how talented or careless this Galaeron Nihmedu is, he's not going to breach the Sharn Wall—and certainly not by accident."

Khelben frowned. "What are you saying? That the shadow shaper did it on purpose?"

"That would make more sense than some accident, would it not?" asked Elminster. "Think on it. The Netherese have been dead and gone for these fifteen hundred years—"

"Save for Shade," Khelben pointed out. Shade was an ancient Netherese city that had reputedly escaped the fall of Netheril by transporting itself into the plane of shadow. "No one knows what happened to Shade, but if this shadow shaper is Netherese. . . ."

"My point exactly," said Elminster. "Whether he is a lone survivor—which would make him an archwizard of truly awe-inspiring might—or an expatriate seeking revenge, would it not make sense for him to make the phaerimm *our* problem?"

No one needed to ask what Melegaunt might be seeking vengeance for. The Netherese Empire had consisted primarily of floating cities, built upon the upturned bottoms of truncated mountaintops and kept aloft by the incredible magic of the empire's archwizards. Unbeknownst to them, their profligate abuse of magic was destroying the underground home of the entire phaerimm race, which depended on the inherent magic of nature for survival. To save themselves, the phaerimm had developed a powerful spell that drained the life from Netherese lands, turning their fields to sand dunes and their lakes to arid flats of cracked mud.

As the farms grew less fertile, the empire found it difficult to feed its people, and eventually the stress led to a strange series of wars. Some were fought for sport to keep the restless populace entertained, and some were fought to claim the remaining patches of arable land. The result was an ever-escalating magic arms race that culminated in the mad attempt of the empire's greatest archwizard, Karsus, to steal the mantle of divinity from the goddess of magic, Mystryl herself.

Sadly for all, Karsus was not up to the job. The sudden influx of godly knowledge left him too stunned to perform the most important role entrusted to the deity of magic—that of constantly reworking the Weave of life and mystic power that was the source of Faerûn's magic. The Weave began to unravel.

To save it, the goddess—Mystryl—was forced to sacrifice herself, temporarily severing the link between Faerûn and its magic Weave. Without magic to keep them afloat, the cities of Netheril plummeted to the ground. Karsus himself died imbued with the knowledge of what he had done, plummeting to the ground in the form of a huge red butte. Save for Shade, which had somehow foreseen the disaster in time to withdraw into the plane of shadow, the rest of the empire perished with him. By the time Mystryl could reincarnate herself as Mystra, the new goddess of magic, the empire was gone.

All were silent as they contemplated Elminster's suggestion, until Laeral voiced the question on all their minds.

"Surely, not even a Netherese—survivor or descendant—would unleash the phaerimm merely to have his revenge."

To Khelben's surprise, it was Imesfor who shook his head. "That would not be my sense of it all. This Melegaunt risked much to save my life and Kiinyon's, and his determination seems not to be in destroying the phaerimm, but to set right what he and Galaeron did wrong."

"And this Galaeron?" asked Khelben. "Forgive me, but it is not entirely unheard of for an elf to betray his own kind."

"I know," agreed Imesfor. "I have given the matter no little thought, but I have known father and son for more than a century. Though the Nihmedu family is noble more by name than rank or power, Aubric is thought of so well that he has served the Swords of Evereska as blademajor for five decades now."

"It is the son we are speaking of here," said Elminster.

"That I know," said Imesfor. "Galaeron was known for his arrogance and stubbornness in both academies of the College of Magic and Arms, but he has served on the Desert Border without complaint for twenty years. Were he the betraying kind, he would have done it before now. I thought enough of his integrity to entrust my own Louenghris to his patrol, and even now I blame him for my son's death no more than any father would."

Elminster looked back to Imesfor. "If ye can tell me one thing, then will I rest easy this night."

Imesfor nodded. "I'll try."

"How was it that this Melegaunt could snatch ye and the others from beneath the phaerimm's very noses? They see magic the way dwarves see body heat. And how was it that he shadow-walked ye right out of the Sharaedim, when neither Khelben nor myself nor any of the Chosen can so much as set foot inside its borders?"

Imesfor could only shake his head. "I wish I knew."

Khelben began to have a queasy feeling. "Then we must consider at least one other possibility." He felt Laeral's hand slip into his and was suddenly glad for its warmth. "When the illithid attacked you, where was Melegaunt?"

Imesfor frowned. "We had just parted ways. I was leaving the shadow way to teleport here, and he . . ." The elf let his sentence trail off. "The human bastard!"

"He sent it after ye, did he?" asked Elminster.

"Not *it*," said Imesfor. "Them."

CHAPTER ELEVEN

26 Nightal, the Year of the Unstrung Harp

Even with a veil of storm clouds sliding along the cliff tops and a snow squall blasting through the gorge, Thousand Faces was more museum than pass. At the entrance stood the statues of two stone giant warriors, so lifelike that their chests seemed to rise and fall with breath. Beyond these guardians stretched the sculpture of an entire stone giant steading, carved into the canyon wall in high relief. There was a smith hammering an axe blank, a hunter carrying a pair of mountain elk by their ankles, a mother watching two sons wrestle, and a hundred other figures farther in, increasingly obscured by the howling blizzard. Above the giants wheeled sculpted snow finches and boulder hawks, the finches darting through a breathtaking maze of tree limbs, the hawks soaring across sublime mountain peaks. There were no beholders in sight, but neither were there any stone giants—at least none of flesh and bone.

"Where did you see these beholders?" whispered Melegaunt.

The wizard was lying between Galaeron and Malik, peering into the canyon from beneath the ground-hugging branches of a spruce tree. Vala was on Galaeron's other side, her body touching his at shoulder and hip.

"Find the law keeper," said Malik. "Look into the door on the right."

Galaeron searched the canyon until he came to an elderly stone giant holding a tablet in one hand and a dagger in the other. Next to him stood a doorway flanked by two columns. It ran only a couple of paces before ending in a wall at the same depth as the rest of the sculpture background, cleverly concealing the portal as a relief of itself. So convincing was the effect that had Galaeron not noticed a swarm of tiny eye-shaped reflections gleaming out of one shadowy corner, he would never have guessed the entrance to be real.

Armed with this insight into the wonder of the giants' art, he reexamined the canyon wall and spotted several other openings. There were two more doorways—one actually disguised as a door and another as the hollow between two trees—and half a dozen windows. A swarm of beholder eyes peered from most of them.

"Malik, you saved our lives," said Galaeron. "Thank you."

"I don't know that he saved our lives," grumbled Melegaunt, "but he did save us some trouble. There are more beholders than I expected."

"How can there be so many?" asked Vala. "All the beholders I have fought were solitary."

"You live far from beholder civilization," said Melegaunt. "The phaerimm have enslaved a whole city."

"Phaerimm?" gasped Malik. The little man backed out from beneath the tree. "Perhaps it is not so far around the mountains after all."

Melegaunt grabbed the newcomer's cloak. "There aren't any phaerimm here, and I can sneak us past the beholders."

He started to back out from beneath the tree, and Vala said, "You're just going to abandon the stone giants?"

Melegaunt did not stop. "They're dead or gone."

"Not all of them."

Vala pointed near the cliff top, where a distant pair of gray legs extended down out of the clouds to balance on the stone wing of a sculpted eagle. As the companions watched, one foot moved up the cliff in search of a foothold, but found none and reluctantly returned to its former place.

"That complicates things." Melegaunt pushed himself out from beneath the tree. "We'll have to hurry, if we are to save him."

"I beg a thousand pardons, but you have clearly lost your mind." Malik crawled after the wizard. "Dead men save no lives!"

"You're free to try another way, of course." Melegaunt stood and started around the shoulder of a small hill. "But there's nothing to worry about. You and the others will go through as I planned. I'll just take a small detour and help the giant off the mountain."

Galaeron found himself racing both Malik and Vala as he scrambled after the wizard into a sheltered draw where they had left their gear and Malik's horse.

"You can't do that," Galaeron said.

Melegaunt faced him frowning. "I'll not abandon anyone to become a beholder's plaything, not when it's within my power to prevent it."

"Granted, but you're the only one who knows where we're going and who we're looking for," said Vala, all but taking the words out of Galaeron's mouth. "If something should go wrong. . . ."

Melegaunt looked insulted. "We're only talking about a few beholders."

"I can't let you take that chance, not when the fate of

Evereska hangs in the balance," said Galaeron. Despite the objection, Melegaunt's determination to rescue the giant quelled many of the doubts the elf had been having about the wizard. "I'll rescue the giant, unless you'd rather tell me how to find whoever it is we're looking for."

The wizard's expression turned darker than usual. "Be careful what you wish for, young elf." He looked from Galaeron to Vala, then back to Galaeron again. "Very well, we'll do it your way, provided you can still use the other magic I showed you."

Malik's ears perked up at this. "What do you mean, 'other magic?' "

"It doesn't concern you." Melegaunt turned his back on the little man. "And even if it did, there's no time to explain now."

"I understand completely." Malik slipped around to place himself directly between Galaeron and Melegaunt. "Only, I have always been given to believe that the Weave is the only source of magic."

Melegaunt scowled at him. "Why should this interest you? Are you a wizard?"

"I am a man of many interests," said Malik. "And magic is among them, for my master—"

"We'll talk later," interrupted Melegaunt.

He glanced in Vala's direction. She grabbed Malik by the collar and, even as he tried to explain his interest, dragged him away. Her treatment was rough enough to draw a low whinny of warning from the sad-eyed horse.

Melegaunt turned back to Galaeron. "About the other magic—"

"Still available to me," said Galaeron, deciding to keep to himself for the moment just *how* available. "Here's what I was thinking."

Galaeron outlined his plan.

When he finished, Malik called, "You can cast the same spells twice?" He asked this from near his horse, where Vala had dragged him. "How did you know to study those spells more than once? Or can you do this because of the 'other' magic?"

"Quiet!" Melegaunt hissed.

He turned to glower, but Vala was already locking an arm around Malik's neck. She slapped her other hand over the newcomer's mouth and deftly put him between herself and his horse when the beast turned to nip at her.

"Are you *trying* to give us away?" she asked.

Malik's face paled, and he shook his head.

Melegaunt returned to Galaeron. "Remember, the beholders are less able to detect your shadow magic than the phaerimm, but they can still dispel it. If they notice your presence, stay clear of the rays from their central eyes."

"That lesson I learned from the first one we fought," said Galaeron.

"Good." Melegaunt reached into his sleeve and produced a small wisp of what looked like black fog. "This is shadow silk, the primary element of much shadow-shaping magic. Let me show you a spell that may prove useful, and we'll be on our way."

The wizard started to run through the gestures, then noticed Malik watching. He turned his back to the little man, confiding to Galaeron, "There's something about him I just don't trust."

"Yes, mysterious humans *do* have a way of raising suspicions," said Galaeron, resisting the temptation to comment on his own uneasiness with the wizard. "You were showing me a variation on a web spell?"

Melegaunt cocked his brow. "I hadn't really thought of it as a web, but yes, I suppose that's the heart of the matter."

The wizard finished his demonstration. Galaeron repeated the words and gestures to make certain he understood them correctly.

"Amazing." Melegaunt could only shake his head. "Magic shouldn't be that easy for anyone."

"It isn't, really," Galaeron confided. "I must practice like anyone else to learn something new. But when it's basically a spell I already know, it's no big trouble to understand a few changes and what they do."

"A few changes?" Melegaunt shook his head incredulously. "No big trouble indeed!"

He went over to Malik and Vala, then circled his hand over the ground, creating a floating shadow disk similar to the one they had used to transport the wounded elves. Malik watched with interest, then undid the girth strap and placed the saddle in the center of the floating circle.

When the little man removed the bit from her mouth, Melegaunt said, "It's not necessary to leave your horse behind. If we cover her eyes, she'll never know we're moving."

"You misunderstand. Kelda needs no blinders." Malik grabbed the mare by the soft halter and had no trouble convincing her to jump onto the disk. "But she has always been a faithful horse, and if you madmen are determined to see us all dead on account of one cowardly giant lacking the courage to die with the rest of his tribe, then I will not have her starving in these mountains because I was too stupid to remove her saddle and bit."

The little man clambered onto the disk and kissed his horse full on the snout. Galaeron looked to the other humans and saw by their expressions that they found this behavior as puzzling as he did. Melegaunt and Vala climbed up with Malik, and the wizard cast another spell, turning the platform and everything on it invisible. There was a startled whinny, followed by a whispered request from Malik to please be silent and not get them all killed. A puff of wind stirred the blowing snow into a white eddy, which started down the draw toward the trail and vanished into the general blizzard.

"We'll see you on the other side, Galaeron," called Vala. "And be careful."

"You may count on it," said Galaeron. "But if something happens—"

"You'll be on your own," said Melegaunt. "Don't worry."

"And that is the most sensible thing any of you have said since I saved you with my fire," added Malik.

Galaeron allowed them another minute to drift safely ahead, then cast two spells on himself. To his surprise, he discovered that the cold magic did not rush into him as it had during the bugbear attack. To make it come, he had to think of his shadow self—to embrace it, really—and open himself to the cold magic's presence. Whether this sluggishness was due to the lack of shadows in the blizzard or because he was not presently overcome by the heat of battle, he did not know. He was just happy to discover he retained more control over his magic than he had thought.

Galaeron launched himself over the spruce tree with a gentle leap, then swung toward Thousand Faces well above the heads of the two stone giant guard statues. To avert the possibility of colliding with each other, they had agreed that Galaeron would fly higher than a giant and Melegaunt would stay lower. This put the wizard and the others more directly in the area watched by the beholders, but there was no avoiding it. The platform would float no more than a dozen feet off the ground.

Galaeron paused at the canyon entrance and used a spell to search for magic wards. He could see a dozen beholders lurking in the grotto's shadowy portals, the reflections of their eyes flitting about like swarms of golden fireflies. With so many eyes turned in his direction, Galaeron was nervous enough that the cold magic came to him very easily. Though the presence of two sculpted guardians would suggest defensive wards in most elf communities, not so with stone giants. The statues were just that, decorative artworks designed to greet—or perhaps intimidate—anyone entering the canyon.

Galaeron flew on, climbing toward the rim of the gorge. The giant's legs were completely hidden behind a low cloud sliding along the cliff tops, but the elf could still see the stony eagle his feet stood upon. Twenty paces from the great bird,

Galaeron was astonished to see a swarm of eyes peering out from a window hidden beneath the bird's great wing. Perhaps the little human had been right, after all. By Tomb Guard doctrine, at least, Galaeron should not even try to rescue the giant. The saving of one life simply did not justify the risking of four.

It was good thing no one followed that particular precept.

Galaeron reached the wall and ascended into the clouds, running a hand along the cliff to orient himself in the gray haze. He felt the eagle's wing pass beneath his fingertips, then rose past the blurry silhouette of a foot as long as his forearm. How the enormous toes could cling to such a small ledge he could not imagine, but the huge ankle was trembling with fatigue. Galaeron ascended alongside the giant leg to a giant waist, where he had to swing around a tool belt hung with steel hammers of various sizes, then continued up the giant's flank. He circled away from a cavernous armpit, looped over gnarled biceps, passed a neck as thick as a pillar, and found himself staring into a pair of eyes as big as dinner plates.

Galaeron took a piece of copper filament from his pocket and rubbed it between his thumb and forefinger. The shadow magic flooded into him, then he pointed at the giant's head and began to whisper.

"Don't cry out, giant. You have nothing to fear."

The giant flinched, lost a toe hold, and groaned. Galaeron cursed the big fellow's lack of self-discipline, then slipped a few arm lengths across the cliff and grabbed the shadow silk Melegaunt had given him. A glimmer of hope appeared in the giant's face, and his big eyes roved about in search of his savior.

"Be careful!" Though the giant's whisper seemed as loud as rushing wind, Galaeron did not worry about it being overheard. The spell he had cast would prevent that. "Where are you?"

Before Galaeron could answer, a beholder floated up between him and the giant. The thing was close enough to kick, with several of the small eyestalks waving in the elf's direction, but the creature did not seem to notice Galaeron's invisible presence.

A cone of blue light shot from its huge central eye and began to sweep over the stone giant's body. Galaeron raised his hands to cast the spell Melegaunt had taught him, but stopped when the giant continued to cling to the cliff and showed no more fear than previously. Clearly, neither the giant nor the eye tyrant were surprised to see each other, and Galaeron realized their foes knew Melegaunt better than the wizard thought.

The beholder shifted its beam to the cliff and swept it back and forth at random. Keeping a careful watch on the creature's many eyes, Galaeron floated around behind it. By all rights, he should have left instantly, for he knew better than to think he could escape any trap designed to capture Melegaunt. But it was too late. He had already seen the hope in the giant's eyes.

The beholder finished its scan of the cliff face and spun around, flashing its beam back and forth through the cloud. Galaeron tucked in the other side of the giant's torso.

Finally, the beholder gave up and turned to the giant. "What was that groan for?"

"I slipped," the giant said.

"You wouldn't lie to poor Kanabar would you?" As the beholder spoke, one of its smaller eyes swung toward the giant. "Not when Kanabar told the others he had a use for you? You wouldn't lie to Kanabar when he saved your life, would you?"

"No, I wouldn't lie."

The giant's body tensed as he tried to resist the eye tyrant's charm magic, and Galaeron began to worry. Vala's beholder had slain one of his best scouts with nine eyes cloaked. What hope did he have against one able to use all eleven?

The giant spoke again, this time in a higher, almost

singsong voice. "Aris would never lie to his friend Kanabar."

Galaeron pushed away from the cliff, then looked across the giant's broad back in time to see a crooked smile come to the beholder's toothy mouth.

"That's right," the beholder said. "So, why did Aris groan?"

The giant's body trembled visibly. "B-b-because his foot slipped."

"And why did his foot slip?" asked the beholder. "Tell your friend Kanabar."

As the eye tyrant said this, Galaeron flung a strand of shadow silk in its direction and spoke the incantation Melegaunt had taught him. The beholder's eyes swung toward the sound of his voice, but the spell was a quick one, and in an instant, Kanabar was cloaked in a gummy mass of shadow.

"Hey!" Aris thundered. He turned his head and looked directly at Galaeron, who had turned visible the instant he attacked. "What'd you do to my friend, you stupid elf?"

"He's not your friend," Galaeron said, trying to figure out how he would rescue a becharmed giant. "I am."

Galaeron started to reach for his sword, then had a better idea when he saw the beholder's magic-destroying ray burn through the gummy shadow over its central eye. He rattled off a series of vaguely mystic syllables and tucked in behind the giant's body. Desperate to interrupt Galaeron's spell, the beholder swung toward him and ran its blue beam across the giant's back.

The beam flashed across Galaeron's shoulder. He began to fall, but spared himself a long plummet by catching hold of Aris's tool belt. The beholder tried to cry the alarm, but, with its mouth full of shadow gum, managed only a garbled babble.

Looping one arm through the giant's belt, Galaeron drew his sword and braced himself to fight the monster—then gasped as Aris's far hand descended out of the haze and grabbed Kanabar. The beholder looked like a riys melon in the giant's palm.

"Friend indeed!" growled the giant.

The beholder mumbled something unintelligible as Aris smashed it into the cliff.

"Thank the leaflord!" Galaeron gasped. "I didn't know if his ray would work on his own charm magic."

"It did," said Aris. "But I fear you have doomed yourself for naught, elf."

The giant pointed to a trio of round forms drifting toward them out of the haze. Galaeron looked behind him and saw another pair, and yet two more rising into the cloud beneath them. He sheathed his sword, then plucked two more threads off the shadow silk Melegaunt had given him.

"This seemed like a better idea from down there."

"I imagine so," said Aris. "Should they becharm me again. . . ."

"No offense taken," said Galaeron. "Do as I say, and it won't come to that."

He dropped first one, then two shadow threads and repeated Melegaunt's spell twice in rapid succession. Though he had learned to do multiple castings at the Academy of Magic, it was the one technique that had not come easily for him—and that had prompted him to practice it until it came even more naturally than everything else. The two enchantments worked perfectly, though he was starting to grow tired and felt like the coldness of the new magic would crack his bones.

An alarmed gurgle rose from the beholders as they were engulfed in shadow morass, then they collided with each other and stuck fast. Without waiting to see what effect this would have on the others—though he prayed it would give them pause—Galaeron pointed toward the far end of the pass and cast his most powerful spell. A numbing wave of cold magic rushed through his bones, then a black square appeared just below him and to the side.

"Through the door!" he ordered.

Aris peered down. "I can't fit—"

"Now!" Still holding onto the belt, Galaeron leaped for the square and hoped the giant would follow. "Jump!"

With a deep bellow, Aris released the cliff and obeyed. Galaeron glimpsed a blue ray sweeping through the clouds toward his magic door, then they plummeted into darkness.

A sudden chill bit at his flesh, and there was a dark eternity of falling. Galaeron grew queasy and weak, heard the stillness of his own heart. His head reeled, his thoughts dissolved into a jumble of ill-defined fears, and he was back in the world, plunging through a howling tempest of white. A deafening bellow filled the air behind him. Galaeron glanced back to find a huge gray figure plummeting alongside him, then a circle of treetops flashed past and the world erupted into a cacophony of cracking and snapping. They tumbled groundward, flipping first one way, then another as they were snagged by passing branches. Galaeron tried to push away from the mountainous figure and found he could not.

In the next instant, he crashed down on the giant and lay in a daze, struggling to recall where he was and where he had come from. A low groan shook the air around him, then he started to swing groundward as the enormous body rolled to its back.

The spell's afterdaze vanished in a flash, and Galaeron knew instantly where he was—and who he was with. "Aris, wait!"

The giant gave a startled cry and stopped mid roll. "Elf?"

"The very one." Galaeron pulled his arm free and dropped into the snow. "Are you all right?"

"For now." The giant pointed into the storm.

Galaeron scrambled up and peered over Aris's hip. The moon-shaped silhouette of a beholder was careening toward them through the storm, coming so fast it was bouncing into tree trunks.

"Do something!" Aris urged. "Another spell!"

"I don't think I can." Galaeron was so exhausted from the cold magic that had already passed through him that he could not stop shivering. "I'm too tired."

"Tired?" Aris boomed, clawing through the snow in search of a boulder. "Rest when you're dead!"

Seeing the wisdom in the giant's argument, Galaeron plucked another thread off his ribbon of shadow silk. He tossed it the beholder's direction and started the spell—then cried out in shock as the cold magic gushed into him. His entire body went icy numb and puffed up to half-again its normal size. When he continued the spell, his skin went as rigid as marble and turned as pale as snow. He choked out another word, and his lips grew so stiff and cold that he could barely utter the last syllable.

The beholder instantly became a massive ball of gummy black shadow—then returned to normal when a cone of blue light shot through the blizzard to engulf it from behind.

"There!" Aris pointed at a smaller, more indistinct silhouette trailing the first. "Do two, like you did before!"

"I-I can't."

Even as Galaeron said it, he was pulling two more strands off the shadow silk. This time, when he opened himself to the new magic, it blasted straight through him, and his body erupted into molten pain. Galaeron hurled himself screaming into the snow and rolled back and forth. There was no sizzle of melting snow nor hiss of rising steam, but the world suddenly turned very gray and dark, as though he were looking at it through a veil of smoke.

"Elf?" Aris glanced back and gave a bewildered frown, then rolled to his knees with a boulder in his hand. "Elf, do you have a friend here?"

Fighting through the pain, Galaeron pushed himself up and looked in the direction of the beholders. His smoky vision made everything look doubly hazy in the blizzard, but even given that, the first eye tyrant was so close the eyestalks were visibly writhing atop its head. The second was close enough that he could make out the shape of its big central eye, and behind it—*far* behind—was a figure on horseback. It was hardly a ghost, too faint to tell whether it was Vala or Melegaunt, but one of them.

"The fool!" He struggled to his feet and drew his sword. "Yes, that would be my friend—a friend who shouldn't be here, but a truer one for it."

"What very good news." The giant sounded less exhilarated than he might have. "Then all we must do is survive until he arrives."

Aris hurled his boulder, which soared through the woods and arced down toward the lead beholder. An eye swiveled on the top of its head, then a ray of silver light shot up to intercept the attack. The rock exploded into a spray of pebbles. Judging that they had about two seconds until the creature was close enough to use the ray on them, Galaeron lurched over behind a tree. His legs were numb and sluggish, and the sword in his hand felt more like an awkward orcish blade than one forged in elven fire.

"Keep attacking!" said Galaeron. "Keep their attention focused on us."

"That shouldn't be hard."

The giant hurled another boulder, only to have it demolished by another silver ray. Galaeron dashed forward and took shelter behind a slender canyon spruce, then nearly lost his head as a silver beam slashed through the trunk. The top crashed down in front of the beholders, creating a small camouflage barrier. Galaeron hurled himself beneath the boughs and lay very still, relying on the camouflaging magic of his cloak to conceal him until he could attack.

"Elf!" Aris sounded panicked. "What are you doing?"

Galaeron didn't answer, until the blue light of an antimagic ray washed over his shoulder and neutralized his cloak's concealing magic. He rolled out on Aris's side of the fallen tree just as the large beholder sank down on the other side, now using its silver ray to disintegrate a ten-foot swath of boughs.

Galaeron sprang back at the beholder, crashing through the boughs atop the trunk, touching down long enough to spring over and come down on top of the beholder. He brought his sword around and cut half a dozen eyestalks off the head, then whipped the blade around in an arc and drove it into the eye tyrant's skull.

The blade sank to the depth of his thumb, then stopped cold.

"Elf!" Aris let out a sharp huff as he hurled another boulder, then bellowed, "Are you mad?"

Galaeron felt more than saw the boulder sailing past his head, then heard it crackle into a thousand pieces and realized the second beholder was close on him. He flung himself off the first, pulling his weapon free as he dived. His arm skipped over a rock, then he landed headfirst, rolled, came up beneath a big spruce, and found both beholders facing him. If the big one was troubled by the green gore pumping from its severed eyestalks, it showed no sign.

Galaeron raised his sword—and promptly found his view blocked by Melegaunt's broad back. There was just enough time to notice how strange it seemed that the wizard had a dark, well defined shadow in the flat blizzard light before both beholders blasted the dusky man with their silver rays.

"No!" Galaeron raised his sword and sprang forward to avenge what he knew would be the end of Evereska. Something snagged his foot as he tried to cross Melegaunt's shadow, and he fell flat on his face. "By the Red Moon!"

Quite certain the next instant would be his last, he looked down and found the wizard's shadow holding his ankle.

"You've done your part," said Melegaunt's familiar voice.

No sooner had the wizard spoken than a set of muffled hoof beats came pounding through the forest. Instead of attacking Galaeron, the big beholder spun to face the sound—then died without a shriek as Vala's black sword came flying from the opposite direction and cleaved it down the center.

The smaller beholder spun all ten eye tentacles in the direction from which the sword had come, only to be driven to the ground when Malik came flying off his horse from behind and began slashing eyestalks with his dagger.

Galaeron scrambled to his feet and rushed to help, but by then Vala was already on the creature. She extended one hand to summon her sword, used the other to crush an eye when the stalk swung in her direction, then caught the weapon and drove the tip through the beholder's skull. Unlike Galaeron's blade, hers sank to the hilt.

"Elf?" Aris's looming figure peered over the fallen tree, a big boulder grasped in each hand. "Elf, are you alive?"

"For now."

Galaeron turned to see Melegaunt's mangled body dissolving into shadow, and his shadow coalescing into a healthy body.

"Melegaunt, you were not to risk your life," Galaeron said. "We agreed for the sake of Evereska."

"Aye," said the wizard. "But after you troubled yourself so dearly to save him, how could I let the giant die?"

CHAPTER TWELVE

27 Nightal, the Year of the Unstrung Harp

Galaeron felt himself jerk, then felt the hand clamped over his shoulder and knew that—impossibly—an intruder had crept up on him during his own watch. He rolled away from the tree he had been leaning against and tangled in a heavy cloak in which he did not recall covering himself.

"To your weapons!" Even as he yelled the alarm, he feared he was too late. "They're on us!"

Despite the entangling cloak, Galaeron somehow rolled to his knees and faced his attacker. He found himself looking at three bewildered humans and a very concerned stone giant.

"It's only us, Galaeron," said Vala. "That must have been some dream."

"Dream?" Galaeron threw off the cloak and, searching the woods behind them, reached for his sword. "I wasn't dreaming. How could I have been dreaming?"

Vala rolled her eyes. "That's what people do when they sleep."

"That's what *humans* do when they sleep," Galaeron corrected. He was not sure which implication he resented more, that humans were Tel'Quess—of the People—or that he had neglected his duty by sleeping on his watch. "And I was not sleeping!"

"No?" It was the little round-faced man with the bulging eyes who asked this. Galaeron needed a moment recall what he was doing with them. "Then what are you doing when you close your eyes and snore?"

The night did seem oddly bright, Galaeron realized. He frowned and looked eastward, where an amorphous sphere of light hung just above the Greypeak Mountains. Even through the thick mantle of concealing snow clouds, there could be little doubt that the glowing pearl was the morning sun.

"I fell asleep?" The alarm in Galaeron's voice was unmistakable. "In the middle of my watch?"

"Don't feel bad." Vala gathered his cloak off the snow and offered it to him. "Malik took over, and you needed the rest."

Galaeron accepted the cloak and dropped to his haunches. After two days without a Reverie, there was no denying he needed rest. But to fall asleep—by *accident*? He suddenly began to feel lost and hollow, as though something inside had vanished.

"Why so worried?" Melegaunt came to his side. "Elves *do* sleep. I've seen them."

"Occasionally," said Galaeron. "When we're sick or wounded, sometimes when we're despondent or fall prey to the Gloom, more often as we grow older and the time to go West draws near."

Vala nodded. "When you need to escape your pain and rest. Not so different from humans."

"Much the same," allowed Galaeron, "except that we never *fall* asleep. It's a purposeful act."

"What a joy that must be," exclaimed Malik. "Me, I am always lying awake when I should be sleeping and sleeping when I should be awake. This year alone, it has nearly cost me my life a dozen times." He hesitated a moment, his mouth contorting oddly as he struggled not to say more, then he blurted, "I hardly dare close my eyes for fear of having my throat cut by that Harper witch Ruha!"

Galaeron frowned. The Harpers were among the few humans generally accorded admittance to Evereska, and the mere fact that one of them counted Malik an enemy was reason to be suspicious of him. On the other hand, the little man *had* risked his own life to save Galaeron and Aris from the beholders, and any trouble between humans was no business of the tomb guard's or Evereska's.

Vala and Melegaunt seemed even less interested in Malik's revelation than Galaeron. Vala pursed her lips as though wondering why the little man thought they should care, and Melegaunt merely tugged his beard and studied Galaeron.

Finally, he said, "Things didn't go exactly as we planned with Aris's rescue. How much did you strain yourself with the magic I showed you?"

"I think of it as the cold magic," said Galaeron. "A lot. There was no choice."

Melegaunt's face turned instantly stormy. "Fool! Did I not warn you against testing yourself with this magic?"

"I wasn't testing," said Galaeron. "There was no other choice."

"There is always another choice," said Melegaunt. "It would be better to surrender your body to the beholders than to surrender your spirit to your shadow."

Melegaunt came forward and grabbed Galaeron's head, then tipped it back and pulled his eyelids open.

"There it is. You've let your shadow inside."

Galaeron's stomach turned to ice. "Then get it out!"

"I can't." Melegaunt released Galaeron's eyelids and

stepped back. "You must learn to control it, before it learns to control you."

"Control it? How?"

"Carefully—very carefully," said Melegaunt. "Shadows are subtle things. It will try to subvert your nature, to make you see the dark in everything around you."

"See the dark?" asked Galaeron. "You mean dark motives?"

"In a way, yes. For every light, there is a shadow. It will make you look at the shadow instead of the light, to see how every noble act might be selfish. Gradually, you will come to see the darkness before the light. When that happens, you are your shadow."

Galaeron's throat went dry, and he could not bring himself to speak again.

"Galaeron, you must learn to do the hardest thing of all," said Melegaunt. "You must always make sure you see the light before you see the shadow."

"That will be hard." Galaeron thought of the suspicions that had been plaguing him the past few days, and of his decision to keep secret the way the cold magic had rushed into him during the battle against the bugbears. "Why did you ever show me this magic, Melegaunt?"

"Are you that weak?" Melegaunt grabbed his arm and pulled him to his feet. "I give you the most precious gift in the world, and you call it poison? Your shadow is winning already, elf."

The words hit Galaeron like a blow, for his trouble entering the Reverie had come with his doubts about Melegaunt's character. Had the shadow been inside even then? Despite the cold, he felt flushed and sweaty.

"There's something I should have told you about the bugbear battle," Galaeron said.

"The new magic came to you?"

"Unbidden," Galaeron replied. "When I cast my spells, it rushed in of its own accord. I had to concentrate to keep it out."

Melegaunt nodded. "Looming death has a way of bringing

you closer to your shadow self." The wizard stared at him. "It is more troubling that you kept it from me."

"You keep so many secrets of your own." Even to Galaeron, his tone sounded defensive. "And after you sicked the illithids on Lord Imesfor, I *did* have reason to doubt you."

"We talked about that. If you were not satisfied with my explanation, you should have said so." Melegaunt's voice lacked its usual patience. "This will be a struggle, elf, and I don't know that you will win."

Galaeron's heart sank. "I don't want this magic. There must be something you can do."

"There is." Melegaunt glanced meaningfully toward Vala's sword. "And should you fail, I will."

"It would be that bad?"

"It would," said Melegaunt. "And I am not here to release yet another evil on this world."

"Nor would I want that. I will take your word as a promise." Galaeron turned to Vala. "And one from you, as well."

She raised her brow and glanced at Melegaunt. When the wizard nodded grimly, she shrugged and seemed a little sad. "I hope you know what you're asking."

"He is only asking what is right," said Melegaunt. He cast a wary eye eastward, where Thousand Faces stood hidden by snow and trees and far fewer miles than any of them would have liked. "We must be on our way. The beholders will come looking for us—"

"I will show you a safe way." It was the first Aris had spoken. "You are going to the Delimbyr River?"

"A little beyond, yes," said Melegaunt, "but that would be a good start."

"Then follow."

Aris turned up the narrow side gulch where they had made camp and started through the blizzard. Melegaunt led the way after him through knee-deep snow. With Malik's horse breaking trail, they were just able to keep the giant's looming silhouette from vanishing into the storm.

As they climbed, Galaeron barely noticed the slope growing steeper. He could not help being frightened—frightened of what he might become, more frightened of what he might cease being. Elves who could not enter the Reverie soon became something else altogether. Unable to share in a communion of like hearts, they grew immeasurably sad and lonely. Eventually, such lone wolves withered of despair or abandoned their home, preferring a life alone—or even among humans—to the constant reminder of the bliss they could no longer share.

Without that connection to his fellows, Galaeron did not know if he would have the strength to control his shadow. Even now, it seemed reasonable to be wary of Melegaunt. Humans were well known for treachery, and the wizard's furtiveness certainly invited misgivings. Why wouldn't he say who he hoped to find, or why he had been studying the phaerimm, or where this new magic came from?

It occurred to Galaeron that Melegaunt's warning might be a scheme to make him doubt his own misgivings. Certainly, there could be no better way to quell a person's suspicions than to make them an object of fear. Hardly had this thought flashed through the elf's mind before another followed suggesting his shadow had planted the previous one. Galaeron had entered a maze of spirals, where every idea turned back on itself and no opinion could be trusted. He felt as though the ground had vanished from beneath the snow, leaving him to flail around helplessly until he grew tired of struggling and simply let the blizzard take him.

After a time, they crossed a high white meadow and came to a steep gully packed full of snow. Aris instructed them to stand well off to one side, then cupped his hands and gave a booming yell. There was a soft rumble so quiet and low Galaeron felt it more than heard it. In the next instant, a tremendous avalanche swept out of the gully and spread across the meadow.

Aris waited a few minutes for the snow to stabilize, then

pointed up the chute. "The ridge on top descends into the Delimbyr Valley. Stay on the crest and follow it to the river. The trees are tall and thick, so you won't be seen by any but a few stone giants traveling the same path. Don't hide from them, and tell them what you did for me, and they will do you no harm."

"And what of you, Aris?" asked Galaeron. "Will you be all right?"

"I think not." Aris's voice was so angry and low that it felt like another avalanche barreling down the chute. He snapped the top off a thirty foot pine, then began to strip away the branches. "The massacre of my steading was a terrible thing, but what those eyes did to the Saga Caves . . . for destroying the work of two thousand years, I will make them pay."

"Sadly, you will not," said Melegaunt. "At least not alone. Will others of your kind help?"

The giant shook his head. "I would not ask such a thing. The responsibility is not theirs."

"No, but it is ours," said Melegaunt. "Perhaps even more than it is yours."

Malik's eyes grew wide. "Think what you are saying—and who you are saying it to!" He craned his neck up at the giant. "The wizard speaks for himself."

The giant paid no attention to the little man and kneeled down over Melegaunt. "Explain."

"Do you know of the phaerimm?" asked the wizard.

Aris nodded. "I have seen their shapes in some of the old murals. A fell and powerful race, by the hewn stories."

"And a cunning race," said the wizard. "Though the beholders may not realize it themselves, the phaerimm are their masters. The phaerimm sent them to Thousand Faces to find us."

"There is no fool like an honest one!" exclaimed Malik, clambering onto his horse. "I pray you have not killed us all!"

Neither Aris nor anyone else paid any attention to the little man. The giant merely considered the wizard's words for a time, then rubbed his long chin and turned to Galaeron.

"And even knowing they were looking for you, you risked all your lives to save mine?"

Galaeron nodded. "I could not have left you and lived with myself."

"You nearly did not survive saving me," said the giant. "That was not a wise thing to do."

"It was wiser than you returning alone to face the beholders," said Melegaunt. "We would join you if we could, but there is greater evil afoot, and we must continue on our way."

The giant nodded. "It is enough that you rescued me."

"You would be doing us a service not to waste our efforts by attacking so many beholders alone," said Melegaunt. "You would be lucky to kill one or two."

"Then that would be justice to one or two." Aris glanced in Galaeron's direction, then rose. "How could I live with myself, were I to fail my steading even in the little I could do to avenge its loss?"

"By doing more," said Galaeron. He knew what the giant was feeling, for he had felt much the same thing as the phaerimm encircled Evereska. "Would it not serve your steading better to strike a blow against the ones responsible for what happened to Thousand Faces?"

The stone giant furrowed his heavy brow. "How can I do that?"

"By coming with us," said Melegaunt, following Galaeron's lead. "We are sworn to destroy the phaerimm—the same phaerimm who sent their beholders to Thousand Faces."

Aris considered this for no more than ten minutes, a very short time for a stone giant, then said, "You must give me a promise in return."

"If it's within my power," said Melegaunt.

"I think it is," said the giant. "You must promise to accept my help until the end. If Thousand Faces is to be avenged, I must be part of it."

"Done," said Melegaunt. "And I promise you this as well,

that the beholders who have taken your home are not long for this world. Before all is done, they will rue the day they laid eyes on your steading."

"Then it is a pact." Aris stooped down to pluck Malik out of his saddle.

"What are you doing?" Malik pulled a tiny dagger from inside his cloak and flourished it. "I must warn you—"

"The hill is a steep one," said Aris. Paying no attention to the tiny dagger, he placed Malik on the ground and scooped up the little man's horse. "I will carry this for you."

Aris tucked the mare under his arm and started up the chute, not seeming to notice the beast's flailing hooves and terrified whinnies. Malik scrambled after them, alternating warning the giant not to harm his Kelda and cooing words of comfort to the horse.

Galaeron and the others followed, and soon they were descending a snowy ridge toward the vast Delimbyr Valley. With Aris breaking trail, travel was fast. It required only a day and a half of solid walking to reach the base of the mountains, and the journey would have taken no more than a day had they not made two "brief" stops so Aris could warn giants coming in the opposite direction about the beholders.

As Galaeron listened to Aris's sorrowful descriptions of the fate of Thousand Faces, he found himself thinking of Evereska. Surely, his own city remained untouched. Even the phaerimm could not breach the magic of the mythal—at least not so quickly. Or could they? According to Melegaunt, the phaerimm of Myth Drannor were drawn to the area because of the mythal, and they were great magic-users in their own right. What if they knew how to unweave its defenses? Once they entered the city, even the Spellguard would be unable to turn them back. Galaeron would become like Aris, a lone survivor with nothing to live for except vengeance. In a stone giant, such an existence was sad beyond words. In an elf, especially one struggling with his own shadow, it would become an unspeakable evil.

Galaeron longed to move faster, to insist that Melegaunt use his magic to speed them along—even to journey into the Shadow Fringe again—but he knew better than to suggest such a thing. After the battle at Thousand Faces, the phaerimm would be scouring the area for any hint of spell use, and even Melegaunt's strange magic would leave subtle incongruities in the world that would attract the attention of a careful searcher. Better to avoid magic altogether and let the blizzard conceal them.

The trip through the valley proved more trying. They were about halfway across when the blizzard blew itself out, catching them in the open a mile short of the river. Without a steady wind to fill their tracks, a party of bugbears soon spotted their trail and began to pursue. Instead of using magic to eliminate the threat, the companions rushed to the river and crossed the ice. When the bugbears followed, Aris hurled a few boulders into their midst, shattering the ice and plunging the entire band into the cold waters.

The companions were not so lucky the next afternoon, when two gray circles appeared just above the horizon. At first, the companions pretended not to notice their pursuers, hoping the pair would be foolish enough to catch up and attack. When the eye tyrants refused to take the bait, Melegaunt turned to cast a spell. The beholders vanished from sight. Perhaps a half-hour later, Galaeron glimpsed one creature still trailing them. The other was nowhere to be seen.

"He's gone for help," Vala surmised.

Galaeron nodded. "With luck, it will only be beholders."

"*Only* beholders?" Malik gasped. "You are as mad as a cuckold in his harem!"

"Beholders would be better than phaerimm," said Melegaunt. "Unless you intend to make our fight your own, now would be a good time to part ways."

"So you can send your foes after me?" Malik's dark eyes shined with indignation. "I am hardly the fool I look, old man."

Melegaunt shrugged. "You were warned."

The wizard pulled a scrap of shadow silk from his cloak and traced a shadowy maze on the snow. When he finished, he and Galaeron cast flying spells on everyone in the group—including Malik's astonished horse—and the companions streaked off toward the High Forest. The beholder avoided Melegaunt's shadow maze by circling wide, then became an ominous presence that appeared on the horizon now and again to remind them of their approaching danger.

Finally, they reached the High Forest and slipped into the woods. The beholder stopped behind a hill and hovered there with one eyestalk peering over the summit. Several of the other stalks flitted in and out of view, looking in all directions in search of help.

"Now we have them," said Melegaunt. He pulled a piece of shadow silk from his cloak and tore off a strand, then strung it between two trees. "We're almost to Karse."

"Karse?" gasped Malik. "Why are we going there?"

"*We* are not." Melegaunt handed Galaeron a second piece of shadow silk and motioned for him to begin stringing strands. "Once we have finished here, it will be safe to part ways. I'm sure you're as eager to be about your business as we are ours."

"I have no business." Malik paused as though that was all he meant to say, then slowly cocked his head to one side and added, "Except you."

"Us?" Melegaunt continued to string shadow strands between trees. "And what would your business be with us?"

Malik paled and said, "Nothing . . . except—"

The rest of the explanation was lost to a tremendous crashing from the forest behind them. Galaeron spun around to see an enormous oak stomping up, its branches waving madly and a huge trunk cavity twisted in an angry snarl.

"No!" the tree boomed. It swept a branch down past Galaeron's head at the strands he had been stringing between tree trunks. The limb passed through the shadowy fibers without effect. A fierce shudder ran through the oak's crown of golden leaves, and it shook a bough in Galaeron's face. "Not in my wood!"

"We mean no harm to the f-forest," Galaeron stammered. Now that he had recovered from his surprise, he recognized the oak as the oldest treant he had ever seen, with a long beard of green moss and a trunk easily a dozen feet around. Realizing the creature would view Aris's wooden club with a dim eye, Galaeron motioned the giant to keep watch at the edge of the forest, then turned back to the treant. "We must take measures to protect ourselves. We're being pursued by beholders."

"By *one* beholder. Eyes I have." To prove it, the treant blinked a pair of knotholes more than fifteen feet up his trunk. "And your welfare is no concern of mine. There is a wrongness to your magic, and in my wood I will not have it."

"It is, indeed, magic of a different sort," said Melegaunt, "but that does not make it wrong."

"That makes it wrong for the High Forest." The treant tried again to drag down the shadow web, then turned to Galaeron when he failed. "Take this down."

Galaeron began to gather the shadow silk into a ball, drawing a disapproving scowl from Melegaunt.

"What are you doing?"

"This is Turlang's home," said Galaeron, guessing at the treant's identity. Only Turlang, the renowned ruler of the High Forest, could be so huge and old. "We must respect his wishes."

Melegaunt rolled his eyes. "You do know that means they'll catch us?" He glanced at Turlang, then added, "And there would be a battle."

"Fuorn's whispers spoke of your gift to the Forest Forgotten, Duskbeard, so one threat I will forgive." The treant creaked down to peer into Melegaunt's eyes. "His whispers also spoke of the trouble that hunts you, and I will have no magicgrubs in my forest."

"Then you would do well to help us." Melegaunt waved his hand at Galaeron and the others. "We have all sworn to return the phaerimm to their prison, and the help we need lies inside your forest, in the temple of Karse."

Turlang drew himself to his full height. "What help can you need from Wulgreth? That you count a lich your friend only proves the evil I taste in your air."

A chill ran down Galaeron's spine. "Lich?" he echoed, finally understanding the reason Melegaunt had been so secretive about the help they were seeking. "What other lies have you been telling us?"

Melegaunt wagged a finger at Galaeron. "Be careful of that shadow, my friend." Looking back to Turlang, the wizard said, "Wulgreth is no friend of mine, but every treasure has its guardian, and I do mean to deal with him—though not in the way you believe."

Turlang fell silent and motionless, presumably weighing Melegaunt's words against the evil "taste" of their party. As suspicious as Galaeron was of Melegaunt, he feared the malevolence the treant sensed lay in his own dark spirit. Try as he might, the elf could not help attributing the most selfish motives to every action. Melegaunt hoped to strike a bargain with an evil lich. Malik wanted to steal the secret of shadow magic. Turlang refused to help them because he feared the wrath of the phaerimm. Galaeron was losing the fight against his shadow.

He stepped forward and placed himself squarely in front of the treant. "The Turlang my mother speaks of would never turn away a tree-friend."

"Nor would the one standing before you," said the treant. "Were he certain they were tree-friends."

"Then you will not turn us away." When Galaeron waved a hand at his companions, he found only Melegaunt, Vala, and, still standing watch at the edge of the forest, Aris. Malik and his horse were nowhere to be seen, apparently having decided to accept Melegaunt's advice and depart. "On my life,

I promise no one here will harm the High Forest, nor allow any harm to come to it through anything he does or does not do."

Turlang regarded him for a long time, then said, "Your life means nothing to me. I know you for an Evereskan by your dress and speech, but there is a darkness in you I do not trust."

"There are more eye-devils coming," Aris called from the edge of the forest.

"How many?" Vala called back, ever the battle chief.

"Too far to say," said the giant. "They are only specks, but there's also something that resembles a dust devil."

Galaeron and Vala exchanged nervous glances, and Melegaunt ran out of patience.

"We're out of time, tree," the wizard growled. "There is more at risk than your forest, and we *will* pass through—"

"What we will do is abide by Turlang's will," Galaeron interrupted. Even were Melegaunt powerful enough to defeat Turlang and his many allies—and Galaeron suspected the battle would be closer than the wizard knew—for an elf to defy a treant in his own forest would be an act of wickedness as terrible as treason. Galaeron turned back to the treant. "If the great Turlang places no value in my promise, I am certain he will value my mother's."

"You would offer your mother's life in place of your own?" Turlang's voice was condemning. "Who is this lucky elf?"

Galaeron had to bite back a wave of anger. "Morgwais Nightmeadow."

The burls above Turlang's eyes rose. "Morgwais?"

Galaeron nodded. "Known to the people of the High Forest as Morgwais the Red."

Vala and Melegaunt looked to each other with expressions of surprise. The treant considered Galaeron's claim for a long time, during which Aris kept up a running account of what he saw.

"They're tiny circles . . . six of them, and something like a funnel with a tail. The one behind the hill is flying back to join them . . ."

Finally, Turlang spoke. "If you are lying about this, your lives are forfeit." He glanced to Vala and Melegaunt, then added, "All of them."

"Agreed," said Galaeron.

Vala and Melegaunt were quick to nod their own agreement, and Aris said, "My life is Galaeron's to pledge."

"Then we have a bargain." Turlang lowered two branches. "I will need your weapons . . . and your pledge not to use your dark magic until you enter the Dire Wood."

Galaeron removed his scabbard and laid it into a tangle of gnarled sticks. "As you wish."

Vala removed her belt and wrapped it around the hilt of the weapon to prevent the black blade from slipping free, then laid it next to Galaeron's sword. Melegaunt pulled his sheathed dagger from its place, but hesitated before laying it alongside the other weapons.

"The dagger I'll yield happily," said the wizard, "but the magic I may need to confuse our foes."

"They will be confused," said Turlang. "I will see to that."

"These are no ordinary beings," Melegaunt warned. "The phaerimm will not be fooled by normal magic, and the beholders can dispel it with a glance."

"It will not be magic that misleads them." Turlang's tone was uncharacteristically peevish for a treant. "Will you promise or not?"

Melegaunt gave Galaeron a hesitant look.

"Decide now," said Galaeron. "It will mean my mother's life if you lie."

At the edge of the forest, Aris called out, "They're spreading out, and turning invisible—the cowards!"

Melegaunt continued to look at Galaeron. "You're sure?"

"It's the only way," Galaeron answered.

Melegaunt shrugged. "Very well, I promise."

Turlang studied the wizard for nearly a minute before

shifting his gaze to Aris. "Are you ready, giant?"

For a moment, Aris continued to stare across the valley, his lip curled into a hateful snarl. When he finally nodded and stepped into the forest, his gray eyes were as cold as ice.

"Let's go."

Turlang stretched a branch toward the giant's wooden club. "Your weapon."

Aris passed the club over. The treant held it at limb's length and inspected it for a moment, then he seemed to realize that it had been fashioned from an entire tree trunk. His face twisted into a strange expression of sadness and revulsion, and he dropped the weapon into the snow. The wood grew instantly brown and soft and crumbled into humus.

"Now we may go."

Turlang started into the dark forest, his enormous bulk gliding through trees as gracefully as any elf. Galaeron motioned the others after him, then took a place beside Vala at the end of the line.

She leaned close to him. "Did you see what became of Malik?"

"Not a hoof print," Galaeron replied. He glanced back and was not surprised to see a dozen trees arranging themselves into a boscage, while a like number of druids slipped quietly to and fro, eradicating all trace of the group's passing and laying a false trail in the opposite direction. "But I do hope he didn't go south."

CHAPTER THIRTEEN

28 Nightal, the Year of the Unstrung Harp

The scout and his hippogriff wheeled down out of the gray sky, a ghostly rider on a ghostly mount, almost impossible to see against the steely clouds even with detection magics fully raised. Khelben glanced over at Laerm Ryence, his counterpart and co-commander of the Swift Cavalry, and found the elf's silver eyes fixed on the trail ahead. Here they were, racing toward an army of phaerimm as fast as their spell-driven mounts could gallop, and the fool still had not bothered to cast his detection magic. Such negligence did not speak well for Evermeet's expeditionary company.

The scout swept up alongside the column, his hippogriff's wings thrumming air as he slowed. Lord Ryence jumped visibly, his free hand dropping to his belt of wands, his neck craning to look over the wrong shoulder.

"No need for alarm," Khelben yelled, his voice falling into the rhythm of his galloping mount. He wrapped his reins around his saddle's pommel, then worked a spell to mute the thundering hooves of the four hundred horses behind him. "It's my scout."

Ryence's fingers finally flashed through a detection spell. "So . . . I . . . see." Like most of the elves, he seemed ill-at-ease on the powerful chargers Lord Piergeiron had selected for their journey. "I am not blind."

Ignoring the testy reply, Khelben turned to his scout. "What is your report?"

The rider, a long-faced man with a two-day growth of beard, said, "About two miles ahead, the Winding Water bends within an arrow's flight of the High Moor. Not a thousand paces beyond, the Serpent's Tail forks north and blocks your way."

"A good place for an ambush?"

"The best. You'd be trapped against the Winding Water, with the Serpent's Tail blocking the way ahead."

Khelben glanced at the steep slope flanking them to the north. Though the escarpment rose only a hundred feet to the High Moor, its face was soggy and slick—difficult climbing under the best of circumstances, impossible with arrows and lightning bolts raining down from above. Opposite the moor lay the Winding Water, easily two hundred paces across, with a dark central channel purling between two banks of solid ice.

"We'll need to cross." Khelben nodded toward the river. "I can bridge the distance with a space-folding door, but we'd have to feed riders through one at a time. It might be faster for your Selu'taar to fashion a good-sized bridge."

Ryence tried to look surprised. "What makes you think there are high mages here?"

"You try my patience, Lord Ryence," Khelben said darkly. Were Laeral there, she would have been proud of him for not calling the elf a liar. "Now is a poor time to insist on polite little secrets."

It was Ryence's aide, a venerable Gold male named Bladuid, who answered, "A bridging spell would not be difficult. Half an hour would be sufficient."

"Too much time," grouched Ryence, annoyed that Bladuid had betrayed his identity. The elf commander pointed his chin toward the wall of snow-caked trees along the river's southern bank. "And we would only have to cross again, or have the Forest of Wyrms to worry us for the next hundred miles."

"Better to lose an hour or two crossing rivers than half a company fighting an ambush."

Ryence's eyes flashed white, and he looked to Khelben's scout. "Did you see any ambushers atop the moor?"

Somewhat reluctantly, the rider shook his head.

"He wouldn't," said Khelben. "Not if the phaerimm are using their magic."

"I'm willing to take that chance."

"I'm not," said Khelben. "There must be enough of us left to hold after we raise our end of the gate. If the phaerimm destroy it, it will take a month for the army to reach Evereska."

"I am not surprised to hear such talk from a human," said Ryence. "The phaerimm are not threatening one of your cities."

"It may not be a human city they are attacking, but plenty of human blood will be spilled defending it." Khelben struggled to conceal the full depth of his contempt for this elf. He had witnessed enough noble ambition to recognize a lord trying to make a name for himself, and he knew that such fools rarely had the good taste to get only themselves killed. "You'd do well not to waste it."

"No elf has asked you to waste anything," said Bladuid, urging his horse alongside Ryence's. "As far as we are concerned, this an elf matter."

Though Khelben was well aware of the disdain in which most Gold elves held humans, he was unaccustomed to feeling its sting himself. Drawing himself to his full height, he glared past Ryence at the high mage.

"Perhaps you have forgotten who I am. My father was Arun Maerdrym, noble son to House Maerdrym of Myth Drannor." What Khelben did not add—though it was obvious by his entirely human appearance—was that Arun had been a half-elf, and as such the first son of mixed race to be acknowledged by a noble house. "And I, personally, am one of the few—human, elf, or otherwise—who actually recalls living in Myth Drannor."

"Then you should know what happens when elves and humans mix," the high mage replied. "How long ago was it that Myth Drannor fell?"

"More recently than Aryvandar," Khelben shot back. "And you can hardly blame humans for that."

The gibe drew an angry snarl from Ryence and a black glare from Bladuid. No elf—especially no Gold elf—liked to be reminded of how the Crown Wars had shattered the golden age of elven civilization.

Khelben softened his tone. "Fortunately, the spirit of Myth Drannor still lives in some—even in Evereska. I myself have always found a warm welcome in the vale."

"Yes. Perhaps if more humans risked their lives *helping* elves instead of robbing their tombs, they would receive the same welcome you did." The high mage was referring to the time—nearly a thousand years earlier—that Khelben had almost died saving three Evereskans from a phaerimm ambush. When the grateful elves took him home to recover from his wounds, he became the first human ever allowed to see Evereska.

"If I may be so bold," said Khelben's scout, still flying just above his shoulder, "we are trying to help *now*."

"How very noble of you," Bladuid said. "And your generosity has nothing to do with what will become of human lands if the phaerimm succeed?"

"Waterdeep is a long way from Evereska, mage." The

scout looked back to Khelben and pointed up the trail. "There's the bend, milord. If you're going to cross, you'd better do it soon."

Khelben looked over to Ryence. "What say you? Will you humor me this once?"

The elf lord considered his request only a second. "There's no need. We must be two hundred miles from Evereska. The phaerimm are not going to ambush us here."

"Then I wish you well," said Khelben, pulling his horse out of line.

Ryence's eyes widened. "What are you . . ."

That was all Khelben heard before Ryence was carried out of earshot. He raised his hand to call Waterdeep's riders to him, then watched with a heavy heart as the elf warriors streaked past, their heads swinging around to look in his direction. He would have felt better, had their expressions had been less indignant and more perplexed.

The scout landed beside Khelben, keeping a tight rein on his hippogriff so it did not try to snack on the gathering horses.

"A wise choice, milord." In the thickening cloud of steaming horse breath, the scout's invisible form was barely discernible even to Khelben. "That elf is too eager to find his death."

"Let us hope he finds it later rather than sooner. Ryence may be a fool and Bladuid a bigot, but their warriors are brave and worthy, else they would not have traveled so far to fight someone else's battle." Khelben looked away from the elves and fixed his attention on the scout. "Shandar, is it not?"

"An excellent memory, Lord Blackstaff."

"There are only a dozen of you," said Khelben, dismissing the compliment with a wave of his hand. "Tell me how the moor looked when you flew over it. Can a horse cross it?"

"The ground looked frozen enough, but it was too broken. I fear we'd cripple as many as we didn't."

The last of the elf riders passed by, leaving the archmage

alone with his company of volunteers—barely a hundred warriors and a quarter that many battle mages. The men looked nervously from one to another, waiting in silence for their commander to explain why he had divided the Swift Cavalry. Khelben paid them no attention, convinced they would learn the reason soon enough, but hoping they would not.

Shantar finally grew impatient. "Lord Blackstaff? The river?"

Khelben looked across the Winding Water to the barren trees, knowing how difficult it would be to return across the river if the elves were ambushed.

"We can't chance the river." Khelben dismounted and passed his reins to a nearby rider, then drew his staff from its holster and started up the slope. "We'll have need of those elves."

The first hint of the village was the fruity reek of fireweed smoke, a stench that had led Galaeron to the camp of more than one shiftless, tomb-robbing wizard unable to forgo his indulgence for a few nights. This particular smoke happened to be especially foul, and he had a sudden vision of his mother and her friends squatting in the snow outside their storm-lodge, their hands cupped around white meerschaum bowls and their heads swaddled in clouds of brown fume. Wood elves were the most capricious of Tel'Quess, ever ready to test some new delight or enliven a party with a touch of intemperance, and he could easily imagine them becoming slaves to the pipe after seeing some human wizard blow smoke rings through a yellow-stained beard.

As Turlang led the small company deeper into the village, they heard a male voice singing a bawdy tale of one-night love. A rush of laughter punctuated each verse, and it was not long before Galaeron could identify his own mother's voice among them. As always, it stirred in him a youthful longing he had long thought past—and also deeper, angrier emotions upon which he dared not dwell if he meant to keep his shadow at bay.

Like most Sy'Tel'Quess settlements, the winter village of Rheitheillaethor was more of a camp than a town. On the ground stood rough huts of log and mud meant only to deceive intruders, while the elves' true homes sat high among the trees. Modest both in size and construction, the nestings were usually no more than a waxed leather tent covering a platform of dead-fall logs. Often, the walls were decorated with elaborate dye-work grisaille depicting winter scenes, usually rendered so that the art enhanced the camouflage. To spare the residents the effort of descending to the forest floor when they wanted to go somewhere, the entire hamlet was linked by an intricate network of catwalks and swing-ropes, all cleverly disguised as crisscrossing limbs and draping vines. With a fresh twilight snow on the ground, as there was now, a careless observer might easily cross all of Rheitheillathor and never see the real village.

Galaeron's companions were not careless observers. Vala and Melegaunt pretended not to notice the eyes peering down from the sentry hollows, but the care they took to avoid fields of fire suggested they knew exactly where Rheitheillaethor stationed its archers. Aris was not so subtle. The stone giant simply stomped from one tree to another, studying the grisaille and mumbling to himself as he admired the most inspiring of the works. If he noticed the startled elf mothers herding their wide-eyed children out the opposite sides of the nestings, he showed no sign.

At last, they reached the village center. Turlang stepped aside, revealing Rheitheillaethor's only permanent building, a white marble longhouse. Aris was instantly on his hands and knees, studying the sculpted frieze work ringing the building.

Fifty paces beyond the longhouse, a hundred Wood elves sat on snow-cushioned deadfall logs, swilling triplewild mead and listening to the bawdy song the companions had been hearing. The lyrics were being sung by a throaty-voiced human seated on the Honor Chair—a flat-topped boulder nestled in a crook along the bank of the Heartblood River. The fellow's face was thin and weathered, with dancing eyes and a flowing beard stained yellow around the mouth. One hand held a long-stemmed pipe that had single-handedly covered the clearing with a cloud of turquoise smoke, while the other was cupping the fanny of the laughing Wood elf woman who sat on his lap.

With amber eyes, waist-length hair as richly golden as honey, and a face so deeply copper it could only be called red, the Lady of the Wood looked as strikingly beautiful as ever, and it took Galaeron a moment to accept that it was actually his mother on the human's lap. Though Morgwais scorned humans even more than did most Wood elves—and the Wood elf abhorrence of humans was legendary—she did not seem to dislike this man. She had one arm wrapped around his neck and her bosom pressed to his cheek, and if she was troubled by the wrinkled hand on her behind, she hid the fact well.

Turlang waited while the human finished his song, then rustled his branches. "Forgive the intrusion, tree-friends."

At the sound of the treant's voice, Galaeron's mother smiled broadly and turned to look, the delight in her eyes bespeaking the regard all elves held for the forest master.

"Turlang?"

"I have need of words, Lady Morgwais."

"Of course," Morgwais called. She jumped off the human's lap, then spread her arms wide and started forward. "Welcome."

The treant dipped his leafy crown. "Always a joy."

"What brings you to Rheitheillaethor, my friend?" As she slipped past the other elves, she finally seemed to notice Aris kneeling beside the stormlodge. "And who is your tall friend?"

"Aris is neither friend nor foe to me—yet." Turlang

lowered a limb toward Galaeron. "He is companion to one claiming to be your son."

"Galaeron?" Morgwais's gaze shifted to where Galaeron stood beneath Turlang's shadowy boughs, and she slipped past the treant to embrace him. "I didn't feel you enter the wood!"

"No?" The comment caused Galaeron to feel strangely resentful, as though she were accusing him of trying to surprise her. He cast a bitter glance toward the white-bearded human, now trailing his mother forward like a hart after his hind. "Perhaps you were distracted by your man-friend."

Morgwais retreated to arm's length and cocked a chastening eyebrow. "Did Aubric send you to look in on my virtue? Because I am certain your father has more important things to worry about."

This drew a chorus of titters from the Wood elves, who considered jealousy perverse. Galaeron felt the heat rise to his cheeks and started to grow angry with his mother for embarrassing him, then realized he had brought the ridicule on himself. To Sy'Tel'Quess, flirtation was as much a part of a good life as savory food and abundant drink, and even his father would not have been upset to find Morgwais sitting on someone else's lap. The cause of Galaeron's indignation was not her behavior; it was something much deeper and darker.

"I apologize," said Galaeron. "I doubt Father even knows I'm here. I was just so astonished to find you keeping a human's company I didn't know what to think."

The smile that returned to Morgwais's lips was only half doubtful. She took Galaeron's hand and motioned the white-bearded man forward. "Elminster is no ordinary human."

"Elminster?" It was Melegaunt who gasped this. "Of Shadowdale?"

"The very." As the old man stepped to Morgwais's side, the twinkle in his eye turned fiery. "And ye be Melegaunt Tanthul, I believe."

Melegaunt's eyes narrowed, and his expression changed

from one of concern to something between awe and terror. "I am he—but you know that already."

Elminster puffed his pipe. "Thy efforts have not gone unnoticed, lad. There is talk of all ye've done for Evereska."

"And that's why you are here?" Galaeron was as dazed by the idea that anyone would call Melegaunt "lad" as he was excited to hear that Elminster himself had taken notice of his home's plight. "To help us?"

Elminster continued to look at Melegaunt. "That depends on what ye seek in Karse."

Melegaunt arched his brow. "What makes you think . . . ?" He seemed to suddenly realize the answer, then said, "The stone giants, of course—and Lord Imesfor thinks I'm Netherese."

"And I am not convinced he is wrong."

"Believe what you wish, but if you spoke to the stone giants, you must also know the phaerimm are desperate to stop us. That alone should convince you we serve the same goal."

Elminster's tone grew sharp. "I'd be more convinced, had there not been an illithid after Lord Imesfor's brain when he arrived at Khelben's. He said ye set a whole band on him."

"Then he is well." Though Melegaunt's reply was a statement, his audacity did not prevent him from cringing in the face of Elminster's ire. "Sometimes right and wrong are not so clear. Imesfor had to suffer that Evereska might live."

"Is that so?" Elminster's tone suggested it was not. "Had he arrived with no holes in his skull, methinks Khelben would have been on his way that much sooner."

"Khelben is going to Evereska?" Galaeron asked. "Khelben *Arunsun*?"

"Of course, lad. Did ye think he'd let the phaerimm take it?" The wizard pointed his pipe southward. "As we stand here talking, he's leading a company across the western plains to raise a translocational gate."

"What kind of company?" There was alarm and sorrow in

Melegaunt's voice. "You are only sending live men after dead."

Elminster's irritation showed in his eyes. "Ye should not underestimate Khelben Arunsun."

"Never, but he is no more a match for the phaerimm than the Evereskans." Melegaunt gestured to Galaeron. "And young Nihmedu will tell you what became of them."

Galaeron met Elminster's eye and nodded. "The tomb guard, the border guard, the spell guard—"

"Yes, yes—and half the high mages as well." Elminster dismissed Galaeron's account with a wave of his pipe. "Imesfor told us all about it, but Khelben has certain, ah, resources unavailable even to thy high mages."

Galaeron did not ask the old wizard to elaborate. At least in Evereska, it was well known that like Elminster himself, Khelben was one of Mystra's "Chosen." Nobody knew exactly what being Chosen meant, but it seemed fairly well accepted that these individuals were invested with some of the goddess of magic's divine power. According to rumor, they were nearly immortal and could call upon the power they carried to perform fantastic feats of magic. Certainly, it was good to have the Chosen taking Evereska's side—but still Galaeron did not think one would be enough.

"Good mage, you'd do well to listen to Melegaunt in this," said Galaeron. "If it's not too late to contact Lord Kh—"

"There be few men as stubborn Khelben Arunsun." Elminster cocked his brow and fixed a questioning eye on Galaeron. "But it could be that I can call him off—if the reason be good enough."

"I can only tell you that without Melegaunt Tanthul, Lord Imesfor would be hatching an egg for the phaerimm right now," said Galaeron. "Melegaunt is the only one who seems able to engage our enemies on an equal footing."

Elminster shook his head. "Khelben is a proud man, I fear. Perhaps if ye could tell me what ye seek in Karse."

"Something to defeat the phaerimm." Galaeron looked to

Melegaunt to elaborate, but the shadowmage kept his gaze fixed on Elminster and pretended not to notice. "That's all he's told me."

"Ye are a trusting spirit, lad," said Elminster. "It speaks well of thy own honesty—if not thy cunning wit."

"The phaerimm have been close on our trail the entire time," explained Melegaunt. "I thought it best to keep the plan to myself, lest bad come to worse."

"A wise precaution." Elminster stepped closer to Melegaunt and offered his ear. "But ye can tell me."

Melegaunt retreated, and Vala interposed herself between her master and his interrogator. Elminster might have missed the subtle tension that came to her body, but Galaeron did not.

"I can handle matters here," said Melegaunt. "If you truly want to do some good, you'll join Khelben in the south. A second hand flinging Mystra's silver fire would go far toward saving his company."

This drew a wry smile from Elminster. "Ye know more about me than I about thee . . . and I can see ye mean to keep it so."

"Your deeds have made a great name for you," said Melegaunt. "I have lived a quieter life, but Galaeron can tell you my intentions are good."

Elminster's voice turned hard. "I keep my own counsel about such things."

"That is your privilege," said Melegaunt. "Just as it is mine."

Elminster waited for him to elaborate, then finally sighed and shook his head. "Ah, well, I had hoped to do this a simpler way."

He slipped a hand into his pocket. Vala was instantly moving, one hand chopping for his throat and the other reaching for the offending arm.

A few hairs shy of his body, a blue aura flashed beneath her hands. She cried out in shock and pulled her arms back, then took one glance at her smoking fingertips and plunged them into the snow. Elminster gave her a bemused look, then pulled a small wad of fireweed out of his pocket and refilled his pipe.

"What'd ye think, girl? That I meant to enchant his secrets from him?" Elminster snapped his fingers, then held a small flame over the bowl of his pipe. "I've better ways than that."

The wizard puffed on his fireweed and glowered at Melegaunt through the awful-smelling smoke. The gaze Melegaunt returned was too nervous to be called a glare, but neither did he look away. Galaeron and the others watched in tense silence, reassured by Turlang's presence—and the great boughs he stretched over the pair's heads—that the matter would not come to a duel of spells, yet worried enough that they hardly dared breathe for fear of touching off a fight. Even Aris tore himself away from the stormlodge to come loom over the standoff.

Galaeron did not know what to make of the situation. Elminster was, by all accounts, a loyal elf-friend and a man of character, yet he seemed to presume a great deal in the demands he made of Melegaunt. On the other hand, Melegaunt had used Lord Imesfor to lure the illithids away—an act destined to be viewed in a dim light by anyone who did not understand how important their escape had been. Even knowing that Imesfor had survived, the thought still sent a guilty shudder down Galaeron's spine. How could Elminster, who had never seen Melegaunt risk his own life for others, react to the shadowmage's furtive nature with anything *but* suspicion?

Galaeron interposed himself between the mages. "It pains me to see you two off to such a bad start." He turned first to Elminster. "Given what happened to Lord Imesfor, your suspicions are reasonable, but Melegaunt did nothing wrong. Imesfor's life was Melegaunt's to do with as he pleased."

Elminster's were not the only human eyes to grow wide, but the mage was almost as quick as Lady Morgwais to take Galaeron's meaning.

"The Rule of Saving?" Elminster said. "I haven't heard that invoked in five hundred years!"

"Handsome as you are, you are not an elf," said Morgwais. She sidled up to Elminster and gave his beard a meaningful tug. "If Melegaunt saved Imesfor's life. . . ."

"And he did." Galaeron deliberately left out mention of his own part in the rescue. "I saw that much with my own eyes."

"You see? Melegaunt did nothing wrong!" Morgwais flashed Elminster a brilliant smile, then took him by the hand and started toward the river bank. "Let's go back to the party and drink this misunderstanding under."

Elminster flashed Melegaunt a scowl that said their meeting was far from over, but he was too well-mannered to refuse such a request from the Lady of the Wood. He allowed himself to be passed off to a young elf maiden and led back toward the Honor Chair. Morgwais turned to the treant.

"My thanks for bringing my son to Rheitheillaethor, Turlang. Do join us."

Turlang shook his leafy crown. "That cannot be. A magic-grub followed your son and these others into the forest, and I must return to watch it." He lowered a bough toward Galaeron. "I want only to be certain this one is who he claims. There is a darkness in him I do not trust, and I would know if you will vouchsafe his conduct, and that of his friends."

The light faded from Morgwais's face. "A darkness, you say?"

She took Galaeron's hand, then looked past his shoulder. Her gaze grew unfocused, as it would during the Reverie, and a single furrow appeared in her unblemished brow. She remained that way for several moments, then finally opened her eyes and nodded.

"It's true. You seem lost to me, child. It is as though you are . . ." She started to look away as though embarrassed, then hesitated and forced herself to look back. "It feels as though are *asleep*."

The comment struck Galaeron like a blow, and he realized

with a start that he did not feel the other elves either. The absence had seemed normal enough during his travels with the humans—especially given his trouble falling into the Reverie—but he should have sensed other elves as they traveled deeper into the High Forest. Instead, there had been nothing—no sense of welcome, no warmth, no safety. He had felt nothing—nothing but the anger and jealousy he had experienced upon seeing his mother on Elminster's lap.

Galaeron forced himself to meet his mother's gaze. "I have been through some trying times, and it may be that even I shouldn't trust myself." He gestured to Melegaunt and Vala and added, "But I do know I can trust these humans."

Morgwais studied the humans for several moments, her gaze lingering on Vala longer than on Melegaunt, then she finally cracked a melancholy smile and stepped toward Vala.

"Vala," said Vala, extending her hand. "Vala Thorsdotter." Unfamiliar with human customs, Morgwais stared in confusion at the out-thrust arm. "You will watch after Galaeron?"

Vala glanced briefly at Melegaunt, then gave a solemn nod. "That promise I have already made."

Morgwais shrugged and turned to Turlang. "I am Galaeron's mother." She glanced at Vala, then her smile broadened, and she said, "Of course, I will vouchsafe their conduct!"

She took Vala's hand and thrust it into Galaeron's, and that was when a svelte Wood elf in a brown Tomb Guard cloak pushed through the crowd. She had a familiar cupid's bow smile and a pair of doe-brown eyes Galaeron would have recognized through a keyhole. The instant she stepped to Morgwais's side, her gaze dropped to the hands clasped between Galaeron and Vala.

"T-Takari!" Galaeron gasped.

Takari's gaze rose, the light already fading from her eyes. Her face remained hollow-cheeked and sallow from her wound, and her cloak hung more loosely than usual on her bony shoulders.

"I really shouldn't be surprised," said Takari, looking Vala up and down. She sighed dramatically, then reached past the human to pull Galaeron to her lips. "But she'll have to share!"

CHAPTER FOURTEEN

28 Nightal, the Year of the Unstrung Harp

Khelben had barely crested the slope before the first crack of war thunder rumbled across the frozen tussocks. Less than a mile distant, a rank of figures became visible along the moor's edge, their invisibility spells fading as they hurled sling stones and magic bolts down on Lord Ryence's elves. Khelben used thumb and forefinger to make a circle over his eye and uttered a spell. The figures resolved themselves into a couple of hundred bugbears, perhaps twenty beholders, and a dozen mind flayers. A pair of phaerimm hovered together near the center.

"As you predicted, milord," said the scout Shantar, landing his invisible hippogriff beside Khelben. "We'll ambush the ambushers and be done with it."

"Our enemies would not make things so easy," observed Naneatha Suaril, cresting the slope beside

Khelben. A blonde beauty whose pearly smile and shining eyes belied her fifty winters, Naneatha was Priestess of the High Moonlight of the House of the Moon in Waterdeep—and the unofficial commander of the small band of priests accompanying Khelben. "They are creatures of darkness, full of treachery and deception."

Khelben nodded and glanced over his shoulder. The rest of the company was scrambling up the slope, wands and bows at the ready. He directed the Sword Captain to form a combat line and the Wand master to scatter the battle mages behind it, then turned back to Naneatha and Shantar.

"The other scouts will be returning to the sound of battle?"

Shantar nodded. "They'll be here any minute."

"And your mounts can carry extra riders?" Khelben asked.

"For a short while." Shantar's eyes showed curiosity. "And lance work will be out of the question."

"Spells will serve you better," said Khelben. "Have the scouts assemble behind the battle line and take up Naneatha's priests. They are to circle high, half a mile behind us. That will keep even phaerimm from seeing through your invisibility."

Naneatha frowned. "A priest's place is in battle."

"And so it shall be." Khelben pointed his staff toward a scraggly pine hummock, then toward a cluster of moss-covered boulders. "Watch there for their rear guard. You and the scouts must strike them from behind—and strike hard."

Naneatha's scowl remained. "And if there is no rear guard?"

"There will be." Khelben turned to Shantar. "Do your *sending*, then wait until Lady Suaril is free to join you."

"As you command."

Shantar flicked his thumb over his scout's ring to activate its sending magic, and Khelben turned to find his small force ready. The archmage laid his staff aside, then he and Naneatha began to cast combat guards over the company. The spells required several minutes to complete, but Khelben did not even consider advancing until they were finished. Without spell shields, sending men against phaerimm would be murder.

Once the last spell was completed, Khelben sent Naneatha off with Shantar, then took up his staff and led the way forward at a run. The company followed in silence, the normal clamor muted by his war magic. Despite the frozen tussocks and wind whistling into their faces, they covered the ground swiftly, invigorated as much by approaching battle as by the prayers Naneatha had said over them.

Even Khelben, who had fought too many battles to enjoy the prospect of another, felt his pulse pounding wildly. This was the rousing part of war, the anticipation of the victory, the fear of a violent end, the reckless joy of a mortal gamble. Later came the hundred stenches of death, the grieving, the maimed bodies. The company passed the scraggly pine hummock Khelben had pointed out to Naneatha, closing to within three hundred paces of the enemy. The archmage slowed to a walk and raised his staff, signaling his archers to nock their arrows.

A pair of thunderclaps erupted from the pine hummock, and two lightning bolts exploded into the company spell shield and filled the sky with silver light. Next came a chorus of bugbear grunts, followed by a stone rain. The sling stones struck the missile guard and bounced away, but a dozen of Khelben's archers shot arrows into the ground.

Not bothering to look back, Khelben brought his company to a halt and lowered his staff. The archers loosed a cloud of dark shafts into the air. Half the arrows fell short and the others came to a sudden halt, hanging motionless twenty feet above their targets. The phaerimm tipped their toothy maws toward Khelben, but seemed the only ones who noticed the attack. The bugbears and beholders with them continued to hurl death down from the moor's edge, paying no attention as the reciprocating barrage of elven magic burst harmlessly against their spell shields.

Another flurry of sling stones and lightning bolts struck

Khelben's own missile guard from the rear, then Naneatha's priests sent a cacophony of crackles and booms rolling across the frozen moor as they unleashed their wrath. The answering chorus of anguished bellows left no doubt about the fate of the rear guard. Khelben leveled his staff at the phaerimm and advanced at a deliberate walk, assailing them with a stream of fiery missiles and magic blasts. The attacks exploded into fire storms and starbursts against the enemy spell shields, causing no damage, but blinding the phaerimm to Naneatha and the other hippogriff riders.

The phaerimm used their own fireballs and lightning bolts to disorient the humans, and a small band of beholders and bugbears turned to face Khelben's advance. He felt almost insulted. He had destroyed the phaerimm's rear guard and arrived behind their line uncontested, and still the creatures believed they could destroy his company with a handful of spells.

The beholders floated forward behind a screen of bugbears, using the hairy giants like shields until they closed to two hundred and forty paces—close enough to use their magic-disrupting beams on Khelben's spell guards. He brought his company to a halt, then planted his staff at his side and pulled a piece of amber from his pocket. After rubbing this against his beard, he began to stroke a handful of silver pins over the amber one by one.

By the time he finished, the leading bugbears had closed to within a hundred and seventy paces, well outside the phaerimm spell guards. He tossed the pins into the air and uttered a mystic syllable, then groaned as a bolt of lightning exploded from his chest and arced to the closest bugbear. The huge creature exploded into red haze and scorched fur, as did the beholder behind him and the next two bugbears, then the bolt continued down the line in a blinding flash that seemed to last forever. A second beholder and two more bugbears burst into flames, then another half dozen creatures spawned smoking holes in the centers of their bodies.

Had any other wizard cast the spell, the bolt's rampage would have fizzled there, but Khelben was no ordinary mage. He was Chosen of the goddess of magic herself, imbued with the power of the Weave and—at over nine hundred years old—nearly immortal himself, capable of withstanding energies that would incinerate any common man. The lightning continued, blasting through another dozen victims before the first dozen hit the ground. With each strike, the smoking holes shrank from the size of melons to fists to acorns. Finally, there were no more holes. One bugbear and two beholders died of nothing but shock. The last bugbear escaped altogether, stumbling three steps back and grabbing for his chest.

After the spell sputtered out, all that remained to carry on were half a dozen bugbears and two wide-eyed beholders. The bugbears turned to flee and perished instantly in a curtain of fire—phaerimm did not tolerate cowardice in their thralls. The two beholders focused their big central eyes on one another, encasing each other in a purple cone of magic-dispelling radiance.

"Arrows at the beholders!" Khelben commanded.

A flight of shafts leaped toward the beholders. The creatures had no choice but to deactivate their magic-dispelling rays and bring their other eyestalks around to defend themselves. Khelben's battle mages unleashed a veritable shower of magic, and the eye tyrants vanished into a roiling storm of fire.

"Forward walk!" Khelben called.

As the company started forward, the phaerimm assailed Khelben's spell shield with a tempest of fire and magic. Though the accompanying dazzle made it impossible to see what was happening ahead, Khelben was glad to have his foes finally showing him some respect. A little caution would do much to ease the attacks against the elves.

Had he wished, Khelben could probably have frightened the pair into a full withdrawal. As one of Mystra's Chosen, he carried within him a small part of the goddess's power—a power which manifested itself as *Silver Fire*. He could call upon silver fire to protect himself from most sorts of harm—hence his nine hundred years—and to assail his enemies with a blast of white, pure Weave magic. Even the mightiest magic-users quavered at its sight, for they usually recognized its true nature and knew what it meant for their survival, but Khelben was not ready to reveal all his secrets. The two phaerimm would teleport away the instant the battle turned against them, and he did not want them telling their friends back at Evereska what they were facing.

Khelben and his battle mages returned the phaerimm assault in kind, filling the area between them with a blinding wall of starburst radiance. Eventually, they would draw close enough to assail each other's spell guards with dispelling magic, and the killing would begin.

Khelben flicked his thumb over his signet ring, activating its sending magic. He pictured Shantar's face in his mind, then spoke to the scout with thoughts. *Can't see. What's happening?*

Elves regrouping slowly. Shantar's reply came to Khelben in his mind's voice. *A hundred and fifty paces to hand-to-hand. Half their company is turning to face you.*

Khelben sighed in relief, then boomed an order, "Ready arrows—and it will be to the swords."

A hundred warriors nocked a hundred shafts and continued to advance. A black fog appeared over their spell shield. Khelben blew it aside with a magical wind.

"Mages halt—let the warriors screen you!"

The mages stopped in their tracks, adjusting their wands to arc fireballs and ice storms over the heads of their advancing comrades. Khelben himself slipped in behind a pair of archers and continued forward. He judged he would be close enough to dispel the enemy spell shields in thirty steps.

"Steady now," he called.

Half a dozen beholders zipped out of the enemy ranks,

forsaking the safety of the phaerimm spell shields for a field of lightning and fire. Amidst all the flashing and streaking, they looked like mere cloud shadows, but that did not prevent Khelben's followers from peppering them with fiery bolts and hissing shafts. Three creatures erupted into flames the instant they left their spell guards, and two more fell to arrows.

The sixth eye tyrant dodged and weaved its way forward by flashing its magic-dispelling gaze on and off so its other eyestalks could spray the sky ahead with their various magics. It destroyed several arrows with its disintegration beam and deflected a whole cloud with its telekinesis rays, but even that was not enough. It sprouted a dozen shafts and plummeted to the ground, then rolled forward three paces and came up facing Khelben.

A cone of blue light shot from the creature's huge central eye and touched the front wall of Khelben's spell guards, creating an oval of shimmering radiance. The circle flickered, then swept over the rest of the shield in a flash of magic-dispelling brilliance. The enemy spells changed from dissipating starbursts to crackling bolts and sulfur-stinking ribbons. Men began to scream, flesh to sizzle, the frozen ground to rumble. Suddenly, the moor stank of charred flesh and opened entrails, sling stones hailed from the sky, and warriors fell by the dozen.

"*Charge!*" Khelben boomed, using a cantrip to make himself heard. "*Charge or die!*"

Khelben had barely given the order before the air turned silver and fresh-smelling around him. The man beside him erupted into a spray of boiling blood, then a lightning bolt blasted through the archmage and struck the next man in line. Khelben was hit in the head by a disembodied shoulder and knocked to the ground. By the time he could raise his head, the lightning bolt was already sputtering to a stop ten men away.

Before rolling to his feet, Khelben screened himself

behind his charging warriors. He was protected from lightning strikes and magic bolts by Mystra's silver fire, but every second the phaerimm delayed him cost a dozen human lives. He scrambled forward on hands and feet, then laid his staff aside and stood. Though the phaerimm spell guards still blazed with the dazzling starbursts of dissipating magic, a dark line of bugbear silhouettes stood just inside the barrier, axes raised and ready to meet the charge. The last few beholders—Khelben counted four—hovered along the line at even intervals, their eyestalks whipping this way and that as they sprayed the charging line with death rays of a dozen varieties. Only the mind flayers were nowhere to be seen. Khelben raised his hands toward the enemy spell guard and spoke three mystic syllables.

The barrier flickered once, then faded. Khelben's battle mages rushed forward, using their war wands to assail the bugbears and beholders with lightning bolts and fireballs. The two phaerimm responded with a horrifying array of flame geysers and needle showers, black fogs and acid clouds, steaming pits and strangling tentacles. Half a dozen wizards fell in as many steps.

Khelben wrapped a pinch of coal in a swatch of gingham and flicked it in the general direction of the phaerimm. When the nugget landed, he raised a hand to point and began his incantation. As he rattled off the mystic syllables, he was careful to keep his finger aimed at the ground instead of at the creatures themselves. Centuries earlier, Khelben had learned that phaerimm were beings of magic and naturally resistant to its power. Any spell striking their bodies had a good chance of ricocheting back at the caster or being used to heal their wounds, so he was careful to use magic that affected the area around the phaerimm instead of the creatures themselves. He finished his spell, and a sphere of black gauze billowed up around the pair, encasing them in a cocoon of inky fibers. Though their spell flurry continued unabated, it was to far less effect.

The swiftest of Khelben's swordsmen were within fifty paces of their foes, where the bugbears seemed content to wait in rank. It was a mistake they would regret. Khelben retrieved his staff.

"Mages, redcloud!"

The battle mages exchanged their war wands for red candlewicks and began their incantations. As they spoke, they used simple cantrips to ignite the wicks, then held the burning strands at arm's length.

Determined to keep the phaerimm from interfering with the redcloud, Khelben rolled a parchment spell scroll into a cone and held it to his mouth. When he began to boom out the syllables of another spell, his voice sounded much closer to, and on the other side of, the black cocoon.

The phaerimm did not respond, even when the spell he had uttered turned the cocoon into a block of solid stone. Either they were not fooled, or they had decided it was time to flee. Khelben hoped it was the latter.

The first of the battle mages' candlewicks burned out. Above the heads of the bugbears appeared a single wisp of red haze, crackling so softly that only a handful of the creatures looked up. As more wicks burned themselves out, the red wisp became a ropy bank of crimson fog, and the crackling grew louder. Whole bands of bugbears glanced upward, and the eyestalks of the few remaining beholders swiveled overhead. By then, the last candlewicks were expiring, and the fog had coalesced into a roaring cloud of flame.

"Now!" Khelben boomed.

The battle mages crumpled the candlewicks' sooty remains, and a curtain of flame rolled down from the red cloud.

A single beholder managed to whirl itself backward and bring its magic-dispelling eye to bear, opening a small gap in the long wall of fire. Khelben leveled his staff at the creature's exposed underside and blasted it with a fireball. The resulting eruption engulfed not only the eye tyrant itself, but the handful of bugbears whose lives it had spared.

With nothing ahead but a swirling curtain of flame, the charging swordsmen drew up short. There were far too many gaps in their line to please Khelben, for the phaerimm had taken a terrible toll. Fully a third of his warriors had fallen, and perhaps a quarter of his battle mages. Another "victory" like that one, and he would not have enough men left to defend the gate—even if Ryence had managed to keep his high mages alive to establish it.

Khelben raised his arms to dispel the fire curtain so he could take the survivors of his company and save Ryence's elves—then he saw a bushy-bearded warrior kneeling behind a frozen tussock. The man cried out and lifted the corpse of a dead comrade to his armored breast. When the archmage saw that nothing remained of the body beneath the shoulders, he lowered his arms and reached into his cloak for a feather instead. His men had done enough for the elves that day.

Khelben! Come quick! This time, Shantar's message came in the form of a soft whisper. The scout could use the sending magic in his ring only once per day, but, as one of Mystra's Chosen, Khelben could hear the next sentence or so when someone spoke his name anywhere on Toril. *They're after the high mages!*

Khelben did not ask who "they" were. Unlike a sending spell, his eavesdropping gift did not allow a reply. Besides, he had a sinking feeling he knew who the scout meant. He brushed the feather over his arms and legs, then spoke an incantation and launched himself into the air.

After flying over the wall of fire, he found himself above a slope of peat that fell sharply away to the sheer banks at the confluence of the Serpent's Tail and Winding Water. Judging by the number of pointy-eared corpses strewn along the lower half of the pitch, Ryence had tried to screen his crossing by sending part of his force to attack uphill. That the final line of bodies lay near the top of the slope spoke well of the elves' courage— if not of their commander's wisdom.

An enemy charge had caught the main body of the company preparing to cross the stream. The elves had felled most of the mind flayers and easily half of the bugbears on the way down, leaving the lower half of the slope strewn with almost as many foes as elves. The survivors had slammed into the rest of the company atop the gravelly bank of the Serpent's Tail, where a terrific melee continued to rage, with the bugbears trying to shield their last two mind flayers from an onslaught of gleaming elven steel. Nearly two dozen of Evermeet's swordmages lay writhing on the ground, their palms pressed to their ears in a futile attempt to shut out illithid mind blasts, but Khelben did not pause to hurl any spells into that quarter of combat. Even as he swooped down toward the battle, a pair of bugbears fell with elven steel through their hearts, and a trio of golden bolts shot through the resulting gap to blast the nearest mind flayer.

The scene in the middle of the Serpent's Tail was far less encouraging. Ryence sat astride his horse, tumbling ever so slowly to the water. Just ahead of him, Bladuid and two other Gold elves—presumably the rest of Ryence's high mages—were also slipping from their horses, one bent almost in two by the torpidly-rising water column of a spell blast. They were followed by several dozen slow-motion bodyguards, all caught in mid twist as they turned in their saddles to fling bolts and blasts at two phaerimm hovering behind them.

One of the phaerimm was moving as slowly as the elves, as much a victim of its companion's powerful reality-altering magic as Ryence and the high mages. The caster of the spell was floating forward through the contingent of bodyguards, its four arms lashing out to rip open their throats as it bumped its way forward toward Ryence. Had Khelben believed the target to be Ryence alone, he would have tried mightily to save the elf, to blast the phaerimm with a death spell or banish it to the depths of the ninth hell.

But Ryence was not alone. He was with the high mages, and Khelben could not take the chance that his spell would be reflected or absorbed by the phaerimm. He needed something powerful and direct, something that would burn through even a phaerimm's natural magic resistance.

He needed his silver fire.

Not for the first time, Khelben cursed the name of Laerm Ryence. The phaerimm cleared the last of the guards, reaching for Ryence's throat with one arm and for Bladuid with the other three. Khelben swooped down behind the creature, plummeting headfirst down from the sky, pointing one hand at the thing's open mouth and summoning his silver fire. A blissful pain hissed through his body, gathered for an instant in the pit of his stomach, then left his arm in a long streak of roaring fire. The phaerimm spun toward the sound on its tail, and the silver flame shot straight down its gullet. The creature came apart in a halo of white flame.

The reality-altering spell ended with the thing's death. Ryence and his high mages completed their falls, hitting the water with a loud series of splashes. Khelben wheeled toward the remaining phaerimm, frantically searching his mind for the safest way to destroy the thing quickly. It would take an hour for his body to reabsorb enough of Mystra's raw magic to use his silver fire again, so he would have to chance a spell.

A thunderous chugging filled the air, and elves began to wail. A scintillating tornado of gem-colored light appeared below him and began to dance across the river, raking the bodyguards of the high mages with spinning tentacles of death-dealing radiance. Each color brought an end more terrible than the previous. Those struck by red erupted into flames. The flesh of anyone touched by green sizzled away in a cloud of emerald gas. Blue brought death by choking, yellow by the foulest of stinking diseases, orange by spontaneous bleeding from every pore. Those touched by a black tentacle oozed away putrid part by putrid part, while those caught by white froze solid and floated away in the cold current.

Khelben had never before seen such a war spell. Nearly half the bodyguards already lay dead or dying, and the other half were scattering in every direction. The phaerimm itself did not seem to be aware of him, high in the air above it. Leaving the tornado to wander on its own, the creature glided toward the splashing forms of the high mages.

It was too late to be safe. Khelben stopped to hover and summoned to mind his most deadly spell. The phaerimm paused above a tangle of elf corpses, then reached down beside an ice-capped boulder to retrieve its companion's shredded tail. Khelben turned his palm toward the creature and barked out a syllable.

The phaerimm did not wave its arms or try to swing itself upright, nor even to make a last, desperate counterattack. At the sound of Khelben's voice, it simply teleported away, leaving his spell to splash harmlessly into the icy stream.

Damn, but they were fast.

CHAPTER FIFTEEN

28 Nightal, the Year of the Unstrung Harp

The celebration was an uneasy one, and not only because Elminster spent the evening glowering at Melegaunt. Galaeron kept glimpsing a dark shape just beyond the glowcircle, a stout little figure that vanished into the shadows the instant he turned to look upon it. Were it not for the agitation of the sentries, he would have dismissed the apparition as the product of a weary mind, but the night watchers kept flitting about up under the stars, swinging from tree to tree or rushing silently along barren limbs to scrutinize something on the ground. Still, they never gave the owl call, so perhaps it was no more than the playmagic of mischievous Wood elf children, and Galaeron was content to take his cue from his mother's people.

The moon rose silver and bright, filling the wood

with a milky snowlight, and out came the starlutes. The melodies were airy and cheerful, as always among Wood elves. Takari made a show of dragging Galaeron away from his mother—and coincidentally also Melegaunt and Vala— and being the first to dance. Though the song would have been more suited to a feather step, she pressed herself into Galaeron's arms and began a matched gambol.

"Don't overdo it," Galaeron said, struggling to stay in step as they skipped through the moonlit snow. "You still look weak."

"I'm well enough." Takari pursed her lips into a playful pout. "The only wound that troubles me is the one in my heart—the one you put there tonight."

"I'm sorry." Galaeron's apology was sincere, for he had been so absorbed with Elminster, Turlang, and the rest that he had not even thought of inquiring as to whether Takari had arrived. "I should have stopped by your nesting as we came in."

"My nesting?" Takari raked her heel down his shin. "I'm talking about Vala, orc nose! What's wrong with you, taking a human for your mate . . . over me?"

"Vala?" Galaeron's foot nearly slipped from beneath him. "I haven't taken her!"

Takari gave him a doubtful look. "Not even once?"

Now Galaeron did slip, stumbling over a half-buried log and bringing them both down in the snow. The fall drew a chorus of laughter, and the musicians embarrassed them further by slipping into a slow meter.

"Not even once," Galaeron whispered, lying in the snow. "Though it's not really your business who I take."

Takari gave him a frisky smile. "But it could be." With that, she leaped to her feet and took a good-natured bow, then stretched a hand toward Vala. "Come help me, human. This one is such a hoof-foot it will take two to keep him in step."

Before Vala could object, Morgwais pushed her out to join Takari and Galaeron, and soon the three of them were whirling around the glowcircle arm-in-arm. Vala could keep even the quickest meter, but her steps were heavy and conspicuous by elf standards. Nevertheless, their antics proved inspirational, and soon the rest of the Wood elves were gliding about the glowcircle in whirling trios, stomping the beat and pumping their knees like centaurs on parade. Even Lady Morgwais joined the merriment, slipping one arm around Elminster's waist and the other around Melegaunt's—no easy task, given the girth of the pair.

Sometime during the festivities, Aris dropped a six-foot boulder next to the Honor Chair and set to work, hammering and clinking to the music. The boulder quickly assumed the rough shape of three whirling bodies, and it was not long before dancers began to spin past to check his progress. The figures emerged as if by magic, the giant not so much giving them form as finding it within the stone, and it soon grew apparent Aris would be leaving his hosts with a treasure worthy of Rheitheillaethor's greatest masters.

Half a night later, the eyes of the humans began to droop, as did Galaeron's. Not wishing to admit publicly that he now felt the need to sleep, he excused himself on the pretext of showing his companions to someplace they could rest— Takari was quick to volunteer her nesting—and they fell asleep to the sound of Aris's clinking and elven star lutes.

Galaeron awoke to darkness and silence, no snoring from Melegaunt's corner, no more of Vala murmuring her son's name in her sleep, no star lutes in the distance, none of Aris's hammering. There was only the breeze rustling against the walls and the creaking trees, and, farther off, the Heartblood gurgling down its channel. A hand touched his shoulder and gave it a tentative shake. Galaeron opened his eyes, then found his dark sight blurred by a thin film of mucus and wiped his eyes. That was one of the many hard things for him to accept about sleeping, the half second of thinking he was going blind whenever he woke.

When his sight cleared, he found Takari kneeling beside him, the corners of her cupid's bow mouth turned up in a slight sneer. There was no one else in the nesting.

"The others are outside," she explained, following his gaze. "They needed time to get down quietly, and I wanted to watch you sleep."

Galaeron grimaced. He had seen drool running from the corner of human mouths often enough to know what sleep looked like. "Not a pretty sight."

"Awful," Takari agreed, twisting her nose up. "Why do you do it?"

Why indeed? Galaeron wondered. "A bad habit I picked up from Melegaunt, I think." He sat up and shrugged, then found himself running his palms over his face the way humans sometimes did. He tore his hands down. "What's going on?"

"There are beholders coming."

Galaeron was on his feet and instantly awake. "But the owl calls—"

"The night watchers don't know yet." Though Takari wore her tomb guard's cloak, she made no move to rise as he shrugged into his chain mail. "Your frog-eyed friend warned me."

"Frog-eyed friend?"

"I think his name was Malik," Takari said. "Why didn't you bring him to the celebration?"

"I didn't know he was still with us," Galaeron confessed, struggling to make sense of what he was hearing. "Did he mention phaerimm?"

"He said there was one. Melegaunt thought it best to leave quietly and draw them into the Dire Wood."

Galaeron nodded, then pulled his cloak over his shoulders and reached for his sword belt. Having seen what the creatures had done to Thousand Faces, Galaeron was not eager to have a battle fought in Rheitheillaethor—not even with the great Elminster there to help.

Takari caught his hand. "Melegaunt said he can go without you. The rest would do you good."

"That doesn't sound like Melegaunt. Are you sure?"

"Look at yourself," said Takari, not answering. "You're turning into a human, sleeping half the night and struggling with something inside. Lady Morgwais isn't far wrong, you know. Maybe you are falling in love with Vala."

"Hardly." Galaeron's voice was sharper than he meant. He freed his belt from her grasp and started for the door. "But I do need to see this through with the humans. I'm the one who breached the Sharn Wall."

"You were doing your duty."

Galaeron slipped through the door without answering.

Takari followed him out onto the branch. "And you weren't the only one there."

In the creamy moonlight, Galaeron could see the edge of her leather scout's armor showing above the collar of her cloak. "You're still not strong enough. And if Melegaunt doesn't need me, he doesn't need you."

"He certainly does." Takari sprang off the limb and caught a rope, then slid toward the snowy ground. "Unless you think you can find the Dire Wood?"

Galaeron knew by how she had asked the question that he could not. As an elf, he felt reasonably at home in most forests, but he also knew how maddening it could be to navigate through an endless expanse of trees—especially if one's goal happened to be concealed by protective magic. Offering no further argument, he caught hold of the rope, then started down after Takari.

They touched ground not far from the glowcircle, where Melegaunt, Vala, and Malik stood waiting beside Aris and his sculpture. The statue depicted Galaeron dancing with Vala and Takari, and it was every bit the masterpiece he had expected—if a little embarrassing. Vala's body was pressed close against his, her scabbard and legs almost horizontal as she whirled on his hip. Her chin was raised slightly, as though they were about to kiss, and the smile on her face seemed both beguiling and tender. On Galaeron's other side, Takari was wrapped into his arm, their bodies not quite touching, her head thrown back in wild abandon. Though her mouth was open in laughter, there was a wistfulness to her expression that Galaeron had seen on a Wood elf's face only once, when his mother called the family together to tell how her heart ached to return to Rheitheillaethor.

Galaeron's own smile seemed lost and lonely, his gaze fixed a short distance away. Though caught physically between the two women, he was separated from them in mood by a lowered brow and narrowed eyes. The expression made him look sullen and hinted at a darker struggle within, but it was impossible to say whether Aris had actually captured this or whether Galaeron was reading it into the work on his own.

Takari circled the statue for a long time, then finally stopped at Vala's side and took her hand. Vala cocked her brow and looked down at their intertwined fingers, but did not try to free herself.

"It's remarkable!" Takari gasped. She turned to Aris and, finding herself staring at his knee, tipped her head back. "That is the most beautiful stone I have ever seen!"

This drew a meager smile from the stone giant. "The beauty was in the dance." Though he did not speak loudly, his deep voice rolled through the trees like thunder. "It is only a small matter to capture what one sees."

Melegaunt held his finger to his lips. "Quiet, or we will be what is captured." He turned to Takari. "Unless Elminster left?"

"Have no fear of him," said Malik. "Elminster will not be waking soon."

Melegaunt's face grew alarmed. "What? You didn't do any-thing—"

"Me? An assassin?" scoffed Malik. "I cannot even tell a decent lie! I mean only that he is asleep in the stormlodge."

"Asleep?" Melegaunt frowned at this. "You're sure it was Elminster?"

"Of course I am sure," said Malik. "I saw him myself, tucked under his furs with two women."

"Triplewild will do that to a man," chuckled Takari.

Galaeron was not quite so amused. "*Elf* women?" A cold anger was welling up inside him. "*Which* women?"

The jealousy in his voice drew a frown from Takari. "Not your mother. I saw Lady Morgwais leave for her nesting alone."

"That means nothing." The words slipped from Galaeron's mouth almost before he realized he was speaking. "She might have sneaked back."

Takari's scowl changed from disapproval to shock, but it was Melegaunt who spoke.

"Careful of that shadow, my friend." He nodded to Takari. "Perhaps we should go, if we want to lay another trail for the beholders."

"Fine by me." Takari continued to look at Galaeron. "I think Galaeron has had his fill of Rheitheillaethor."

She led them away from the river, passing close enough to the stormlodge that Galaeron could hear wet human snoring. He veered over to look inside, but felt a hand on his shoulder.

"You are doing yourself harm," said Melegaunt. "Suspicion is the food of wrath."

"If Lady Morgwais is not there, my suspicions will be allayed."

"They won't." Melegaunt released Galaeron's shoulder, leaving him free to do as he chose. "You'll doubt what you saw, or you will think that even if she wasn't there when you looked, she could have been there the night before. Doubt is the way of the shadow, and it is a powerful way indeed. Only trust can defeat it."

Melegaunt walked after the others, leaving Galaeron to his decision.

"Go ahead and look," said Malik, coming up behind

Galaeron. "In my experience, you cannot watch a woman too closely. They are all faithless harlots who will betray their husbands every chance they have."

"And you know this how?" asked Galaeron.

"As I told you, by my experience," said Malik. "My own wife I always kept safely locked in my house in Calimshan, and still she betrayed me at the first opportunity."

"Truly?" Shaking his head at the strangeness of human customs, Galaeron started after the others. "Then I shall take a lesson from you."

Malik looked puzzled, but fell in at Galaeron's side. "I suppose there are things a man does not want to know about his mother."

"Fortunately, I am an elf." Though Galaeron resented the human's witless slighting of his mother, he held his tongue for fear of giving his shadow another foothold. "My mother's decisions are her own to make. She and my father have not shared a house for thirty years."

Malik nodded knowingly. "I'm sorry to hear that. It must be hard for your father to see your name besmirched in such low fashion."

"Besmirched?" Galaeron felt himself growing angry over the disgrace—and knew instantly that the ire was not his own. No elf would consider it dishonorable for a woman to follow her heart. "It is not the same with elves as humans. There was no dishonor in her decision."

"Truly? I was not aware that elves were so free with their women." Malik looked into the dark forest, muttering something about there being no honor among fools.

They passed the village boundary, where the night watchers were observing from their perches in the trees. Takari offered no explanation for their furtive departure. Inhabitants and guests of Rheitheillaethor were free to come and go as they wished, so long as they did nothing to betray the village. Nor did she or Galaeron return the waves of farewell that came their way. With humans present, it would have been unthinkable to betray the positions of the sentries.

A hundred paces beyond the village, Galaeron asked, "Didn't you have a horse, Malik?"

"Her name is Kelda."

Malik opened his hand to display a set of reins, and suddenly the mare was behind him, her breath shooting white plumes over her master's shoulder. Galaeron looked back at the silvery snow and was astonished to see a long line of hoof prints alongside their own.

"I am beginning to see how you sneaked into Rheitheillaethor," said Galaeron. "Very impressive."

Malik shrugged. "It is a gift of the One."

"The One?"

Malik pretended not to hear the question, which only raised Galaeron's curiosity to the height of suspicion. He began to imagine the little man being the agent of some powerful archwizard or merciless tyrant—or even of the phaerimm themselves—but of course that was ridiculous. Malik hardly seemed able to attend to himself and his horse, much the less the business of some powerful and nefarious master. Such suspicions could only be the work of Galaeron's shadow.

They continued in silence for some distance, then Galaeron said, "Thank you for coming back to warn us about the beholders. If we can spare Rheitheillaethor their depredations, you will have the gratitude of every elf in the High Forest."

"You must think nothing of it," said Malik. "It was no great trouble. Because you cannot see a man does not mean he is not there."

Galaeron spent a few moments sorting through the statement, then asked, "You were with us the whole time?"

"A little distance behind," said Malik. "Talking trees have always made Kelda nervous."

Galaeron frowned. "If you were with us, then how could you know the beholders escaped Turlang?"

"I don't know they have," answered Malik, "only that they will be here soon."

Galaeron grew irritated. "How do you know?"

"Because Turlang's followers did not misdirect all of our pursuers," explained Malik. "One of the beholders was a very beautiful and cunning one. It lagged behind the rest and entered the wood a little north of the others and found, er—" He seemed to struggle with the words, then said, "Truly, the thing was a genius! I did not see it until it was on me, staring at me with all those wonderful eyes."

Galaeron had a sinking feeling. "How did you escape?"

"I, uh . . . Kelda is very . . ." Malik struggled to recall, then finally gave up and shrugged. "Why is that important? All that matters is I am here to warn you."

The qualmish feeling in Galaeron's stomach changed to fear, and he felt his hands curl into fists. "And what happened to the beholder? The one with the wonderful eyes?"

"It went after the others, I think. It wouldn't have been safe for it to go after you alone."

The grinding of his own teeth filled Galaeron's ears. "And how did you mark our trail?"

"What?" Malik's hand slipped inside his cloak, no doubt reaching for a hidden dagger. "You accuse me of betraying you?"

"Of course not." Certain that the anger he felt was as much his shadow's as his own, Galaeron reminded himself of how the beholder had beguiled Aris in Thousand Faces. Even if Malik had laid a trail, he was not to blame for his actions. "But why do you think the beholder let you go?"

"I see what you are thinking." Malik slipped a hand under his turban to scratch at something on his brow. "I am not that big a fool. Beholders are certainly cunning and handsome creatures, but I am a man of great will and stronger mind. I could never be tricked by one."

"Oh, never."

As Galaeron spoke, he waved his hand across Malik's face, and taking care not to use Melegaunt's coldmagic, started the incantation of a magic-dismissing spell.

"Murdering sorcerer!" Malik's hand dropped from his turban into his cloak and came out with a curved dagger. "Hold your tongue!"

Galaeron finished his incantation in time to jump back and avoid being sliced open. A torrent of fear and excitement raced through him, and with it came his shadow self, welling up from the darkness deep inside him. He saw his foot lash out and catch Malik behind the knee, dropping him to his back. Then Galaeron was over him, standing nose-to-snout with an angry-looking Kelda, using one foot to pin the little man's dagger hand in the snow.

"Stay your hand, I beg you!" Malik raised his free arm to shield his head. "I swear on my life, I never meant to betray you or your friends!"

Vala caught hold of Galaeron's arm. "What in the name of the Red Gauntlet are you doing?"

Galaeron pushed Kelda's snout aside, then stepped off Malik's trapped wrist. "One of the beholders beguiled him. I had to dispel its magic."

Vala glanced down at the arm she held. "So why do you need that?"

Galaeron looked down and was astonished to find his hand holding a half-drawn sword.

"By the Moon Harp!" Galaeron swore. He was so shaken he could only stare at the weapon. He had no memory of reaching for the weapon, even less of what he intended to do with it. He let the blade slide back into its scabbard, then began to fumble at his weapon belt, his hands trembling so hard he could not undo the clasp. "I could have killed him!"

"Yes, and you would have been lost." Melegaunt slipped past Vala and stood beside Galaeron. "Did I not warn you about using magic?"

"I didn't use coldmagic, only my own."

"No magic is your own," Melegaunt said. Despite the sternness of his words, his voice was soft. "All magic is power borrowed, and ever has unearned power opened the door to ruin."

Galaeron's hands finally stopped trembling long enough to undo his belt.

"Leave it," Melegaunt said. "Better to reach for a sword than a spell."

"That is easy for you to say." Malik pushed himself upright. "You are not the one he attacked."

"At least his sword is still in its scabbard," said Vala, eyeing Malik's dagger. "I would say neither of you had his wits about him."

Malik seemed as surprised as Galaeron to find a weapon in his hand. He shrugged. "A man must defend himself."

Aris and Takari arrived, Aris kneeling down behind Vala and still looming over the group, Takari stopping at Vala's side and raising her brow at the sight of Malik's horse. Before standing, Malik gathered a fold in his robe and drew his dagger through it to dry the blade. As it emerged, Galaeron noticed a resinous smear on the face of the blade.

"Malik, did you mark our trail with a blaze?"

"A blaze?" Malik asked. "What is that?"

He opened his robe to put the dagger away, but Takari snatched it from his hand. She ran her finger over the sticky resin several times, then held it to her nose.

"This blade has sap on it." Takari looked as though she might sheathe it in Malik's chest. "You've been cutting bark."

Malik's eyes bugged out like a pair of bird eggs. "By the Black Sun—the beholders! I marked our trail for them!"

"The Black Sun?" demanded Vala, who looked like she might kill Malik before Takari had the chance. "You worship Cyric?"

Malik winced, then closed his eyes and nodded. "But I beg you, do me no harm! It is not on his account I betrayed you."

"No one will harm you," said Aris. The giant stood the little man on his feet. "I myself have felt the beguiling magic of beholders."

Malik dared to look up. "You will protect me?"

"The blame is not yours," said Aris. "Their magic is powerful."

"But he *did* cut Turlang's trees—and we brought him into the forest," said Vala. She looked to Galaeron. "What will that mean for your mother?"

It was Takari who answered. "Turlang will never trust Lady Morgwais's word again, but if the village attends to the wounded trees and doesn't let them die, I think he will permit us to stay."

"Permit you to stay?" Galaeron drew a calming breath, then turned to Malik. "When was the last time you saw the beholder?"

Malik thought for a moment, then shuddered. "After the dancing ended. They are waiting up . . ." He paused and looked ahead, searching the forest for a familiar landmark, then gestured vaguely ahead. "Up where the trail turns toward the village. I, uh, 'blazed' that trail, too."

Takari glanced at Galaeron with a question in her eye, but he gave a quick shake of his head and looked away. Both knew exactly where Malik meant, but Galaeron did not want to tell the humans about the trailmaze—not when he had already done so much to endanger Rheitheillaethor.

"There's nothing to be done about the blazes now," said Galaeron. "And every minute we hesitate only makes it more likely they'll try to find the village itself. We have to leave another way and draw them after us."

Takari pointed at Malik. "What about that one? You are responsible for him by the pledge that Lady Morgwais vouchsafed to Turlang."

Vala set a hand on the pommel of her darksword. "I can think of a solution."

"That would not be fair," rumbled Aris. "I do not know about this Black Sun he worships, but he has been a true friend to me."

"Then I suppose we have no choice except to take him

along," said Melegaunt. "We certainly can't leave him running lose in Turlang's forest."

"No?" The smile that creased Malik's face was suspiciously broad—or so it seemed to Galaeron. "May the One rain a thousand blessings down on you all!"

"I'd leave well enough alone, were I you," growled Vala. "Aris only owes you one life, as best I can figure."

Galaeron fell in at the end of the line behind Vala, then suggested to Melegaunt that he and Aris follow a few dozen paces behind Takari. As they angled off to the north, Galaeron looked behind them and saw the trail Malik had blazed. Within a few hours, someone from the village would discover the atrocity and dress the wounds with special salves to aid the healing bark, but the damage would never fade. For as long as the trees remained standing, the long line of blazes would point straight toward the Heartblood River, where Rheitheillaethor stood hidden on the bent shore. Not for the first time, he wondered just how high a price he would be forced to pay to save Evereska.

A few minutes later, they crossed into a region of impenetrable thorn hedges and hidden precipices where the only safe footing was down the center of the snowy path. A bewildering array of forks and branches split off the main trail, winding along the rims of hedge-capped abysses and down bramblewalled tunnels, but the humans failed to notice any of the alternatives. The labyrinth's magic worked counter to intuition. Instead of presenting the intruder with a bewildering array of choices, the trailmaze allowed intruders to see only the path they happened to be following at the time. All of these trails twined back on each other in a tangled snarl of endless loops, slyly feeding the interloper from one circle to another without his knowledge. Though Rheitheillaethor suffered few invaders, those who did assault the village were usually found in the maze, either dead of starvation or trapped in the bottom of a hidden pit.

At last, they emerged from the trailmaze, the humans

none the wiser. The gray light of a winter dawn was brightening the sky behind the eastern treetops, filling the forest with shadows so faint they almost did not exist. They traveled a little more than a mile, then Galaeron called to Takari with the *wit wit wit* of a cardinal. She responded with a buzzing chick-a-dee call, and Galaeron knew she had located their foes. He studied the wood to the south and saw nothing except an endless tangle of snow-caked branches. Along the Desert Border, he might have hoped to match Takari's sharp eye—but here in her home, he would have to leave matters in her hands. He told her as much by repeating the cardinal's call twice more, and she led the way onward.

They traveled in single file, stepping only in Takari's tracks to avoid snapping an unseen stick or rustling a jumble of twigs. Aris's footfalls were as silent as Galaeron's, but Malik and his mount were by far the quietest in the group, Kelda placing her hooves more like those of a unicorn than a horse. There was more to Malik than being a simple Cyric worshiper, Galaeron felt certain—but he did not dwell on his suspicions, lest he invite a badly-timed attack from his shadow self.

The morning shadows were just growing darker when Takari began to move more rapidly, leading them just fast enough so that it became difficult to travel without making noise. Melegaunt sent a shiver up their spines by stepping on a stick and filling the air with a low crunch. Vala slipped on a slope and fell to her knees with a soft thud and muffled curse. As they crossed a broad creek, Aris broke through the ice, and a loud splash purled through the trees. Galaeron did not need to look to know their foes were following somewhere behind. Takari had increased the pace to attract their attention, and now she was leading them closer to the Dire Wood.

The sun finally made a full appearance, an orange disk hanging low in the trees, shining down into the forest and striping the snow with trunk-shadows as long as some roads. Takari began to vary the pace, slowing for a time and wandering an erratic course, then plowing ahead in a sudden, steady surge. Galaeron knew without looking that their enemies were preparing to attack, trying to slip unseen along their flanks to cut the party off. Takari was using the same trick that a band of Darkhold Zhentarim had once used against Galaeron's patrol, feigning fatigue and poor discipline so the pursuers would hold their attack in hopes of catching the quarry at rest. Galaeron tried to help by acting the part, gulping down handfuls of snow and quietly instructing the others to do likewise. Once or twice, he even lagged behind, trying to convince the beholders that with enough patience, they might pick off a straggler and make their job that much easier.

At last, the forest seemed to thin ahead, the barren trunks of the sugar maples and shadowtops giving way to a broad, blurry expanse of white. At first, Galaeron thought they might be coming to a meadow or snow-covered lake, but as they drew closer, the pale blur resolved itself into a wall of albino oak trees. Amazingly, they were still in full leaf, and they were completely white, from the bases of their alabaster trunks to the height of their blonde crowns. Galaeron could even see a few ivory acorns hanging from their white stalks.

Takari gave a series of sharp siskin *shicks*, and Galaeron realized he was looking at the Dire Wood. He had expected it to be darker, more ominous—twisted, somehow, and tangibly evil. Instead, it looked like something out of an elven myth, beautiful and illusory and ancient beyond the ages. Galaeron answered with his cardinal's *wit wit wit*, and Takari stopped, nocking an arrow and spinning to fire in the same quick motion.

"Run for the white trees!" Galaeron shoved Vala forward. "Melegaunt can use his magic there."

Takari's arrow hissed past Galaeron's head and thudded into something soft. He pulled his bow from his back and dived over a log, then came up with his own arrow nocked and pointed in the same direction.

A shrieking beholder hovered seventy paces distant, its eyestalks spraying colored rays in every direction, the fletching of Takari's arrow protruding from its big central eye. Galaeron leveled his shaft at the same target—then, twenty paces ahead of the creature, glimpsed a plume of snow rising from the ground as some invisible foe raced for the Dire Wood. In a breath, Galaeron adjusted his aim and loosed the arrow.

The shaft flashed across the plume at about rib height, then drew a startled cry before it ricocheted away and sank into the snow. Galaeron uttered a curse on all phaerimm, then leaped up on the log behind which he was hiding and pointed in the direction he had fired.

"Watch over there!" he yelled. "The phaerimm's invisible, with an arrow shield!"

He was rewarded for his bravery by a black flash from one of the beholder's eyes, but he was already diving for cover behind a snowy boulder. The log he had been standing on shriveled into a mass of rotten pulp, then the eye tyrant screeched again as another of Takari's arrows sank into its body. Galaeron nocked another arrow and hurled himself from his hiding place, aiming as he rolled. A cone of golden light flashed from one of the beholder's eyestalks, and the boulder dissolved into dust. Galaeron loosed his arrow at the creature's big eye and saw it sink out of sight.

This time, the beholder did not cry out. It simply dropped into the snow, its eyestalks drooping over its body like so many withered vines. Galaeron and Takari each planted a guarantee arrow into the lifeless orb and darted to new hiding places, and only then did they raise their heads to take stock.

Malik and his horse were nowhere to be seen, of course. Aris was charging in the direction Galaeron had pointed, swinging a ten-foot deadfall log back and forth in a noble, if somewhat misguided, effort to smash their invisible foe through sheer chance. Vala and Melegaunt were running in the wrong direction, charging through the snow toward Galaeron and Takari.

He waved them back, only to have them stop and gesture him in their direction. He tried again, this time more urgently. Once Melegaunt reached the Dire Wood, he would be free to use his shadow magic—and if they stood any chance at all of escaping the phaerimm and its minions, it was the arch-wizard's magic.

Vala ignored him, instead pointing her darksword at the fallen beholder. "It was only the scout," she yelled. "Now, will you two stop clowning around and get your pointy ears over here?"

When no rays of any color leaped out to silence her, Galaeron dared to look behind him. Much to his relief, the rest of the beholders were a hundred paces distant, coming up fast, but still fist-sized spheres weaving through the trees. Behind them hovered the tornado-shaped figure of a phaerimm, no larger than Galaeron's thumb, yet terrifying enough even at that distance.

A dull thump echoed through the wood as Aris connected with their invisible foe. To Galaeron's amazement, the stone giant did not instantly erupt into a pillar of flame or drop dead with a gaping hole through his torso. Instead, he gave a deep groan of satisfaction and started forward again, shaking the snow from the trees around him as he beat the ground with his makeshift club.

"Aris!" thundered Melegaunt. "Stop that at once!"

A series of colored flashes filled the air in front of Galaeron as the approaching beholders began to test the range of their eye rays. They were not close enough to strike yet, but it would not be long before the beams began to hit. Seeing that the foolish humans were determined to enter the Dire Wood together or not at all, he whistled to Takari and turned toward them. Even at their best pace, he doubted they would be fast enough to outrun the beholders' eye rays, but with a little dodging and weaving, they stood a reasonable—well, acceptable—chance of reaching the wood alive.

As Galaeron and Takari approached, Vala grabbed their hands and pulled them behind a tree. The beholder rays were starting to blast through the forest around them now, boring holes through massive shadowtop trunks and withering whole maples. Turlang would not be happy about the damage done to his forest, but as long as Melegaunt did not use his shadow magic within the wood, the treant would not hold them—or Lady Morgwais—responsible.

As Aris approached, a golden ray caught him square in the leg. The beam would have taken the torso off a normal man, but it merely drilled a melon-sized hole through the stone giant's thigh. He let out a great bellow and collapsed, shaking the ground beneath their feet as he crashed down behind Melegaunt.

"That will do!" yelled Melegaunt, directing himself to Vala.

Vala grabbed Galaeron's hand and pressed it into Takari's, then looped her own arm through his and grabbed hold of Melegaunt's with the other. The archwizard locked her hand in the crook of his elbow, then pressed his other palm to the giant's biceps and began the incantation to a shadow spell.

Galaeron jerked free of Vala's grasp. "What are you doing? If he breaks his word to Turlang—"

"Look to the shadow, elf!" Vala grabbed hold of Galaeron again, then used her chin to gesture along the length of the trunk-shadow in which they all stood. "He's drawing his magic through the Dire Wood."

Galaeron looked in the direction she indicated and saw that the tree's shadow extended clear through the ring of white oaks. Though he wasn't sure Melegaunt was living up to the letter of his pledge to Turlang, there was no time to debate the matter. A half dozen beholders appeared to either side of them, lacing the air with gleaming beams of destruction.

The rays shot past without touching anyone in the party, and only then did Galaeron notice how dim and hazy the eye tyrants appeared. Several of the creatures passed by within an arm's reach of the party and did not seem to notice them.

"Don't lose touch with me," warned Melegaunt. "At the moment, we are only shadows to them . . . and that is all that protects us."

"Then let's get out of here," said Takari. "The Dire Wood is not a hundred paces away."

"And may as well be a hundred miles," said Aris. "Look ahead."

An ankle-high curtain of black fire had arisen at the edge of the white forest. Though Galaeron guessed the flames would be invisible to anyone outside the Fringe, he saw no reason it could not be dispersed by a wizard of Melegaunt's power.

"We cannot hide in the shadows forever," he said. "Dispel it and let us be on our way."

"Gladly—were that not what Elminster expects," said Melegaunt.

"Elminster?" demanded Aris. "But he was sleeping—"

"Mystra's Chosen do not sleep," interrupted Melegaunt. He pointed in the general direction of the giant's feet and ran his fingers through the motions of a detection spell. "And they most certainly do not snore."

A ghostly figure in a floppy hat appeared twenty paces beyond Aris's feet. He was slowly creeping toward the Dire Wood, peering over his shoulder at the main body of beholders, then farther back at the hovering phaerimm, and finally at the eye tyrant scouts still passing back and forth through the shadow where Galaeron and his companions stood hiding in Melegaunt's spell.

A knowing twinkle came to Elminster's eye, and he started toward their hiding place. Melegaunt finished his spell, directing a finger in the archmage's direction. Almost at once, the beholders swung their eyestalks toward Elminster and began to assail him with rays both black and golden. Without exception, the attacks exploded into harmless starbursts against the archmage's spell shields, but the flurry was enough to stop the old man in his tracks. He lowered his bushy eyebrows, and Melegaunt uttered another spell. Instead of stopping a foot short, as had all the other attacks, the next beam—a golden one—struck the ancient wizard broadside and sent him cartwheeling across the snow.

"What are you doing?" Galaeron came near to releasing Takari to grab Melegaunt's arm. "You'll get him killed!"

"Hardly."

Elminster tumbled to a stop and came up glaring in Melegaunt's direction. He raised a shaming finger—and the phaerimm came floating up, waving all four arms in his direction.

Elminster vanished in cloud of crimson flame, and Melegaunt immediately uttered the reverse of a teleport spell.

In the next instant, Elminster's ancient figure appeared fifty yards to the east, cloaked in fire and shaking a long finger of flame. Though the gesture was directed roughly in Melegaunt's direction, it was easily ten degrees to the left, leaving no doubt in Galaeron's mind, at least, that the greatest mage in all Faerûn could not see through the simplest of the shadow wizard's spells.

The phaerimm streaked off toward the archmage, whistling something angry in its breezy language that drew the beholders after it. Elminster turned and fled, covering his retreat with a wall of scintillating colors. The phaerimm and beholders paused long enough to dispel the wall, then flew after the archwizard.

Melegaunt smiled. "*Now* we are ready for the Dire Wood."

CHAPTER SIXTEEN

29 Nightal, the Year of the Unstrung Harp

The Dire Wood was much darker and ominous than it appeared outside. Within a dozen paces, the pristine snow turned to soggy peat, and the albino oaks gave way to the shadowy depths of a petrified forest. The trees were as black as coal, with ebony limbs that ended in jagged stumps and twisted trunks propped against each other at every odd angle. The ground beneath the trees was as red as blood, full of scum and rot and the smell of decay. Galaeron could not imagine how they would ever wade through such a morass—much less find and reach Karse.

He looked to Takari and asked, "Which way?"

She shrugged. "I've never been beyond the Pale Ring, but no need to worry. Jhingleshod will find *us.*"

"Jhingleshod?"

Takari gave him an enigmatic smile. "Wulgreth's servant."

"His *servant*?" exclaimed Malik. Once the phaerimm and beholders had gone off chasing Elminster, the little man had appeared alongside their hiding place, whispering after them until Takari jerked him into the shadow. He still had not forgiven her for the indignity his fright caused him to visit upon his pants. "It might be easier to attract Wulgreth's attention by finding some trumpets to blow."

"Not every servant loves his master," replied Takari.

"While that is certainly true, it does not mean he will love us."

"We'll worry about Jhingleshod later," said Galaeron, looking back toward Turlang's forest. "But we can't wait here. Sooner or later, either Elminster or the phaerimm will be back—maybe both. We'll leave as soon as Aris is ready."

Kelda eyed the bog and snorted, prompting Malik to pat her neck. "There is nothing to worry about, girl. Aris will be happy to carry you."

Galaeron was not so sure the giant would be able to carry himself, much less Malik's horse. Aris was seated along the inner edge of the Pale Ring, madly chipping at a small rock into a granite cylinder just small enough to fill the hole the beholder's disintegration ray had left through his thigh. He blew the dust off, held the stone over the wound for a moment, tapped a couple of flakes off one side, then passed it down to Vala, who carefully lowered the rock into the wound.

The giant winced in pain, then laid his hammer over the wound and rumbled an incomprehensible prayer to the dour god of his race. A plume of crimson steam shot from the hole on both sides of his leg, then Aris pressed his back against an oak and held the hammer in place as the wound filled with stone-colored flesh. Though his clenched jaw betrayed how much the healing hurt, he remained stoic and silent.

When the rising vapor paled to pink, Aris returned his hammer to his pouch. The wound was still a puckered mess, but there was nothing tentative about his movements when he pushed himself to his feet and reached down for Kelda. The mare nickered, and dragging Malik along, backed toward the Pale Ring.

"You won't need to carry her," said Melegaunt. He turned to Takari and held out a palm. "If you will lend me your sword."

Takari glanced at Galaeron, then reluctantly passed her weapon over. Melegaunt tipped it toward the sun and uttered a conjuration spell, all the while passing his palm over the underside of the blade. The side facing his hand grew black and hazy, while the steel facing the sun gleamed with silver sunlight. Takari scowled and started to reach for her weapon, but Galaeron waved her off. Though he had never seen anything quite like this spell, he recognized the general form as a Making, and he doubted it would harm Takari's weapon.

By the time Melegaunt finished, the dark side of the blade was as black and deep as a fissure in a cavern floor, while the light side shone too brilliantly to look at. He turned the dark face toward the bog, and a black stripe appeared on the surface of the water. When he adjusted the angle, the stripe broadened to a width of two feet and stretched to thirty paces.

Melegaunt returned the sword to Takari. "Lay the shadow where you wish. It will keep our feet dry."

Takari accepted the weapon with a gaping mouth, then stepped gingerly onto the shadow. When her foot did not pass through into water, she started forward.

Melegaunt motioned the others onto the black band. "Quickly. The path lasts only a few moments."

Vala drew her sword and started along the trail without hesitation, followed by Malik and Kelda, who was persuaded to step onto the shadowy trail only by the threat of being picked up again. Aris took two precarious steps before announcing it was like walking on thread and stepped off to wade alongside. Melegaunt went next, and Galaeron brought up the rear.

The bog was more of a mess than it looked, with a muddy

bottom that sucked at Aris's boots and filled the petrified forest with a steady cadence of slurping. Takari's trail was by necessity crooked and irregular, detouring around blockades of tangled trees, occasionally narrowing to mere inches as it passed beneath a half-fallen trunk. The air was damp and biting, numbing their faces and stiffening their fingers with cold. They were all shivering within a hundred steps, and the anemic rays of the rising sun were too thin to warm them.

"I have been in howling blizzards warmer than this swamp!" complained Malik. "How can the water not be ice?"

"It is not cold you are feeling, it is death," said Melegaunt. "Death ancient and mad and mighty, death sorrowful and ashamed."

"Then what are we doing here?" demanded Malik. "If this Wulgreth is mighty enough to drain the heat from an entire swamp, we have no chance at all."

"Not Wulgreth," said Melegaunt. "I am speaking of Karsus. It is his magic that makes the Dire Wood, and his mad regret that twists everything within it."

Karsus was a name that Galaeron, at least, recognized from his years at the Academy of Magic. Karsus was the foolish Netherese wizard who had tried to steal the Weave from the goddess of magic and brought the floating cities of Netheril crashing to the ground.

Daring to hope he was finally beginning to understand Melegaunt's plan, Galaeron asked, "So it is Karsus's magic you mean to use against the phaerimm?"

"In a manner of speaking, yes." Melegaunt ducked under a tree trunk and came face-to-flank with Malik's horse, which had slowed as the little man paused to eavesdrop. The wizard slapped the horse on the rump, urging her forward and nearly knocking Malik off the trail, then said quietly, "You will see."

Galaeron silently cursed the Cyricist, then found himself debating the merits of killing him and being done with it. Takari would not think much of the idea, but Melegaunt clearly had his suspicions about the fellow, and the wizard had proven on more than one occasion that he would not balk at doing whatever was necessary to save Evereska. Vala would agree to whatever Melegaunt decided, so the only problem was Aris, and if it came to that, even Galaeron's magic was powerful enough to . . . the thought brought him to a stunned halt, scarcely able to believe how easily his shadow had crept up on him. The dark thoughts had seemed so normal.

So shocked was Galaeron that he barely noticed Melegaunt disappearing around the next tangle of stony trees, but he did notice when the path vanished beneath his feet and plunged him to his waist in icy water.

His breath left him in a shriek, and his feet turned instantly to blocks of numb flesh. His knees began to ache with cold, his thighs felt like slabs of ice, and his body drained into the swamp. He staggered a single step and nearly fell when the mud refused to release his boot. Something large and soft bumped his leg and stayed. He cried out again and pulled his dagger, but could not bring himself to reach into the icy water to find out what it was.

Galaeron heard another splash and looked forward to see Melegaunt dropping into the water as the shadow trail vanished beneath him. The wizard let out a surprised roar, then spread his hands and levitated himself out of the water. The path was fast disappearing behind Malik and his horse, but with Vala and Takari spinning around to look toward Galaeron, they were helpless to continue forward.

Galaeron waved them on. "K-k-k-keep m-m-moving!"

The trail vanished beneath Kelda's rear hooves, and that was all the impetus the mare needed to nose Malik forward. He gave Vala an urgent shove, and they were moving again, staying a few bare steps ahead of the vanishing shadow trail. Takari started to lay a crooked course back toward Galaeron, but Aris gestured them forward again.

"Go." The giant plucked Melegaunt from the air, then sloshed back to Galaeron. "I'll get them."

The soft thing on Galaeron's leg slithered around his thigh, a tiny set of scales or barbs or whatever ticking against his elven chain mail. He took a deep breath, then reached into the water with both hands and felt something huge and fleshy around his leg. He jabbed his dagger into its body, then pulled it from the water and immediately wished he had not.

The thing was as long as his arm, with a slimy black body tapering from a round head to a narrow tail. He could not imagine what it was until he turned it over and saw a ring of sharp little teeth surrounded by a fleshy-lipped sucker.

"By the Fey Wand!" He held the thing at arm's length. "It's a leech."

"More my size, I'd say." Aris stooped down and crushed the creature between two fingers, then plucked Galaeron up in his free hand. "And you should see the dragonflies up here."

Galaeron saw a lacy blur nearly four feet across dart past the giant's head, then said, "As l-long as there aren't any s-spiders." Though the swamp was no longer draining his body heat, he could not seem to stop shivering, and even Melegaunt looked a little blue around the lips. "Can you c-cast a warming spell?"

Melegaunt gave a wry smile. "Unfortunately, sh-shadow magic does not create heat." He shivered, then added, "From normal cold I can protect us, but from this life-draining chill . . ." He only shook his head.

Galaeron hesitated, already knowing Melegaunt's response, then said anyway, "I can use the Weave—"

"How often must I warn you?" Melegaunt glared at Galaeron a moment, then looked up at Aris. "You do not seem troubled."

"Nor do I seem troubled by the leeches—but seeming does not make a thing so." He raised a foot out of the water to display the bloated black forms dangling to his ankle. "If we can find a stone, I can ask Skoreaus Stonebones to make it warm for us."

Galaeron eyed the petrified trees they were passing, but decided not to suggest using one of them. The magic that had stolen their lives seemed as corrupt as the shadow trying to steal his.

Aris weaved through the petrified tangle until he caught the others, then placed Galaeron behind Takari and Melegaunt behind Vala, leaving Malik and his horse to bring up the rear. Recalling that Cyric was the human god of strife and murder, Galaeron was not so certain he liked the idea of having Malik behind everyone else—but a few stumbling steps convinced him he was too weak to assume the post himself.

Conscious that the phaerimm and beholders—or perhaps even Elminster—would soon be coming up behind them, they continued westward at their best pace, Aris now assuming the duty of watching for foes behind. The strength continued to drain from Galaeron's body, and he began to shiver uncontrollably. Vala sheathed her sword and carried him in her arms long enough to strip him out of his wet clothes, then volunteered her own cloak to keep him warm instead. When that did not work, Takari volunteered hers, and even Malik produced a heavy woolen cape. The extra weight only seemed to tire Galaeron all the more. He began to feel queasy and lethargic, and it became a regular duty for Vala to catch him by the arm.

Melegaunt and Aris fared better, though the swamp had clearly taken its toll on them as well. The archwizard stumbled along mumbling to himself about hearts and heavy magic, and even became muddled enough to explain a little of his shadow magic to Malik. Aris simply started to slow, pausing now and again to brace himself against a petrified tree and check back for enemies.

The sun was high overhead when the trees finally vanished and the bog became a broad river that seemed to flow one direction on the near side and the opposite way along the other side. The far bank sloped up from the water in a gentle slope covered with gnarled black oaks—no doubt as petrified as the bog trees—but at least standing on dry ground.

Takari laid the shadow path perhaps halfway across the river and started across, only to watch the swirl of a dark eddy catch it near the end and sucked it beneath the surface. She saved them all by flipping the sword around and severing the trail with a flash from the bright side of the blade, then quickly laid another path and tried again. This time, the eddy caught the trail only a dozen paces ahead, barely giving her time to flip the blade.

The horse whinnied from the back of the line, and Malik called, "Keep going! There is an eel behind us large enough to eat Kelda!"

Takari laid a trail along the edge of the river and, when the shadowy ribbon did not swirl away in a new eddy, raced forward to give the others room.

"Given what the bog did to Galaeron, I don't fancy taking a swim in the river," she called over her shoulder. "I don't suppose you've another way to cross, Melegaunt?"

"Cer . . . tainly."

Melegaunt's voice was so weak and thick-tongued that Galaeron hazarded a glance over his shoulder—prompting Vala to extend a guiding hand as the trail rounded a bend in the river.

"Why don't we use that bridge?"

"Bridge?" Galaeron asked, confused.

"There's always a bridge," said Vala, pointing past Galaeron's nose.

Galaeron looked forward again and saw the river purling over a stretch of dark, submerged stone. At each end of the stretch stood ruined bridge towers, their crowns jagged and broken, their windows black and unbarred. In front of the near tower stood a hazy figure in plate armor, his hands wrapped around the hilt of a huge two-handed sword resting tip-down in front of him.

"And a knight," called Malik. "There is always a knight."

Galaeron drew his sword and heard the others doing the

same, but Takari waved their weapons down. As they drew closer to the knight, it grew apparent he stood ankle deep in the river, water gurgling around his feet and mist swirling around him. His armor was coated in rust, while the face peering out from his raised visor seemed nothing but moldering bone and watchful, coal-dark eyes.

As they approached, he unsheathed his great sword and held it before him, the tip pointed at Takari. She stopped in her tracks and lowered her own sword.

"Well met, old Jhingleshod," she said. "Oft have I watched your wanderings from the Pale Ring."

"And there you should have stayed, elf. You have no business in the land of death."

"Not I, but my friends." Takari stepped aside and gestured to Galaeron. "They come in need of your aid."

"My aid?" Jhingleshod's black eyes shifted to Galaeron. "What aid can I give thee but a quick death?"

From the end of the line came a pair of splashes, then a startled whinny and hissed curse as the shadow vanished beneath Malik and his horse. Jhingleshod lifted his chin at the sound, but kept his attention—and his great sword—fixed on Galaeron.

"We have need of Karsus's magic," Galaeron said. "If you can show us—"

"Not we." Jhingleshod jabbed his sword at Galaeron's chest. "You. What come you seeking?"

"I come to save—"

"Think well, elf," Jhingleshod warned. "To answer wrong is worse than death."

Galaeron paused to consider the question. He had been about to say he came to save Evereska, but Jhingleshod's reaction left little doubt that the answer would not have been the one the dead knight wished to hear. Another splash came from the end of the line, and this time it was Melegaunt's voice that cried out.

Jhingleshod paid the noise no attention and kept his dead

gaze fixed on Galaeron. "Your answer? You have come far, elf—you must know what you are seeking."

"I do." Galaeron glanced at Takari, then over his shoulder to Vala. "Absolution. I seek pardon for my mistake."

A black light flared in Jhingleshod's eyes, and his skeleton's jaw opened as though smiling. "There is a boon I would ask for my help, elf. Will you give it?"

Galaeron started to ask what the boon was, then thought better of it. Jhingleshod would not react well to pointless barter. He demanded unflinching honesty of those who sought his help, and the truth was that Galaeron would pay anything to absolve his mistake. He simply nodded.

Jhingleshod's eyes shifted to Takari as though to ask something, but seemed to find the answer they were seeking in her frightened expression and looked back to Galaeron.

"Go," the knight said. He pointed through the rusted-out remains of a portcullis to the submerged bridge. "If you have the strength to reach the other side, I will do what can be done to help you."

Galaeron left the shadow trail and stepped through the portcullis without hesitation, but stopped on the other side. "My friends—"

Jhingleshod whirled on him, bringing his great sword around so swiftly that Galaeron could not have blocked the rusty weapon had he tried. The flat of the blade caught him full in the shoulder and slammed him into the musty tower wall.

"Go!" Jhingleshod motioned again toward the bridge. "My bargain with you is done."

Galaeron felt an angry darkness well up inside him and gathered himself to spring, but Takari desperately shook her head and flicked her eyes toward the bridge. Galaeron remained crouched, trying to fight down the black fury within. Together, he and his companions might be able to destroy Jhingleshod, but what then? Takari had said he could guide them to Karse, and Galaeron had seen enough of the

Dire Wood to know how valuable such assistance would be. He gathered himself, and letting his aching arm dangle at his side, staggered through the cold water.

Jhingleshod turned to Aris next, and as Galaeron passed through the shadowed archway asked, "What seek you?"

Galaeron stepped out of the tower onto the mossy surface of a submerged bridge. Though no more than three inches of water ran over the surface, the river's purling drowned out Aris's answer. Reluctant to anger Jhingleshod by tarrying, Galaeron continued forward.

The stone was as slick as ice, so that even the shallow flow threatened to sweep his feet from beneath him. He sheathed his sword and dropped to a low crouch, carefully sliding one foot ahead of the other and twisting it into the mossy surface. He could feel the heat of his body rushing down through his feet into the water. A light fog rose around him, veiling the far shore behind a pale haze, and he grew dizzy from the cold.

As Galaeron crossed the midpoint of the bridge, the river changed direction and began to flow across from the other side. The effect was more than a little disorienting, making him feel he had somehow gotten himself turned around and was now approaching the wrong tower. He closed his eyes and continued blind until the current's new direction felt right.

Galaeron was nearly across when the purling changed pitch, and the water began to surge over his feet erratically. A flicker of dark motion next to the bridge caught his attention, then he saw the bloated body of a drowned human floating on the surface, bobbing in place as the current pitched him repeatedly against the bridge.

Dressed in knee high boots and black leather armor, the man was bearded and large, with a crooked nose and skin as blue as his open eyes. There were no signs of any wounds or broken bones, though the absence of a helm and weapons belt suggested there had been time to shed both before drowning. Galaeron shuddered, wondering if the fellow had fallen victim to the river's life-stealing waters and simply fell in. The man's eyes rolled toward Galaeron, then a blue hand rose out of the water, stretching out as though reaching for help.

Galaeron cried out and sprang back, landing on his seat when his feet slipped out from beneath him. The current immediately threatened to sweep him into the riffle on the other side of the mossy bridge. He rolled to his stomach and flung his arms out, catching hold of the bridge on the upstream side. The current whirled him around, spinning him so that his feet hung over the downstream edge. The river poured over his head and down his throat, chilling him to the bone and threatening to fill his lungs. He clamped his jaw shut and felt the water bubbling into his nose, a mad, animate killer determined to have his life. Already his body was growing weary and stiff, the life draining out of him everywhere the river touched. He blew the air from his lungs, forcing the water out through his mouth and nose, then drew a stiff leg up so he could stand—and felt the dead man's hand clamp his wrist.

Screaming, Galaeron shook the water from his head and found himself staring into the man's undead eyes. The fellow's lips drew back in a gruesome grin, displaying a mouthful of broken fangs and a black wagging tongue. A dozen spells leaped at once to Galaeron's mind. As a tomb guard recruit, he had been well-drilled in the weaknesses of the undead—almost as well-drilled as he had been in horrors awaiting those who fell to them. He thrust a hand into the creature's face and opened himself to the Weave—then felt the icy ache of shadow magic rushing into him instead. Galaeron let the spell drop, and holding onto the bridge only with his free hand, rolled his wrist around against the creature's thumb.

A living man would have released Galaeron's arm and pulled his hand away in pain. The ghoul continued to hold, trying to use strength against leverage. So weak was

Galaeron that the tactic nearly succeeded. The first time he tried, the strength simply left his arm, and his hand stopped halfway through the motion, hanging palm up between him and his blue-faced attacker.

Galaeron shoved the arm forward, jabbing a fingertip into the creature's eye. Even a dead man had to flinch, and Galaeron finished his motion, bringing his hand over and down behind the ghoul's. The thing's thumb snapped with a sharp crack, folding over backward to expose a jagged spear of coal black bone.

Galaeron shot his hand up behind its neck and caught it by the back of the skull. He slammed its head into the side of the bridge, at the same time pulling himself back onto the walkway and swinging his feet up beneath him.

The ghoul lashed out madly with both arms, catching Galaeron behind the ankles and trying to sweep his feet from under him. The elf drew his knees straight up, and reaching across his body for his sword, came down kicking. One heel caught the ghoul in the back of the head. The other landed on the mossy bridge and slipped free, dropping Galaeron to a knee directly in front of the beast. His sword cleared his scabbard and struck the ghoul's face in the same motion, its gleaming elven steel slicing through the head just above the jawline.

Galaeron followed through gracefully, his head turning to follow the sweep of his blade tip, and saw a second creature springing out of the water in front of him. This one was smaller than the first, with a female's rounder curves, long black claws, and the yellow eyes of a wight. She was also much faster, stomping Galaeron's sword arm down on the bridge and pinning it there as she snapped her other foot around in a vicious kick.

Thinking to trap her foot with a hook block, Galaeron caught the blow on his forearm—but he was simply too tired and weak. The impact knocked him to his back, then the current spun his feet downstream again, leaving him affixed to the bridge only by his pinned sword arm.

The wight crouched down above his head and grabbed his throat, her icy claws piercing his flesh in so many places he was surprised not to see warm blood spurting up before his eyes. She bared two long rows of sharp teeth and pulled him toward her, twisting her head around to bite.

Galaeron tried to break free and roll away. He was too weak even to push his free hand into the crook of the wight's arm. He tried to kick his feet up to wrap her head in a leg-lock, but his legs felt as numb and heavy as gold. His life was seeping out by the second, being sucked out by the spirit-stealing touch of the undead, being robbed from him by the vigor-draining waters of the shadowed river.

The wight pressed her teeth to Galaeron's throat. He spun toward her with the little strength remaining to him, thrusting his free hand into her face and summoning the incantation to a spell of light. A surge of icy power flooded Galaeron's body as it filled with coldmagic, but he had more pressing worries than his shadow at the moment. He called out the mystic syllable, and a brilliant beam of silver light shot from his palm.

The wight screeched madly and spun away, leaving Galaeron to float across the bridge. He rolled after the wight, digging the numb fingers of his free hand into the cold moss and whipping his sword across the back of the creature's feet with the other. The thing stumbled two steps forward before crashing into the water with a pair of severed heels. Galaeron pulled himself to his knees and brought his sword down across the wight's back. The blow was clean and, had there been any strength to it, he would have cleaved the thing in half. As it was, his elven steel bit deep enough to maim even a beast of the undead.

The wight stiffened and tried to roll toward her foe, but succeeded only in twisting her torso open along the wound. As she looked down in bewilderment, Galaeron raised a hand and spoke a single mystic syllable. This time, he barely noticed as the coldmagic flooded his body, nor did he care that the bolts shooting from his hand were as black and frigid as shadow. It only mattered to him that the undead thing before him had finally gone limp and lost her hold on the bridge, and that the murky current was at last carrying her away over the riffle.

The gate tower stood only a dozen paces away, the dry ground beyond its shadowed archway offering warmth and refuge, or at least an escape from the cold battle on the bridge. Galaeron staggered to his feet and discovered he did not feel nearly as weak as he had several minutes before. To the contrary, while he felt tired and cold, his strength seemed to be returning. There was a peculiar ardor burning inside him, not so much anger as resolve, not so much brutality as ruthlessness.

When no more undead appeared to attack him, he started toward the gate tower, no longer concerned about the slick moss underfoot, thinking only of the battles to come and the magic he would find in Karse—then he recalled Melegaunt following behind, and the others he was traveling with, all following in his footsteps, all trying to cross the dark bridge behind him.

Galaeron spun on his heel and saw Takari slipping and sliding toward him, pushing her sword into its scabbard. Twenty paces behind her, Vala was spinning and whirling across the bridge, her black blade weaving a dark mesh around her and Melegaunt as she slashed at the translucent figures of two withered, shrewish-looking ghosts trying to dart past her flashing defenses. Beyond them, a pair of inky silhouettes were flitting around Aris's steam-shrouded head, darting in to slash at his eyes and ears with black talons. Malik and his horse were nowhere to be seen, of course, but Jhingleshod was not far behind the others, a hazy glimmer of orange that appeared briefly every time the stone giant took a step.

Galaeron pointed his sword over Takari's shoulder. "The others!" He staggered a few steps back across the bridge, his numb legs and weary body stirring themselves for another fight. "They need help!"

"Are you mad?" Takari intercepted him and pressed her hand to where the wight had clasped his throat. Her palm was as hot as fire against his skin. "The humans can take care of themselves. We need to get you to shore."

"Shore? What do you take me for?" Galaeron jerked her hand down. "A coward?"

Takari's eyes flashed. "Only a fool." She thrust her palm into his face, displaying a coating of blood so dark it was almost black. "Half your throat is ripped away, your face is as pale as glass, and all you can think about is a human minx with wild eyes and milkbags the size of a thkaerth's!"

Too stunned to reply, Galaeron raised a hand to his throat and felt a gash four fingers wide. How the wound had missed his veins he could not imagine, any more than he could understand how he had the strength to continue standing. There was no pain, no dizziness, no sign of the injury except an overwhelming sense of cold, and even that seemed to be fading.

Takari drew her sword and, grasping Melegaunt's arm, turned back to help the others. "Let's go, then—but I'll never forgive you if you get yourself killed over a human."

They had barely taken two steps before Vala's darksword found one of the ghosts, cleaving it down the center. The creature came apart with a horrid screech, the two halves of its gossamer form paling into wisps of fading light. Melegaunt reached over her shoulder, spraying a string of shadowy darts through the second ghost. The black bolts vanished inside the creature with no visible effect.

Seeing what had become of its fellow, the ghost darted away from Vala and hovered alongside the bridge, well out of her reach. It stretched a hand toward her sword, then flowed into the dark glass and vanished from sight. Galaeron stretched out his arm, trying to slap the weapon from her grasp with the flat of his own blade. His reach fell just short.

"Vala, drop your sword!"

Even as Galaeron called out, Vala's eyes went glassy and white. She whirled on Melegaunt, her movements now fitful and rigid as she raised her arm for an overhand chop. Jaw dropping, the wizard pivoted into the clumsy attack, throwing his arms out in a desperate block and catching Vala square in the chest. He bellowed two syllables and sent her body blasting past. She landed two paces away on the downstream side of the bridge, flat on her back and dazed from the explosion.

Vala's hand began to open, and the darksword dipped into the water.

"Grab her sword!" As Galaeron tried to spring past Melegaunt, he slipped on the mossy stone and fell to a knee. "It has her soul!"

Melegaunt stooped down and reached for the weapon, then her white eyes flicked in his direction, and he abruptly drew back. "She'll kill me!"

Vala slipped over the riffle and started a lazy spin downstream, quickly starting to sink as her scale armor pulled her beneath the surface. Ignoring the fact that even elven chain mail was not light, Galaeron dropped his own sword on the bridge and sprang over Melegaunt after her.

He entered the icy river headfirst and pulled himself down through the riffle with two quick strokes, then caught a handful of hair and continued to kick deeper. It would do no good to save Vala if he allowed the darksword to sink with her soul. He drew himself down by her hair, stretching his free hand toward the glass sword—then suddenly found the point driving up through the water toward his heart.

Still holding onto her hair, Galaeron rolled behind her and changed hands, then reached around her shoulder to grab her sword arm from behind. Vala whirled and kicked, trying to spin free, but managing only to drive them a few feet upward before they began to sink again. Galaeron released her hair and slipped his arm around her throat, using the crook of his elbow to clamp down on the vulnerable veins in her neck.

Vala went limp almost instantly. Her head tipped to one side and her eyes rolled back in their sockets, and the hand holding the darksword came open even before Galaeron could twist the weapon free. He caught it by the hilt and kicked for the surface, already so cold he barely noticed its freezing touch.

Had he been fresh, or had Vala's scale armor been as light as elven chain, he might have pulled them both to the surface. As it was, he barely had the strength to keep from sinking deeper—and that strength was fading fast. Slipping her darksword back into her scabbard, he drew his dagger and began to cut the buckles on her heavy breast plate.

Galaeron had just finished one side when he saw Malik's chubby silhouette drift past above. He thought for a moment that he was merely imagining things, or that the cold water had finally taken him. The little human did not strike him as the heroic type, but there had been that time in Thousand Faces, and now here he was again, his turban unwinding behind him as he dived for them from above. Not taking the time to sheathe his dagger, Galaeron let it fall and raised his hand.

Malik ignored it and circled around behind them, trailing a thin rope. Galaeron felt the human pushing something under his arm and took the line from his grasp, then passed it around Vala and back to his rescuer. Malik tied a quick knot, then the current began to pull at them as the cord caught. Wrapping his legs around Vala for extra security, Galaeron grabbed the rope with both hands and pulled.

He had barely begun before the rope jerked them to the surface, and his breath returned in a series of cold coughs. He felt Malik clinging to his belt, crying out in terror and all but dragging him back beneath the surface as he struggled to reach the rope. Galaeron caught hold of the little man's collar and pulled him up.

"Malik! Our thanks!" Galaeron guided his hand to the rope. "That was a brave thing you did."

"Think nothing of it," coughed the little man. "I have a bad habit of doing brave things in bad causes."

Unsure of just how to take this, Galaeron rolled Vala onto her back, then finally looked upstream, to where the other end of the rope was attached to Kelda's saddle. The mare was just trotting into the archway beneath the bridge tower, pulling them diagonally across the current as she moved. Takari and Melegaunt were slipping and sliding along the bridge as they scrambled after her, while Aris, having somehow freed himself of the two shades, was kneeling at the edge of the bridge, stretching a long arm out to grab the line.

He finally succeeded, then pulled them to the side of the bridge and hoisted them to safety. Malik whistled Kelda to a stop, and Galaeron set to work on Vala. Her armor was scorched and dented from the spell that had launched her into the river, but any injuries the blast had caused her appeared less important than her near drowning. He turned her on her side and, bracing her between his knees, pushed on her back to force out the water. She began to cough, spewing cold river water from her lungs, and started to breathe on her own.

"She'll live," pronounced Aris.

"But not recover." This from Jhingleshod, who was stepping around Aris's far side. "Not until she is free of this river."

Galaeron glared up at the ghostly knight, barely able to restrain his dark anger. "You might have warned us."

"And what would you have learned by that?" Jhingleshod looked away and continued forward, following Melegaunt and Takari into the shadows beneath the next bridge tower. "Were you not strong enough to defeat the servants, I do not think you would have been strong enough to defeat the master."

Galaeron glared after the rusty knight for a moment, then scooped Vala up and started after him. As they passed into the shadows beneath the bridge tower, she began to stir, her arm slipping around his neck, her eyes fluttering open.

"G-Galaeron?" She seemed barely conscious, hardly able to utter his name. "You . . . came after me?"

"Did you think I would let you drown?"

"Then we're alive?"

"At the moment, yes."

He smiled, and, as they stepped out onto the dry road, Vala's lips were suddenly pressed to his, her warm tongue dancing softly against his. Surprised as he was, he would not have minded, were it not for the guilty shame in Melegaunt's eyes—or the hurt in Takari's.

CHAPTER SEVENTEEN

30 Nightal, the Year of the Unstrung Harp

A bevy of meadow quail broke from the grass some miles distant, two dozen plump flecks scattering into the air. The sight of so many juicy birds brought the water to Aubric Nihmedu's mouth—as it did to the mouths of all the Noble Blades and Lordly Wands tucked into their spider holes across the sun-baked hillside. For a nearly tenday now, the Swords of Evereska had subsisted on crisped lizard and spell-baked mouse, forsaking even cacti and wolfroot for fear that the phaerimm would notice any plant-gathering. It was hardly the ordeal proud aristocrats envisioned when they joined the Swords of Evereska, but no one complained. Since forsaking open combat for ambushes and surprise attacks, they had cut their losses from staggering to merely heavy, and they had killed more than twenty phaerimm. By Aubric's estimate, the Swords would need only ten lives apiece to eradicate the remaining phaerimm from the Shaeradim.

Two hundred paces ahead of the quail, a pair of moon foxes darted across a stream, herding four young kits along between them. There was something out there, slinking into the eastern end of the Blazevale—the broad, sand-scoured valley that separated the Sharaedim from the Greycloak Hills to the north. Though curious, Aubric resisted the temptation to augment his keen elf sight with magic. Not two hours before, sentries had sent the Swords scrambling for cover with news of an approaching company. Aubric had to settle for staring out across the plain with his naked eye, waiting patiently for the next hint of the creature's presence.

Soon enough, he noticed a narrow riffle in the grass. The disturbance was advancing steadily toward a high, bowl-shaped outcrop known as Rocnest, a natural citadel that had housed elf garrisons for nearly a thousand years during the Crown Wars. Though the fortress had been abandoned after the fall of Aryvandaar, its location between Evereska and the Greycloak Hills had lately prompted talk of reclaiming it as a watch post.

Aubric's heart began to pound faster. The riffle was easily half a mile front to back, too long to be caused by an animal and far too straight. It advanced steadily toward the natural fortress, pausing neither to search for prey or check for predators. There was only one creature that traveled so efficiently, so confidently in the open plain. Aubric flipped the top off his spider hole and turned up the hill, flashing the signal to prepare for battle.

Rhydwych Bourmays, the company artmaster, poked her sable-tressed head out of the next hole. "You cannot be thinking to attack!" she hissed. "Ten thornbacks is too many—especially with illithids and beholders to back them up."

"Tell your wands to prepare themselves," Aubric said, sidestepping the argument. "There is help for Evereska out there, and I won't stand idle while the phaerimm ambush it."

Rhydwych arched her thin eyebrows and looked across the plain. "Invisible is good." She studied the line a few seconds longer, then said, "And fast, I'll give them that. But help is an exaggeration. There can't be two hundred riders in the column."

"We don't know who those two hundred are, Artmaster—or what they intend." His tone was sharper than he intended, perhaps because of the disappointment Rhydwych's question had engendered in his own heart. By the Swords' best estimate—an estimate they had been unable to communicate to Evereska or anyone else—there were two hundred *phaerimm* in the Sharaedim. "Will you signal your wands, or must I?"

"No need to get nasty, Lord Nihmedu," snipped Rhydwych. "I know the ladder of authority—though you may be sure the House of Swords will review it if matters go badly."

"If matters go badly, they will have no need."

He shooed Rhydwych off with a wave, then turned to find a watchman bounding down the shoulder of the hill. Aubric signaled his Noble Blades to hold steady, then began to tighten his armor. By the time he finished, the sentry was beside him, and a hundred Swords stood scattered across the hill.

"The phaerimm weren't hunting *us*, Aubric." As a superior noble, it would have been beneath the Gold elf to address Aubric by his title. "They're on the move."

"Down the Blazevale, Lord Dureth?"

Dureth nodded. "How—"

"Someone is trying to reach Rocnest." Aubric pointed toward the grass riffle. "It may be help."

The elf looked in the direction indicated. "If it is, it's not much." Dureth narrowed his eyes, then said, "Unless . . ."

"Your thoughts do me no good unless you speak them."

"I'm wondering about the Rocnest," explained Dureth. "Why trap yourself there—"

"Unless you'll be able to fight your way out—"

"But you need to defend yourself until you can," finished Dureth. "Could they be erecting a gate?"

Aubric nodded. "It's all that makes sense."

Dureth pointed toward the hill's western shoulder, which descended gently to the plain near the mouth of the Blazevale. "We'd better hurry. They'll be closing on the Deadwall."

Aubric signaled the Swords to follow Dureth. "Lead the way—and quickly."

The Noble Blade started forward at a steady jog, and Aubric hurried after him. The Deadwall was the intangible barrier the phaerimm had erected around the Sharaedim and Greycloak Hills. It had earned its name not because it killed everything that tried to walk or fly through it—though it did—but because it blocked all magical communication and travel with the outside world. Rhydwych and her mages spent every spare hour trying to defeat the barrier, but had yet to succeed.

The Swords bounded up the slope in utter silence. At the top of the ridge, Dureth, Aubric, and Rhydwych crawled to the crest and peered into the Blazevale.

They found themselves a few hundred paces above the phaerimm, who were advancing toward Rocnest. In addition to the ten thornbacks, there were a dozen illithids, a like number of beholders, and two hundred mindslaves. The slaves were a mixed bunch, mostly humans and bugbears, but with an alarming number of elves as well. A fair number of elves wore the elaborate, beast-head helmets favored by Evereskan nobles. It filled Aubric with despair to recognize a gilt hawk and two stylish lions as the helms of Noble Blades.

Leaving Dureth to skulk along behind the crest and watch the enemy, Aubric and Rhydwych slipped down the slope and led the Swords along a parallel course. Soon enough, the ridge fell to a bare seven feet, and the enemy company streamed out beyond the shoulder to the line of decomposing birds and rabbits that marked the Deadwall. Aubric signaled his company to wait.

On the plain, the ruffle had closed to within four hundred paces of Rocnest. Though it was impossible to tell whether the invisible newcomers had seen the enemy, the phaerimm were making no secret of their presence. They stopped at the Deadwall only long enough for one of their number to run his four hands through a spell, creating a shimmering half-disk of greenish light.

"Four hands! No wonder we couldn't find the spell!" whispered Rhydwych.

The first two phaerimm pressed themselves to the shimmering doorway and melted through it, their bodies spreading across one side, then oozing out the other. Aubric grimaced. The slow process precluded a mad dash to take the enemy from behind. They would have to fight for the doorway and hold it, like an army claiming a crucial bridge.

The other phaerimm floated through the portal one after the other, leaving the illithids and beholders to herd the mindslaves through. Arrogant as always in their power within the Sharaedim, they were not even worried about being attacked from behind—an unfortunate testament, Aubric realized, to how little damage the Swords had truly inflicted on their enemies.

By the time the last phaerimm had crossed the barrier, the fast-moving newcomers had reached the base of Rocnest—or at least their riffle had. In front of the tor, a steady progression of birds began to take wing as invisible warriors fanned out to set up an advanced defense line.

The phaerimm huddled together arguing, filling the air with strange whistles and angry gestures. After a few wasted moments, they returned to the Deadwall and created nine more shimmering portals. The beholders and illithids began to shove mindslaves through en masse, while the thornbacks worked frantically to arrange them into battle ranks. Aubric could not help smiling. It was the first time he had seen anyone disrupt a phaerimm plan.

The newcomers seemed eager to press. A dozen golden

meteors arced away from Rocnest, landing short of the phaer-imm lines, but exploding into huge curtains of amber fire.

"That's Vhoorflame!" hissed Rhydwych.

Aubric raised a finger to his lips, drawing an irritated—but silent—scowl. He did not take offense, for he understood the excitement that had led to her exclamation. Vhoorflame was a specialty of Evermeet's fleet mages, invented for the rare occasions when the island nation found it necessary to defend itself at sea.

A stiff wind—no doubt magical—rose behind the flames and drove it toward the Blazevale. The mindslaves grew agitated and more difficult to arrange, angering the phaerimm enough that they killed a handful as an example. That only sent the others into a panic, and several dozen turned to flee through the portals back into the Sharaedim.

A pair of the smaller phaerimm left the group and called up an opposing wind that stopped the Vhoorflames three hundred paces from the Deadwall. When the blaze continued to burn, they called rain down from a clear sky. The water merely turned to steam. They used a ground-moving spell to flip a huge wall of dirt back onto the fire. The Vhoorflames continued to burn, consuming the dirt as though it were coal. The fire began to advance again.

Finally, one phaerimm tried to dispel the magic that had created the fire curtain. Normally, dismissing the spell of a fleet mage was no easy task, but the phaerimm were far more than normal magic-users. The creature had barely stopped waving its arms before a section of flame faded, leaving a thirty foot breach in the blazing curtain.

A blinding bolt of silver fire came streaking through the gap to catch the phaerimm in the torso. The thing erupted in a dazzling flash, hurling thorns and arms thirty feet into the air.

"In the name of Angharradh!" hissed Aubric, turning to Rhydwych. "What manner of spell was that?"

Rhydwych only gestured to the plain, where a robed man

stood with a black staff in one hand. Aubric was just starting to make out the shadow of a thick beard when another ball of Vhoorflame streaked down to seal the gap in the fire curtain.

"It appears our help may not be needed," whispered Rhydwych.

"I pray we will be so lucky," said Aubric, "but we must be ready. Prepare the eye shield."

"There is no harm in being prepared." Rhydwych turned away to join her small cluster of Lordly Wands.

If the newcomers thought the destruction of one phaerimm would discourage the others, they were badly mistaken. The creatures merely spread out and floated forward in a line, then dispelled the entire wall of Vhoorflame at once.

This time, there were no streams of silver fire, only a flurry of lightning and golden bolts. The phaerimm vanished inside nine columns of roaring magic, each one pelted by such a tempest of spells that the ground split and the sky shook. One creature spun madly around and dropped in a heap of gashed flesh, but the others floated firm where they were, returning the attacks in kind.

A long rank of wizards—some looked human, others elf—was approaching through the fading smoke, all visible now that they had attacked. They fell in twos and threes, or sometimes just vanished into blood and smoke. Fearing his allies were not as well-prepared as he'd thought, Aubric longed to call out to them to change tactics, for he and his Swords had discovered the hard way that spells hurled at phaerimm had a nasty habit of ricocheting back at the caster. On the other hand, there was value in keeping the thornbacks busy, and perhaps that was all the newcomers intended. Clearly, they had come with a plan—and at least a few surprises.

Aubric tried to find the bearded figure again, but quickly realized it was hopeless. Deciding the time had come for Evereska to unveil a surprise of her own, he stood and drew his sword.

"Arrows and spells!" he yelled. "Loose at will, slow advance!"

Bowstrings thrummed the air, sending a wall of hissing death down into the mindslaves trapped against the Dead-wall. The first volley and most of the second dropped the illithids before they had a chance to whirl and use their mind blasts against the company's spellcasters. The Lordly Wands hurled a few fireballs and ice storms to keep the enemy off balance, but eight of the dozen remained quiet and assumed positions in the first rank of advance.

When the beholders finally recovered and turned their death-dealing eyes toward the invaders, Rhydwych called, "Eye shield!"

Together, the Wands uttered an incantation and poured a handful of powdered silver to the ground. The air in front of them shimmered with mirrorlike brilliance, and the behold-ers' rays ricocheted off in all directions. Aubric's archers took aim at the eye tyrants and waited, then, when the creatures spun their big magic-dispelling eyes around to dispel the eye shield, they loosed their arrows. Most of the beholders dropped to the first volley. The handful that survived perished in the second.

The confused mindslaves, now on their own, turned to meet the attack in a jumble.

"Spare them if you can, but be quick!" Aubric cried. "We must show our friends at the Rocnest how to kill phaerimm!"

Rhydwych and her Wands unleashed a flurry of spells, dropping a full third of the mindslaves into a deep slumber. Another twenty fell into helpless fits of laughter, and dozens more dropped their weapons and simply wandered off. A handful went blind and fell to their knees screaming. Unfor-tunately, a full two-dozen warriors remained to block the Swords' advance.

Aubric led the crash into them, using his elven sword to parry the wild axe of a vacant-eyed human, then slipping inside to knock the man unconscious with a mailed fist to the jaw. As he spun away, he snatched the fellow's axe and hurled it into a charging bugbear, dived under the monster's legs, and came up flinging sand into the eyes of three elves standing in front of the portal.

"Rest well," he said, adding the arcane syllable that gave his command its magical force.

The knees of two elves buckled, but the third danced forward in the practiced steps of a bladesinger—a pattern that Aubric Nihmedu had often taught his most promising students at the College of Arms. He should have backed away and called to one of Rhydwych's Wands for a killing spell, but he could not do that to one of his own pupils. Knowing what would come next, and trusting his own skill to defeat it, he blocked the low attack, slipped the lunge, parried the returning backhand, and knocked the fellow unconscious with an elbow to the jaw—then felt something hot and sharp pushing through his chain mail.

Aubric looked down to find a silver dagger protruding from his flank. "Oh, very good." He pressed himself into the shimmering Deadwall portal. "Very sneaky."

The world grew hot and flat looking. He experienced a strange instant of infinite expansiveness and intoxicating energy, then his side erupted in pain, and he fell.

The pain, Aubric promptly shunted to one side of his consciousness, to a place where he would be aware of what it told him, but not dominated by it. The falling, he threw himself into, flinging himself over his shoulders and rolling to his feet, his own blade and the dislodged dagger weaving a defensive pattern around him. He felt his sword slice across a body behind him and knew a human was trying to rush up on his left, which meant someone else was coming from the right. He flipped the dagger under his sword arm, aiming high for the throat and a quick kill. A strangled gurgle betokened an intuition still as sharp as two centuries before, but Aubric barely noticed. He had fallen into the grasp of the blood dance now, his mind and his body becoming one, an instrument being played by a will indistinguishable from the mad whirl of combat around him. His foot lashed out in a blind back kick, drawing a pained howl from the man he had wounded an instant earlier.

Aubric spun, blade flashing, blood coursing. It would have been wrong to say he became a bladesinger again—such a thing was impossible for an elf of so many responsibilities and so little time—but a gift hard won and long nourished returned. He became stronger, quicker, more supple—if not quite the dancing sword with whom Morgwais had fallen in love those few centuries ago, then at least once more a whirling blade. The old battle song tolled in his ears, and he began to feel in the Weave everything happening on the field of combat. He saw the wall of glassy-eyed mindslaves rushing up to attack, felt Lady Bourmays and Lord Dureth pushing through the Deadwall behind him, heard the voices of Lordly Wands calling out incantations to both sides of him. In the plain ahead, he saw the phaerimm streaking forward through a tempest of blades and bolts, heard one of the creatures fife its pain as an iron spear impaled it, felt the crackling energy as a blue force-dome rose up to cover all of Rocnest.

A strand of silk appeared in Aubric's hand of its own accord. He flung it at a dozen charging mindslaves and called three arcane syllables. A golden web engulfed their legs and brought their charge to a halt. Pounding feet sounded to his left. He dropped to a whirling crouch and swept his attacker's legs with an extended foot, then knocked the woman senseless with a heel kick to the head. The smell of musk saturated the air, and he launched himself backward, somersaulting into the legs of an astonished bugbear, thrusting his blade up through its guts, rolling free before the gore came showering down. He sprang up and heard a pair of light feet approaching from his wounded side.

Aubric lowered his sword, then seeing no more mindslaves to attack, stooped down to clean the blade on a human's tunic.

"Impressive," said Rhydwych. She thrust a healing potion into his hands. "But you might want to leave the bladesinging to younger nobles."

"Old habits die hard." Aubric allowed himself a wince, then drank the potion down. Its healing warmth coursed through his weary body, but there remained a chill deep in his wounded side. "Damn, that's one youngblade I wish I hadn't taught so well."

Rhydwych cocked her brow. "If you are too badly hurt—"

"When I am in too much pain to defend Evereska, you will know it by the pieces on the ground."

Aubric glanced over his shoulder and found the rest of the company assembling. They had lost perhaps twenty Noble Blades, but still had all twelve Wands. He waved his sword toward Rocnest and started after the phaerimm.

"For Evereska!"

"For Evereska!"

If the reply was weaker and softer than Aubric would have liked, so was his own voice. The pain was spreading, filling his abdomen with cramping fire. The blade had pierced something vital, but there was nothing to do about it. Both of the company's healers had long since been killed, so he could either fight through to Evereska's allies and hope they had a good healer, or he could sit down and die.

Aubric closed off all awareness of the pain, calling on his old bladesinger talents to draw strength from the Weave and lead the charge across the charred plain. As they drew closer to Rocnest, he was astonished at the newcomers' losses. Elves and humans alike lay scattered by the dozens, most motionless and quiet, some writhing and groaning. He saw at least seventy or eighty casualties himself, and guessed the total could easily be twice that number. He assigned half a dozen of his own walking wounded to do what they could for the injured, though everyone knew that would be all too little.

Seventy paces from the enemy, a tremendous crack echoed across the plain. The newcomers' blue dome flickered and dimmed, then flashed out of existence. The phaerimm started forward again, only to be met by a volley of arrows and spears from Rocnest. The dark shafts struck in a clattering cloud, many ricocheting harmlessly off the thorn-backs' scales, but a few finding soft seams. One monster dropped to the ground with the butt of an elven spear in its mouth, and two more trilled in anguish, but most showed no reaction at all to the sticks bristling in their bodies.

A hundred warriors appeared atop Rocnest, visible now that they had attacked and turning to scramble down behind the jagged lip. They made it only a step before the rim erupted into curtains of golden fire and showers of fuming black rain. There was a cacophony of crackling flame and anguished screaming, then another sound—four roaring voices booming out the same intricate spell, complementing each other, working jointly to twine together separate strands of the Weave in one creation.

"It's a Circle!" Rhydwych said, coming to Aubric's side. "The high mages are trying to open the gate!"

"How long?" Aubric asked.

"Too long." Rhydwych pointed at the surviving phaerimm, who were plucking the last of the arrows from their bodies and rising toward Rocnest. "Ten minutes, at least."

Aubric's heart sank. The whole battle so far had taken only fifteen minutes, and the newcomers had done well to delay the phaerimm that long. He thrust his arm into the air, extending his thumb and smallest finger in the "bow" signal.

"Arrows!" He turned to Rhydwych. "How many of us can you magic up there?"

"None, if you expect us to put up a fight," she said. "There's a moment of confusion after any translocational spell—and a moment would be all the phaerimm need."

Aubric nodded, then closed his fist and lowered his arm, calling the Swords to a halt. "Dying that way would do no good, but we must buy them time. Take your Lordly Wands and do whatever you can. The Blades will follow as we can."

Rhydwych's face paled, but she nodded. "For Evereska."

"For Evereska—and all the elves remaining to Faerûn." Aubric's stomach turned hollow and queasy. It was one thing to lead the charge into peril, quite another to order a dozen brave elves to their certain deaths. "May the Harp Archer watch over you."

"And you as well, Lord Nihmedu." Rhydwych gave him a weak smile, then kissed his cheek. "Don't let them make a mindslave of me."

"Nor you of me," answered Aubric.

Rhydwych drew a pair of battle wands, then closed her eyes and used her magic to mindspeak with her fellow wizards.

Aubric looked toward Rocnest again, where five healthy phaerimm were already halfway to the rim. The other two remained closer to the ground, wobbling about on their tails as they tried to recover their wits.

"Loose and advance!" Aubric yelled.

A volley of arrows darkened the sky, a dozen flying toward each phaerimm. Perhaps a quarter of the shafts directed against the injured creatures struck home, lodging themselves deep between their scales or in the pulpy rim of the mouth. One thornback dropped writhing and flopped like a trout out of water. The second vanished in the glimmer of teleport magic. The other flights streaked to within a few inches of their targets, then struck some invisible shield and bounced harmlessly away.

By the time the arrows tumbled to the ground, Rhydwych and her Wands were in the air, streaking after the phaerimm like sparrows after hawks. Aubric started to raise a hand to call a ground charge, then saw a dark-bearded human step onto a jagged spur atop Rocnest. He held a black mage's staff and wore heavy winter robes, and Aubric felt certain he was the same man whose silver flames had destroyed the first phaerimm.

Hit them again, my friend, and this time your arrows will strike home. On my signal.

Aubric did not question how the voice came to his head, nor hesitate to implement its command. He raised his thumb and little finger in the "bow" signal and called a halt.

"Nock and aim!" he yelled. "Choose your targets well."

Even as he yelled this, the phaerimm unleashed a tempest of magic at the figure atop the rock. There were fireballs and ice storms, swirling clouds of vapor and black bolts of death, lightning forks and even a great disembodied hand. The human stood through it all, his arms spread wide, his black staff raised high above his head, its body surrounded by a purple aura as it drew attack after attack down into its shaft.

The figure could only be Khelben Arunsun. Aubric's spirits rose at once, for with one of the Chosen fighting in Evereska's defense, surely it could only be a matter of time before the phaerimm were driven from the Sharaedim. He waited patiently for the promised signal, all the while watching his Wands draw closer to the phaerimm, and the phaerimm closer to Rocnest, until he began to worry about distance and accuracy, and to fear that his archer's shafts might strike the Swords' own wizards.

Finally, the bearded figure lowered his staff. Though it was impossible to hear the archmage's voice over the booming chant of the high mages and the general battle roar, Aubric saw the human's fingers flashing through the familiar gestures of a magic dispelling spell. He lowered his arm.

"Loose!"

The thrum of eighty bowstrings sounded as one, and a cloud of arrows hissed through the sky. As they neared the phaerimm, the shafts bunched into swarms, almost like wasps streaking out to sting the fools who dared disturb their nests.

The flights struck with an almost audible thud, driving the phaerimm closer to Rocnest's basalt cliffs and a little downward. Fully half the arrows snapped against the creatures' scaly armor, but the others sank deep, adding their feathery tails to the forest of spines already rising on the backs of the phaerimm.

The Lordly Wands adjusted their course and swooped to

engage, but were brought up short when a handful of battered human mages appeared alongside Khelben to hurl a fusillade of bolts and flashes at the phaerimm. Several blasts ricocheted off their intended targets and streaked back to the caster, and a full half dozen merely vanished without causing visible harm. The other spells hit on mark, spraying cracked scales and broken thorns in every direction.

One phaerimm lost an arm and went tumbling groundward, only to vanish in a silver flash. The other four fought back in kind, swinging out to spray Rocnest's scorched rim with every color of hissing bolt. There were lightning blasts and fire streams and storms of exploding hail, but the most destructive attack was a surge of invisible force that slammed into the cliff itself, creating a boom so loud it hit Aubric like a punch. A web of fissures shot across the rocky face, bringing the rim down in a crashing mass of stone and black dust.

Rhydwych and her Wands swooped into the roiling cloud somewhere beneath the phaerimm. Aubric raised his arm to signal the blade charge and was startled to realize he was already half a dozen steps behind everyone else. Determined not to dishonor his position by being the last into battle, he reached out to the Weave and felt its strength surge into him—but he found also that his legs would not rise faster, nor his lungs draw deeper, nor his heart pump harder. He could not understand what was wrong—until he noticed the dull burning in his abdomen and felt the wet warmth pouring down his leg. The pain he had shunted aside, but one could demand only so much from a body, and he had long ago passed that threshold.

As the landslide settled, brilliant flashes and deep rumblings filled the dust cloud. A Lordly Wand tumbled out of the roiling mass in a dozen pieces and rained to ground amidst the Noble Blades. They paid no attention and vanished, screaming, into the swirling murk.

Aubric raced after them, lungs aching and muscles burning. The plain turned into a hazy field of jumbled stone and ghostly silhouettes, and the air grew thick with choking dust, filling his throat with racking coughs. It occurred to him he might not survive to thank Evereska's new allies, and his thoughts turned briefly to Morgwais—the Red Lady, with skin so bronze it was scarlet—and he was sorry he had not gone with her into the High Forest, not because he feared what was about to befall him, nor even because he knew he would never see her again, but because he had let her think that his duty meant more to him than she did.

Aubric came to the base of the landslide and saw his ghostly Blades scrambling up the boulders, chasing after handfuls of long gray cords dragging across the stones. One elf sprang off a stone, and letting his sword fall free, caught hold of the rope. He began to climb, and the line dragged across the ground more slowly. Another warrior caught hold and dropped to his seat, bracing himself between two boulders to hold it in place.

Coughing and hacking so hard he could hardly hold himself straight, Aubric ran his gaze fifty feet up the line to the amorphous blob above. In the swirling dust, it looked like some sort of jellyfish, with a shapeless body and a string of long tentacles dangling below. It took the blademajor a moment to recognize what he was seeing, to identify the tangled knot of limbs as the grotesquely broken arms and legs of three Lordly Wands, wrapped tight to their foe by the sticky white strands of a magic web.

A rolling ball of flame engulfed the phaerimm, drawing an anguished shriek from a lone elf voice. Aubric thought for a moment that Khelben or a human wizard had hurled the spell down from above. When the creature did not come crashing to the ground, he realized that the fireball had been no more than a desperate attempt to free itself—but elven ropes did not burn. A half dozen Noble Blades grabbed hold with the other two warriors and hauled their foe down toward its death. The thornback had other ideas and vanished in a twinkling of silver spell light.

A second phaerimm, still reeling from the fury of earlier attacks, was not so lucky. A trio of elves caught its ropes, then drew it down while their fellows poured arrows into it. By the time the dazed creature finally thought to raise a shield, they had it on the ground, dragging it past a teetering boulder. When their fellows pushed the monolith over, the spray of green blood left no doubt about its fate.

Aubric clambered over the rocks toward Rocnest, searching the sky for the last two creatures. The booming voices of the high mages continued unabated, as did the cries of the wounded and the rumble of shifting stone, but an ominous pause had descended over the battle itself. By the time he reached the base of the cliff, the dust cloud had thinned to a mere haze.

Dureth came up beside him. "Aubric, you look in a bad way."

Aubric nodded and searched the landslide below. "Did you see what became of the last two phaerimm?"

A worried look came to Dureth's eye. "No."

"Then tell those who can to hurry." Aubric turned toward the cliff. There was perhaps fifty feet of vertical face, then another hundred of steep bowl where the avalanche had caved away. He sheathed his sword and looped a coil of rope over his shoulder. "I'll see you above."

Dureth caught his arm. "You can't do this, my friend," he said. "Not alone."

"How can I not?" Climbing as nimbly as a spider despite his wound, Aubric started up the cliff. "I doubt there is anyone left who can keep up."

"Aubric, no one expects the blademajor to—"

But Aubric was already twenty feet up, his fingers and toes moving quickly from one hold to another. Dureth began to yell at the others to regroup, asking if anyone had a spell of flight. By the time the high lord had everyone gathered, Aubric was pulling himself off the vertical face onto the treacherous slope left by the landslide. He yelled for the others to stand clear and scrambled up through the loose stone, twice falling and nearly sliding to his death.

The high mages continued their spellcasting, their voices rising to a fevered pitch as they neared completion. When the top of the slide basin came into view, Aubric began to think Rhydwych had killed the other two phaerimm herself—and that, of course, was when the crackle of a war spell rumbled over the crest of the slope. He tied the rope off to a spar of rock and tossed the free end to the others, then drew his sword and scrambled into the saddle.

At the top, Aubric dropped to his belly and peered into Rocnest. All that remained of the ancient fortress were a few sections of elf-raised wall along the jagged rim. But down in the basin stood a rectangle of lustrous black stone, still shining with the magic that had drawn it from the ground. In front of the block stood a gossamer-robed Gold elf female, her voice ringing heavenward as she plucked strands of Weave from the air and plaited them into the dark monolith. She was fashioning an elegant keel arch, its purple depths growing ever darker and richer. With every fiber she laid, the mage herself seemed to grow wispy, translucent, as though she were braiding herself into her work. Aubric thought it so, for though the high mages kept their art to themselves, he had heard that their magic often involved the binding of their own spirits.

Arrayed around the elf woman were three male mages, their bodies as black and opaque as the female's was translucent. They held their arms spread skyward, spraying shimmering arcs of magic into the circle. Their voices were booming to a crescendo, each calling out a separate spell of support, yet weaving their incantations together in music-like harmony.

The slope directly below Aubric was more dirt than rock, strewn with bodies both human and elf—many writhing in agony, none able to stand. Halfway down hovered the two phaerimm, still swaddled in Rhydwych's magic webs and flinging spells at a scintillating dome of colors. Though Aubric recognized the dome as one of the most powerful defenses taught by Evereska's Academy of Magic, he could not understand why the phaerimm were wasting their time destroying it when the high mages were so close to completing the gate.

Khelben Arunsun stepped out of the dome, hurled a spell at one of the creatures, and dived back into his sphere. The stricken phaerimm froze and began to sink into the ground. Whistling in alarm, the other floated around the sphere and dispelled the magic drawing its fellow down into the stone.

In the basin below, the voices of the high mages rose to a thunderous roar. The archway glowed deep purple, and the female elf faded to a shimmer.

Khelben popped out of the dome again and cast a ray of black death at the second phaerimm, only to have the magic reflected back at him. He tried to bring his black staff down to intercept the spell, but even Mystra's Chosen could not catch their own spells. The bolt took him in the chest, hurling him a dozen paces up the slope. He landed in a heap, brown vapor rising from the puckered hole in his chest.

Aubric was already bounding down the rocks, his knees quivering with weakness, his breath coming in hot, wet wheezes. As he passed Khelben, he was relieved to see the edges of the hole already closing, but it seemed clear the archmage would be of no further use in this battle. The closest phaerimm spun to meet Aubric's charge, its barbed tail tangling in its skirt of elven ropes. The second creature extracted itself from the ground and started down the slope toward the high mages.

Aubric sprang six feet to the right, then right again, as though trying to work his way around the first creature. When he gathered himself for a third leap, his foe took the bait, spraying his path with sizzling black acid. Aubric jumped left, drawing on the Weave's magic to launch himself into a glorious flying somersault, his sword whirling about him as his panicked target filled the air with flashing magic.

In the basin below, the voices of the high mages fell silent. The female vanished in a brilliant burst of purple radiance, and the gateway glowed with a magic so deeply violet it was black.

A magic bolt caught Aubric in the shoulder, but he twisted around, launched himself off the phaerimm's fleshy lip—one of the few areas not covered with magic web—and dived over the scintillating dome. The startled creature whistled an alarm, and its fellow spun on its tail, splicing the air with a sheet of scything magic.

Aubric was already on the ground, rolling to his feet and dancing toward the phaerimm in a tornado of flashing steel. The creature called to its fellow and moved to block the elf's path across the hill. Aubric feigned an attempt to circle above it, then saw the weary mages below lower their arms and knew the gate was complete. He changed directions, barely escaping as a nest of tentacles sprang from the ground to snatch at his legs. The second phaerimm streaked by, trilling in anger as it swept down into the basin.

"Watch yourselves!" Weak and croaking as it was, the call sent Aubric into a spasm of coughing. Bright blood sprayed from his mouth, taking with it what little remained of his strength. He dropped to his knees, then tried again to warn the high mages.

"Behind you!"

Whether or not they heard the cry was impossible to say, for the elves turned almost sedately to look up the slope. Their golden faces had gone sallow and gaunt with exhaustion, and when they raised their arms, it almost seemed they were trying to ward off a blow instead of preparing to cast a spell.

The phaerimm was faster. Still wrapped in its amorphous cocoon of magic web, it stopped at the bottom of the slope and struck the ground with its tail. A deafening crash shook the entire Rocnest, then a network of magma-belching fissures shot across the basin floor toward the black gate.

The high mages crossed their arms in front of them and calmly awaited the assault. The fissures shot to within a dozen feet of the trio, then turned aside and scribed a fiery loop around the floor of the basin. The phaerimm warbled its frustration and struck the ground again, causing a blinding ring of magma to roar dozens of feet into the air.

The archway's black silhouette remained visible through it all, but when the fiery curtain sank back into its crevices, all that remained of the three mages were fuming black robes, lying rumpled and empty along the edge of their circle.

Though it seemed minutes had passed, Aubric knew by his labored breathing and trembling muscles it could only have been seconds. He looked away from the receding fires more disheartened than awed. The gate had been raised—but to what purpose? Even if others wanted to help, Evereska remained as alone as ever. Any forces sent by Evermeet or Waterdeep would be destroyed the instant they left the gate—or, worse, added to the ranks of the phaerimm mind-slaves.

A shadow fell across the ground before Aubric, then he heard something wispy and sibilant inside his mind. *Come along quietly, and you will live.*

It was all Aubric could do to find the strength to look at the dusty, web-swaddled mass before him. "I doubt it."

Do not. I have a fondness for you brave ones. You hatch strong larvae.

Aubric heard a soft rustle and brought his sword up beside him, catching the phaerimm's tail just above the barb as it came whipping in at his flank. There was a wet slashing sound, then the feel of hot blood as the severed tail sprayed his face.

Leaving his pain to come flooding into him, Aubric called upon his last tiny reserve of strength to launch himself into a mad, cart wheeling attack.

He did not make it, of course. The phaerimm floated aside and let him tumble down the slope, and the searing spray of green vapor came sizzling down on him from above.

Aubric hardly noticed, for the strength had fled from his body. He felt the sword slip from his grasp, and the last thing he saw was the luminous face of the female mage watching him from the mouth of the black gate, and he was struck by how much her smile looked like that of his beloved Morgwais.

CHAPTER EIGHTEEN

30 Nightal, the Year of the Unstrung Harp

To Galaeron's eye, Malik looked a touch ill at the prospect of letting Melegaunt cast any spell on him, much less a spell involving a darkdagger and rope. His gaze kept darting from the bridge into the black wood beside them, where the others were breaking camp after a dry night's rest around a magic-heated boulder.

"Have no fear, my friend," said Galaeron, knotting his elven rope around Malik's wrists. "You may trust Melegaunt."

Malik looked over his shoulder. "*You* may, but I heard what he said to Jhingleshod before crossing the bridge."

Galaeron wanted to ask for an explanation, but saw Melegaunt approaching with his darkdagger and knew there was no time. He leaned closer to

Malik's ear. "Then you may trust me, human. I do not allow those who save my life to be murdered—even if they are Cyric worshipers."

"That is little enough reassurance," said Malik, "considering who is the student and who is the master."

Melegaunt stopped before them and glowered down at the little man. "I could not find you in the dawn shadows." He paused, allowing Malik to consider the implications. "If you don't wish to continue—"

"Oh no, you are not leaving me!" Malik glanced at the darkdagger, then raised his chin. "Do what you must."

Melegaunt cast an inquiring look in Galaeron's direction, and receiving a curt nod, kneeled at Malik's feet. Beginning a long incantation, he laid a small pair of braided shadow-silk manacles in the little man's shadow. The shadow instantly grew broad of chest and slender of waist, with a strange pair of what looked like antlers on its head and a blurry area of white in the center of its chest. Malik's teeth ground together loudly, but he did not try to flee as the shadowmage had warned he might.

Melegaunt cocked a bushy brow. Still chanting his spell, he drew his dagger along the edge of Malik's feet. The shadow came free, peeling itself off the stones to stand looming over them all, brown sky showing through the hazy-edged hole in its chest.

Malik gasped and would have collapsed, had Galaeron not been there to slip his hands under the little man's arms.

A pair of crimson eyes appeared in the shadow's head and peered at Melegaunt. "I am bound to your will." Its voice was as resonant as Malik's was nasal. "Though you do me a grave disservice. I know your purpose and would aid it gladly."

"All the same, we will keep matters as they are." Melegaunt pointed across the bridge. "I wish you to keep watch. You know our enemies?"

"The phaerimm—or Elminster?" the shadow asked.

"Both, and their servants as well," replied Melegaunt. "When you see any of them, return to Malik and give us warning."

The shadow inclined its head. "As you command."

Melegaunt studied the silhouette for a moment, then turned back toward camp. Galaeron started after him, pulling an awestricken Malik along beside him. The little man glanced at his feet and back to the shadow, then turned to Galaeron.

"That demon cannot be anything of mine!"

"Exactly." Doubtful he could explain the shadowself as well as Melegaunt, Galaeron did not even try. "You don't seem very disturbed. The first time I saw my shadow, I was terrified."

"Oh, I have seen things worse than my own shadow," scoffed Malik. "After all, I am much favored of the One."

They joined the others in camp, where Vala and Takari stood over a half-sized relief Aris had sculpted into an expanse of bedrock. Depicting Malik's rescue of Galaeron and Vala, the work was amazingly fluid and detailed. Malik's character looked more confused than resolute, and perhaps a little angry at himself for being foolish enough to jump into the river. Vala was unconscious in the crook of Galaeron's arm, more dead than alive. Galaeron was holding the rope and glancing down at Vala, his expression leaving no doubt that the terrible fear in his eyes was for her alone.

Takari and Vala were huddled together on the opposite side of the work, talking quietly and studying the relief so intently they did not see the others approach.

". . . don't want either of you hurt," Takari was saying. "You've seen yourself why it can never be."

"I have?" Despite her curtness, Vala's voice was surprisingly mild. "When was that?"

"You met his father," Takari explained. "You saw what became of Aubric when Morgwais returned to the forest."

"We're getting ahead of matters here, but I'm no Wood

elf," Vala said. "Were I to make a life pledge, I would honor it as my mother and father honored theirs."

"And how long would that be?"

Vala raised her chin. "My parents have been sharing the fur for forty years and three."

"A blessing for them both, but forty years and three is not the same to an elf." Takari laid a hand on Vala's arm. "Forty years from now, Galaeron will still be young, with four centuries before him."

When Vala did not answer, Galaeron said, "There's no need to poison her against me, Takari." He waited for the pair to turn, then gestured at Aris's relief. "It's only art— and what business is it of yours? I'm your princep, not your nestmate."

The flash that came to Takari's eyes was more sorrowful than angry. "And no fun as either." She turned and slipped through the black tree trunks. "Sorry to forget my place."

Vala shot a scowl at Galaeron. "I only kissed you," she growled, starting after Takari. "I have done more with half the men in my clan!"

This drew a crooked smile from Melegaunt, but he made no comment and turned to Jhingleshod, who stood studying the work with the enigmatic gaze of the dead.

"It appears we are ready to go," Melegaunt said.

"You are ready," said the knight. "But there is still the matter of my payment."

Galaeron cast an anxious glance after the departing women. "If the bridge is any example, you are not worth much of a price," the elf said.

"You learned what you needed to learn," replied Jhingleshod. "If you recall what happened there, you may survive to claim what you seek."

"I have no fondness for these games of yours," said Galaeron. "If you would have something from us, then you must tell us what we need—"

Melegaunt stepped in front of Galaeron. "We have already

agreed to your price, Sir Knight. If you wish to tell us what it is, we are listening."

"I ask little," said Jhingleshod. "Only your word that you will do what already you must."

"Yes?" asked Melegaunt.

"Destroy Wulgreth, my master, as I once attempted."

"As you once attempted?" Galaeron asked, more wary than before. "If you betrayed your master, how are we to know you won't betray us?"

"I have no care for what you know or do not know, elf," said Jhingleshod. "But I tell you this: I bear no small part of the blame for the evil here, and I am damned to wander the Dire Wood until what I should have done then is done at last."

"How is Wulgreth's crime your doing?" asked Melegaunt. "I sense no great evil in you."

"But I relished the bounty of his shadow," said Jhingleshod, "and so I stood by. After Wulgreth summoned the demons to Ascalhorn, for six decades I watched their evil and did not raise my voice against them. When the demons turned on him at last, I followed Wulgreth into the wilderness and sat in his shadow feasting on stolen bread and drinking the wine of murdered wayfarers. And after he came here to Karse, I was waiting outside the black crypt when he returned with its dark power."

Jhingleshod let his chin fall.

"And yet, you found the strength to slay him," prompted Melegaunt.

"It was despair, nothing more," said Jhingleshod. "The power was twisted and evil, and it corrupted all it touched. First, the forest died and turned to black stone, then the ruins became a city of the dead. When I begged Wulgreth to send the monsters away and build a city for the living, he struck me blows, saying he would never be avenged on the demons with a living army. Seeing that my dream was not to be, I felt betrayed and vowed he would never again bring ruin to any city. I killed him in his sleep that night."

"Which proved unwise," surmised Melegaunt.

Jhingleshod nodded. "He caught me as I fled the city, a cackling dead thing of heinous power. He chased me through the forest, using his magic to flay me an inch at time, until I ran myself to death. I awoke as I am now, condemned to wander the Dire Wood until the vow I made is kept." He turned to Galaeron. "And that is why I won't betray you."

"And if we fail you as Wulgreth did?" asked Galaeron. "Will you turn against us, too?"

Before Jhingleshod could answer, Melegaunt said, "What you say can't be right. Wulgreth was a Netherese arcanist, killed much earlier when a magical experiment went awry and Karsus had to push an orb of heavy magic off his enclave."

"Heavy magic?" Galaeron asked. He knew "enclaves" to be the legendary floating cities of ancient Netheril, and Karsus was the deranged archwizard who had caused the empire's fall by trying to steal Mystryl's godhead, but Galaeron had never heard of "heavy magic."

"A powerful sort of magic discovered by Karsus—and nothing I want you playing with until you bring that shadow under control." Melegaunt fixed Galaeron with a disapproving eye. "It's appallingly dangerous, a force-made-tangible that Netherese archwizards once used to heighten their other magic."

"Once used?" asked Malik. "Then you do not have any of this 'heavy magic'?"

Melegaunt glowered at the little man. "No. It vanished with the Netherese." He turned back to Jhingleshod. "But it was Karsus's heavy magic that turned Wulgreth into a lich, not your attack."

"Netheril fell a thousand years before I lived," said Jhingleshod. "And Wulgreth was much alive when I served him. One does not turn from a lich into a man and back to a lich again."

"There is no record of such a thing in the Tomb Guard chronicles," said Galaeron. Recalling Malik's cryptic comment about what Melegaunt had told Jhingleshod before crossing the bridge, he studied the wizard with narrowed eyes. "The Tomb Guard *would* have a record."

Melegaunt's eyes grew stormy. "You accuse me of lying?"

"I ask for an explanation."

"You—or your shadow?" Melegaunt countered.

"I have my shadow in hand," said Galaeron. "It has not troubled me since the sunken bridge."

"Why should it?" Melegaunt turned back to Jhingleshod. "I am not mistaken about my dates. Wulgreth never forgave Karsus for the accident, and there are records of him plaguing Netherese enclaves for decades afterward. It's the reason Wulgreth haunts the Dire Wood at all."

"Wulgreth haunts this wood because I killed him here," Jhingleshod insisted. "The Dire Wood did not exist before that."

"But Karse did," countered Melegaunt. "The city was founded over sixteen centuries ago, a little after Karsus brought Netheril down. A refugee group was drawn to his corpse by dream visions and began to worship his dead body—and *that* really angered Wulgreth. He destroyed the entire city and moved into the ruins so it would never be rebuilt."

Jhingleshod fixed his dead eyes on the sorcerer. "I know nothing about heavy magic and worshiping dead bodies. I killed Wulgreth, and he became a lich."

"If I may, the answer is plain enough," said Malik. "In a thousand years, there were certainly many wizards named Wulgreth. Does it seem so unlikely that two ended up here?"

Melegaunt raised his brow, then nodded thoughtfully, but Jhingleshod did not seem to hear the suggestion. In fact, Galaeron realized, though Jhingleshod's gaze was fixed on the same point as Melegaunt's—Malik's face—the knight's eyes were focused on the ground behind the little man, and the slight tilt of his helmet suggested he might be wondering what the wizard was looking at.

"I think we can trust Jhingleshod's account of events."

Galaeron chose his words carefully. "But we'd better be off before Takari and Vala get too far ahead of us."

Jhingleshod's dead gaze shifted to Galaeron. "Then you give your word?"

Galaeron nodded. "I will destroy Wulgreth, if we can find him."

"He will find you," said Jhingleshod.

The ghoulish knight walked across Aris's sculpture, leaving the river stained with rusty footprints, into the trees. The forest here was dark, tangled, and dead—much the same as the bog, save that it stood on dry ground and did not drain their strength. The group soon caught up to Takari and Vala, and Jhingleshod took the lead, clinking and squeaking his way deeper into the tangled wood.

Huge webs of yellow-green filaments began to appear in the branches. Galaeron kept watch for ball-shaped silhouettes and sticklike legs. Instead of spiders, he started to see slender leaves and moldy pods clinging to the tendrils. As they climbed away from the river, the vines grew longer and the vegetation thicker, until it became difficult to see more than a few paces. It was impossible to walk without brushing against the vines, and soon after their hands and faces erupted into white boils. Aris used his prayer magic to powder a stone and create an ointment that reduced the sores to an itchy rash, though Malik refused the salve out of fear of offending his god. To the amazement of all, he continued at as strong a pace as anyone, even when the blisters began weeping and he had to cut his eyelids to keep them from swelling shut.

The vines began to grow in broken squares and straight meshwork, taking the shape of the ruins beneath. Jhingleshod walked more quietly and carefully now, prompting Galaeron to send Takari ahead to scout and take a position beside Vala. Malik and Melegaunt remained in the center, with Aris in the rear. As they advanced deeper into the city, the patterns grew more regular and even, arranging themselves into crooked streets and sunlit meadows that had once been plazas.

Vala kept her hand on her sword, her eyes following Takari's stealthy figure with remarkable ease for a human. After a time, she said to Galaeron, "You shouldn't have said that to Takari. She's only trying to protect you—and me."

"That's not what it sounded like to me."

"Maybe not," said Vala. "But then, you didn't hear what she told Jhingleshod about why she wanted to cross the bridge."

"Whatever she said, it is not her place to protect me from our relationship." Galaeron glanced over at Vala. "Not that there *is* a relationship."

"No?" Vala glanced at him sidelong, her mouth cocked in a crooked smile. "Then why should you care what she says about it?"

"I prefer to make those choices myself," said Galaeron. "As I'm sure you do."

"We have a saying in Vaasa," she said. "In love and death, only the gods choose."

"It sounds a handy excuse," said Galaeron.

Vala gave him a roguish smile. "One that makes life interesting." She watched Takari poking her sword into a tangled mass of vine, then asked Galaeron, "When you told Jhingleshod you were seeking pardon for your mistake, was that the truth?"

"More than I knew," Galaeron said. "It had to be, or I doubt Jhingleshod would have let me pass."

"I thought so." Vala remained quiet for a moment, then said, "I had to think carefully, but Takari didn't hesitate."

"I take it the answer concerned me?"

Vala nodded. "Takari said she had to cross because you're her spirit-deep mate . . . and you refused to see it."

"She . . ." Galaeron closed his eyes. "She knows I don't return her affections."

"Because of your father's pain," Vala said carefully. "Or so she says."

"That's part of it," said Galaeron. "Moon and Wood elves

live different lives. When they join, sooner or later there will always be sadness."

"Of course." Vala sounded almost irritated with him. "Sooner or later, every joy comes to an end—but that is a poor reason to turn your back on the gifts the gods *do* send your way."

"I'm just being prudent," said Galaeron. "I'm not turning my back on any gift from the gods."

"Oh, I think you are." Vala's voice turned teasing. "And you will be sorry. There is no fury worse than Sune's when she has been rejected!"

"Fortunately, I am an elf," laughed Galaeron. "I doubt our Hanali Celanil is so vengeful as your Sune."

"Maybe, but Takari isn't the only woman I've been talking about, you know."

An owl hoot rang out ahead, bringing their conversation to an abrupt end. Galaeron drew his sword and saw a vine web fluttering as Takari vanished into the trees. Jhingleshod was continuing up the street, paying no heed to whatever had alarmed Takari. Galaeron suspected their guide of betraying them—until a half-rotten corpse dashed out of a side lane and hurled itself headlong into the iron knight's flank.

Jhingleshod rocked up as though he might fall, then brought his axe down and split the ghoul through the side. He turned to Galaeron and pointed down the lane.

"Beware those dead, elf." There was a hint of mockery in the knight's bleak voice. "They have a hatred of the living."

Vala at his side, Galaeron started forward to block the attack, but heard a warning chirp from Takari's tree and turned in the opposite direction. He found himself staring at an alley full of monks, their eyes sunken and their robes in tatters, but looking as alive as Galaeron. Behind him, Vala's sword hissed through the air on the opposite side of the street. There was a wet slash, the thud of a falling body, another slash, another thud.

Galaeron pointed his sword at the first monk, now less

than a dozen paces away. "Stand and name yourselves!"

The entire company of monks stretched their arms out, turning their hands palm up as though begging alms. When they continued forward without speaking, Galaeron whistled the clear *tee-yeer* of a meadowlark. He was answered by the hum of a bowstring, and a warning arrow appeared in the dirt in front of the leading monk.

The monks stopped, their gazes following the angle of the arrow into the nest of vines from which it had come, but Galaeron knew without looking that Takari was already gone. He quietly pulled a ball of sulfur wax from his pocket.

"Name yourselves or go."

The first monk responded to the challenge with an incomprehensible moan. Behind Galaeron, Vala's sword continued its gruesome work, and now he heard Aris's mighty club and Melegaunt's bellowing voice as well. Malik remained as silent as usual during battle, but the elf had no doubt the little man would appear when needed most.

The lead monk cautiously stepped around the arrow and continued forward, his cupped hands still stretched before him. Finally convinced he was looking at undead impostors, Galaeron tossed his sulfur ball into the group and spoke his incantation. The cold magic filled him for an instant, and the alley erupted into black fire. Galaeron backed away from a long tongue of dark flame, then beheaded a pair of blazing monks as they staggered from the alley.

A powerful hand clamped Galaeron's shoulder. Surprised, he jammed his elbow back and drove his attacker off a step, then spun with sword flying. By the time he realized it was Melegaunt, his edge was an inch from the wizard's head. Galaeron tried to pull the attack, but to no avail. The blade caught Melegaunt square in the temple.

There was a black flash and dull ping as the edge stopped. Pain sizzled up Galaeron's arm, then his hand opened and let the sword fall to the ground.

Melegaunt touched three fingertips to his head and came

away with a thin smear of blood. "Is this how you repay my gift? By defying me at every turn?"

"I can hardly be blamed for your stupidity." Still trembling, Galaeron stooped down to retrieve his sword. "Grabbing a warrior in the middle of a fight—what's wrong with you?"

Melegaunt stepped on Galaeron's sword. "That's not what I'm talking about."

"I used the magic, yes. It was necessary."

Behind Melegaunt, a ghoul slipped past Vala. One of Takari's arrows took it square in the forehead and knocked it off its feet, but the creature merely rolled to its knees and snapped off the shaft.

Galaeron tried to jerk his sword free, but found the wizard's foot impossible to move. "The magic hasn't hurt me. I'm more in control than before."

"Yes, I have seen how well you are mastering your shadow." Melegaunt touched his head again, then flung a hand in the ghoul's direction and blasted it into a dozen pieces. "Leave the magic to me."

The wizard started up the street after Jhingleshod, calmly directing Vala and Aris against individual ghouls and wights while he blasted larger concentrations with shadow magic. Galaeron gathered his sword and followed behind, quietly venting his anger on any creatures foolish enough to come his way. The undead continued to assault them in erratic fits, occasionally stopping a short distance away to attack with a spell, screech, or gaze. Sneaking along through the treetops, Takari prevented such attacks from succeeding, usually by distracting the creature with an arrow until Melegaunt could blast it. Twice, Malik saved the company by appearing out of nowhere to harry a lurking wight or ghoul until someone more adept could destroy it.

Eventually, the attacks grew less frequent, then, when an enormous butte of red stone began to loom over the treetops, ceased altogether. Jhingleshod guided them to a barren plaza near the head of the butte. There was no sign of the black pyramid he had described Wulgreth entering.

"I believe that is what you seek."

"It is," said Melegaunt. "The fallen body of Karsus."

The butte did resemble a body—albeit a broken and twisted one. The small knoll closest to them looked like a head resting on its side, with a round oversized forehead, hooked nose, and thin-lipped mouth over a weak chin. There was a bent and crooked arm coiled at an unnatural angle, a sunken chest and the round swell of a pot belly—at nearly a hundred feet above the surrounding ground, easily the butte's highest point. From the side of the chest, at about heart level, gushed the source of the Heartblood River, a frothy red spring that flowed away in a meandering stream.

"I see why the refugees took it for a dead god," said Vala. "It certainly looks like a god's body."

"It is a god's body—though Karsus was a god for only an instant," said Melegaunt.

"And this dead god will save Evereska *how*?" asked Galaeron, seeing no sign of the help Melegaunt had promised. "You can't mean to resurrect him."

"In a manner of speaking, yes," said Melegaunt. "But first we must find the black pyramid."

"First, you must find Wulgreth," said Jhingleshod. "You cannot enter the pyramid until you keep your promise."

"As you wish." Despite Melegaunt's words, his tone was impatient. "Tell us where to look."

Jhingleshod ran his gaze over the plaza. "He should have made his presence known by now."

Melegaunt turned to Galaeron. "You're the tomb guard. What's Wulgreth planning?"

"Maybe nothing." Galaeron turned to Jhingleshod and asked, "How long has it been since you last saw him?"

Jhingleshod looked at the sky. "Time is difficult to judge, but several winters. It might have been eight or nine—or a dozen. It is hard to know."

"But it *has* been some time?" asked Takari.

Jhingleshod nodded. "Since before Tianna Skyflower and her ilk began to roam the Dire Wood."

"That makes it nearly a decade," said Takari. She looked to Galaeron. "What do you think?"

Galaeron shrugged, knowing without asking what she was thinking. Often, liches evolved into beings of pure spirit, forsaking their bodies to wander other worlds beyond Toril. When that happened, their corpses began to decay, until all that remained was a skull and some dust to which the lich had only the most tenuous attachment. It was often easier to destroy such creatures than younger liches, but Galaeron knew better than to think they would be that lucky—especially if Wulgreth had only been gone a decade.

Galaeron shook his head. "We'll keep it in mind, but there's too much that doesn't make sense here. The Netherese Wulgreth is certainly old enough, but not the one Jhingleshod served—and there's that time gap to consider."

"So what do we do?" asked Malik.

"The only thing we can do," said Galaeron. "Draw it out."

CHAPTER NINETEEN

30 Nightal, the Year of the Unstrung Harp

From atop the Karsus Butte, the ruins of Karse seemed one huge mold blossom, sickly yellow and reeking of decay, studded with shadowtop snags and crisscrossed by dragonflies the size of eagles. There was a tornado of crimson mist whirling down the Heartblood River and a curtain of smoking hail sweeping across the ruins, but Galaeron had been assured by Jhingleshod that such "wizard weather" had nothing to do with the lich. Strange storms had plagued the area since long before Wulgreth's death.

Galaeron and the others were standing on Karsus's "chest," outside a two-story pyramid of black marble. Though the building's darkness and gloss were a stark contrast to butte's coarse sandstone, the pyramid seemed melded to the rock, almost as though it had been grown instead of built. Aris was studying the workmanship, but everyone else was keeping watch for Wulgreth.

"Anything?" Galaeron asked.

"Flaming rain and green lightning," reported Vala.

"Silver snow by the steaming lake," said Takari. "It can't be more than a couple of miles. Maybe a bath—"

"No!"

Melegaunt and Jhingleshod spoke over each other, the wizard declaring they had important business at hand and Jhingleshod claiming that distances within the Dire Wood were deceiving.

Takari pouted. "We've already wasted an hour."

"An hour you do not have," said a wispy voice.

Galaeron and everyone else spun toward the sound and found themselves looking at a pale, quivering Malik.

"On my life, I said nothing!"

Galaeron frowned—since the sunken bridge, it seemed people were always giving him reason to be suspicious—then he noticed a powerful-looking silhouette at Malik's feet. Galaeron gestured with his sword.

"Malik, your shadow has returned."

Malik looked down. "What a joy to have you back!"

"You must know I cannot say the same." As the shadow spoke, its antlers grew thinner, and the fuzzy hole in its chest began to close. "It is bad enough to follow a man about like a slave one's whole life, but when that man is the inept seraph of a—"

"Enough!" growled Melegaunt. "You have something to report, shadow?"

"I do." The antlers grew as thin as twigs, and the crimson eyes turned pale. "There was a fight in the swamp, but only one creature survived."

"Which one?"

"A human." The shadow's voice was soft and wispy, almost inaudible. "With the pipe and . . ."

"Elminster?"

The silhouette's eyes closed, then it melded into Malik's pearlike figure and was just a shadow once more.

"We must go inside." Melegaunt started around the pyramid.

Jhingleshod clanged after him. "This Elminster is not my concern. You must destroy Wulgreth first."

"And we will." Galaeron scrambled after the pair. "But Melegaunt's right. It's time to go inside."

Jhingleshod turned his lidless eyes on Galaeron. "You are not lying?" Though he asked it as a question, to Galaeron the words felt more like a command. "You will keep your word?"

"If this is Wulgreth's lair, we'll find him inside," said Galaeron. "If he's not there already, he'll come when we enter."

Jhingleshod studied Galaeron with his vacant eyes for a moment, then followed Melegaunt and Vala into the crooked entrance corridor. Galaeron had Aris call upon his god to bless a full skin of water, then took Takari and Malik after the others. Too large to enter with them, the giant waited outside.

The darkness and close confines reminded Galaeron of the cairns in the Sharaedim, though the passageway smelled more like blood than dust, with just a hint of sulfur and steam. Within a few steps, the corridor opened into a vestibule lit by silver spell light. In the moment it took Galaeron's eyes to adjust to the harsh light, he heard Melegaunt saying, "Jhingleshod, here is your Wulgreth. Nothing but dust and bones."

Galaeron glimpsed the wizard's burly shape stooping to pick something up, then heard Takari hissing a spell and knew she had realized the same thing he had.

"Don't touch—"

Takari's spell erupted in a terrible ringing, causing Melegaunt and Vala to cover their ears and spin toward the clamor. Galaeron pushed his way past the pair and found a cloud of dust whirling in the corner, a gray skull rising into the air atop it. He motioned the others away, then breathed a silent sigh of relief when Takari canceled her spell.

"What spell was that?" he asked, keeping a wary eye on the dust pillar. "You nearly broke my eardrums."

"It was supposed to be a silence spell," Takari answered. "Something went wrong."

"Wild magic," explained Jhingleshod. "The Dire Wood is full of it, and the closer to the pyramid, the worse it grows."

"Then let me be the first to suggest we are in terrible trouble," said Malik. Hanging the skin of blessed water over his shoulder, he drew his curved dagger and waved it at the spinning dust, which was now taking a vaguely human shape. "I fear we have found Wulgreth."

"There is nothing to fear." Melegaunt took out a sliver of obsidian and pinched it between his thumb and forefinger. "My spells are not affected by wild magic."

"No!" Galaeron and Takari yelled, then Galaeron added, "Whatever it does, do nothing in return."

"Nothing?" Malik gasped.

"It's a demilich," Galaeron explained. "It will absorb your attacks and use the energy to return to this world."

"A *demi*lich?" echoed Malik. "Then it will be easier to destroy?"

"Trickier," Takari said. "If we strike too early, we bring it back. If we strike too late . . ."

"Yes?" Malik raised his brow. "If we strike too late?"

Galaeron answered, "The Tomb Guard has accounts of demiliches killing an entire company with a single screech."

"*Accounts?*" Malik said. "I thought you had fought many of these things!"

Galaeron and Takari exchanged looks, then he said, "There was one lich."

Malik's face was not the only one that went pale, and even Jhingleshod's lidless eyes seemed to bulge. The dust coalesced into a skeletal figure clothed in rotting silks.

"That is not Wulgreth," Jhingleshod said. "Wulgreth wore no such robes."

Jhingleshod stepped toward Galaeron, but stopped when

the demilich cut him off. The creature flailed at the knight's skeletal face, prompting him to step away and heft his axe.

"Don't!" Galaeron yelled.

Jhingleshod checked his swing, and the demilich's claws burst into harmless clouds of dust as they struck. Fiery points of light began to burn in its empty eye sockets, then it held the stumps of its arms before its face, let out a powdery snort, and whirled on Galaeron. He lowered his sword, and the creature stepped to within a hand's breadth of him, a handful of brown-crusted gems glimmering dully in the place of several teeth. It smelled of musty dirt and stale air, and the hiss of alien winds whispered on its breath. Though Galaeron's whole body went cold and clammy, he forced himself to meet its burning gaze and show no fear.

The demilich raised an arm, where a dusty hand was forming anew, and pressed a fingertip to Galaeron's face. Though the claw did not cut, the otherworldly cold of its touch traced a line of numbness down his cheek. The elf willed himself to stand fast, and though he knew it would anger Melegaunt, readied the necessary spell. The thing opened its mouth and spewed a plume of dust into his face. Caught by surprise, he began to cough and choke, stumbling back as he tried to spit the powdery stuff from his mouth.

"Poison!" Malik started for the exit.

Vala dropped an arm to block his way. "We may have need of that holy water you're carrying."

Galaeron snorted the dust from his nose, then felt his gorge rise as the reek of decay filled the room. A fringe of red, straw-coarse hair sprouted from the lich's head, then a mask of shriveled skin began to creep over its face. The open nasal cavities did nothing to improve the thing's appearance, but with a rounded forehead, overhanging brows, and hideously-skewed jaw, it would have been grotesque even with a nose.

A terrible aura of cold filled the room, and Galaeron knew the demilich's spirit had finally returned to its body. He stepped forward and circled his palm before its face.

"*Forget.*" He spoke in the ancient language of magic, calling upon Melegaunt's coldmagic to empower the spell. "*Return to your rest.*"

The demilich lashed out, catching Galaeron by his chain mail and ripping a handful of magic-forged loops from over his breast. Vala leaped forward to attack, but the links were already falling through the creature's hand. Galaeron raised a hand to check her attack, then watched as the thing's body dissolved back into dust. When the skull sank to the floor, he motioned her forward.

"Now, Vala—before the spirit flees. Cleave it in one blow."

Vala's sword descended in a black flash, splitting the skull lengthwise and dividing both sides again before they toppled to the floor. A crimson flamelight shot from the bones and streaked through Vala's body, then circled the room with a blood-curdling keen. Her jaw dropped and she looked as though she might collapse of shock, then a cold wind ripped through the room and the whirling flamelight faded from view.

Galaeron glanced around the room. "Where's Malik?"

The little man stepped out of a shadowy corner, dagger clutched in his trembling hand. "Have no fear on my account."

Galaeron motioned at the skull fragments. "Douse them well—and hold your breath."

Malik did as he was asked, and the blessed water began to eat through the skull fragments, filling the room with an evil-smelling fume that troubled the little man not in the least. Everyone else withdrew to the tunnel and took turns gulping down fresh air. The bone fragments dissolved, mixing with the dust in a single muddy heap. Malik continued to pour, but no matter how much he stirred, the whole mess adhered together like bread dough. Finally, when no chips of the skull remained visible, Galaeron returned and prepared another spell.

Melegaunt caught his arm. "Allow me."

"If you're not too weary, old man." Galaeron was surprised to feel his lip curl into a disparaging sneer. "All you need do is dispel the magic."

Melegaunt glowered at him. "I can manage. And I could have handled the forgetting magic as well."

The archwizard muttered a few syllables and waved his hand. A purple shadow fell over the doughy mass, then the mud lost its cohesiveness and spread across the floor. Malik dropped the waterskin, and on the pretext of stooping to pick it up, deftly swept up the six brown-crusted gems that had been in the demilich's mouth. Having no interest in the stones himself, Galaeron pretended not to notice.

Jhingleshod came to their side, then propped his axe on the floor and looked at his iron palm. When the gauntlet showed no sign of flaking or disintegrating, he turned to Galaeron.

"What next?"

"I don't know." Galaeron glanced around the chamber, searching in vain for some hint of a forgotten step. "The lich is gone."

"What of its phylactery?" Malik quietly pocketed the gems. "I have heard it said that liches hide their life-forces in repositories—usually an item of great worth?"

"They do," said Galaeron. "But not so with a demilich. They have abandoned their repositories for worlds beyond, and remain connected to Toril only through their remains."

"Liar! Do you think your excuses can fool me?" There was a note of desperation in Jhingleshod's voice. "Had you destroyed the lich, I would not be here now."

"Unless we destroyed the wrong one," said Galaeron, recalling the argument between Melegaunt and Jhingleshod over the lich's true identity. "Malik, let me see those gems you took."

"Gems?" asked the little man. "What gems are those?"

"These."

Vala slipped an arm around Malik's throat and used the other to pluck the brown nuggets from his pocket. Galaeron took them and carefully scraped the brown crust from their faces. He was down to the sixth, a deep ruby, before he found the inner light for which he had been searching. Returning the others to Malik, he displayed this one to his companions.

"The chronicles suggest that this will be an imprisoned spirit," he said. "If we free it, perhaps it can help us."

Melegaunt cast an impatient eye toward the tunnel. "How long?"

"Not as long as trying to defend yourself from my axe," warned Jhingleshod.

"It will need a body," said Galaeron. "Perhaps one of the undead?"

"I can make a body for it," said Melegaunt. "One that will be safer for it—and us."

The archwizard took a piece of shadow silk from his cloak and laid it on Vala's shoulder. Repeating a long incantation over and over, he began to knead the stuff with his fingers, spreading the dark substance over her, carefully covering her flanks, limbs, even her head and face. When he finally finished, Vala resembled a living, breathing sculpture of the blackest basalt.

Melegaunt took her hand and pulled. She emerged from the shadow as though from a dark corner, leaving a dark likeness as perfectly shaped as one of Aris's sculptures.

"If the spirit is troublesome, we can dismiss it with a little light."

Galaeron laid the gem next to the figure, then waved Jhingleshod over. "If you would smash it."

"If this is one of your tricks. . . ."

"By the shadow deep!" Melegaunt cursed. "We haven't time for trickery."

Melegaunt brought his heel down and ground the gem to powder. A crimson radiance flowed out from beneath his heel and began to climb his leg.

"Oh no, my friend!"

The archwizard plunged his foot into the body he had created, then sighed in relief as the luminescence melded into the shadow. A glossy sheen spread over the figure's black flesh, then the eyes opened and stared at the ceiling. It raised a leg, and twisting it around at an impossible angle, studied its heel. Then, seemingly unaware of the arms hanging motionless at its side, did the same with the other leg—and crashed to the floor.

Galaeron rushed to its side. "We didn't know what kind of creature you were." He waved at the body. "We made this in our own fashion."

The shadow sprouted a pair of eyes on the side of its head. "You did well. The color is right."

Galaeron glanced at Melegaunt and found the wizard staring at the dark figure with a dropped jaw. When the elf looked back to the creature, it had wrapped its arms around its legs, and all four limbs were melding into the body.

"We were wondering if you could tell us . . ." Galaeron looked away. He could not quite keep from asking, "What are you?"

"A sharn." It was Melegaunt who said this. "At least that is what I think."

A smiling mouth appeared in the flank of the drop-shaped body. "You think right, wizard." Another mouth appeared on Galaeron's side. "What is it you want to know? I am obviously in your debt."

Galaeron was too stunned to answer, as was everyone except Jhingleshod.

"We would know who captured you, and whether he has been entirely destroyed."

The sharn rose off the floor and floated toward the door. "That was the lich Wulgreth, who took my soul when I came thinking to end his depredations against the empire."

"Wulgreth?" echoed Jhingleshod. "*Which* Wulgreth?"

"The only Wulgreth that is a lich," replied the sharn. "How many do you think there can be?"

Iron shoulders slumping, Jhingleshod whirled on Galaeron. "You have not destroyed him, not completely."

"Wulgreth is completely destroyed," said the sharn, now struggling to squeeze itself into the exit tunnel. "Were that not so, I would not be free."

Jhingleshod whirled on the sharn. "Liar! If Wulgreth were destroyed—"

"Jhingleshod, wait," Galaeron said, stepping in front of the iron knight. "You asked the wrong question."

"Then ask the right one—and quickly." The sharn paused in the tunnel mouth, peering out from a bulbous extrusion that might or might not have been a head. "Grateful as I am, I hunger for better company than yours."

"Which empire were you trying to protect?" Galaeron asked.

"Which *empire*?" The sharn withdrew completely into the tunnel. "Why, the *only* empire of course—unless you mean to include your quaint elven confederacies."

"The Netherese Empire?" Galaeron pressed.

"The very one." The sharn's voice faded as it retreated up the passageway. "And now, if you'll excuse me, I shall return later to repay the favor you have done me."

"Wait!" Melegaunt stepped forward, speaking in a language of strange syllables. When the sharn did not reply, he turned back to the others, shaking his head sadly. "He doesn't know. It's all gone, and he doesn't know."

"The sharn were Netherese?" Galaeron gasped.

The question jolted Melegaunt out of his despair. "I don't know." He shrugged. "No one does, I suspect. There are some who claim they were Netherese arcanists who transformed themselves in order to battle the phaerimm. Others claim they came from another world. What is clear is that they had a hatred of phaerimm, or they would not have erected the Sharn Wall."

At the mention of the Sharn Wall, Galaeron cast a hopeful look up the tunnel, but Melegaunt shook his head. "He's gone, my friend—and even were he not, I doubt he could help us. Before we can patch the hole, we must fight our way through the phaerimm who have already escaped."

Though it angered Galaeron to concede the argument, he nodded and turned toward the back of the chamber. "Then let's find the help we need and get to it."

Keya Nihmedu stood atop the Livery Gate watchtower, slightly self-conscious in her form-fitted chain mail and painfully aware that the magic pike in her hand was no defense at all against phaerimm. Her eyes were as sharp as any in Evereska, and she had seen enough of the battle in the High Vale to know that fifty years of half-hearted blade drill—suffered daily at her father's insistence, Hanali bless him—would stand her in poor stead against the thornbacks. The unsightly monsters had already turned the high slopes into a forest of bare-limbed scarecrows, and now they were working their way onto the upper terraces of the Vine Vale, using their hideous magic to turn the vineyards into dead tangles of thorn hedges.

Most of the Long Watch felt their duties were of little real importance to the war, that they were only standing a post to free the real soldiers to fight, but Keya was not so sure. She had it from Manynests—if she understood his scattered peeptalk correctly—that the Cloudtop Magi Circle had divined the phaerimm's plan. They intended to capture Evereska much the same way they had destroyed the Netherese Empire, by using their life-draining magic to devitalize Evereska Vale. Without the surrounding lands to sustain it, the city's mythal would slowly lose its magic, and eventually it would grow too weak to keep out the thornbacks.

At first, Lord Duirsar had not been overly worried. The groves and lands within the mythal were large enough to sustain its power for a year or two, by which time help would surely arrive. Then the high mages of the Bellcrest Spire had reminded him that plants need light and water, and the Moondark Circle had named a dozen spells that could shut off both. According to Manynests, Lord Duirsar had decided on the spot to create the Long Watch, and that was how Keya knew her duty to be as important as whatever her father and Galaeron were off doing—wherever they were off doing it.

Keya selected a wand from her belt and dutifully swept it across the four quarters of the sky, studying its wake of blue radiance for any telltale glimmers of invisibility magic. The wand was one of a trio quietly supplied to each member of the Long Watch by the three towers of high mages. Keya had not known there were that many circles in Evereska until Manynests had "slipped" during a rather curious visit to inform her that Lord Duirsar had not heard from her father and the Swords—a fact well known to all of Evereska.

After a day's reflection, Keya had dutifully let it slip in gossip that she had heard from a reliable source that Evereska still had three full towers of high mages. This had done much to reassure her friends, who had promptly spread the secret so efficiently that it was repeated to her twice over the next two days—exactly as Lord Duirsar had intended, she was sure. What she had not passed along was the high mages' concern about the mythal, since she felt certain the bird had, in fact, not meant to reveal that bit of bad news.

When Keya found no invisible phaerimm lurking above the mythal, she returned the wand to her belt and started a slow, top-to-bottom scan of the encircling cliffs with her naked eye. She was about halfway around when she noticed a crag hawk circling its nest, claws extended as though it would like to attack but could not. As she had been taught, Keya did not dwell on the spot or immediately reach for a wand, but marked the place in her mind and continued her routine to fool any watching phaerimm. Then, feigning boredom—also a part of Long Watch's meticulously rehearsed routine—she yawned and shook her head, studied her nails for a moment, and glanced back to the spot.

The bird was still circling.

Keya retreated casually down the stairs and found a window from which she could see the hawk. Standing in the shadows, she pulled the first wand from her belt and swept it over the area. She was rewarded with a row of telltale sparkles. For the first time, her heart began to pound with excitement. Though she descended the stairs a dozen times every watch to check on something, this was the first time she had ever found anything suspicious. She pulled her second wand and waved it at the street-side window.

The image of a beautiful Gold elf appeared in the window. "What is it, Keya? If you are thirsty, I can send a boy with some wine."

"No wine, Zharilee." Keya could not keep the excitement from her voice. "I've something to report."

The Gold elf arched her brow. "You're sure?"

"Crawling down the face of Snagglefang," she said, trying to remember the elements of a good report: what doing what, where, when, how many. "A group of invisibles. Maybe a dozen, side-by-side. Just passing the crag hawk's nest."

"Crawling, you say? Why would they crawl?"

Keya looked back to the cliff, where the invisibles continued to descend in crooked row. "It might be a battle line."

Zharilee frowned doubtfully. "Phaerimm don't need to crawl. Why wouldn't they just float . . ." She let the sentence trail off and grew more serious. "I'll send word to Cloudtop. Keep watching."

The image faded, leaving Keya to her invisibles. They were descending rapidly, three of the twelve bunched together. She waved a different wand. The cliff drew close enough to see individual crags and crevices, but the wands would not work together and the twinkles were no longer visible. She went back to the first.

The invisibles reached the base of the cliff and started

down the jumbled talus boulders beneath. Several of the other twinkles gathered around the close-bunched trio, helping them over the rough terrain. Was the trio carrying something? No—more likely, they were two carrying a third. A pair of warriors carrying a wounded comrade.

Any lingering doubts about their identity vanished. Even had it been phaerimm crawling down the cliff, they would not be carrying wounded. From what she had seen of the thornbacks, they did not carry their wounded anywhere—least of all *into* an attack. The invisibles had to be elves—or elf-friends—trying to reach Evereska.

Keya reported her observations to Zharilee, then switched wands and examined the surrounding mountainside. As she had feared, there were five phaerimm and a dozen times that many beholders and illithids scurrying through the denuded forest to intercept the band. She reported that as well.

Zharilee said she was passing the information to Cloudtop Tower, and that she was sorry, but Keya would have to watch what followed. Keya replied that watching was the least she could do. Seeing that there was no longer a danger of giving the party away, she returned to the roof for a better view. Though she would appear only a speck to the invisibles even if they knew where to look for her, she pointed toward the ambush.

The warning proved unnecessary. The invisibles paused at the bottom of the talus, then one sprayed the wood ahead with a stream of silver fire so brilliant it spotted Keya's vision from more than a thousand paces away. The five phaerimm reeled away, pouring columns of smoke into the air and slapping at their burning bodies with all four hands, and the invisibles followed the assault with a volley of enchanted arrows. As each of the shafts struck their targets, they exploded in golden flashes of magic and filled the wood with blazing red smoke.

When Keya used her wand to report this development, the too-gaunt face of Kiinyon Colbathin appeared next to Zharilee.

"This silver fire—who cast it?" he demanded. "Was it a human?"

After losing the entire tomb guard in the initial battles with the phaerimm, Kiinyon had apologized to all of Evereska and tried to resign. Lord Duirsar had refused the resignation and placed him in charge of the vale's defenses, saying that Evereska had need both of his experience and the wisdom he had earned by it.

"I can't see," Keya reported. "The smoke is too thick."

"Well look, damn it!"

Keya looked, but, as she said, the smoke was impervious to sight and magic—at least any magic she had been given. All she could see was the curtain of smoke billowing across the hill, a handful of illithids scrambling up into the talus—and it occurred to her what she did *not* see. The invisibles had attacked, so now they should be visible—but she still couldn't see them, not with any of her wands. Realizing how well the small band had planned its attack, Keya swept her gaze down the mountainside.

She found them halfway down the Vine Vale, staggering out of a small black door in the middle of an arbor-covered terrace. The first was a bearded human in scorched robes, the hair on his bare chest singed away around a grotesque brown scar. The second was a Gold elf in the elaborate armor of an Evereskan noble, as were the third, fourth, and all the others that followed.

"It's the Swords!" Keya cried. "They're back!"

"The Swords?" gasped Kiinyon. "Of Evereska?"

"Well, some—a few." No sooner had Keya said this than she thought of her father and began to search the faces in the party. "I see Lord Dureth, and Janispar Orthorion, and a black-bearded human."

"That human, could it be Khelben Arunsun?" This time it was Lord Duirsar himself asking. "And tell us how you can see them, damn it! The tower mages can't find them in that wretched smoke."

"I'm sorry, milord—they're down in the Vine Vale, in the ThistleHoney Vineyard," said Keya. "And I don't know Khelben Arunsun, but the human is carrying a black . . . by the golden rose, no!"

"What?" demanded Lord Duirsar. " 'No,' what?"

Keya did not answer, for the last two elves emerging from the black door held a litter bearing the shrouded figure of a dead body. She could not see who lay beneath the shroud, but there was no mistaking the acid-pitted helmet lashed across the figure's chest. A simple basinet of silvery mithral steel, it was by far the plainest of any worn by the Noble Blades. It belonged to Aubric Nihmedu.

"Watcher!" roared Kiinyon. "Answer Lord Duirsar!"

"I—I apologize, milords," said Keya. "The human has a black beard and black staff, and he shows sign of a grave injury. More than that, I cannot tell you of him."

"And why did you cry out?" prompted Zharilee. "Lord Duirsar asked about that as well."

"I saw . . ." Keya paused to clear the catch in her throat and saw a patrol of elves rushing past the Swords to meet two phaerimm that had teleported in to attack the battered company from behind. "Excuse me, but if you want to see Khelben Arunsun alive, you must send some war mages to help."

Before she had finished the sentence, a circle of high mages appeared between the fleeing elves and their would-be attackers. With a sweep of her hand, the center erected a wall of golden radiance and sent it rolling toward the enemy. The phaerimm countered by sending a cone of cold blasting through the wall to strike down one of the mages, then it teleported away. The surviving Swords were swept up by the patrol and hurried toward the protection of the mythal. So went the battles for Evereska, swift and deadly and never-ending.

"We'll see to the Swords, Keya." Now that things appeared to be under control, Lord Duirsar's voice was gentler. "Tell us what you saw."

"Lord Nihmedu . . ." She stopped to choke back a sob,

then realized that her brother was now Lord Nihmedu and began to wonder what had become of him, and she could not stop the tears. "I'm sorry to report the Swords' blademajor has fallen."

"Your father?" Zharilee gasped.

Keya nodded and looked away from the wand-window.

"I'm sorry, Keya. He was a good friend and a loyal Evereskan," said Lord Duirsar. His voice grew softer, and he spoke to Kiinyon Colbathin. "Under the circumstances, Vale Marshall, I wonder if the Long Watcher might be excused."

"Of course," said Kiinyon. "Feel free to retire, Watcher."

"Thank you, milord." Keya wiped the tears from her eyes and turned to the wand-window. "Do you have someone to relieve me, Zharilee?"

The Gold elf hesitated. "We're well-covered in other posts."

"But none of the other posts reported the Swords' return?" Keya asked.

Zharilee shook her head. "There are a couple that should have seen it, but no."

"Then I'll stay." Keya turned back toward the High Vale. "The Long Watch has its duty, too."

CHAPTER TWENTY

30 Nightal, the Year of the Unstrung Harp

Wulgreth number two."

"Definitely two." Peering around the chamber, Galaeron nodded his agreement with Takari's conclusion. "This has to be Jhingleshod's Wulgreth."

The pyramid's second room was as dusty as the first, but packed with implements required by any practicing wizard. There were mortars and kettles and vials, balances, braziers, and bottles, tablets, scrolls, and librams—many librams, all lined up on shelves and safely protected behind glass doors. There was also a thick tome of spells, resting on a stand beneath a hovering glowball, open to a spell near the back and not at all covered in dust.

A loud grating sound came from the far corner. Galaeron turned to see Takari springing away from a small crawlway, sword in hand and the first syllable of a fire spell gliding off her tongue. When nothing sprang out to attack, she gestured at a depressed trigger-stone in the floor.

"That was easy."

"Too easy." Galaeron kicked a loose stone into the crawl-way, then winced as a wall of green magic descended behind it. "This lich is a tricky one."

"Something he learned from the demons of Ascalhorn," agreed Jhingleshod, stepping into the room. "Easier to lead a victim to his doom than to push him into it."

"A lesson Galaeron would do well to remember," Mele-gaunt said. He followed the others into the room, and seeing the open spellbook, shook his head in scorn. "A little too inviting, I would say." He flicked a hand at the stand, and a pall of shadow fell over the pages. "To guard against a straying glance."

Though Galaeron suspected the comment was directed at him, he did not object. The open book was too obvious an invitation. Sooner or later, someone would glance over to see what Wulgreth had been studying and would find himself compelled to continue reading, activating some spell of possession or imprisonment. He was beginning to understand this lich. Unlike the first, which had wanted to drive them off, this one wanted to control them.

The glowball brightened of its own accord, filling the chamber with harsh light and deep shadows. Along the back wall stood a small collection of gilt armor and bejeweled weapons, all enchanted so heavily that an aura of magic showed through the thick coating of dust. Next to the weaponry stood a rack of wands and staves, and next to that sat a row of treasure chests. In front of one chest kneeled Malik, his hands plunged to his wrists in a bed of jewels, his gaze blank and empty.

Galaeron pulled the little man from the chest, spraying jewels across the floor, and slammed the coffer shut. "Don't!"

Malik blinked several times, then reached for his dagger.

"No need to be greedy, elf. There are gems enough here to make rich men of us all!"

"To make us Wulgreth's slaves." Galaeron looked to the others. "Don't touch it. This is bait."

"Bait?" Vala was eyeing a suit of gleaming chain mail.

Galaeron stepped in front of her. "It's how he recruits his undead servants, I think. You saw Malik's eyes."

She nodded.

"A clever scheme." Takari eyed the treasure as though it were offal. "If we can't touch anything without becoming slaves, we can't sort through it to find his phylactery."

"Unless we dispel the magic first," said Melegaunt.

"Then dispel it," Jhingleshod said.

"My magic is not unlimited." Melegaunt eyed the wall of magic items. "It will take someone more powerful than I to dispel all this."

"I am no fool," said Jhingleshod. "You cannot have what you want until I have what I want."

"It's not possible," said Melegaunt. "I've already used that spell once today. I can cast it one more time, but after that I must spend the night imprinting the magic on my mind many times over. By the time I finish, Elminster will be here."

"Perhaps Elminster could dispel it," suggested Jhingleshod.

"You don't have a bargain with Elminster," said Galaeron, "and I doubt he'll be inclined to rescue the one who helped Wulgreth bring demons to Ascalhorn. You can only trust Melegaunt."

"Trust *him*?" The veins in Jhingleshod's eyes grew red and thick. "I am not so naive as you."

"Naive?" Galaeron's gaze flashed to Melegaunt, then back to Jhingleshod. "What do you mean by that?"

"Galaeron, a man can intend two things at once." Melegaunt tried to interpose himself between Galaeron and Jhingleshod. "I am still Evereska's only hope."

Galaeron continued to look at Jhingleshod. "Tell me."

"There is no need to tell you what you already know," said Jhingleshod. "You saw him betray Vala on the bridge. You should not be surprised to learn he has been lying to you."

Galaeron whirled on the archwizard and found Vala blocking his path, one hand on her sword. "No, Galaeron." She pushed him back gently. "You know I can't let you."

Galaeron felt something in his hand and realized he was holding his own sword. He released it, turned to Jhingleshod, and asked, "What did Melegaunt tell you?"

"After Wulgreth is destroyed," the knight promised.

Galaeron turned next to Malik and said, "You heard it."

"I told Jhingleshod I came to save my people," said Melegaunt. "You, of all people, should understand that."

Galaeron continued to look at Malik. The little man sighed and nodded. "First he claimed he came to save Evereska, and for that lie he received the same blow you did. Then he said he came to save his people, that he needed the Karsestone to return shade to his home."

"Not *my* home, *it's* home." Melegaunt shook his head in frustration, then sighed and said, "Shade was a Netherese city. Our shadow masters read the empire's fall in the dawn shadows and took us to safety in the Demiplane of Shadow. We've been trying to return to our home—you call it Anauroch—ever since."

"Seventeen centuries is a long time trying," Takari said.

"Time is not the same in the Demiplane of Shadow," Melegaunt said. "Nor the task of returning a simple one."

"Not with the phaerimm in your way," said Galaeron. The anger in his voice prompted Vala to draw her sword. "First, you had to move them someplace else!"

"It was not meant to be Evereska," said Melegaunt, now growing as angry as Galaeron. "But what if it had been? For seventeen of your centuries, we have been trapped in a dark hell, unable to return because of the phaerimm. For the first millennium, we kept our freedom by paying tribute in lives to the demon lords who thought to make us their own, and for the last seven hundred we have fought the Malaugrym for our very survival. Would it be too much to ask of Evereska—and the rest of the world—that they help us destroy the phaerimm so we could return in peace?"

"You didn't ask," said Galaeron.

"Not Evereska." Melegaunt shouldered Vala aside and drew himself to his full height, reminding everyone present—including Galaeron—that he had little to fear from an angry elf. "But what would the answer have been, had a Netherese city asked your Hill Elders for help?"

The question sent a cold bolt through Galaeron, for the answer was as obvious to him as to Melegaunt. The ancient elves had disapproved of Netheril's careless magic, and as he knew from ancient writings in the Academy of Magic, taken a secret delight in the fall of the ancient empire.

"You can be sure I am doing more for Evereska than Evereska would for Shade," said Melegaunt. "Whether you believe that is up to you—and your shadowself."

Without awaiting Galaeron's reply, the wizard spun on Jhingleshod. "I presume the Karsestone to be beneath this pyramid. If there is an easier way to reach it, do not make me waste precious time and magic opening a shadow tunnel."

Jhingleshod's eyes flared angrily. "Your promise—"

"Whether you value Melegaunt's promise or not, you may trust mine." Galaeron did not know whether the all-too-human fury in his heart was his own or that of his shadowself, but he did know that much of the criticism Melegaunt had leveled at Evereska was true. He turned to the wizard and said, "Were the circumstances of our cities reversed, perhaps I would do as much to save Evereska. But know this, wizard, I will hold you to your promise. If Evereska falls, I will see to it that Shade suffers a fate many times worse."

Melegaunt gave him a dark smile. "It already has, elf. It was never our intention to loose the phaerimm on your city—and they remain more our enemy than yours. There is no need to worry on that account."

Galaeron turned to Jhingleshod. "My promise stands as before."

Jhingleshod studied Galaeron for a moment, then nodded. "Do not fail me, I warn you."

He went to the crawlway Takari had discovered and swung through feet first, his body erupting into a cloud of dust as it passed through the green barrier. Galaeron and the others looked at each other with dropped jaws.

Finally, Takari said, "An illusion. This lich is a very clever one, indeed."

She stepped over to the passage and swung her legs through the opening, then vanished in a cloud of dust. Galaeron went next and found himself plummeting into a high, silver-lit cavern. He glimpsed a colonnade of curved pillars arcing up to a central support, then splashed into a pool of foul-smelling liquid the color and consistency of quicksilver. A small hand caught him by the hair and dragged him to one side just as Vala hit beside him. Next came Melegaunt, fluttering down on the magic of a slow-fall spell, and Malik plummeted into the pool screaming.

A moment later, the group found itself standing waist-deep in a silvery pond, staring across a mirror-bright surface at a luminous white boulder the size Malik's horse. From a jagged crack in the center poured a steady stream of the shimmering fluid, filling the pool and slowly disappearing down a whirlpool at the far end. As the liquid swirled down the hole, it assumed a crimson tinge and began to steam, almost like blood.

"It's touching," said Takari, ever the romantic. "Karsus's heart bleeds for what he did."

"You might say that, though Karsus was too mad for true remorse," said Melegaunt. "The Weave filled him to bursting when he tried to steal Mystryl's godhead. What you see pouring from the Karsestone is all that remains of that ancient whole magic."

"*Whole* magic?" It was Malik who asked this. "Since when has magic been less than whole?"

"Since the Fall of Netheril," Galaeron surmised, thinking back to the tiresome texts he had studied at the Academy of Magic. After the fall, Mystryl had saved the Weave by reincarnating herself as Mystra, but the surviving archwizards had quickly discovered that without the goddess's direct intervention—a very rare occurrence indeed—they could no longer cast their most powerful spells. Most sages conjectured that Mystra was simply limiting magic to protect the Weave from another disaster, but Galaeron saw that another explanation made more sense—and explained the source of Melegaunt's cold magic. "It split," he said.

Melegaunt was too busy pressing strands of shadow silk onto the Karsestone to answer, but Malik was hanging on every word.

"What split?" the little man asked. "Do you mean the Weave?"

Galaeron started to answer, then recalled Malik's previous interest in shadow magic and thought better of it. "You ask too many questions, human." He started toward the little man. "You're no wizard. What is it to you if the Weave split?"

Malik's eyes grew wide, and he began to retreat. "Remember your shadow, my friend. You are placing yourself in grave danger with these questions!"

"But I'm not," said Vala, approaching from the other side. "And I've been wondering myself. It wasn't any coincidence that we found you camped outside Thousand Faces, was it?"

"You would threaten *me*?" Malik gasped. "After I risked my own life to save yours?"

"I'd like to know why." Vala rested a hand on her sword. "In my experience, Cyricists are rarely so selfless."

"Don't kill him—I'm going to need him," said Melegaunt, still working his way around the Karsestone. "His presence is no mystery. He's investigating my magic for Cyric."

Malik's jaw dropped. "You knew?"

Melegaunt peered out from behind the Karsestone. "Do I strike you as an idiot?" The archwizard pointed his chin at

Malik's turban. "Pull that off, and you'll find his antlers. Our companion is no ordinary thief—he's the Seraph of Lies."

Galaeron did as Melegaunt instructed and found a pair of small antlers—they looked more like cuckold's horns—then asked, "You knew, and you let him stay?"

"Better the spy you know than the one you don't—and he has proven useful, wouldn't you say?" Melegaunt began to point to spots in a circle about six feet from the Karsestone. "Now spread yourselves out, and we'll call the power we need to save Evereska."

The companions did as Melegaunt requested, leaving a sixth spot open for him. The archwizard grabbed two handfuls of silvery magic from the pool, then floated into the air above the Karsestone. He hung the globes about six feet apart and touched a plain copper ring that he wore on his left had to each. A magical light spread upon the orbs, which began to glow with the blinding radiance of the sun. Galaeron turned away with spots in his eyes.

As his vision cleared, he saw a pair of shadows lying on the silvery surface of the pool, both so black and deep they looked at once like solid bodies and empty wells. Galaeron reached to find out which was his, and his fingers vanished in the darkness without creating a ripple on the pool's surface. When he pulled them back, all four digits were missing above the middle knuckle. There was no pain, no impression of heat or cold, no sensation at all. The fingers simply weren't there.

Gasping in alarm, Galaeron spun to berate Melegaunt for not warning him—then saw the translucent shape of his fingers outlined against the brilliant glow of the lights and realized he had been assuming the worst again. Atop the Karsestone, Melegaunt completed a spell he had been casting and noticed Galaeron watching him.

"Only a moment now," the wizard said. "All is ready."

Melegaunt stepped off the Karsestone and floated to his place in the circle. He asked the group to join hands, then spoke a few words in a strange language Galaeron assumed to be Netherese. Next to him, Vala hissed in surprise as a tingling stream of energy passed from her hand into Galaeron's, then Malik gasped aloud as the stream passed into him. Galaeron began to feel lightheaded, and growing suspicious, opened his hand.

"Don't break the circle!" Melegaunt commanded. "Let no one break it, or we will all be pulled into Shadow."

Vala clamped down on Galaeron's hand with astonishing strength. "Trust us, not your shadow!"

Galaeron's two shadows began to grow longer and broader, taking on a shape completely unlike his own. One assumed the form of an armored human with immense shoulders and a narrow waist. A pair of curved horns sprouted from his blocky head, then a pair of yellow eyes appeared in his dark face. The second silhouette was as large as the first, though squarer of body and clothed in swirling robes of darkness. Though it sprouted no horns, its profile revealed a grotesquely square chin and a crescent-shaped mouth full of sharp teeth.

Both shadows sank beneath the silvery surface and disappeared, only to reappear a moment later as huge, murkswaddled figures. When Galaeron glanced around the circle, he found a pair of similar figures standing in front of each of his trembling companions. He could not quite decide whether he was looking at men or demons.

Melegaunt opened his hands and bowed so deeply that his brow touched the silvery pond. "My Princes, welcome back to Faerûn."

"Stand, young brother." The largest, a copper-eyed brute nearly three heads taller than Vala, motioned Melegaunt upright. "That is the heavy magic?"

"It is," said Melegaunt.

Paying no mind to the others in the chamber, the rest of the princes waded to Melegaunt's side. Galaeron and the others followed, but stopped a respectful distance away.

"All has gone according to plan?" asked the copper-eyed figure. "We are ready to proceed?"

Melegaunt's face betrayed the barest hesitation. "All has gone well, my lord Escanor, but one matter may trouble us."

The horn-helmeted prince cast an admonishing glance at Galaeron's hip. Galaeron looked down, but did not realize what the dark warrior was staring at until he felt Takari pull his hand away from his sword.

"I think that would be foolish, my princep," she whispered.

The murky warrior looked back to Melegaunt without comment.

The one called Escanor said, "Yes, young brother?"

"I have spoken of one called Elminster," said Melegaunt.

"The gray-bearded Chosen," said the horned warrior. "We have observed him. A powerful ally—or an inconvenient enemy. Which?"

"That is yet to be decided, my lord Rivalen, but I fear unexpected events have turned him a little against us. As you know, his parents were slain by a shadow mage, and that has made him suspicious of us. Only two days ago, he tried to stop us from entering the Dire Wood, and I have been informed by a darksentry that even now he comes after us. I fear he would think to interfere with the Return—and he has the power to do it."

Rivalen and Escanor glanced at each other.

"We will need to set matters straight with him before proceeding, that is all," said Escanor. "And these unexpected events?"

Melegaunt motioned Galaeron into the circle. "Galaeron Nihmedu is in a shadow crisis and losing badly." Several princes cast knowing looks at each, and Melegaunt continued, "He has done much to aid our cause. Through no fault of his, he and I opened the Sharn Wall in Evereska instead of Hartsvale."

"The phaerimm are out already?" gasped Rivalen.

Melegaunt hung his head. "My fault entirely. I chose a poor place to meet my darkswords, and Galaeron's patrol took us for tomb robbers. They were not to blame."

"There is no blame here," said Escanor. "We will adjust

our plan, that is all." He looked to Galaeron. "We cannot undo the anguish your people have already suffered, but your home will be saved—have no fear of that."

"The war will be farther south," Rivalen said. "Unfortunate, but no great disaster."

"Evereska has a mythal," warned Melegaunt.

Rivalen shrugged. "And it will take a little longer than planned." He clasped Galaeron's shoulder. "But it will be won. On that, you have the word of the Twelve Princes of Shade."

Galaeron's first thought was of what the prince left unsaid. "At what cost to Evereska? It is well and good to slay the phaerimm, but not if you mean to fight the war on elf lands."

Rivalen exchanged a concerned look with the others, then a third prince, the square-chinned one who had arisen in front of Galaeron, stepped forward.

"I know it is difficult during your shadow-struggle, but you must trust us. Evereska will suffer—it has already suffered, as you must know—and we will do what we can to help. But it is the phaerimm who attack your land, not us. We did not set them to it any more than you did."

"But *I* did," Galaeron said, nearly collapsing beneath the weight of his mistake. "I ordered the wrong spell."

"You did your duty," said the prince. "You would have been remiss not to attack to your best judgement. Any blame you feel comes from your shadow, no one else. You must ignore it, or you are lost."

The prince's words lifted the burden from Galaeron's heart a little—but not as much as when Takari slipped her arm through his.

"Listen to the murky one, my princep. He is telling you what everyone who was there already knows."

Galaeron nodded. "I'll try."

"Good," said Melegaunt. "And we'll be there to help—so long as you stop casting spells."

"And I will see to that," said Vala, coming to take Galaeron's other arm.

Rivalen smiled, baring a pair of fangs that would not have looked out of place on a vampire. "Good. Now, we must be off."

"What of Wulgreth?" Jhingleshod shoved his way into the circle and glared at Melegaunt. "Do not think—"

"I would not think of it," said the archwizard. He turned to Escanor. "There is the matter of a small promise I made to this spirit. Can you dispel all the magic in the room above?"

Escanor eyed the iron knight, then motioned the other princes toward the ceiling exit. "As you wish." He started to rise after the others. "We'll do it on our way out."

"On your way out?" Melegaunt waved a hand at the Karse-stone.

"We must deal with these little problems," said Rivalen. "And from the sound of it, the sooner the better."

"But what of the Return?"

Escanor smiled broadly, baring a mouthful of needle-thin fangs. "That honor is for you, young brother. Levitate the boulder into the sky, then use your magic to call our people home."

"Me?" Melegaunt gasped. "I am the lowest of us all!"

"But the most worthy," said Escanor. "You cannot have forgotten the words."

"Never." Now it was Melegaunt who smiled. "Hear me now, people of Shade. Follow me now, for the Return is at hand!"

CHAPTER TWENTY-ONE

30 Nightal, the Year of the Unstrung Harp

A hoarse phaerimm whistle rasped through the stone trees above Elminster, prompting him to hurl his ample bulk through a tangle of the Dire Wood's poison vines. He rolled out the other side with astonishing grace for a man of his considerable age, then spun around to find a cascade of harmless gray spiders fluttering to the ground before him. The archmage spied a pair of fiery lich-eyes peering over a vine-shrouded wall opposite him and countered with a swarm of meteors that turned into a colony of bees, then the phaerimm—there were two of them, floating through the treetops above the street— unleashed their own flurry of magic. Three silver rays disintegrated into scintillating rainbows, two black death beams became winged snakes and flew off, and one spell actually worked, a lightning bolt that dissipated against Elminster's spellguard in a silver flash.

Such was any battle in a wild magic area, nine parts futility and one part danger. Seeing Wulgreth starting to rise into view—with a fringe of coarse hair, noseless rotting face, and lipless skeleton's mouth, the lich looked much the same as the hundreds Elminster had disposed of during his long lifetime—the archmage spun around and crashed down a vine-choked ally. At the corner, he turned toward the center of the city, hoping to circle back to the main road and follow the trail of mangled corpses to Melegaunt and the others.

That the shadow wizard had destroyed so many undead in the middle of the largest wild magic area on Faerûn spoke volumes to Elminster. It also raised some disturbing questions—many, many disturbing questions. He had faced enough shadow mages to know they drew their magic from some dark power that slowly corrupted them, inexorably twisting them into monstrous mockeries of themselves. He had long suspected that the dark power was not part of the Weave, a suspicion now confirmed by the fact that Melegaunt's magic worked well in an area where the lingering effects of Karsus's madness had twisted the Weave into an unpredictable snarl.

What Elminster did not know and hoped to learn before this day ended was the exact nature of that other source of magic—and which god controlled it. He had his suspicions, of course. As Mystra's enemy, Cyric would go to great lengths to create a source of magic other than the Weave, and Talos the Destroyer had long been attempting to wrest a part of the Weave from her control. The now certain knowledge that someone had succeeded was enough to make even Elminster's silver fire-warmed blood run cold. There was already more than enough evil in the world to keep the Balance—even without its own special source of magic.

Elminster darted down a vine-choked lane back to the main street, and stepping over the cleaved body of a wight, renewed his pursuit. After his fight against the phaerimm outside the Dire Wood and the running battle he had been waging against Wulgreth since crossing the bridge, there was nothing he would have enjoyed more than nice spell of flying—he just didn't want to turn into a butterfly. He continued down the road in a heavy-footed jog, keeping one hand close to his wand belt and hazarding a glance over his shoulder every ten paces.

The silhouette of Karse Butte was just beginning to loom above the treetops when a chirrupy voice sounded inside his mind. *Elminster, haven't . . . Khelben . . . days . . . should . . . try Rocnest . . . twenty . . . wizards.*

Garbled as the sending was by wild magic, Elminster understood enough that he forgot to watch his feet and tripped. He landed sprawled on his hands and knees, huffing for breath and shaking with fatigue. *Only twenty, Laeral?*

If Laeral answered, it was lost in the cacophony of clanging and banging that erupted around him. Elminster rolled and found himself being buried under an avalanche of cake steel. Heavy as the ingots were, they merely bounced off his body shield and piled around him, but he was more concerned to find Wulgreth standing outside the shower, ready to attack the instant it was safe. The touch of a lich could paralyze even one of the Chosen, which would instantly trigger his evasion magic and—under normal circumstances—whisk him to his Safehold to recover. Given the wild magic in the area, however, he doubted even Mystra herself could say where he would find himself.

Better to try something over which he might have more control. Elminster envisioned the vine-tangle he had left a few moments earlier, then uttered a single mystic word.

There was a brief moment of black timeless falling, then he found himself staring at an overgrown street through a tangle of thin-leaved vines. He was familiar enough with the afterdaze of teleporting to recognize the effects instantly and trust that he would remember where he was and why he was there in a moment, but something seemed especially strange about this time. He felt both hugely large and unable to move, and for some reason he seemed to be holding his arms spread wide.

He saw a pair of phaerimm come floating past about a dozen feet below his nose and remembered if not *what* he was, at least where he was—in a wild magic area in the Dire Wood, fighting a running battle against Wulgreth and trying to escape an army of pursuing phaerimm—and something had gone wrong.

The phaerimm were about a quarter the size they should have been, and the overgrown street was no wider than a foot path, and the petrified trees looked no larger than a man. One of the huge dragonflies buzzed past, snatching a small black finch that looked no larger than a mosquito, and Elminster had a sinking feeling in his . . . no, it wasn't his stomach. It was more like his trunk. He tried to turn his head and discovered he could not.

The dragonfly buzzed back by and landed on an outspread branch, its mandibles popping as it consumed the black finch. Elminster let out a sigh too deep to be heard by any creature that was not a tree, then saw the phaerimm zip past in the wrong direction and vanish into the tangled wood.

Elminster stood motionless and quiet for a moment—it was about all he could do—trying to imagine what kind of magic a mere lich could possibly have summoned that would frighten two phaerimm so. Then he heard a murky voice call his name and realized Wulgreth had not frightened the creatures at all. Another voice called for him, then yet a third. He recognized a little of Melegaunt's accent and timbre in both, but they were deeper and more powerful, and more assured of themselves—far more assured.

Too wise to reveal himself in his present condition, Elminster did not even try to speak. He could escape with a mere thought, so the tree seemed a safe enough place to hide for now. The deep voices continued to call out, drawing closer each time, and twelve murk-swaddled figures soon marched into view.

They looked vaguely human, but with the grotesque features he had long ago learned to associate with shadow magic, and they were by far the largest, most powerful looking men he had ever seen. Most wore the dress of warriors, several the cloaks of wizards, and two were shrouded in clerical robes. They all had the brightly-colored eyes of creatures from the lower planes, and an aura of darkness seemed to swirl around them like fog.

The largest, a copper-eyed brute as tall as an ogre, stopped and turned to the others. "If he is here, he is hidden well. I see nothing in the shadows."

A figure in a horned helm spread his palms in resignation. "Then we must make him find us."

"How so, Rivalen?" asked the first. "He is not one to be so easily manipulated, and we have other problems to attend to."

"Let three of us go to Evereska, and three to Hidden Lake," said Rivalen. "That will leave six for Shadowdale. I am sure Elminster will find us then."

It had to be the loneliest camp in Faerûn, a single tent in the heart of a barren salt pan, a young father staring across the horizon at the white winter sun, a haggard mother dripping water into her children's mouths one sip at a time, a bony camel so sick and weary it did not even groan. Earlier in the day, the camel had collapsed on the waterskin, and the children had pressed their faces to the salt and made themselves sick trying to lap up the last drops of water. The mother had wailed and beat her husband's chest, and the husband had struck her and turned away to hide his tears. That much the princes had read in the twilight shadows, and they could guess what would come tomorrow. Even in winter, no one crossed the Shoal of Thirst without water.

The irony was not lost on the three princes. To the east, a mantle of shadowy clouds was already coalescing out of the empty twilight. They were bringing water—enough to mire the camel, enough to sweep away the tent and all it contained—but water would not save the family. Quite the opposite. Even if these desert nomads knew how to swim, they could not swim for miles.

The princes rolled to their sides, peeling themselves out of the tent's shadow, then rose to their feet in a silent motion. There was a deep bristling as their bodies returned to shape, followed by the cold nausea that always accompanied a flight through the shadow deep.

It took only an instant for the feelings to pass, but by then the camel had raised its nose to test the air, and that was the only alarm the family required. The mother called her children and disappeared into the tent, and the husband leaped to his feet, his scimitar clearing its scabbard.

Brennus spread his palms to show they were empty. "By the Little Gods, friend, we mean no harm."

The nomad looked past the three princes across the darkening salt pan, then peered around the other side of the tent to make certain no accomplices lurked there. Only then, when he was sure they were alone, did he speak.

"What would you have of me, *djinn*? As you can see, I have nothing worth stealing—save my daughter, and I will slay her myself before I let you make her a slave."

"That won't be necessary." Brennus bent at his waist. "We beg your forgiveness, but a small party cannot be too careful in a place such as this."

The nomad eyed the trio warily. "You do not have the look of those who need worry."

Brennus avoided the temptation to smile, knowing his ceremonial fangs would alarm the nomad. "It is often a mistake to judge men by their appearance. We are not djinn."

"I have no desire to argue the point," the nomad replied. "Name your business or be gone."

"You would do well to curb that tongue," said Brennus's brother Lamorak. With night almost upon them, Lamorak's swarthy face had assumed an almost spectral murkiness. "It makes no difference to us whether you live or die."

The knuckles on the nomad's sword hand whitened, and Brennus realized the threat angered the man more than frightened him.

"We are not here to hurt you, only to warn you," Brennus said. "Pack your things quickly. This place will soon be a mire."

"The Shoal of Thirst? A mire?" The nomad looked at the first stars twinkling in the west. "I do not think so. The heavens themselves do not hold that much water."

"The heavens hold more water than you know." Brennus pointed east, where a wall of purple clouds was already sweeping in from the dusky mountains. "Enough to fill the Shoal of Thirst and sweep away your tent. Enough to drown your camel and your children, too."

"There is no reason to believe it will all fall here," the nomad said stubbornly. "Only a djinn would claim to know otherwise."

"Call us what you will," growled Lamorak. "We know."

"Surely you noticed the casting," said the third prince, Yder. "You could hardly have missed it."

"That was your doing?" The nomad's swarthy face grew sallow and yellow. "That ground-shaking thunder, and the black bolt that tore the sky?"

"We didn't know you were camped in Hidden Lake." As Brennus spoke, whirling clouds of salt-laden air began to skip through the camp, drawing an alarmed groan from the camel and gasps of surprise from inside the tent. "You must hurry. The rain will soon be falling in sheets."

"Sheets of rain?" The nomad looked east and saw the black wall of rain. "By the light of Elah!"

The wife pushed her head out of the tent, her face veiled by a purple scarf, her eyes rimmed in kohl. "Shall I pack, my husband?"

"What good would it do?" the nomad gasped. "We cannot

outrun the wind! Better to wait in the *khreima* while it passes."

"If you wait in your khreima, you will drown in your khreima," said Brennus.

The nomad narrowed his eyes. "Surely, those who can summon the rains can send them back?"

"Do you think such magic is easy to work?" demanded Lamorak. "A matter of a few syllables and a handful of powdered silver?" He turned to the woman, pointing a talonlike finger at her veiled face. "If you wish to live, pack your things."

The woman's eyes grew round, and she looked to her husband for instruction. He glared at Lamorak. "What would you have us do? Fly to the Sister of Rains?"

Brennus interposed himself between the man and his brother. "And if you could?"

"Men do not have wings, *berrani.*"

"They do not need them." Brennus took a strand of shadow silk from his pocket and shaped it into a small ring, then tossed it on the ground and spoke a single mystic word. The circle swelled to the size of small wagon, then darkened and floated off the ground. "There are other ways."

"Not for the Bedine." The nomad brought his scimitar down on the flying disk, slicing it down the center. "The Bedine do not abide the magic of devils!"

The two halves dropped to the ground and melted into the twilight darkness. Brennus watched the pieces disappear, then looked back to the nomad.

"As you wish."

The winds arrived in a whistling flurry of salt and mist, and Brennus signaled his brothers. They backed away from the camp, fading into the darkness with silent acts of will.

"We Princes of Shade are hardly devils," Brennus said. "Not even close."

Elminster returned to find Shadowdale blanketed in war smoke. Exhausted as he was by his long fight against Wulgreth, the archmage circled the village, reconnoitering the battle before joining himself. The clang and crackle of hard-fought combat rose from a dozen places along a great circle scribed by Toad Knoll, Castle Krag, and Harper's Hill. Golden bolts of magic flashed back and forth along the length of Shadow Ridge, silver lightning limned the walls of Castle Krag, swarms of meteors flew over the Ashaba down by Mirrorman's Mill.

Much as he longed to swoop to the defense of each embattled townsman, Elminster bided his time. His battle against Wulgreth had left him exhausted physically and magically. He had used half his spells before becoming trapped in the tree, and most of the rest—including his emergency evasion spell, the last of his teleports, and both worldwalking spells—escaping Wulgreth (again) in the wild magic area. He left the Dire Wood with only three magic-dispelling spells, a single set of golden bolts, three speed enchantments, and the ability to fly.

These last four spells he had expended on a triple-hasted flight across Anauroch—with a long detour around the Shoal of Thirst, where the most furious storm he had ever seen was pouring water into the ancient lake bed—and a breakneck descent into the Dales . . . where nothing made sense. Elminster had expected to find Rivalen and five other princes attacking Shadowdale, yet he could see a dozen separate battles raging in the woods. Moreover, he saw no sign of shadow magic, only the standard bolts and blasts, with a little bit of arrow- and axe-work for good measure. If Rivalen and his brothers were here, they were disguising themselves well.

Finally, Elminster spied the blinding swarm of bolts for which he had been searching and dropped through the trees onto Mistledale Mount, where a small line of warriors were working their way through the undergrowth toward a charred phaerimm. In their midst ran the tall, smoky, as-always-stunning figure of Storm Silverhand.

Too weary to run, Elminster called, "Storm, lass! Wait for me."

Storm whirled, eyes flashing and ready to fling fire. "Elminster, there you are!" Her voice was not exactly joyful, and she was slow to lower her spell-ready hand. "Would you please tell me what in the Nine Hells you're doing?"

"Me?" Elminster gasped. "I've been in the Dire Wood chasing a shadow mage—or twelve, as it happens—too long a story to tell now." He waved at the phaerimm's crisped form. "What's this? Have the phaerimm decided Evereska is not enough to chew in a bite?"

"I doubt they care what is happening in Evereska." Storm was looking as puzzled as Elminster felt. "These phaerimm came from Myth Drannor, demanding that you stop your assassinations."

"What?" Elminster jammed his pipe into his mouth. "These killings, do they continue?"

"I assume so, since the phaerimm continue to attack." Storm sounded less angry than intrigued. "There've been seven so far."

Elminster cocked a brow. "Been doing well, have I not?"

"I *thought* so," Storm answered cautiously.

Elminster lit his pipe with the flick of a finger. "How are matters here?"

"Not bad," she said. "Between Sylune, Mourngrym, and myself, we have killed nearly a dozen, and I don't think the phaerimm want this any more than we do."

"I imagine not." Elminster took a long puff, then extinguished his pipe with a word. "Well, let's put a stop to it then. Stay out of sight and follow me."

"Follow you where?" Storm asked.

But Elminster was already in the air, streaking toward his tower to collect a few necessaries for the upcoming battle. The princes were clearly trying to lure him to Myth Drannor, no doubt reasoning it would be wiser to attack him away from his home territory. With a little luck, their ambush would be set up along the Ashaba somewhere near Shadowdale, and he and Storm would be gone only a short time.

Given his luck over the past couple of days, Elminster should have known better. As he approached his tower, a half dozen murky figures stepped out of the shadows and arrayed themselves before the entrances. There was the horn-helmed one called Rivalen, a square-chinned one in wizard robes, a cleric with a face as round as a dark moon, and three more swaddled in dark tabards that might have been covering armor or mere flesh.

Like all good assassins, they wasted no time with preliminaries. The square-chinned wizard took the lead, launching himself straight at Elminster, his dark fingers already flashing through a spell to dismiss his foe's magic shields. Elminster countered with his own dispelling enchantment, and Storm sent a ball of silver fire over his shoulder toward the wizard.

Elminster had a bare moment to wonder if that was a good idea, then the sphere of blazing raw magic struck the shadow mage's spell shield. Instead of blasting through the barrier, as it would have any normal protection, the silver fire spread over the wizard's shadowy shield, silhouetting his body in white radiance. The shadow mage howled and covered his eyes, then the silver fire imploded, crushing the fellow in its iron grip and shrinking to a brilliant orb barely the size of an eyeball.

The remaining shadow princes countered with a volley of dark bolts and black flame. For the first time in a century—perhaps twice that—Elminster actually cringed at the thought of what might happen next. The attacks came roaring and thundering at him—then suddenly curved toward the silvery sphere and vanished from sight.

A deafening rip filled the air, and the silvery orb stretched into a jagged line. Elminster pulled his thumb away from the ring it had been rubbing and pointed at the ground.

Too late. The blue ray extended only feet from his hand, then curved upward and vanished into the crooked streak of brilliance—as did the lightning bolt Storm sent dancing over his shoulder. There was another zipping sound, so powerful Elminster felt it in his guts. The jagged line expanded into a rift—a deep, silver-sided crevasse with crimson flames at its bottom—and continued to expand.

"By all the holy gods, it's—it's ripping!"

It took Elminster a moment to realize he was the one yelling—and even he was not sure exactly *what* was ripping. He knew only that he had seen those fuming swirls once before, when, searching for a lover as cherished as she was flawed, he had dared look where no man should.

And now those same flames were licking at Shadowdale, boiling out of the Nine Hells to lap at his beloved home. The raw magic of his silver fire had fused with the shadow mage's dark magic and imploded, tearing a hole in the world fabric itself. It was, he realized, exactly what had happened when Galaeron's magic bolt struck Melegaunt's shadow magic at the Sharn Wall—but the things that might flee this breach would make the phaerimm look like mere cantrip-tossing goblins.

When the rift continued to open, the shadow princes drew their dark weapons and began to circle warily. Though hardly concerned about Shadowdale's safety, they were as surprised by the breach as Elminster—and hardly eager to get themselves knocked inside. Storm took advantage of their hesitation to unsheathe her own sword and start forward.

Elminster raised an arm to stop her. "No."

"But these shadow princes—"

"Are welcome to follow me, if they dare." Elminster glared at the circling princes. Seeing no sign that any of them intended to accept his invitation, he shooed Storm away. "See ye to the phaerimm. I'll tend to this other trouble from the inside."

"From the *inside*?" Storm stopped outside the circle of shadow princes and cast a wary eye toward the widening rift. "Elminster, tell me you're not—"

"But I must, dear Storm." Elminster started forward. "I can't have the Nine Hells erupting beneath my own tower, can I?"

The flames leaped up, a lot like a lover's arms reaching for an old friend, and Elminster flew into Hell.

CHAPTER TWENTY-TWO

30 Nightal, the Year of the Unstrung Harp

Galaeron spread the last coffer of gems across the table. Melegaunt passed first one hand, then the other over the stones. Finding nothing, he worked his way around the table, repeating the process from all sides to be certain his hand passed over every stone. Finally, he shook his head.

"No magic, no evil. If Wulgreth's life-force is here, it's undetectable by my best magic."

Unable to control his frustration, Galaeron swept the gems onto the pile of scintillating wealth already heaped on the floor. Malik, kneeling half-buried in the heap, winced as they struck him, then began to sort with a expert eye, pitching the most valuable stones into the second of two large coffers he intended his beloved horse to carry back. Vala, who had grown more distrustful since learning he was the Seraph of Lies, eyed him suspiciously.

"Have you taken anything that wasn't checked?"

"I have touched nothing that did not come from the table," Malik replied. "Do you think I am eager to keep a lich in the treasury of my new manor?"

"If you're lying—"

"How many times must I tell you?" Malik demanded. "I was crippled by that harlot Mystra's truth magic and cannot lie! You may inspect everything I have taken."

Vala reached for a coffer, but Galaeron put out a hand.

"He hasn't lied to us yet, which is more than we can say for Melegaunt," he said. "The phylactery's not here, or Wulgreth would be on us like a spider on flies."

Takari turned to Jhingleshod. "Is there another place he lairs?" When the knight did not seem to register the question, she gingerly pushed his arm. "Are you still with us?"

The iron knight disappointed them all by meeting her gaze. "There is no other place. He stays near the butte."

"Then he would store the phylactery somewhere visible from here." Galaeron glanced toward the door. "As overgrown as the ruins are, it will take time to find."

Melegaunt stepped in front of Jhingleshod. "I have done everything possible to keep my word, but there is more at issue here than Wulgreth. We *will* find the phylactery, I promise you, but Aris should be finished with his passage by now. Would it not be possible to take the Karsestone outside and summon Shade? There are thousands in the city, and they will help us search."

Jhingleshod looked to Galaeron.

"It would be best," Galaeron said. "Otherwise, it could take months."

"Months?" The disappointment in Jhingleshod's eyes was as easy to read as Galaeron had prayed it would be. The promise of the end to any ordeal could make days seem like tendays, and this looked to be as true for Jhingleshod as for an elf.

Glancing at his weary companions, Galaeron added, "I don't know that we could survive that long."

Jhingleshod waved Melegaunt toward the crawlway in the corner and said, "Summon your city."

"A wise choice." Though Melegaunt tried to sound restrained, the joy in his voice was unmistakable. "You won't regret it."

Giving Jhingleshod no time to change his mind, the wizard led the way through the green barrier. Vala, Takari, and Malik followed, with the iron knight next and Galaeron last.

As the elf dropped through the door, a booming crash shook the cavern below. He looked down to see Melegaunt skittering across the silver pool on his back, limbs flaying and forks of magic dissipating against his spell guard. Leaping off the Karsestone after him was a skeletal form with a rotting, noseless face and lipless mouth. The filth-stained claws and fiery pinpoints in its empty eye sockets left no doubt that they had finally found Wulgreth.

Hurling himself into an oblique somersault, Galaeron grabbed his sword and had it half drawn by the time he splashed into the pool. He swam half a dozen strokes toward the rear of the cavern, then surfaced behind Jhingleshod.

The iron knight was splashing toward the battle behind Vala and Takari, his big axe raised to strike. At first Galaeron thought their guide was rushing to attack Wulgreth, but something inside much wiser and darker suggested otherwise. Jhingleshod had been trying to exterminate them since the sunken bridge. Had he not forced them to cross separately, so it would be easier for the undead to attack? After they survived that, he had led them through a savage gauntlet of wights and wraiths. When even that failed, he had found excuse after excuse to stall until Wulgreth returned. Probably, it had even been Jhingleshod who alerted the lich to their presence in the first place—after all, they had only his word that he had ever killed Wulgreth at all.

Galaeron swung at Jhingleshod's neck. Even sharp elven

steel did not bite deep into the iron flesh, but it did catch the knight's attention. He whirled around, his gruesome jaw hanging almost as low as his guard. Galaeron sprang for the opening, driving his sword at the knight's exposed throat.

Jhingleshod's arm flashed up, deflecting the attack almost before the elf saw it move. "Are you mad?"

"Hardly!" Galaeron slipped his free hand into his sleeve. "I see how you have been playing us."

"Playing you?" A long crackle sounded from the melee behind Jhingleshod, prompting the knight to glance over his shoulder. "I am not one to play at anything."

Galaeron pulled his hand from his sleeve, cupping a small glass rod, but Malik's chubby arm knocked it away before the elf could cast the spell.

"Matters are bad enough without this shadow folly!" Malik pointed to the artistic trefoil passage Aris had cut into the side of the butte. "The giant told me there are phaerimm coming!"

Galaeron realized he should have been disappointed in himself, but he was not. After learning of Melegaunt's lies, the line between his shadow and himself had blurred. Suspicions that might have seemed groundless before were suddenly reasonable. He peered past Jhingleshod and saw that matters were, indeed, bad enough. Melegaunt was kneeling in the pool, beard scorched away and eyes glazed with pain. Only the constant attacks of Vala and Takari, harrying the lich from opposite sides, kept Wulgreth from finishing the wizard in a blow.

Jhingleshod let out an eerie wail and hefted his axe. Trusting more to Malik's word than his own instincts, Galaeron pointed at Wulgreth's head and summoned a spell. Vala lunged in, blocking Galaeron's lightning bolt, and Takari attacked from the opposite side.

The lich flicked a finger and sent Takari stumbling away, wailing and shaking her head, eyes red with blood and fixed blindly ahead. Vala's darksword took some small vengeance, slashing off a moldering arm, then whipping around to open Wulgreth's side from spine to navel. Hissing and spitting in anger, the lich grabbed her by the throat with its good arm.

Vala went instantly rigid, mouth gaping, eyes rolling back. Jhingleshod buried his axe deep into Wulgreth's back, driving both the lich and the woman down beneath the pool's silvery skin. The iron knight hefted his axe again, lidless eyes bulging as he tried to see beneath the surface. He began to shuffle through the basin, trying to locate his quarry with a series of savage kicks.

"Jhingleshod, you'll break her ribs!"

"Galaeron?" This from Takari, who stood with her back to the wall and her sword weaving a blind-fighting pattern before her. "I can't see."

"You're fine," Galaeron said, realizing Vala was in the most danger. Even if the lich released her, its touch would leave her paralyzed and unable to return to the surface. "Stay there."

"But Galaeron—"

She was interrupted by a startled cry from Melegaunt. The archwizard pointed his hand into the basin and started a spell, then vanished beneath the surface. Galaeron rushed forward, sweeping his sword back and forth across the bottom, trying to think of some spell that would allow him to find Vala before she drowned. Jhingleshod opted for a more direct method and dived under the surface.

A muffled crack rumbled out of the pool, then Melegaunt's body floated to the surface, the smell of charred flesh rising from a hole in his back.

"Galaeron?" Takari called.

"Stand still," Galaeron ordered, starting after the wizard. "Stab anything near you."

His sword touched a body on the bottom of the pool. When it did not attack, he ducked down and grabbed hold of an armored elbow, then pulled Vala to the surface. She began coughing, spewing liquid magic from her nostrils and mouth. Dragging her along beside him, Galaeron went to Melegaunt's side and rolled the archwizard over.

The spell had blown open Melegaunt's whole chest. Incredibly, the archwizard's heart continued to beat. Galaeron could see it.

"Meleg-ghaunt!" coughed Vala, more or less recovered from her near drowning. "He needs help!" She spun her head around the room. "Malik!"

Malik appeared in the mouth of Aris's tunnel. "Quiet!" he hissed. "The phaerimm are already coming out of the forest."

"We need to get him to Aris." Vala motioned to Melegaunt.

"Waste . . . of . . . time." It was Melegaunt who gasped this. He grabbed Galaeron and pulled him close. "Promise me—"

A flurry of splashing near Takari interrupted the archwizard. She cried out and began to hack blindly at the pool.

"Where is it, Galaeron?" she yelled. "Which way?"

"To your—"

"Elf!" Melegaunt boomed, jerking Galaeron to him with a strength born of his dying magic.

"Don't worry, Melegaunt," Galaeron said, trying to rise. "I remember: 'Hear me now, People of Shade—' "

"No!" Melegaunt gasped, now loosing his strength. "You must leave it . . . to the princes, or you'll be . . . lost."

Galaeron started to promise, but stopped when the sour clang of a breaking sword sounded from the far wall. Takari cried out—no longer calling for him, just shrieking—and he turned to find her slashing at the pool with a broken sword, Jhingleshod and Wulgreth rolling across the surface in front of her.

Vala started across the pool. "Move left, Takari!" she yelled. "And don't panic. I'm coming."

"Malik!" Galaeron started toward the battle. "Hold Melegaunt."

"Galaeron!" Melegaunt demanded. "No more spells."

"Yes, I promise."

Seeing Malik approach, Galaeron started to push Melegaunt over—until the archwizard's fingers dug deep into his arm, drawing blood and pouring a dark river of anguish into him. Galaeron's knees buckled, and he slipped beneath the surface, swallowing a mouthful of silvery liquid. Swirling shadows filled his mind, then he began to feel weightless and weak, and his last conscious thought was that Melegaunt had finally betrayed him, that the archwizard had used his shadow magic to switch bodies.

Then Malik was pounding him on the back, yelling in his ear. "Cough it out, stupid elf!"

A heavy blow landed on Galaeron's back, then he opened his eyes to find Melegaunt floating in front of him, lifeless eyes staring at the ceiling. He had no memory after his mind began to fill with swirling shadows, no idea how long he had been beneath the surface with Melegaunt—or of what had happened there. His mind felt heavy and clouded with darkness, his head ached as though it would split, and his lungs were burning for air. He had to have been under for a good long while.

Another blow landed on Galaeron's back, and he realized the little man was holding him up by the collar, trying to hide behind the Karsestone while Jhingleshod continued to wrestle with Wulgreth. Vala stood pressed against the wall, one hand ineptly flailing at the lich with her sword, the other holding Takari's broken and bloodied body above the surface.

"What happened?" Galaeron gasped. He could not help wondering just what Melegaunt had done to him—but now was hardly the time to puzzle it out, not with Takari wounded and the phaerimm on the way. The last time he saw Takari, she was blind but still healthy. "What happened to my scout?"

"What do you think happened?" Malik released him. "Wulgreth struck her while you were doing your pool dance with Melegaunt's corpse."

"Pool dance?" Galaeron gasped. "Never mind! Keep a watch on the phaerimm."

Galaeron shoved Malik toward the tunnel, then pushed off the Karsestone—and that was when he understood why they had not been able to find Wulgreth's phylactery. Liches always stored their life-forces in something of great worth, something hard to destroy and harder to find.

Jhingleshod went limp and vanished beneath the surface. Wulgreth spun toward Galaeron, tiny forks of green lightning dancing on the fingertips of his one remaining arm. For an instant—for more than an instant—Galaeron thought the lich had finally destroyed its ancient servant. The elf thought he would be next.

Then Jhingleshod came up beneath Wulgreth, lifting him out of the pool. The lich twisted his one arm around behind his back, fingers spraying his life-stealing magic into Jhingleshod's iron breastplate. A loud, watery knelling echoed off the cavern walls, and Jhingleshod wailed in unearthly pain. Had the magic been powerful enough to destroy him, Galaeron knew, the lifeless knight would gladly have endured the suffering. As it was, it only melted a hole in his armor and filled the air with a forgelike stench. Galaeron sloshed forward and plunged his magic sword into the lich's fiery eye socket.

Wulgreth howled in rage, and the elven steel began to melt and sag. Galaeron started to blast the lich with his magic bolts, then remembered his promise to Melegaunt and drew his dagger, flinging it into the other eye in one smooth motion.

The blade sank deep—then vanished in a flash of blue flame.

"Galaeron!"

Galaeron glanced toward the voice and saw Vala's black sword spinning toward him. The pool swirled around his legs as Wulgreth kicked at him. He dodged sideways, caught the black hilt and winced in pain—it was still as cold as a night hag's kiss—then brought the dark blade across the lich's neck.

Wulgreth's head toppled into the pool, then bobbed to the surface and spun toward Galaeron, eyes still burning with hatred. It shrieked, "You won't destroy—"

And Galaeron brought the darksword down again, cleaving

the head in two, then forced himself to hold the flesh-freezing hilt and hack at the lich's body until all of the pieces sank out of sight. Then, when no counterattack came and he began to believe none would, something bumped his back. He turned to find the two halves of the skull still surging toward him. He cried out and backed away, raising the darksword to strike yet again.

"What are you doing?" Jhingleshod snatched the halves of the skull out of the pool. "We'll need those!"

Galaeron stared at the iron knight in uncomprehending shock, then slowly began to understand that it was over, that Wulgreth had been hacked and blasted into so many pieces that it would take him the better part of a tenday to draw himself together again.

Galaeron lowered the sword. "That's right," he said, realizing that Jhingleshod believed they would destroy this Wulgreth in the same way they had the demilich. "Hold onto those pieces until we find the phylactery."

Even had he the heart, Galaeron knew better than to tell the iron knight what he had surmised about the Karsestone. His heart feeling almost as cold and numb as the hand that held the darksword, he waded over to the wall and returned Vala's blade, then laid his icy hand on Takari's mangled shoulder.

"This will slow the bleeding," he said. "And don't worry. We'll be back in Rheitheillaethor before you know it."

Takari opened her eyes and pushed his hand away. "No, Galaeron. You made your choice."

Another death scream rolled across the brown water, muted by the gossamer curtain of steam, yet still accusatory in its anguish. Laeral ducked beneath the surface and swam toward the voice, using her magic to move almost as fast underwater as she could have through the cold dawn air.

After her garbled sending to Elminster (she still had no idea if he had understood her), she had taken an escort of ten warriors and ten war mages through the new gate to Rocnest—and promptly been ambushed by a half dozen phaerimm. Though they were prepared for that possibility—even expected it—all of their magic protections were dispelled before they cast a single spell.

At that point, Laeral should probably have ordered her small company to teleport back to Waterdeep. Instead, desperate to discover what had become of Khelben and hoping to recapture the gate, she moved her group to the rim of the basin. Four of the phaerimm rushed to press the attack, driving her company into the Marsh of Chelimber before they had time to regroup. In the confusion that followed, the small force became separated, and the phaerimm began to pick them off one at a time. She managed to slay two of the creatures during the long night, but those losses had been more than replaced by reinforcements from Evereska.

The thornbacks were using their magic to heat the marsh. Having raised the temperature to a simmer already, they no doubt intended to either force their prey out of hiding or boil it alive. Neither possibility frightened Laeral, for she could easily teleport back to Waterdeep before either grew necessary—but she was loathe to abandon those who could not.

Laeral pushed her head up to confirm her bearings. The voice was weaker now, having faded to a whimper, but it was also closer—just beyond a willow brake. Fearful of making any noise that would betray her approach, she ducked beneath the surface to circumvent the thicket underwater.

As she rounded the corner, three concussions pulsed down through the water, nearly rupturing her eardrums and jolting her so hard that the last air left her lungs. She pushed off the mucky bottom and launched herself into the air with a flying spell, her fingertips crackling with a silvery ball of her most potent magic.

On the other side of the willows stood a trio of murk-swaddled men, one cradling the mangled figure of a Waterdhavian warrior, the other two using black glaives to pin down the writhing remains of a spell-blasted phaerimm. The men were all the size of bugbears, with brilliant gem-colored eyes and flesh as dark as shadow. While their weapons were familiar in form and function, the ebony blades looked more like black glass than steel, and the shafts might have been wood, metal, or neither.

The tallest, a copper-eyed figure in a flowing tabard as dark as night, glanced at the silvery ball on her fingertips.

"If you are who I think you are, it really wouldn't do to throw that at us. We mean you no harm." He used his glaive to raise the phaerimm's twitching tail. "Two more remain, but we have found ten of your men, recovered six more bodies, and have reports of four teleporting away too wounded to fight. Would that be all?"

"So it would seem." Laeral let the magic die on her fingers. "And you are?"

"Escanor Tanthul." The shadowy figure flourished his cape and bowed. "These are my brothers, Aglarel and Clariburnus."

The other two figures bowed and said in unison, "At your service, milady."

Laeral closed her open jaw and returned the gesture with a curtsy. "Laeral, Lady of Blackstaff Tower."

"Yes, we know," said Escanor. "Perhaps we should be gone from here. If you will excuse me for saying so, you seem to have bitten off a bit much even for one of Mystra's Chosen."

Laeral raised her brow. "You seem very well informed . . . for a Netherese."

Escanor flashed a fang-filled smile. "As do you, Milady Blackstaff. I can see that it will be a pleasure to fight at your side in the war to come."

"War?" Laeral began to grow cold at the thought of an alliance with these dark Netherese. "Let's not get ahead of ourselves."

"We are hardly ahead of anything," said Clariburnus. He severed the phaerimm's tail with a flick of his glaive, then tucked the barb into his belt as a trophy. "The war has begun already. Surely you do not expect the phaerimm to surrender without a fight."

"I know they will fight," said Laeral. "They have proven that already, but that does not mean—"

"Our army is already on its way, I am sure," interrupted Escanor. As he spoke, he passed a hand over the face of the wounded Waterdhavian, cloaking the man's eyes in shadow and putting him into a restful sleep. "We will try to limit the destruction to the Shaeradim, but even the Chosen must see that if we hope to defeat the phaerimm, we will need to fight—and fight together."

CHAPTER TWENTY-THREE

1 Hammer,
the Year of Wild Magic (1372 DR)

They had spent the night inside the pyramid. Galaeron had not realized that until they crawled through Aris's artistic trefoil tunnel and saw the rectangular shadows stretching across the overgrown city. He wished he had Melegaunt to look into them and read the coming day, or perhaps not. With two distant phaerimm drifting toward them across the ruins, he could see for himself what the day would bring—at least the short part they were likely to survive.

There were no signs of mind flayers or eye tyrants, nor of Aris and Malik's horse. The illithids and beholders had probably fallen to Elminster or the undead at the sunken bridge. Galaeron could only hope that Aris had recognized how badly events had turned and had managed to sneak quietly away, but he rather doubted it.

"Sooner or later, they'll notice the tunnel," said Vala. She was crouched on her haunches beside Galaeron, with Jhingleshod staring over their shoulders. "We could take the Karsestone out through the river opening."

"What good would that do?" Galaeron looked along the flank of the butte, to where the waterfall poured out of the sandstone and plunged fifty feet into a pool of scarlet water. "They'd only catch us out in the open."

Vala watched him carefully. "It might give you time to summon help."

"You mean Shade," said Galaeron. "I promised Melegaunt I'd wait for the princes."

"Do you think that will be possible?" asked Vala. She turned to Jhingleshod. "Would the Karsestone fit through the river passage?"

"It would be easier to go without it." The knight looked toward the interior mouth of the tunnel, where the scorched cinders of Wulgreth's corpse were already trying to coalesce into a body again. He pushed his axe back to stir the ashes, then said, "And the phaerimm might not care that you escaped."

"They'd care," said Vala, rolling her eyes.

Galaeron suspected that she also understood what Jhingleshod was really saying—that without the Karsestone, they might live long enough to destroy Wulgreth's phylactery. But Galaeron did not know whether Vala also realized that they had the phylactery—that the lich had stored his life-force in the Karsestone.

Galaeron was struggling desperately with what to do after it finally dawned on Jhingleshod that the phylactery and the Karsestone were one in the same. The knight would, undoubtedly, want the stone destroyed, but Galaeron was not even sure such an artifact *could* be destroyed—and that was quite aside from what such a thing would mean for Evereska and Melegaunt's people. It might be possible to extract the lich's life-force from the stone, but that would take time.

When Jhingleshod did not answer her question, Vala said, "The phaerimm have been hunting us since Evereska, Jhingleshod. They aren't going to let us go now, even if we don't have the Karsestone. Can we get it out through the river passage or not?"

"If you can hold your breath so long," said Jhingleshod. "But how will that help you keep your promise to me?"

"By bringing help," said Galaeron. Realizing he had to get Jhingleshod's mind off the Karsestone or lose any chance of saving Evereska, he slipped past the iron knight and started down the tunnel. "You heard what Melegaunt said, and you saw the Twelve Princes. Don't you think a thousand citizens of Shade have a better chance of finding the phylactery than we do?"

"Perhaps so, were Melegaunt here to make them honor his word." Jhingleshod grabbed a handful of Wulgreth cinder and followed Galaeron into the silvery pool. "As it is, I have only your promise."

"Then perhaps I may be of some small use," said Malik. He sat atop of the Karsestone attending to a groaning, half-conscious Takari. "I would be happy to see to the stone's safety—"

"No." Galaeron and Vala spoke simultaneously.

Malik continued unflustered. "I understand your hesitation—namely that I will give the stone to Cyric—but it *would* give you a chance to escape with your friend's life." He lifted Takari's head, but lowered it again when she managed a weak shake. "And a chance to keep your word to Jhingleshod and look for Wulgreth's phylactery."

"Cyric is trouble enough without a toy like this." Galaeron was beginning to believe the seraph's strange claim about being unable to lie. He pulled Takari off the stone and passed her to Vala, then motioned Malik down. "You don't want to be there."

Malik slid into the water. "You have a plan?"

"Perhaps." Galaeron took a piece of shadow silk from his

pocket and pressed it to the side of the stone opposite Aris's tunnel, then went across the pool to the cavern wall. "It occurs to me Aris might not be the only one who can bore a tunnel."

"You're going to use the stone's magic?" gasped Malik. "An excellent plan!"

Galaeron shrugged. "The best I can think of, but it might be better than waiting for the phaerimm to find us here."

"And if it fails?" asked Jhingleshod. A whirling cloud of ash cloaked the hand holding Wulgreth's cinders. "The phaerimm will kill you."

Galaeron nodded grimly, then glanced out Aris's tunnel and saw one of the distant cones coming straight toward them. He arranged a circle of shadow silk on the face of the cavern wall. "Anything you can do to slow them would certainly help."

"Help *you*," said Jhingleshod. "If the phaerimm are as powerful as you say, perhaps *they* could find Wulgreth's phylactery."

The shadow silk slipped from Galaeron's fingers, then vanished into the silvery pool. He turned, slowly, and said, "It seems to me that such selfishness is how you became undead in the first place."

"I do not think promise breakers have any right to rebuke others."

Jhingleshod turned toward Aris's tunnel, but found his way blocked by Malik.

"Selfishness is not always a bad thing," said the little man. "Especially when everyone can be made to see that their own ends are best accomplished by working together. I am sure that if we all put our heads together, we will find the solution lying right in front of us."

Galaeron shook his head urgently, but found the line to Malik's sight blocked by the iron knight's huge form. Forcing himself to move calmly so he did not alarm Jhingleshod, he stepped sideways.

Malik continued, "Wulgreth is certainly a trickster, and I

have been in the counting rooms of enough tricksters to know that they enjoy hiding their treasures in plain sight."

Galaeron shook his head desperately, and when Malik did not see him, he called out, "Malik!"

Jhingleshod raised his hand to silence Galaeron. "This one is making some sense. Perhaps we will can help each other yet."

"If I were Wulgreth, I would have hidden my life-force in the most obvious place," said Malik. "Perhaps in the pyramid itself."

"Would Melegaunt not have detected that from inside?" interrupted Jhingleshod, growing more excited.

Galaeron caught Vala's eye and nodded toward the tunnel. She turned to look, and seeing the phaerimm still approaching slowly, gave him a reassuring nod.

"Maybe in the butte itself," said Malik.

"That's possible," said Jhingleshod.

Letting slip a silent sigh of relief, Galaeron turned to the wall and pressed a fresh circle of shadow silk to the stone.

"What about Jhingleshod himself?" asked Vala. "That might explain why *he* can't die."

"What an excellent thought! Or it might even be that . . ."

Galaeron's stomach sank as the seraph let his sentence trail off. He turned around and found Malik staring at the Karsestone.

"Be what?" demanded Jhingleshod.

Malik's mouth snapped shut, and for a moment Galaeron thought the little man might actually cover his mistake.

Then Jhingleshod demanded again, "Or *what*?"

"Nothing," Malik said, but he seemed unable to stop there. His mouth twisted into a lopsided grimace, and more words began to spill out. "Only that it occurred to me that the thing Wulgreth valued most is right here."

Jhingleshod fell quiet, then turned toward Galaeron. "You were going to take it. You knew, and you were still going to take it."

"I don't *know* anything." Galaeron finished his circle and stepped away from the wall. "And I don't really see what difference—"

"Liar!"

Jhingleshod's axe shot up so quickly Galaeron barely had time to fling himself into the pool before the rusty blade came tumbling past, spraying magic links of elven chain mail in every direction, and the weapon clanged off the wall.

Jhingleshod was already following his weapon across the chamber, hurling himself toward Galaeron. A black sword caught the iron knight from behind, slashing through his armor and cleaving his yellowed shoulder down to his armpit. Roaring in fury, he spun, slamming an iron elbow into Vala's head and bouncing her off the Karsestone. Her eyes rolled back, and she would have fallen, had Jhingleshod's hand not clamped her throat. His fingers started to close, and a wet rasp gurgled from Vala's mouth.

"No!"

Galaeron leveled a hand at the knight's iron back and uttered a mystic syllable. A familiar surge of cold power rushed up through his body, then the silky, liquid fire of the Karsestone's whole magic flooded into him from the silver pool. He gasped in surprise, and Jhingleshod started toward Galaeron, dragging Vala after him. The elf's arm swelled visibly, the muscles convulsing so hard he thought his elbow would snap.

The spell erupted from his hand in a blinding flash of gold light, blasting the nails off his fingers and scorching the tips, then streaking across the cavern into the knight's stomach. There was a deafening clang and the mordant smell of molten iron. Jhingleshod's legs flew in one direction and his torso in the other, eyes bulging and locked on Galaeron's face. The upper half came down a dozen paces away and skipped across the pool's surface, then rolled to its stomach and sank beneath the surface.

Galaeron started toward Vala, who was stooped over holding

her throat, gasping down breath between harsh coughs.

"Galae . . . ron!" Takari's voice was so weak he barely heard it above Vala's wheezing. "Phae-r-rim!"

Placing a hand under Vala's elbow as he passed, he looked across the chamber to Aris's tunnel. Takari was draped across the entrance, pointing down the passage. Outside, two cone-shaped blurs were streaking toward the butte. Galaeron pushed Vala toward the crimson whirlpool in the cavern's far corner.

"Time for your plan, I think," Galaeron said.

He turned to ask Malik to take Takari and found the seraph already wading toward her. To Galaeron's surprise, the little man reached for his treasure coffers instead. Galaeron blasted the coffers with a lightning bolt, blackening his fingertips some more and strewing the tunnel with gems.

Malik whirled with fire in his eyes.

Galaeron merely pointed at Takari and said, "If she dies, so do you."

"As you wish." Malik grabbed her and started toward the whirlpool. "But I will have my fortune from you!"

Galaeron paid him no attention, for the phaerimm were so close now he could make out the sticklike arms surrounding their mouths. He considered staying to ambush them inside, but suspected that even with the power of the Karsestone, he would be little more than a gnat to a pair of wasps. He turned back into the cavern, nearly falling as he tripped over Jhingleshod's disembodied legs, then pointed at the shadow silk on the far wall and spoke an incantation.

Again, he was filled with the silky fire of the Karsestone's magic, the power of the magic turning the skin on his hand black and leathery. The rock wall drew away from the dark circle, fashioning a long tunnel that was, if not as elegant as Aris's, nearly as straight. Turning away even before it broke into the light, Galaeron touched a hand to the Karsestone and uttered a levitation spell. He was beginning to enjoy the feel of the boulder's magic, the power of it flowing through his arm, even the searing tingle it left in his hand.

In response to his summons, the Karsestone rose from the pool. He glanced out Aris's tunnel and saw the phaerimm still coming, so close now he could make out the barbs on their tails. Galaeron started toward the corner, where Vala was already vanishing down the whirlpool. Malik and Takari were close behind, swinging around the rim as the current drew them in.

Galaeron and the Karsestone were a dozen paces behind when an iron hand grasped his ankle. He cried out, then saw Takari glance in his direction before she and Malik vanished down the whirlpool. Galaeron tried to kick free, then stomped down on the unseen wrist.

A second hand snatched at the attacking leg. He jerked away and lunged toward the whirlpool, dragging Jhingleshod's top half along with him. His captured foot twisted, then Galaeron felt—almost heard—a bone snap. His ankle erupted in pain and buckled.

Barely catching himself on his good leg, Galaeron heaved the floating Karsestone ahead of him, then held on tight as the current drew it forward.

Jhingleshod caught him by the second ankle. Galaeron kicked madly, but could not free himself. The ceiling began to spin as the whirlpool caught them. He took a deep breath and glanced toward Aris's tunnel, expecting to find the phaerimm streaking into the chamber, but seeing only Wulgreth's ghostly form coalescing out of his untended ashes.

Galaeron's second ankle snapped, and he nearly passed out from pain. He waited until the ceiling vanished from sight, then released the Karsestone and reached for his buckle. Having lost his sword and dagger against Wulgreth, he had no blades left with which to fight, nor could he use another spell. Most required at least a word of spoken magic, and the only thing speaking would get him now was drowned.

They swirled down into darkness, bumping and scraping along the slick walls of the passage. Galaeron pulled his belt off and stretched it between both hands. Jhingleshod clawed his way up the elf's legs, his fingers digging through the magic chain mail as though it were silk.

They slammed into the Karsestone, which had become lodged in a choke point, and Jhingleshod's truncated waist swung up, smashing Galaeron in the face. The elf thought for a moment his attacker might swirl away, but the iron knight held fast. Galaeron tried to kick free—then nearly drowned when his mouth opened to scream.

The Karsestone twisted in the choke point, and the iron torso drifted away from Galaeron's face. Jhingleshod pulled himself around, lining himself to continue climbing the elf, and Galaeron saw his chance. He stretched the belt across the top of his attacker's arms, then pulled one end underneath the wrists and encircled them in the thick belt. With the deft finger work of any spellcaster, he drew the tail through the buckle and jerked it tight, then circled the knight's iron wrists again and clasped the belt.

The Karsestone slipped past the choke point, freeing the pent-up river to churn down the passage. Jhingleshod's hands came loose, and the undead knight tumbled away, gurgling in outrage. Galaeron caught hold of the boulder and jammed his arm into the crack in its center, then swirled along behind it like a wagging tail. The world turned bright, then the bottom fell out as the river plunged from the butte into the crimson pool below.

Galaeron plummeted after the Karsestone, then slammed into it headlong. His initial thought was that his plan had not worked so well, that the cunning phaerimm had foreseen such an attempt and left someone outside to intercept the artifact—then, when his world did not explode into magic oblivion, he began to slip down the stone's face and recalled the levitation spell he had used to move it in the first place. He wedged his other arm into the crack, and fighting the steady stream of silver liquid that continued to pour out of the stone, dangled beneath the boulder.

As it sank toward the river, Galaeron searched the area for signs of the phaerimm. Vala and the others were bobbing in the crimson pool beneath him, struggling to move away from the expanding ring of ripples that marked the entry of Jhingleshod's torso into the river. An instant later, the knight's legs came tumbling out of the butte and plunged, still kicking, into the water. When a pair of spell flashes brightened the mouth of Aris's tunnel—no doubt the phaerimm's response to Wulgreth's coalescing form—Galaeron finally dared to believe Vala's plan would work.

He settled onto the surface not far from his friends, and continuing to hold onto the Karsestone with both hands, began to drift after them.

"Watch your feet!" he yelled. "Jhingleshod caught me from beneath and—"

Galaeron was interrupted by a tremendous crash from the other side of the butte. He glanced up in time to see a silver bolt of lightning striking down from the heavens, then Aris's deep voice bellowed in rage. The loud crash of a shattering boulder shook the butte, and the golden flare of two more war spells flashed against the sky. The stone giant's bellow changed to a cry of anguish.

Malik swam alongside the Karsestone and pushed Takari's hand toward Galaeron. "My Kelda is over there!"

Galaeron pulled Takari onto the boulder. She looked weak but alert, and the wounds in her shoulder were no longer bleeding. Aris's cries continued to reverberate over the butte, growing more intense. Vala surfaced beside them and pulled herself onto the Karsestone.

"What are they doing to him?" Galaeron asked, unable to look away from the butte.

"Torturing him," said Vala. "They probably think he was covering our escape."

"In that case, I suggest we put his sacrifice to good use," said Malik, struggling to pull himself onto the crowded stone. "My Kelda will find her own way back to the bridge, if she is not there already. We can float down the river to the swamp and pick her up there."

"You would . . . abandon him?" Takari gasped.

A scream of anguish came from the other side of the butte. Galaeron looked to Vala, hoping to see some glimmer of an idea in her green eyes.

She met his gaze steadily. "It's what Melegaunt would do."

Galaeron's heart sank. "I'm not Melegaunt."

"Then you must . . . try," said Takari. "I would not want to live . . . knowing I had deserted one so . . . noble."

Galaeron nodded. "All right, but how?"

"You know how." Vala sheathed her sword and took Takari in her arms, then slipped off the Karsestone. "*We* don't stand a chance against the phaerimm. There's only one way."

Malik's eyes bugged out. "What are you talking about?"

"You know." Galaeron slipped into the river beside Vala and Takari, then turned toward the Karsestone. "Up."

The boulder left the water, Malik still clinging to its side. "Wait!" the seraph called. "There must be another—"

"Up!" Galaeron said again. The boulder rose faster, and Malik let go, dropping into the river beside them. "Up!"

Now the Karsestone fairly shot skyward, the ribbon of silver magic trailing it like a glittering comet tail. The screams from the other side of the butte softened, and the two phaerimm rose into sight, flying skyward after the stone.

"Up!" Galaeron cried again.

The Karsestone pulled away, shrinking to a tiny speck visible only because of the horsetail cascade falling behind it.

"Now," said Takari. "Hear me now . . ."

She let the sentence trail off, too weak to finish.

Vala turned to Galaeron. "Say it. You're the one who sent the stone up. You must be the one who calls them home."

"No doubt," Galaeron said. "Just remember the promise you made to Melegaunt—and to me."

"I do," she said. "And I also remember the one I made to your father. I'll be there to take care of you."

Galaeron nodded, then looked skyward. "Hear me now, people of Shade. Follow me now, for the Return is at hand!"

The silver horse tail vanished, and nothing else happened. Aris's cries faded to muffled groans. The companions swam to the riverbank and dragged themselves to shore. Vala and Malik set Galaeron's broken ankles. Then, with Vala cradling him in her arms and Malik carrying Takari, they started around the head of the butte to see what could be done for Aris.

They were just passing the waterfall when Malik pointed across the pool, to where Jhingleshod was dragging himself to shore. The knight had finally snapped Galaeron's sword belt and recovered his legs. As they watched, he pulled his two halves together and slowly began to work his flesh like clay, kneading it and pushing it together, filling in the gaping hole opened by the elf's spell. He glanced across the pool and glared at Galaeron, then looked skyward, to where a shadowy ribbon of darkness was beginning to swirl down out of the heavens. Tiny flashes of silver and black began to streak back and forth between the end of the ribbon and a pair of specks streaking southward across the sky.

As the companions watched, the specks resolved themselves into tiny cone-shaped figures, the dark ribbon into a long line of bat-winged mounts, each carrying a murky rider armed with a long death-spewing lance.

At last, the phaerimm had their fill of running. They spun on their pursuers, and in a flurry of spellcasting, set the sky alight with flame and magic. A dozen riders vanished into the maelstrom and came tumbling out the bottom, their mounts reduced to charred husks of wing and talon. Still, the riders behind never faltered. One raised his hands, and with a quick gesture, opened a hole in the fiery barrier before them. The rest whirled through the breach on their dark-winged mounts, pelting their quarry with black bolts from their lances.

One of the phaerimm started to writhe about madly and

began to drop—then vanished in a mote of spell light. Taking its lesson from its companion, the second creature also teleported away, leaving the bat-riders to wheel through the air in swirling pinwheels of darkness.

A shadow fell over the butte, then Malik gasped, "By the One! A mountain is falling from the heavens!"

Galaeron looked up to see the summit of craggy black peak hanging upside down above them, just low enough that its jagged tip divided the rising sun. On top of the overturned mountain sat a murk-swaddled city of shimmering black walls and ebony towers, trailing wisps of shadow and layered in bands of hazy black cloud. It was swarming with hundreds—if not thousands—of bat riders, all circling the city in a mad wheeling stream, trailing pennants of royal blue and amethyst and black-red ruby, tipping their lances and performing wild acrobatics for hordes of cheering, gem-eyed citizens gathered along the dark ramparts.

"There is the help Evereska needs," Vala said. When Galaeron did not respond, she looked into his eyes, her brow furrowed in concern. "Galaeron, you should be happy. What's wrong?"

Galaeron did not know how to answer. After breaking his word twice in one day, he had expected to feel disgraced, even corrupt or evil. Instead, he merely felt hollow—hollow and a little cold.

Vala's expression grew hard. "Galaeron?"

He just looked away.

The Battle is Joined!

The Netherese city of Shade has returned from centuries in the Demiplane of Shadow. Evereska is under attack and the High Ice is melting. A seemingly endless torrent is flooding the Shoal of Thirst. Elminster has been banished to the Nine Hells. There are phaerimm everywhere.

And the deadliest threat to the people of Faerûn has yet to make itself known.

The story continues in

RETURN OF THE ARCHWIZARDS

Book II

The Siege

by **Troy Denning**, best-selling author of *Waterdeep* (as Richard Awlinson) and co-author (with Ed Greenwood) of *Death of the Dragon*.

Available December 2001

FORGOTTEN REALMS

For five hundred years,
Elminster has fought evil in the Realms.

Now he must
fight EVIL in HELL itself.

Elminster in Hell

By
Ed Greenwood

An ancient fiend has
imprisoned the Old Mage
in the shackles of Hell.
Bent on supreme power,
the demon is determined
to steal every memory,
every morsel of magic from
the defender of the Realms.
As the secrets
of Elminster's mind are
laid bare, one by one,
he weakens unto death.

August 2001

But Elminster won't go without a fight.

And that is one instance for which his captor may be woefully unprepared.

Counselors and Kings
ELAINE CUNNINGHAM

Under the blazing sun of Halruaa, intrigue stalks the land. Skilled wizards compete for power and wealth, threatening to destroy any who interfere. Only the society of Counselors, impervious to the effects of magic, can maintain balance and order.

Book I: THE MAGEHOUND

Matteo is a rising counselor, intent on serving his wizardly masters well. Yet when a spark of magic is discovered within him, he must flee the wrath of one sworn to root out such talents: the magehound.

Book II: THE FLOODGATE

As Matteo and his companion Tzigone search for clues to their mysterious pasts, Kiva the magehound, now fallen into disgrace, plots in secrecy to destroy those who opposed her. To accomplish her ends, she plans to unleash a power that could sweep away all Halruaa.

April 2001

THREE OF THE MOST POPULAR
FORGOTTEN REALMS
AUTHORS TELL THE STORY
OF FAERÛN'S GREATEST KINGDOM
—AND ITS GREATEST KING.

The Cormyr Saga

CORMYR: A NOVEL
Ed Greenwood & Jeff Grubb
A plot to poison King Azoun IV brings the kingdom to
the brink of disaster.

BEYOND THE HIGH ROAD
Troy Denning
With the threat from within at an end, Cormyr faces an even
greater threat from the barbaric Stonelands, and a princess
begins to understand what it means to rule a kingdom.

DEATH OF THE DRAGON
Ed Greenwood & Troy Denning
Plague, madness, and war sweep through Cormyr and the people
look to their king for salvation. Only the mighty Azoun has the
chance to defeat the horror that will change Cormyr forever.